CRITICAL ACCLAIM FOR
THE TORONTO YOU ARE LEAVING

Gordon's powers of characterization are stunning, creating a large cast of memorable people, each distinct and alive. His sensitive understanding of human emotion is breathtaking. He has fully brought to life a particular time in the story of Toronto and in the history of gay men. His novel is a moving love story and historical document of interest and value. - **Rosemary Aubert, Mystery Writer, 2006.**

The author has captured the spirit of our age; baby boomers coming of age, leaving home to attend university, coming out and living the queer life in Toronto. The characters are beautifully conceived and the descent of AIDS upon their lives is skillfully crafted. In a very real sense...I remember this tale happening. – **Kyle Rae, City Councillor, Toronto City Hall, 2006.**

Anderson's 1970-1980 novel personifies the pride, courage and resilience that he and many other young gay men responded to throughout their lives. With humour and love, this story and its strongly-delineated characters epitomize Gordon's obsession with a full life experienced during too short a day. – **Clair Sedore, 2006.**

Gay and lesbian people, families and friends reach out to the church for help, but often experience a traditional church full of condemnation and judgement. Yet Jesus said, "By this all people will know that you are my disciples, if you love one another". John 13:35. We knock at the doors of the church seeking love, compassion, acceptance and justice. For too long, gay men diagnosed with HIV were left to die, without the love and support from their local House of God. Gordon's book, The Toronto You Are Leaving, indicates a joy of life, the impact of AIDS, and the need for friendship and love within the gay and lesbian community. – **Reverend Brent Hawkes, Senior Pastor, Metropolitan Community Church of Toronto, 2006.**

A dignity is carved out from the commonplace conventions as these young gay men seek their place within society. Every act of kindness is valued, while respect and camaraderie in their dealing with each other keep their hearts alive. – **Al McAuley, 2006.**

G.S. Anderson is wonderfully aware of the subtle and often threatening nuances that distinguish the complex roles in gay life: the friend who "doesn't know", the close friend "who does know", the one-nighter, the roommate, the lover and the ex-lover.

I've lived more than 70 years in Toronto, 45 as a militant gay man, and I've never seen a more lively and realistic depiction of gay life in Canada's gayest city.

My heart goes out to Anderson's richly portrayed characters as they struggle, in realistic dialogue, to negotiate the restless and risky emotions of hidden and open gay life in a non-gay world. - **Dr. John Alan Lee, author of Colours of Love, Getting Sex and Gay Mid-life and Maturity, to name a few, 2006.**

I am pleased and impressed by the novel and its characters. The dialogue is strong, the narrative moves along smoothly and creates interesting tension, the characters are well-developed – the Toronto settings are recognizable...Gordon's writing is clear, friendly and earnest. – **Greg Ioannou, 1996.**

Based in Toronto, the novel introduces David's crush on a straight man, his first friendship with another gay man, and his curiosity and fears about the new world he is entering. The book deals with important issues as homophobia within the Toronto community, the impact of coming-out, the introduction of HIV/AIDS, and the development of caring relationships. – **Bev Walpole, 2006.**

With strong dialogue, fast-paced narrative, and sufficient tension to keep the reader interested, The Toronto You Are Leaving is a tender and direct love story of a young gay man's coming-of-age in Toronto during the 1970's and 1980's. Gordon has written with wit, humour and empathy. – **Todd F. Towery, 2005.**

The Toronto of the 1970's and 1980's is portrayed with humour and pathos. The lively companionship and sexual ribaldry provides an enriched basis for a powerful novel, while it portrays the stark reality of a pandemic which continues to rock our world. – **Dawn Fasken, 2006.**

The warmth and eagerness of Gordon's writing – combined with the vivid, engaging characters and the fascinating story of The Toronto You Are Leaving – cannot fail to touch its readers. – **Natalee Caple, author, 1996.**

No other writer I know has captured the Toronto gay scene in the 1970's like Gordon Stewart Anderson. The Toronto You Are Leaving shows us what it was like to be young in the era of gay liberation, to live the university life, the gay life, the life of youth—and then, suddenly, to be plunged into unimaginable tragedy. One of the indispensable novels about Toronto. – **Ian Young, author of The Stonewall Experiment: A Gay Psychohistory, 2006.**

It remains folly to feel complacent about HIV/AIDS. Social, cultural and economic vulnerabilities create problems in controlling or curing this pandemic. A lack of education to prevent AIDS and a lack of compassion for those suffering from this disease stop our youth from controlling their lives and their health. Ignorance of gay and lesbian relationships create discord and emotional pain. Gordon's book presents insight into the life of a young gay Toronto man and that of his friends. His writing is unflinchingly brave and honest. This book speaks to each of us, and we should listen. – **Joan Anderson, 2006.**

The most powerful section, in my opinion, is 'Jack's Letter'. It has an articulate sense of anger, which I found enormously engrossing and compelling. It's also sweeping—and describes the historical elements in such an intimate way that I found it heart-breaking. Very moving, with an integrity and courage that clings to my mind. – **Stephen LeBlanc, 2006.**

This poem, about Marc Antony's desertion by his protector the god Bacchus when Alexandria was besieged by Octavian, was one of Gordon's favourites. It seems appropriate to include it here.

The god forsakes Antony

When suddenly, at the midnight hour,
an invisible troupe is heard passing with exquisite music, with shouts—
your fortune that fails you now, your works
that have failed, the plans of your life
that have all turned out to be illusions, do not mourn in vain.
As if long prepared, as if courageous,
bid her farewell, the Alexandria that is leaving.
Above all do not be fooled, do not tell yourself
it was a dream, that your ears deceived you;
do not stoop to such vain hopes.
As if long prepared, as if courageous,
as it becomes you who have been worthy of such a city,
approach the window with firm step,
and with emotion, but not
with the entreaties and complaints of the coward,
as a last enjoyment listen to the sounds,
the exquisite instruments of the mystical troupe,
and bid her farewell, the Alexandria you are losing.

Constantine P. Cavafy (1911)

PREFACE

The Toronto You Are Leaving is a smart, homoerotic, wickedly funny coming of age novel about queer life and love in mid-1970's Toronto. Most of the novel is a gay comedy of manners, and the world of this novel is not Toronto the Good but Toronto the Gay. But while it is an evocation of a simpler, more innocent time, there is still the apprehension and angst of coming out in a homophobic, Victorian city. But Toronto at the time was also brimming with easily available gay sex, and gay life was full of care-free promiscuity, which is often presented here very graphically and amusingly. The last two chapters are a dark, painful reminder of the heroic endurance and fortitude required of gay men after the horrific onslaught of AIDS.

In the 1986 sections, Tim and David, the two main characters, must deal with the impossible and lethal challenge. But Anderson does not allow AIDS to triumph, as for him the gay human spirit is indomitable. The surviving characters bravely carry on in the face of what appeared to be a never-ending gay holocaust. The two subjects—the gay coming of age comedy of manners, which occupies most of the book and the graphic evocation of the early years of AIDS—are both reflected in the title, which is an allusion to the 1911 poem, "The god forsakes Antony" by C.P. Cavafy. (See P. Epigram). But there is a lot more here than a poetic acceptance of suffering and death. The main subject and thrust of the novel is its witty depiction of the gay life and sex in Toronto in the 1970's. Surprisingly even now this work is one of the first major gay novels to capture and celebrate, in fiction, the 1970's Toronto queer scene.

The Toronto You Are Leaving is one you wish to linger in, not leave, as it lovingly depicts and mordantly satirizes gay life. Anderson evokes or describes many popular cruising spots in Toronto, including the old Y, the few gay bars, various parks and well-known downtown areas and streets. Including the lectures of Northrop Frye and Jay MacPherson, the buildings of Victoria College and its environs, Toronto—its mindset, mentality, and approach to life, people and traditions—is the life blood of the novel. Toronto has rarely been given this kind of attention and respect in gay literature.

Many of the characters are quintessentially Torontonian. For example, the very handsome 22 year-old Tim Grey is of old "grey" WASP Ontario stock that has some trouble adapting to this brave new Toronto world of many sexual and lifestyle possi-bilities. But the intelligent and resourceful Tim becomes quite the sexual adventurer in his endless search for perfect love. The other main characters—David McTavish, the bespectacled, scholarly 22 year-old Victoria College English student and virgin; Jack Durham, the Philosopher King older gay who is the intellectual centre of the novel and who also gives the reader a voluble vivid glimpse of the pre-Stonewall gay world;

Bobby Riding, the cute 17 year-old boy next door and Kelly, tough boy of the streets—all have their problems in dealing with the often harsh realities of Toronto's gay underworld and life in the 1970's. But they also delight in the incredible sexual diversity and gay life of the city. This is especially true of the sexually-inept David, whose awkward but hilarious coming-out process occupies a large chunk of the novel. It is an entertaining eye-opener of the range of gay life and sex in the '70's Toronto.

The Toronto You are Leaving is an original and impressive literary artifact of a lost time, of a bygone era in Toronto which was a simpler, sexier yet also a deadlier, more dangerous gay environment. The greatest strength of this historically significant novel is its colourful and entertaining depictions of places, people and gay lifestyles of a Toronto now gone.

James R. Dubro, 2006.

(James R. Dubro is the author of five best-selling true crime books and a television documentary producer and writer who has lived, worked and played in the gay village of Toronto since 1970. He has written recently on crime and policing for Xtra.)

The Toronto You Are Leaving

Gordon Stewart Anderson

Editor: B.M. Anderson, Ed.D., Ph.D.

UNTROUBLED HEART INC.

DISCLAIMER
This book is a work of literary fiction. Names, characters, places and incidents are the product of the author's imagination. Any resemblance to actual events, locales, or persons living or dead, is coincidental.

LIBRARY AND ARCHIVES CATALOGUING IN PUBLICATION

Anderson, Gordon Stewart, 1958 – 1991
The Toronto You Are Leaving / Gordon Stewart Anderson
ISBN 0-9780650-1-8
I. Title.
PS8601.N435T67 2006   C813'.6   C2006-901976-2

Printed and Bound in Canada by Coach House Press

Published by Untroubled Heart Inc.
130 Carlton Street, Suite 1101
Toronto, Ontario, Canada M5A 4K3

www.untroubledheart.com
email address: info@untroubledheart.com

DEDICATION

This novel is dedicated to Gordon's family and friends, whose patience and belief in the merits of his manuscript ensured its final publication. It is also dedicated to those who have experienced the impact of HIV/AIDS upon their lives and their loved ones.

WITH THANKS

With gratitude and affection, those who influenced the publication process of this novel are thanked. Gordon's talents and joy will remain with us always. Particular appreciation is offered to the following individuals:

Steve Walker, renowned artist, whose painting entitled Someone To Be Loved graces the front cover, is thanked for his kindness. Steve has had solo exhibitions in Toronto, Philadelphia, Key West, New York and Los Angeles. His paintings embody a political awareness with an acute sensitivity to the relationships between gay individuals. He is fully aware of the impact of HIV/AIDS which makes "the visibility and understanding of the gay community more critically essential than ever before".

Joan A. Anderson, Gordon's only sibling, transferred files from Gordon's computer and fragile floppy discs to create usable, formatted CD's which speeded the printing process. Her computer expertise, calm attitude and assurance in the merit of Gordon's work, made her "labour of love" a vital one.

Jon Lidolt's creativity in the cover and book design, and his unfailing enthusiasm, during each step of this journey were delightful.

Author James Dubro offered generous advice and steered us towards other talented individuals.

BILL anonymously helped to save Gordon's manuscript, located the perfect painting and artist, and encouraged Gordon in his writing. In Gordon's words, "Thanks for smothering me with food and for the last trip to Paris, France".

From Gordon's list and mine, come these names: Stephen LeBlanc, Bruce Dewhirst, Mary Hook, Michael W. Rogozynski, Bev Walpole, Reverend Brent Hawkes, Nick Nolte, John Anderson, Kip Peden, Ray Hemsley, Katie Lane, Lori Campana, Thom Brooks, Alexandra Schmidt, Laurie Colbert, Kerry Cohen, Howard Aster, Cherryl Murdoch, Sandy Horodezky, Shana Dewar and Lucas, Ian Dewar and Kirsten – everyone else who offered support and encouragement, a sincere thanks.

Stan Bevington and his capable crew made this dream a reality.

Despite so many talented helpers, there may remain errors. Should there be any, they are the responsibility of B.M. Anderson, Ed.D., Ph.D., literary executrix of Gordon's manuscript, his Mom and final editor.

TABLE OF CONTENTS

PROLOGUE
Early June, 1986

Somewhere, seemingly far in the distance, a clock radio came on. Raucous music worked its way through the layers of sleep that covered Tim's eyes, removing them one by one, until finally his right lid fluttered half open. The music sounded louder, closer, more insistent, piercing his skull like quick stabs of a needle. 'The Fat Boys', perhaps? His left eye joined his right one, opening ever so slowly, and squinted at the blaring clock radio beside the bed. It was 7:30 in the morning, in the real world. He groaned as he silenced the alarm. The memories were still so clear in his mind, he felt as though he was lying in his same old bed, in the same old room. His jeans were in their regular corner, and his old shirt hung on the closet door. Yesterday's underwear and socks lay where he had left them. It was morning, time to get up, dress and seek some sunshine. Yet, his muddied, sluggish thoughts yearned to dream.

Tim felt secure and relaxed among Alan's familiar furnishings, even though those were now placed in a different setting. This new apartment felt comfortable and welcoming. While Alan toiled at the office, it seemed logical for Tim to gather his things together and bike down to The Beaches. He would find a shady corner close beside the coolness of the water where he could languidly rest. To sleep perhaps, or to think about getting older in a life he didn't know what to do with right now.

But there was someone in the spot he'd been seeing for weeks, even before leaving New York. Yes, he and 'his spot' had become quite close. Just where the trees came almost to the water, a lean form surged up from the grass and resettled on its elbows over its book. His eyes found themselves startled to behold David McTavish, twice before Tim's lover. Had it really been five years since he had seen David? In Toronto for three days now, he'd meant to phone old friends, but found himself going around the city as if he knew no one there, except Alan Connor.

He felt a sudden weariness, the energy he needed to face David threatening to desert him, the sand crumbling under his steps as he kept moving forward.

Suddenly shutting his book, David sat up cross-legged, looking around. He was leaner, tighter, darker – the old David drawn with deeper, harder lines, looking exotic with a day's dark growth of beard.

The familiar long lashes came round to Tim – the eyes beneath them focussed and widened in surprise, or possibly dismay, that quickly gave way to cool recognition. It looked for one moment as though David might not forgive him for coming back. Then his arm came up, with an ironic angle, a greeting with warnings in it.

"Hello. I heard you were in town."

"Oh? I was going to phone, of course. But I don't know how long I'm staying. Can I join you?"

"Of course."

Tim shouldered backwards out of his knapsack, dropped it as he came up by David's towel and leaned over to undo the straps.

"So, David, how are you?"

"Not bad. And how've you been?" There was a pause that kept the two inquiries from balancing each other.

"Since I saw you last? That's a long time!" Tim put on something of an American accent, evoking Manhattan years to hide from David's curiosity. He unfurled his towel, as rich a red as blood glowing through the haze, and laughed as the breeze caught and crumpled it. "A lifetime, almost."

The towel floated down to rest. He stepped out of his shorts and dropped onto it. Untying his running shoes, he was caught short by a yawn. "Excuse me! I was out too late last night, I'm afraid."

"Yes, I know," said David, disconcertingly. "I bumped into Bob Riding this morning, and he said he'd seen you at Desire's. Up on the dance floor. Dancing away."

"Bobby! He's still around? How old is he now?"

"Twenty-seven."

"Bobby Riding twenty-seven? I don't believe it."

"It won't be too hard when you meet him."

Tim turned his runners upside down and watched them rain sand. "David, we're getting *old*." Descending into his T-shirt, he imagined Bobby's round, silent eyes watching while he lost himself in dancing, or tried to, or pretended to.

"But why didn't he say hello?"

"He was a bit shy, I guess. It's been a long time, hasn't it? But where are you staying? That's what we were wondering."

"At Alan's. You probably know, though, the house has been sold, and now Alan's found an apartment, the day before I arrived."

"We thought it might be that. But I was on Michael's side, and so was Bob. I don't know why, exactly, but you certainly had to choose sides."

Allowing a sad one-shouldered shrug for the end of Alan and Michael, Tim got suntan lotion out of his knapsack and began smearing it on his chest. Indifferently he didn't put on desire with this stuff any more. All he wanted was not to burn or get skin cancer.

On a sudden impulse, he thrust the bottle at David. "Do my back?"

For a second, the bottle waited between them uncertainly. David smiled wryly, his eyes closing, an old lover subsiding into a friend, and took it.

Tim shifted, looking south towards the dock and its conferring blondes. And behind, close to his ear, David said with mocking fierceness, "Only you've got to tell us, Timmy, what are you doing here?"

"I'm not sure. I don't know if I'm staying. But I had to get out of New York, find somewhere new. I gave up my apartment. I can't go back there now."

There was a silence behind him. David's touch had always been franker than his words, but the hand pushing up and down Tim's back could have been a stranger's. It was time to ask about David, his work, his life, but somehow it was hard to get started.

"Do you ever hear from Jack Durham?" Tim said. Bringing Jack in to mediate, he realized, to be their wise, older friend. "I haven't, not for years."

David's hand departed for a moment. "Oh, yes," David said. "All the time."

Tim waited for more, but nothing came. "Did he ever find the guy he went down there after, the beautiful what's-his-name? Jim, Jim Fields, the Boy At The End Of The Mind?"

"Yes, actually," David said. "Only it was Jim who found him. Came up in a corner store in the Castro and said hello."

"Really! So what happened?"

David gave an odd, dry laugh. "Well, they're friends now."

"Friends! After all that?"

"That seems to be the pattern."

"I miss Jack, you know," Tim said, apologetically. Would David see that he was talking about David too? "I really do. And I tried to get in touch the times I was in San Francisco. I even found his house, went and knocked on his door. His blue-gray door he sent us photographs of, remember? He and Fred were out of town. The women on the ground floor told me."

David's hand was moving briskly, impatiently applying lotion, as if, perhaps, he and Jack had had another of their strange quarrels. But all he said was: "That must have been a while back, if he was still with Fred."

"So Fred left? That's a shame," Tim said, cautiously. "He was good for Jack. Sensible. Down-to-earth. Good-natured," he said, finishing up with some painterly hand in the air flourishes.

David didn't comment. He dropped the *Bain de Soleil* onto the crimson towel, coughed and said, "Bob and I were down there this spring, for a visit."

"Do you like San Francisco?"

"Yes, doesn't everyone? It was my second visit, actually."

"You know, I'm just remembering something," Tim said, suddenly seeing it again. "I don't know why, exactly, something that happened last year. In the East Village, very late, so late it was getting light again, and I thought I saw Jack lying on the street. I don't know why, I hadn't been thinking about him. But there was an old guy propped up against a wall with garbage all round and glass, broken glass everywhere and I was terrified. I was sure it was Jack. Jack, but a wreck, forty years older. I ran over. I was almost calling his name. I wasn't stoned or drunk or anything, but for a moment or two, I felt like I must have been. I was really thinking, 'Jack, you always took life too hard, and now look at you. Look at you!'"

15

"Jack on the streets?" David said, thoughtfully. "No, I don't really think so." He gave Tim an odd look, and Tim's eyes dropped guiltily to David's book, a small, battered book with one word for its title: *Smoke*.

Why was he telling David this? There had been tears in his eyes as he ran, he remembered, and he had called out Jack's name. Exhaustion, surely, some deadline he'd barely met, or else too much to drink.

"The thing is, David, I couldn't have borne it if it had been him – maybe the hand-some faces, pastel-painted houses and a myriad of thoughts about Jack had merely confused me – but it felt like it had to be him, like I really had to talk to him, right then, at four or five in the morning, no matter what it took. Only it didn't even look like Jack when I got close. Just some old drunk, no mind left, or you hope not, anyway."

David laughed, as if he understood. "But you could just have phoned, couldn't you? He's in the book."

"You know what it's like, David. The years go by. You were always the one who wrote the letters, and then when I was with Kelly – "

"No," David said hastily, "I meant you didn't have to make poor old Jack a derelict just to see him again. In fact, he'll be visiting this summer too. Quite soon, I imagine, if you're sticking around."

"Really?"

"Yes. Staying at Bob Riding's. Because – " David drew it out, it was important news, " despite being in different cities, he and Bob are now officially lovers."

"Jack and Bobby? I don't –" But he laughed, because he did believe it. Life still could surprise him. He laughed again, remembering Jack and Bobby's first encounter, in David's, *in his and David's apartment* on Markham Street. His laughter had found its way out loud, so that the boys on the dock looked up with interest.

"It's only just starting," David said, with a fond, wise smile, a gay parent's fond, wise smile. "They're just like kids: very self-conscious and fragile. And 'we've got to be real-istic' and 'who knows how it will work out?' And they're right, I suppose: eighteen years makes quite a difference."

Then right out of the blue, with a sudden, angry look, David said, "I see you've put on a few pounds."

"Just five," Tim said, off balance. "I've been getting lazy. But at least it shows I'm healthy!"

Would David understand it, this new style of joking dread? People in the bars here didn't, not yet. But then, David had just been to San Francisco.

"Good," David said curtly, as if angry at him for understanding what he meant.

"Don't worry, David," Tim said, quietly. "I'm okay."

"Well, thank heaven," David said, almost angry still.

"Only I feel *old*," he confessed all at once, with an apologetic laugh. Getting back into his own sadness, which was all his own, which at its worst could kill only him.

"At thirty-four?" David's age too, but David's psychology had brought him to a very different thirty-four.

"Are you going to tell me that's silly? Maybe it is, if you're not eighty. Or forty. But aren't I allowed to feel old? And it has nothing to do with wrinkles or fat or being attractive, or diseases, or being gay. Or anything. Somehow, I just feel like feeling old these days. Like I've been young too long."

"Well, go ahead," said David. "But you aren't."

Tim laughed, fondly.

"If you say so, David!"

It was the first time David had spoken out like an ex-lover: privileged to say just what he thought, with the old complications safely in the past. Again it seemed time to ask after David's life and work and lovers, and again Tim put it off.

He let their conversation die away, looking out over the water. Transparent near the shore, it grew a hard, metallic skin farther out, but in between the surface vanished and reappeared, being nothing but light shaping itself over the swell. He imagined drawing it, painting it, but it was becoming a dream – the lake shifting in and out of reality as you watched.

His eyes closed for a moment. He didn't want to see it or dream it, that nothingness. "Let's catch up on everything later, okay David?" he said, in a lower voice. "I need to have a nap."

"A nap?" Sitting straight and taut, David was incredulous.

"Sure. My disco nap, like on Fire Island. I guess Bobby was right: I was overdoing it. But we're going out again tonight, Alan and I. Alan's very restless these days. He thinks he should want a new lover, though anyone can see it's the last thing he wants."

He rolled onto his front. The boys on the dock had arrived at some decision and now came wading and kicking in, as triumphant as if each had caught a fish in his Speedo. Tim closed his eyes as they ran by, drops spattering his face. Past envying their young luck, he rubbed his cheek into the towel, shaping the warm sand, hearing his sleepy heart.

"Remember," he said, "don't let me burn."

"You're safe, Timmy, don't worry," David said, dryly.

A shadow crossed his eyelids, made him open his eyes – David's hand coming down for his book, lifting it away. It was comforting to have David over him again, still reading. Everyone broke up, even Alan and Michael, but David and his book were solid.

"I'm glad I bumped into you, David. Really glad. Of course, I was going to phone." The warm sand made a safe place to say this from.

"But why didn't Bobby say hello to me?" It had been at the back of his mind: if Bobby, famous for hoping, had given up on him, what hope was left? He propped his chin on his hands to say this, focussing on small waves pelting up through stones. "Bob, I mean, if it has to be. He was never shy in a crunch, was he? I'd love to have seen him."

"Of course he wants to see you, but he said you seemed all wrapped up in dancing."

"In dancing? Lord help us!"

Looking down the lakeshore, Tim thought it again, as if the thought hung there like the four smokestacks: *he could die here*. People did, in quiet millions, far to the north of things, and now no rule said he shouldn't be one of them. What was he doing here, David had asked, *But really, David, he thought, the question was what he was doing anywhere at all*. All his life he'd felt welcomed, handsome and talented, a favourite, but then, very slowly, over months and years, it had begun to fall apart. *As if, David (because you like to think this way), there had always been something in him that didn't know if he was meant to live*. That had stopped him, brought his real living to a halt, emptied out the lines of the handsome faces, of the whole world, until he knew.

But after all David had grown older too, had gone out to meet the world and made a living, and perhaps he would say that sooner or later you would get over it and go back to what people in 1986 agree to call life.

He turned his head, burying an ear in the towel again, in the soft booming of his heart, letting his eyelids droop until he saw only brilliant grains of sand: broken rock, you saw, broken glass, ground so fine and soft you could sleep in it.

"I should have kept in touch, David, I know," he said. "With Jack. With you. But..."

THEN WHOEVER IT WAS THIS TIME WAS CALLING HIS NAME.

PART ONE: 1974

"What in man is most delicate, most free, and most threatened –
his dreams - may yet survive."

Gualtieri di San Lazzaro. *Klee, A Study of His Life and Work*, New York, 1964.

CHAPTER I: STRANGERS
Spring, 1974

When Tim first saw David, he wasn't attracted to him.

Waiting alone at the crossing from Queen's Park to the university, he was just an odd stranger, haggard and pale. A baggy raincoat kept his body a secret, except for six feet of height and a sad lean. Dark-brown, messy hair fluttered in the spring breeze. Watching from the bus stop at the other side, Tim wasn't attracted, but he was intrigued, and a little touched. There was a lost look about the stranger, as if his mind was all elsewhere – perhaps inside the heavy, rust-brown volumes he clutched under his arm.

Others, mostly university students from the sprawling St. George campus, were coming up from under the hazy green branches. Three bare-chested runners came loping up and stopped. The blondest paused beside the stranger's book-laden arm. The stranger was still lost to everything: the foot race about to start, the spring around him, its pale-faced chests.

A break in traffic started a hurried crossing, and he was hindmost, the raincoat clinging around his knees, his books sliding back. With a new spate of cars coming on, they dropped to the asphalt. *Abandon them*, Tim thought, but the stranger was squatting, clawing at the books. *Hurry*, Tim urged, afraid of what he might witness. The long, desperate fingers got into the white innards; the stranger rose and ran to the curb, books flapping like dead birds. To the curb, to Tim, who held out his arms a little, smiling.

But as he leapt onto the sidewalk, the stranger's long face was empty. Tim's welcome meant nothing to him. Just as Tim was turning away, a smile emerged: small, shy, sideways. Like the memory of a smile, from the memory of a spring.

PART 2

It didn't look like the beginning of a long friendship.

For his part, David hardly noticed Tim – the person who was going to become Tim, in such fine detail. David was almost blinded by the fear and the love of Chris Leggatt. He had only just persuaded himself to go through the park, because Chris had appeared there several times. He had even stopped the week before to talk about China, kicking a scaly heap of snow. Just now, Chris had appeared, for about five seconds. There was something in the fine cut of his features that let them be seen at a considerable distance, even when they weren't there at all. Chris vanished quickly enough, but David's disappointed heart had lurched into its old, mad pounding regardless, pounding as if it didn't need him, or could hammer out a Chris of its own. It was just slowing down as he waited to cross the road, leaving him exhausted and depressed.

Getting the load of books under control, David went past the fair-haired stranger to the library, where Chris might sometimes appear in the long, dusty ranges of books. As it turned out Chris didn't appear at all that week – only the blond young man, in front of University College, smiling as he went by and saying, "Hi."

Hi? David was taken aback. This stranger had seen him escape the jaws of death, but that wasn't an introduction. The smallest hello escaped him, wrapped in sarcasm.

The next week, waiting for a light at Bloor Street and Avenue Road, he found the blond young man had come up beside him. David gave out a tight, conspiratorial smile, looking straight ahead, pressing one rusty-brown book into his side.

"Hello," the stranger said, nervously.

"'Lo," David croaked. It was the first time he had spoken that day.

"Nice day."

David cleared his throat. He shook the dry folds of his umbrella. "They say it could *pour* this afternoon."

"Really?" The husky baritone went up and softened in protest. "I hope not."

The light turned green and they began crossing, not quite together.

"But if the sun keeps shining," David said, "I'm bound to forget this damn thing somewhere."

It was a test: Was the stranger intelligent enough to be amused – amused in the right way? David didn't hope for much. He was beginning to piece Tim together, with quick side-glances. They were the same age and height, but Tim was more strongly built – "athletic," – David would have said disdainfully. His hair was a dark blond; he had darker eyebrows and brown eyes. A tan had begun to infiltrate the winter pallor of his skin. He wore a dark red cotton shirt, the sleeves shoved breezily back, and soft, tight, washed-out blue jeans. The shirt was stylish and expensive, so far as David could judge. His accent, his manner, were Toronto middle class. And he walked in blue running shoes, light-footedly.

In short, he was quite presentable, but David felt sure he had seen through his "nice day" almost from the start. "Clearly," as Roland Akenside had said, explaining Mr. Eugenides in *The Waste Land*, "clearly, homosexual seduction." Mr. Akenside had paused to breathe in the thrill going around the seminar table: now David felt just as knowing. He could almost feel sorry for this misguided young man, who didn't know how thoroughly previous inquirers had been squelched.

"My name's Tim Grey," the stranger ventured.

David let it hang uncertainly in the air for a moment. For another moment. But it sounded all right.

"I'm David McTavish."

He looked sideways at Tim through 'Tim,' through 'Grey.' He was handsome enough, David supposed. Handsome in the easy way of blonds, unlike Chris, whose looks David thought of as a secret only he had penetrated.

Then, for a second or two, his gaze got stuck on the nape of Tim's neck: golden-brown, with a barely visible feathering of hair.

"What's that you're reading?" Tim asked, glancing at David's book.

"This?" He was embarrassed, almost guilty, remembering Tim had seen him risk his life for its younger sisters. "*Clarissa*. It's an eight-volume eighteenth-century novel, all in letters."

"Interesting?" Tim asked, a little dryly.

But David wouldn't let *Clarissa* be insulted by some hockey fan: she was worth dying for, after all. "*Fascinating*." He added, just to shake him up, "Now she's been raped, poor lady."

"Raped!"

David laughed, delighted. "Yes. In a way, though, you can hardly blame him – Lovelace, the villain. He's been after her for volumes. But then he drugs her – that's not fair, is it? She wakes up and it's too late: the deed's been done."

Tim smiled – he had a wide mouth with well-turned lips, that seemed to allow for many shades of smiling – and said, "The guy I was living with last year was taking a lot of English courses."

"Oh?" Had he been outflanked?

"But he gave it up. He decided it was all irrelevant."

"Oh it is!" David said, gratefully. But his opinion of Tim had gone up: the English student was a good sign.

"In a way," Tim said, thoughtfully, "that's why we broke up."

David looked up at the sky over Bloor Street: innocent blue with inoffensive puffs of white. You don't break up with a mere roommate, do you? He and Mr. Akenside were right, after all. The voice was a bit too soft, too emotional: this nice boy's niceness went too deep. Although, on the other hand, you had to admire his nerve: Tony Shawcross had darkened the air with hints, but never confessed, as Tim just had, to being homosexual.

"I'm hungry," Tim said, stopping them in front of a restaurant, a stylish cafeteria with walls of glass. "Do you feel like lunch? This is where I was headed." He smiled, a little defiantly, as if he'd been reading David's thoughts, and now was throwing down a challenge. "It's just a cafeteria, but it's okay."

"I've never been there," David said, doubtfully. His stomach contracted.

Then Tim produced a wide, reassuring smile, as if promising to be good.

"If it's not too expensive?" David wondered. And as Tim shook his head, "Sure, why not."

After all, if Tim was homosexual, David didn't have to be—in fact, he wasn't, except in the inner world where Chris lived. The graduate student Tim was going to lunch with could be merely a tolerant man of the world. He could learn something about the world too.

But then, holding the door for Tim, he saw there was a tear in the washed-out jeans, a finger's length of white thigh leering at him knowingly. He blinked, not believing it at first, but it was there, it was frayed and old, like the evil double of Tim's reassuring smile. Once inside those glass walls, he would be trapped: Tim Grey could do anything, could become anything. For a second he wanted to let the door close on Tim and run.

They got into line and ordered their meals. Tim said, "He's out in the 'real world' now. Working."

"Who?"

Tim didn't lower his voice. "My old lover, Dennis."

David's coffee tried to leap from its mug, and scalded his fingers. There were people on either side of them. "Damn!" he said imploringly.

"Now he's into being one of those uptown gays you see down here." Tim actually looked around them, out through the glass walls. "Which is okay. He's not bad at it."

"*A chacun son infini*," David mumbled.

Tim only smiled uncomprehendingly, pushing along to the cash register.

After paying, they went outdoors to a small table and sat down, face to face for the first time. If only in self-defense, David took up the social questions. Tim was from Toronto, David from Victoria, B.C. – "Oak Bay, to be precise." Both had been born in 1952, Tim arriving a month sooner. Tim was a student, like David – at the U. of T. before, but now at O.C.A.

It took David a moment or two to pry the initials apart. "Ontario College of Art?"

"Yes."

"Oh." Surprised, impressed, David gave this art student a long look. He must live in art the way David lived in books, in the sound and dark shining of words. For David art was a huge, unvisited museum, one of many famous, grand places on the planet he hadn't got to yet. But now even David's mole-eyed, million-voiced world grew brighter around Tim's blond hair and red shirt. He wanted to ask about O.C.A. but didn't know where to start.

"So what's grad school like at U. of T.?" Tim said. "Dennis toyed with the idea for a few months."

"Oh – boring, frantic, incestuous. We all sit around trading Northrop Frye stories and wondering what they'll hit us with on the Comprehensives."

David speared white asparagus, complacently. Tim said, "So, do you like it?"

"Like it?" David said, cheerfully. "Of course not!"

"Dennis used to do little numbers like that, too."

"Your lover?" David said, with fine, brave tolerance.

"Yes. My ex-lover."

David looked at this young man who had had a lover and could now let the fact escape into the Bloor Street sunshine. He seemed too young to have such a past: it was still a surprise, somehow, that Tim was the older, if only by a few weeks. To have such a past contentedly inside him, like yesterday's lunch, digested and turned into blond flesh and smiling out at you. David had begun to notice that his upper lip was a little ʃhorter than might have been expected, and how this gave his smile a keen, exciting edge.

And then, surprising David, out came laughter, three airy leaps of happiness from his dark insides. The world seemed to loosen and expand around him. Him, them.

"Do you know there's a tear in your jeans?" he said, daringly.

"Of course I know."

David looked across the side street, into a store window full of Danish furniture, jewellery, porcelain. This area of Bloor, west of Yonge, was sardonically referred to as the Mink Mile. Rich-bitches sifted along window-shopping, toting lavishly coloured paper bags emboldened by portable advertising of up-scale shops. The not-so-rich "touchers and ticklers" of merchandise, trudged among them.

"That's thanks to Dennis, actually," Tim explained. "He went through a phase of cutting holes in our clothes in strategic places – he thought they were sexy."

How wasteful, David thought, how irresponsible and how rich. Obviously, Tim was at home on this expensive stretch of Bloor. That finger of white skin had made a hole in his defenses, and David thought of speaking out as he never had with anyone. It might, after all, be a good time to let go of his secret. Or rather, to practice letting go. Tim, after all – too handsome, too blond, too rich ever to fit into David's harried life – was like a stranger beside you on a ship. It was the ferry over to Vancouver that David saw: you could say anything while the islands slid by, sure that he'd disappear on the mainland.

How could he get started? 'You're homosexual. That's interesting, because, as a matter of fact, I wonder if you guessed, but – .' That was impossible: David coughed and looked down at his book, almost giving up. But then he saw his way clear. There would be nothing abrupt or embarrassing, because it could all be done with Chris's help. Chris, or the feeling of Chris, would come along and keep him safe.

"Oddly enough – " but David had to clear his throat, as if this was his first speech of the day" – oddly enough, I was discussing that subject recently. With a friend."

Tim smiled, a little puzzled.

"What subject?"

"You know. Homosexuality." Seven endless syllables: they almost took more breath than David had inside him. But they were out and, being intelligent, Tim must see what they meant. A full confession: total surrender. The most daring thing David had ever done.

Tim's knife screeched a little on his plate.

"Oh? And what did you and your friend decide?"

24

"He did most of the talking, really. He's a Maoist"—David presented this fact gently and proudly – "and he was talking about revolution. It all got started with women's liberation – he'd had an argument with his girlfriend, and he was saying the women's movement had to realize only a real revolution can make any difference. And the same went for the gays, he said."

Chris had thrown in "the gays" as an afterthought: he was being up-to-date, keeping an eye on the signs of the times. Completely unprepared, David flinched. Luckily, Chris was glowering south towards the Queen's Park Legislative Buildings. Kicking the dwindling snow, he went on angrily summoning all oppressed minorities to join him in storming that apoplectic pile. David shrank, afraid Chris would look and see him at last.

But he hadn't: they could go on as before.

Tim's knife screeched again, like an angry peacock.

"Well, you can tell your friend we're not waiting around for the straights to liberate us. Or we'd wait forever."

Disconcertingly, Tim had become as political as Chris.

"And frankly," he went on, "he sounds like the usual middle class, Canadian Marxist to me. And they're about as anti-gay as they come."

"Maoist," David insisted. He was proud that Chris had gone all the way. "His background is middle-class, of course. But he's really passionate about it. He's had big fights with his family."

"You don't need Chairman Mao for that," Tim said, bitterly.

David didn't respond. Tim seemed to have missed the real point completely.

"For instance," Tim said, "try asking him about Cuba. Before the revolution, they were going to be good to the gays there. But now it's all decadence, bourgeois sickness."

"He talks about Cuba, but not that."

"Well – ask him."

It was a command, abrupt and rude. But what did Cuba have to do with anything? Tim was being obtuse, and David was almost ready to give up on him.

"Maybe when I see him," he said, coldly. He looked down at the scraps of his sandwich, suddenly depressed. When would that be, after all? He hadn't been seen for days: he might have left town, for all David knew.

"He's not really a close friend," he admitted.

"Oh?"

"We were just in the same course for a bit. "The Novel and Society, 1814-1914." It was his outside course: he's in political science."

David gave a sad laugh.

"Then he decided Geoffrey Exton had a shitty analysis and dropped out. I still see him around, we talk politics, or he does. It's obvious I'm not really Maoist material, but I guess he thinks he ought to try. To save my soul, I suppose. It's really that

Methodist Victoria College stuff. Did you go there?"

"No, Trinity."

"Anyway, his great-uncle was a famous missionary in China, too. China runs in the family."

"What's his name? Dennis knew some left-wing students."

It was impossible, really: Chris and "one of those uptown gays." But David couldn't resist the chance to say the name out loud, something he could usually do only when alone.

"Chris Leggatt."

Tim gave an odd, knowing smile, as if he had something up his sleeve. David didn't understand it.

"Oh, yes. He really looks like a Marxist. A big, fat guy, balding, bad acne?"

"No!" Tim had almost shoved this repulsive person into his arms. Was he making him up, to tease him? Either way, he had to set the record straight. "No. Chris is shorter than me. Not much, though. Dark brown hair, wire-rimmed glasses, and – "

David looked away, breath taken, unable to utter the colour of Chris's eyes. He looked back into Tim's, which seemed at last to see what he was getting at.

"I've had crushes on straight guys," Tim said gently. "It happens; it's part of being gay."

Now, Tim understood all too well. David sat back, straightening up, putting his arms behind the back of his chair.

"That must have been very awkward," he muttered.

"Oh, it was. Agonizing!" Tim laughed gently, but at him, at David McTavish, for being so foolish as to have 'a crush' (as if that was all it was) 'on a straight guy' (as if Chris was just one among billions). He wondered angrily why he had spoken to Tim at all: certainly not for this slippery sympathy.

Picking up his fork, he cut firmly down into cheesecake, now just another student up to taste the Bloor Street *douceur de vivre* before his next hundred lines of *Beowulf*. Because Tim must see that the time for confessions was over forever, that they had clearly failed to hit it off. David would soon be back in the library, while Tim's smile, still waiting now for some response, faded into the huge city that had produced it.

"Sooner or later," Tim said, "you realize you've got to go on living. That you can, that you aren't the only one in the world."

"Mm," David said, his mouth filled with sweetened cream cheese. Perhaps someday he would come down to the same conclusion, but not this year. Chris had said that he would probably be around during the summer.

Tim began on strawberries and clotted cream. Apparently, he saw at last what David wanted: reflective, comfortable silence about 'homosexuality'. Maybe David could say something polite about Tim's studies, though he'd risk sounding like a frigid lady from Oak Bay.

Then Tim spooned up a strawberry in cream and raised it in a sardonic toast.

"Welcome, David!"

"What do you mean?"

"What you seem to be saying – I hope I'm not wrong," Tim laughed at the thought, "is that you're gay too."

David pouted. If it wasn't perfectly clear by now, Tim must be very dense.

"Well?" Tim said. And he ate the strawberry.

David gave him an angry look. Tim was being a tyrant. And the smile made things worse, knowing too well how winning it was.

Tim leaned forward, attacking. "You aren't in Cuba, you know. You aren't in the eighteenth century. It's *1974*."

Counting out the number, he held himself, there and alive in a crimson shirt, as if showing just what '1974' meant.

"So why can't you say it? *I'm gay*."

Tim had lowered his voice, but not by much. "*I'm gay*," he'd said, meaning himself, meaning David, and the word shrieked, calling everyone around to look at them. At him, David McTavish, exposed at last. He was walled in by staring eyes he didn't dare look at, and the roar of talking, laughing, eating, surged around him, about to close over his head. He opened his mouth, trying to say something about Chris, because whatever he was it was all between Chris and himself. But in his panic, with Tim and the whole angry race staring at him, he couldn't quite remember Chris, couldn't reach down into the feelings he had been hoarding for eight months.

"Can't you talk at all?" Tim said, with rough sympathy.

No, he couldn't. The mob was roaring for his blood, for his soul, and now Tim was part of it. If there was concern in his look, it wasn't nearly enough to trust your life to.

But with David's silence stretching out and out, a look of real fear came into Tim's face. He reached for his arm. Given strength, David pulled away before he could be touched.

"All right. I'm gay," he growled. "But what a *stupid* word!"

"Good, thank heaven," Tim said, relieved.

But now David couldn't stop.

"Of course I am," he went on. "Isn't it obvious? But what is it to you?"

He found he was getting up, not willing it, borne up on a gust of panic.

"Are you going?" Tim said, dismayed.

"Yes, I'm going, damn it. Goodbye."

The fifth volume of *Clarissa* caught his eye: he snatched it away, and the umbrella. "Because who are you, anyway?" he growled. "Just who the hell are you?"

PART 3

And, though Toronto isn't nearly as big a city as David thought, that might easily have been that.

But next week, on a gray afternoon, Tim saw David again, coming out of the College Street Eaton's store in the baggy raincoat, squeezing an Eaton's bag into his chest. David had seen him first, glaring at him through thick glasses, as if he'd begun to go blind. He must have been wearing contact lenses before.

Tim tried an uncertain smile, but it looked as though David would go by in scathing silence. With a flash of impatience, Tim felt willing to let him go, to forget what had happened in the restaurant as an experiment that failed.

When they'd begun talking on the street, Tim hadn't even been sure that David was gay. Certainly, he occupied his world, moved around in it, with inflections of tenderness and diffidence rare in straight, young Canadian males. The real question, Tim saw, was probably how much had got through to David and himself. The dry, sarcastic air, the bachelor fussiness, the prim sarcasm all suggested some decision to step up and back from life into permanent virginal hysteria.

As David had begun letting out wistful looks, and talking about his friend, who brought a soft glow into David's voice, Tim had thought he was doing what was really wanted. He had coaxed out the truth. He had done similar things before, with friends at Trinity, at O.C.A. David wanted to say he was gay, but needed help to get the painful word out. But then, out of nowhere, panic had struck, like a wind of fear and rage, blowing David away down the street. The fear had touched Tim too, alone, abandoned in the restaurant. Feelings he thought he had put behind him in 1974 began to resurface. He'd been angry by the time he left the restaurant a few minutes after, angry and righteous. David might hate him, but he'd given him a push he obviously needed.

They almost passed each other below the walls of the College Street store, but then David's left hand came up out of the deep raincoat pocket and moved briefly through the raw air. The gesture was obviously all Tim was going to get.

"Who's he?" asked Tim's companion, his best friend, Alan Connor.

The doubt in Alan's voice said David hardly seemed to belong to their world. But being good-natured, Alan wasn't quite dismissing him either.

"I guess he's sort of an experiment," Tim said. "Or was." He explained what had happened in the restaurant.

"So what are you up to, Tim?" Alan said.

"I'm not up to anything. It just happened, that's all. I liked him, basically: maybe that's why I was so hard on him. But really, it's like he's sixteen and lovelorn. Like me in Grade Eight, remember, like you and Jamie Blair – but at twenty-two, with some pompous little Maoist twit."

"I wonder how it will turn out?"

"You know how. A year from now I'll see him in a bar– different clothes, a decent haircut – at first I won't recognize him. He won't say hello, he won't forgive me for that scene, and the incredible raincoat and those books all over the road. And I won't really mind: that's how it is, isn't it? Gays use each other that way. You *do* understand – he was doing what was necessary...*surviving*."

"He's probably not that bad looking, actually," Alan said, thoughtfully.

"You think so?" Tim demanded.

Alan laughed. "Well, we'll see. Next year in the bar."

But only a few days later, Tim saw David striding west on Bloor. It was a sunny day, and David was wearing an old blue polo shirt with gray corduroy pants, and the lenses were in again. From behind, a different person seemed to emerge. Seemingly, a different David lived hidden in regions of himself he couldn't oversee or keep up to the mark. His back was tense and intellectual, but it was a good, honest, Canadian back, shouldering its share of northern sky. An expressive back, which made Tim feel that David was alone four thousand miles from home. He ran after him, crossing Avenue Road, and caught up with him beside the Royal Ontario Museum.

"David," he said, coming down from running, breathing faster than he would have expected. "How are you doing?"

David looked sideways, warily, and coughed up a voice.

"Fine, actually."

"I'm really sorry – "

"Oh, no, don't be." David was suddenly friendlier, flattered by Tim's approach, or impressed with his courage. "It was me, really. It was a bit crazy: somehow it felt like everyone could hear every word."

Tim laughed, relieved. "They wouldn't have cared very much if they had. Not in that restaurant. Anyway, I'm sorry. I was being a bit arrogant , I guess."

They went on in silence: healing silence, Tim hoped.

"I haven't seen him today," David said, suddenly. "I never do, along this stretch – it's not his territory. I don't know why."

This was embarrassing: it had an addict's single-mindedness. And Tim had disliked David's friend from the start: he was ridiculous; he was unhealthy.

"Is that all you think about?" Tim protested.

"No. There are other things." David gave him a smile. "My papers. Movies. Records – can I afford them? You."

"Me?"

"Well, I couldn't help wondering, afterward. Who was this person I'd told all my secrets to? Spilled my guts to? He knows everything about me, and..."

David seemed to run out of nerve.

"Fair enough," Tim said. "What secrets would you like to know?"

David smiled, obviously delighted. "Are you living with someone, for instance? Like the one who cut up all your clothes? Dennis, I mean," he added, admitting he hadn't forgotten the name.

"Not now. No."

"Why not?"

Tim laughed. "I've been asking that myself lately. But I've been very busy, finishing my year at O.C.A. – and other projects."

"Yes, I know how it is," David said. "I'm 'way behind, too."

Then he fell silent, thinking of his work, perhaps, or suddenly shy.

"That's where it's all waiting for me," he said suddenly, looking toward a four-storey, brown-brick building. "That's where they keep us – the Graduate Student Residence."

"I've never been inside," Tim said, "but Dennis knew people there. You see some gorgeous men, he said, from all over the world."

"That's true. I suppose you do," David said vaguely. "Anyway, right now, I guess I ought to finish off *Clarissa*. She's dead at last. It was the only way out – but she wrote everyone beforehand, and now it's snowing letters."

They halted in front of the entrance, a gateway leading into a courtyard.

"Well, I guess I'll see you around," Tim said, doubtfully.

"Where are you going now?" David demanded.

"Swimming. To the Y." He was a little embarrassed to admit—if David knew where the Y was – that he'd come out of his way.

David blinked. "Maybe though, you'd like to come up for a drink?"

Seeing Tim's hesitation, he added, "Just tea, I mean. Or instant coffee."

Tim was still reluctant. He'd wanted to make sure that David was all right – that he wasn't still angry and suffering – but did he want such a complicated person for a friend?

But he'd told Alan he liked David, and it was true.

"Sure, great. It's still early."

He followed David in under the gateway. As its shade came over them, David asked, "Do you like Bruckner?"

"What?"

David was patient. "The composer, you know, Anton Bruckner? I'm working my way through him. He wrote nine symphonies, more or less."

"More or less – couldn't he count?"

"There's one that didn't get catalogued at first. So it's called *Due Nullte*."

They were passing a dry fountain planted with sun-shriveled petunias.

"The Nothingth," David went on. "Bruckner can be heavy, but he's very ..."

One of Dennis's gorgeous men came through the door they were heading for, Arab, perhaps, or Iranian, with olive skin and enormous eyes. David didn't notice him, trying to do justice to the composer.

"Grand," he said. "Romantic. Stirring. I'd better lead the way."

They went up stairs and along corridors, till one very short corridor framed a lone blue door. David was fishing out keys.

"I warn you, it's a mess." He opened the door and rushed inside – into a startlingly small room, just big enough for a single bed, a desk, a radiator and a bookshelf. Immediately, he began gathering up clothes, books, records, and a telephone. He pulled up the bedcovers, cranked open the one high window, and turned, grabbing a box of Kleenex from the bed, to confront Tim.

"My small corner," he said. "I should have applied sooner."

It was almost too much to have two six-foot tall men within the little room. Tim regarded the tissue box and its virginal, white blossom, understanding its pathos. David blushed fiercely, tossed it on top of the bookshelf and pulled out the desk chair.

"Welcome," he said. "You can sit here."

PART 4

With Tim about to leave, David feared that he may not have been forgiven.

How could he convince him? His friendship mattered. Tim was very different from the harried graduate students who were almost the only people David knew in Toronto. Besides, now that Tim had his secret, he wanted to keep an eye on him, and talk to him about it. To bring him farther into the world of being in love with Chris. He imagined them meeting, all three of them, all friendly. And afterwards he would ask Tim, "You see? You see what I mean?"

Then, in the corridors, with Tim behind him, unseen and mostly silent, David began to wonder why he had invited Tim to cross his threshold. The room was small: "about the size of Raskolnikov's," as he'd put it to graduate student friends. It was so small it was dangerous. What if the stranger behind him was planning things that David had only read about? Read and masturbated about, as if his lonely cock knew better than he did what goes on out there in the world.

So David had burst in on his room, raiding it like the police, showing just how fierce he could be. Then, turning, he'd seen that Tim's polite upbringing had come down from Forest Hill to watch over them. Even his intelligent glance at the Kleenex was polite. Relieved, David decided not to lay down a barrage of music. He was eager to talk.

There was an awkward silence at first, as if they were waiting for the kettle to speak up first. Then, David coughed and asked about the Y. Tim swam a mile every other day, he said, and the nervous way he moved his shoulders brought the wet lengths into the little room.

"That's a lot. I should swim more," David said, pouring water into the teapot. "But the Hart House pool gets so crowded."

"Well, that can be fun, too! But of course, not if you're a serious swimmer."

David sat on the bed, knees pulled up, tall bony sisters.

"So what are you doing for the summer," he asked. "Aside from paring seconds off your mile?"

"I want to do some painting, on my own," Tim said, suddenly shy. "This is the first time I've had a really free summer. Last year, with Dennis, I had my hands full. The summers before, I was up in Napier, north of here where my parents lived."

"They've moved?"

"No. No, my father's dead. He had a heart attack. Before I started at O.C.A."

"Oh. Oh, I'm sorry." Tim looked young to be fatherless. What was it like, David wondered.

"What about you?" Tim said. "Are you staying for a course?"

"No, but I have papers left over. And I'm reading for the comprehensives. I could do that in Victoria, of course, but well, I thought I'd stay."

"It will be hot in here," Tim said, looking around.

"Yes, but – well, Chris is probably going to be around."

"Is *that* why you're staying? When you could be in Victoria?"

David shifted on the narrow bed. "Yes, basically."

"Really?" Tim looked at him with a kind of sympathetic disgust. "David – why don't you just tell him?"

"Tell him what?"

"Well – that you're going to spend the summer sweltering in this little room, just so you can see him around for a few minutes on the street. Maybe, if you're lucky."

David shrugged, safe, unassailable. He stood up to pour the tea, complacently, as if the tea was all the answer Tim would get. Tim didn't understand: it wasn't a matter of a few minutes. If Chris was in town, he would be around all the time in the air, round all the corners.

"I'd like to tell him," David conceded. "I've thought of it. I've rehearsed it!" He laughed, looking around, embarrassed, at the walls that had heard him. "But who knows how he'd react? Under it all, he's a real Puritan. There are times when those glasses flash just like Northrop Frye's!" He laughed, but it was true. "If I did say something he might be very good about it. Or he might just never say a word to me again."

"Would that really make any difference?"

"Of course it would! I could hardly bear it when he dropped out of "The Novel and Society". I was almost suicidal." David laughed, and ducked into his tea, scared Tim might guess how fondly he'd been thinking about razor blades. "I even gave up one of my other seminars, a class analysis of *The Waste Land*. If Roland Akenside didn't like me, that *would* have been suicide."

"But he's got to be wondering. He knows you don't have a girlfriend, doesn't he?"

"But there are lots of us in graduate school. We haven't discovered girls yet: we're too busy. Some of us never will – do you know how fast the books and articles pile up? But that's all right – we're happy, we're occupied."

"Is he that behind the times? One of the things about gay liberation, David, is that there are no more 'bachelors,' not like that. And obviously he knows there are gays in the world, if he's going to ask us to his revolution."

"He does give me an odd look from time to time..."

"David, you're twenty-two!" Tim said, suddenly. "And a virgin."

"How do you know that?"

"I took a wild guess."

"Well, it isn't Kitty Saunders' fault! But, after all, twenty-two's not old. Yeats lost his virginity when he was thirty-four: you know, the poet. And then he said 'I know all now.'" David laughed. "It didn't hurt him, did it? I figure that gives me twelve years."

Tim shifted in the wooden chair, protestingly. "David, what do you want from all this? All this being in love?"

"Want?"

"Don't you ever want to get him in bed, for instance?"

"No! I've never even *touched* him." And there'd been two times when he might have, probably without a catastrophe: three, if you counted the thread on his duffel coat in February.

"But that's what you really want," Tim declared.

"Is it? Why? You know, you've got an *extremely* simpleminded view of things. What I want is to talk and be friends. The way we are now – that's fine, really, it's enough."

David tried to make this sound final, but he could hear wistful tendrils coming out from under, like roots of a pot-bound plant.

Tim opened his hands, as if he gave up, and David suddenly felt disappointed. It was a pleasure to talk about Chris, whatever he had to say: he didn't want to stop.

As if to escape, Tim turned to the desk, right beside him, picking up a small green hardcover, flagged with torn strips of paper. With big, long-fingered hands, he opened it at the first page. There were flecks of paint along his fingers, David noticed: the bright colours of art. David laughed: Tim looked too big to make his way into the little book.

"What?" Tim demanded, the first sentences of *Mansfield Park* hanging in his eyes.

"I don't know. I was thinking, what would Jane Austen say if she saw you there, in jeans and running shoes in 1974, reading her?"

"You're the English student."

David laughed again. "When Geoffrey Exton said there are only two kinds of people in the world – the people who prefer *Mansfield Park* to *Emma*, and the people who prefer *Emma* to *Mansfield Park* – it nearly drove Chris wild. He said Exton was a twit. So I said, "Yes, of course, but he's a brilliant twit.""

David looked sadly at the green book as Tim put it down again to listen.

"But it didn't help. He still dropped out."

"Poor old David."

"Not really. No. Why? I don't see it that way."

Tim smiled, with a new, hopeful twist to his smile.

"But he still works out at Hart House? That's something."

"Yes – that's why I run, really. From up on that old track you can see down into the whole gym. But I can't figure out his schedule – I don't think he has one."

"But at least you see him."

"Yes, sure, I should count my blessings, you mean."

Tim's smile was stealing up into his cheeks.

"Does he have a nice body?"

David pulled his shins up, defensively.

"He had all his clothes on when I got to know him."

"But it wasn't his clothes that got you interested, was it?"

"It wasn't his body, either. It was him."

"Oh?"

"There was one time," David admitted, hesitantly. "In the showers by the pool, but he was over in the other shower room. And thank God!"

"Why?"

David let out a painful yelp at the memory. "I'd gone in, not expecting anything, and then I saw him there, all – white. It was January, February, the dead of winter. I was so confused I turned the cold on full, and let out a terrific squawk."

He laughed, proudly. His life wasn't nearly as dull as Tim thought.

"He didn't notice. I took a very quick, sort of pretend shower, and ran. Then I came back here and wrote a poem about it. At least, about water and drains and hearts and houses and young men dying in the Great War. He isn't actually mentioned."

He stopped, thinking over the long poem. "It's that subtle," he said, ruefully. He dared to look into Tim's eyes, still eager to see. "To answer your question, yes, I think he does. Have a nice body." He tried to sound judicious, objective. "He's a bit soft in the stomach, maybe – he's not that athletic. He's too busy. But I find I can forgive that – that little pot belly." He stopped himself: he was getting sentimental.

"Is he well-hung?"

The bed squeaked in protest.

"Is that what you mean by gay liberation?"

"Yes."

David took a baleful gulp of tea, delighted and scared.

"Well, is he?"

"I told you I could hardly see. All I can remember now is the steam and the water and the tiles. And the trenches full of corpses, of course."

"I wonder, does your boyfriend have a cock at all?"

"I'm sure he does," David said, coolly. Then a laugh broke out. "God, I hope so!" He pulled himself together. "But that's not what counts. It's him. His personality. His *presence*."

Tim smiled as if ready to come out with some new outrage. Then, disconcertingly, he sighed.

"I know what it's like, David."

It was nostalgic, as if he wanted to talk about love-affairs of his own. To distract him, David leaned and refilled his mug.

"You know what you need, David?" Tim said, taking a drink of tea. "A boyfriend. A real one. One who's got a body."

"I've got one," David said loyally. "I've got what I want."

Tim gave him a long, bemused look. Then he shrugged as if, for now at least, he had given up on him. He stood up, to look at prints on the wall, and stopped at a Klee taped above the desk. Blue depths and clever fish.

"Do you like Klee?" David said.

"Yes. Although, he can be too dry and intellectual."

"Dry?" Did Tim mean him? "That's the *ocean*. I love those dark blues."

"Oh?" Tim turned and looked down at him. David almost said, 'Sit down. You're making me nervous.' Tim stepped over and began to rub the back of David's neck, stiffly, as if he wanted to get rid of his anxiety by thrusting it on David. David looked up at him in fierce silence until Tim took his hand away.

"I like you, David," he said, uncertainly.

Behind his stare, David tried to figure out what to do. He would almost find the tone to say, 'Well, I guess you want to go swimming now, don't you?'

Tim sat down on the bed, beside David. He reached, slowly, giving David every opportunity to object, and put his arm around him. David stiffened, about to pull away, then slumped sideways against Tim, his arms as loose as a puppet's. He hadn't decided what to make of Tim's initiative, but it might be wasteful to turn it down.

Tim leaned and put a small kiss on his cheek. David trained his eyes sideways.

"What *are* you doing?"

It was strange to see a face so close: fine skin, blond stubble, a little mole over the cheekbone.

"What do you want, David?"

It seemed wiser just to stare.

"Anything?" Tim said, offering a way out.

But he didn't take it. He wanted to see what Tim, what life, was capable of.

"Is there anything I should be doing?"

Tim leaned and gave him a kiss close to the mouth. David let out a little laughter. Tim kissed his lips, and David pursed them primly. Tim's tongue shoved between them, while David thought *they really do that*. He pulled back and took a deep breath, or tried to.

"What's wrong?" Tim said. "Are you nervous?"

"Yes."

"I'm glad to hear it."

David stuck out his tongue, and touched it to the golden skin over Tim's cheekbone, experimentally. A sweet saltiness dissolved onto his tongue, back into his mouth. People had a taste: it made sense, when you thought of it, but he didn't know what to feel about it. He tried another small kiss, and suddenly, Tim shoved himself onto David, and began kissing his mouth. Not frightened, but in a kind of sardonic shock, David didn't mean to let the rough tongue in. But on their own his jaws began opening in a kind of wondering, pleasant nausea. Tim's tongue squirmed triumphantly into his mouth. David opened his eyes to see where he was: the walls seemed to be standing farther back, in dismay. Tim shifted farther, getting frankly, heavily on top of David. It was exciting, but it was terrifying too. He couldn't breathe – he could pull in air, despite Tim's weight, but there was a small part right at the centre of his chest that couldn't breathe, that was screaming for air.

"All right!" David gasped, before he was buried in Tim forever. He pulled himself out, and sat up.

Tim was grinning a wide grin with a fierce upper edge on it, as if he thought he'd won.

"So that's what you do," David said.

"That's what we do," Tim said. "You know, the truth is, you're really quite sexy."

"What do you mean?" David said, alarmed, intrigued.

"You're going to find out."

"It takes my breath away, though," David said. He slid along and got off the bed, sitting on the wooden chair, with a defiant look for Tim. Tim ought to be proud of him, though in fact he looked disappointed. David leaned over and switched their mugs. It was like a move in a chess game: Dark's mug takes Fair's.

"Sex is nice, I guess, but rather trying. *Draining.*"

"Well, if you think just that is sex..."

Tim didn't see that he'd given David enough for months. Or weeks, at least: it would take some time to absorb all this. And how could he reconcile it with Chris?

"Come back here," Tim said, his hand trying to scoop him over.

"Why?" David said, with a nervous laugh.

"Oh, come here."

"But I thought you were seducing *me.*"

"Oh? Did you? David, come here."

David shook his head. Tim was asking too much. He could sit on the wooden chair until Tim got the point that he had had enough for now. But had he? He didn't want to drive Tim away, not yet: there might be more to be learned about how people looked, tasted, acted, close up.

Irresolutely, he stood up, not knowing why, remembering the fear that had lifted him in the restaurant, like newspaper in the wind.

"That's it. You can walk."

David took the two small steps across the room. But after them, he didn't know what to do. To sit on the bed might mean unconditional surrender. Instead, he leaned down awkwardly and gave Tim a sort of goodnight kiss on the cheek. He straightened – perhaps he should go back to the chair and specify the things he would and wouldn't do. But that meant talking about them. Tim looked up at him, his smile looking different from above. He put his arms around David's waist and with a little, happy sigh nuzzled his face against David's belly.

Looking down, scared, into the whirl of Tim's hair, David didn't know what to do, holding his useless hands away to the side. Tim gave him an absurd, upward look, like a dog or a saint. Then he put his face against the swollen lump of David's corduroy crotch. David couldn't believe what he saw: Tim's smiling face against his crotch, his eyes closing, blindly letting go. David's open right hand hit him as fast and as hard as it could. For a moment, Tim's head was a living soccer ball with squeezed eyes, flying sideways. Then he pulled back, and David stood paralyzed, sure Tim was going to hit him. Fear flashing into rage came out of Tim's eyes and went just past him: he could almost feel it.

"I'm sorry!" David said, helplessly. "I'm so sorry!" He held his hands out, as if they didn't belong to him. "Did that hurt? Of course it did. But – "

"*You shit!*"

Tim stood up slowly, making David back away, half-sitting on the desk as he bumped into it. Tim strode to the door, pulled it open. David's raincoat swung wildly on its hook.

"Don't go," David said. "I really am sorry. I didn't mean that. It just happened."

Tim's back looked set, final: he wouldn't turn around. Something in his shoulders told David that no one had ever struck him before, not the way David had.

Tim closed the door and turned, his hand still on the knob.

"What did you want?" he demanded. "What the hell were you doing?"

"I don't know. How would I know? I just wanted to see what all that was like. And all of a sudden it got too – ." He squirmed.

"David," Tim said, and took a breath. He spoke with a kind of enraged friendliness. "Keep on trying. But it won't be on me."

"I wasn't trying."

"Whatever it was, next time don't clobber the poor guy when he isn't looking." Tim stared at him for one second, as if he'd finally wrapped his humiliation in enough anger to let David see it. He opened the door again, but stopped for a parting shot.

"Don't give up, though, David. Summer's only starting."

He went out and closed the door, gently. It was a silent slam, closing David into his little room forever. He watched the raincoat swing slowly to rest, pressing into the door, limp as suicide.

"Damn," David said, trying to see if it would help. "*Damn!*" He got face down on his narrow bed with his arms under him and began crying.

He was doomed to spend his life alone like this. He hated people and the strange, terrible things they did: he attacked them when they got close. With earlier suitors it had been sarcastic remarks about Walt Whitman or Noel Coward: but he would have clouted them too, if they'd done what Tim had done. He would be a male old maid, like Hugh Armitage, his parents' and now his forty-year-old bachelor friend. Tim was wrong about bachelors: in twenty years David would sit at the end of a dinner table remembering U. of T. the way Hugh remembered Oxford, and teach promising young men how to savour wine, as if wine had a red, almost human heart. And be speechlessly fond of them, as Hugh was of him.

That time hadn't come yet. For now, he would just go on with Chris, spinning out their romance as long as he could, unfelt ectoplasm brushing Chris's face in the air of Queen's Park or the campus. Tim might think it was ridiculous but it was all he had, it was the best thing he had ever made of his life.

But he kept coming back to Tim's living, friendly weight on top of him. He turned over on his back and re-imagined it. It was a little breathtaking how solid Tim had been – suddenly making solid all the dreamy boys of David's adolescence. Tim's "don't give up" had seemed like the angriest sarcasm, but maybe now David could hear something kind in it. Maybe Tim really would forgive him. But would he ever forgive Tim's closed, happy eyes and whatever lay behind them?

He sat up and brought the box of Kleenex up to blow his nose. He was sitting where Tim had sat, and imagined the evil blow again. Where had it come from? His arm seemed ready to wither as he thought about it now, but he had hit Tim as hard as he could. It certainly wasn't his family. He saw his father in Beacon Hill Park in Victoria telling him something about roses, and gently bending a pink rose forward with his walking stick. It must be some malignity all his own, that cut him off from everyone.

Poor Tim! He'd enjoyed being David's mentor. You could tell that. The hurt to his pride would be the worst thing. Could David make up for it? He didn't know his phone number or his address, and imagined all of the Grays and Greys the bloated Toronto phone book must hold.

When he reached for more Kleenex, he suddenly remembered the understanding look Tim had given that lonely box. It was too much: all the humiliating loneliness of David McTavish was suddenly stripped bare.

"*Damn!*" he shouted, knocking the Kleenex box across the room.

PART 5

In his anger, Tim had got lost. He needed the Y, he needed his wet, cool swimmer's skin and self, but the building kept pedantically thrusting long, dusty, infuriating corridors on him. It felt now as if David meant it all from the start had lured him in to insult him, beat him, humiliate him, then abandon him in this pretentious maze, with Mick Jagger and *Turandot* coming through the walls.

He found some stairs and poured his running shoes down them to a door onto the courtyard. Four students in tennis whites looked at him, at his flaming ear, and he felt another burst of anger. On the street he broke into a run, running all the way to the Y, conspicuous and handsome, gathering in the admiring glances – he needed them all.

When he sat on the edge of the pool to adjust his goggles, he felt the real humiliation. It hadn't just been pity, or kindness, or affection. He wouldn't have done it for those reasons. For a minute or two, there had been something desirable in the long body, in the dark, warning eyes. He had imagined David was attractive! He gave a bitter laugh, and let the water pull him in by the ankles.

After his cool mile, after setups and chin-ups and slow, spraddle-armed pushups, he was still unhappy. He needed a lover: that was what had betrayed him. He'd let his work take him over. He'd been drawing obsessively, daring himself to do paintings, as if this summer would answer once and for all the question of his ambition. Without a lover, he'd become as hysterical as David.

And it was a lover he needed, not a trick. He confirmed that while in the locker-room, looking along the benches at the dressing and undressing, sometimes lingering, sometimes reflective.

He went up Yonge to a bar – a run-down beer barn, but there was nowhere else at four o'clock in the afternoon. It was only half full. Someone just looking in might have imagined he was in some town in the bush where there were no women, where golden mugs of beer were the only lamps in the northern darkness. Taking a table, he looked around for a waiter. There was only one to be seen, far across the room, an old man with a bent back, nursing a tray of empty glasses through a door. Tim would have to wait or go. And perhaps, he thought, he ought to go. There was no one here he knew, or wanted to know.

He felt, like a draught on the side of his face, that he was being watched – watched from the corner of his eye, just where glaucoma begins. He tried not to look back, not caring for an entanglement of eyes, and then, as if on its own, his head turned.

The watcher was sitting about ten yards away. He was a good deal older than Tim: his hair was black, with scattered shots of gray. He had the sort of large, gaunt features which are impressive at a distance, but don't go together when seen close. In the dingy light, Tim was just at the point where they were coming apart or together. He didn't seem to be cruising: his eyes weren't hungry, or else the hunger was too far back to be seen. He was sitting with an Indian boy, who teetered in his chair, his long hair swinging back.

Tim turned away, wisely, then found himself looking again. The deepset eyes were magnetic. Tim didn't know how to feel: he probably ought to be annoyed, but annoyance didn't come.

The man coughed and got up, tall and stooping down from being taller. After a few words to his companion, he came towards Tim. He stopped at a little, measured distance from his table.

"Hello there," he said, in a low, backward voice.

"Hello." With a note of protest in reserve.

"Would you like a drink?" He gestured around with a big hand, as if he thought the gloomy cavern was his party.

"I'd love one – if I can ever get the waiter." He didn't want to have his drink paid for. He looked at the waiter's far-off, white-shirted back, shiny as if from shedding thirsty looks for decades.

"You wonder why *they're* called the waiters, don't you?"

The joke didn't go over, and the man added hastily, "I've seen you around, you know."

"Oh?"

"Could we join you? You'll like Charles. Everybody does."

"Why not?" he said, with a short laugh to show he could laugh at them if he chose.

The man turned to get Charles, and said, over his shoulder, "I'm Jack Durham." As if Tim might have heard of him, but he hadn't.

"I'm Tim Grey."

"Oh, yes, I know."

He went and spoke to the Indian boy, who grumbled a little, for appearance's sake, then tipped forward, leapt up and led the way, his light-footed walk brought up-to-date by crimson running shoes. Jack Durham trudged behind like a white explorer, with a new continent before him.

Another waiter appeared from nowhere at Tim's elbow. He could buy his own beer as the others set theirs down and settled behind them. Jack Durham introduced his friend: "Charles the rightful heir."

Charles's long black eyes slipped away, laughing: his handshake was dry and gentle.

"Be nice to him," Jack said, with an odd, sardonic protectiveness. "He has no hips at all, poor boy."

He swung a big hand across the table for a strong handshake, then sat back and looked at the bar from his new vantage-point.

"Charles doesn't say much," he said, "But he takes it all in."

Charles snorted.

"You'll be getting hungry soon," Jack said, thoughtfully. Then he turned the same thoughtful look on Tim.

"You're what my aunt would call a *husky* boy."

Tim shrugged self-conscious, husky shoulders.

"*Tim,*" Jack said. "A nice name – does it suit you?"

He laughed, startled. "Nobody ever asked." The truth was that as he got older it had begun to seem soft and cute. "I'm used to it."

"I don't mean to be inquisitive, you know. At least, I'm trying to cut down. But – how old are you, Tim?"

"Twenty-two." With his questions, with his strange, cool attention, the man was making him feel younger.

"A very interesting age," Jack Durham said.

"Why?"

"It's the year after twenty-one: you really *can't* go back."

"So how old are you?" It was hard to tell: he could have been in his late twenties or his early forties.

"I'm not that old!" Jack said, quickly. "Let's just say, if the difference in our ages

40

were a boy he'd be a bit too young to take an interest in this place." He looked around, to see what the boy might see. "Maybe he'd be starting to wonder a little. You're at O.C.A.," he said, looking back.

"How did you know?"

"I try to keep up. I was there myself at one stage. We're both, in our ways, artists. I'm a photographer."

"Really?"

"Really. I've had shows."

"Oh?" Tim was intrigued, but Jack protected himself with another question. "Do you have a lover?"

"Not at the moment."

"That's a crime!"

"Well..."

"Get one!" Jack said.

Tim laughed, pleased with his sympathy. "I'd love to, but it isn't that easy."

"Sure it is," Jack said. "Nothing to it."

"Well, today, this afternoon, I was almost literally kicked out of bed." He tried to make it sound funny, but Jack was too perceptive, looking into his face, trying to read the story. Tim touched his ear, afraid it might still be flaming.

"Why?" Jack said, incredulous. "I mean, who on earth?"

"Oh!" He didn't want to talk about his humiliation at David's hands, not in detail. He looked for help to Charles, whose eyes were slipping away again.

"Someone who kicked you out of bed – I'd like to meet him."

"Oh, no, you wouldn't," Tim said.

But Jack had been talking absent-mindedly, staring at Tim's hair. He said: "Is your father balding?"

"No," Tim said, impatiently. "As a matter of fact, my father is dead."

"Oh, I'm sorry!" His eyes met Tim's humbly for a moment and dropped to the table. "I'm sorry." He took two empty beer glasses and traded their positions. Jack was so contrite it was embarrassing, as if he thought his father had died yesterday.

"You must know," Jack said, imploringly, still playing with the glasses. "You start *looking*, and it's impossible to stop." Tim shook his head, impatiently, and a bead of water ran down the back of his neck. He brushed it away with his fingers.

"Swimming at the Y?" Jack said, looking at the wet fingertips.

"Yes."

"You see, what I'm wondering about, Tim, is – your body."

Tim looked to Charles again, teetering back, on the verge of laughter.

"Are you for real?"

Jack looked a little offended. "I try to be. This isn't sex, if that's what you mean. You don't really think it is, do you?"

Tim shrugged.

"Does it *feel* as if a pass is being made?"

"I don't know what it feels like," he said, amused, but a little resentful too.

"You know, you're an introvert," Jack said. "Or maybe you don't know. But that's all right – you'll take time. My models sometimes do."

"Why do you want me?" Tim said, almost helplessly.

"That's what the photographs would be about. Why you?"

He looked at Tim as if for the answer to this, but shyness gathered in his look, shyness verging on shame, and he turned away.

"I'm calling it," he said, "the show, that is, I'm calling it, he took a small, daring breath, "*The Human Body in the Late Seventies*. How does that sound?"

"The *late* seventies?"

"I thought of making it the eighties, but that's too far away, somehow it's got to feel closer than that."

"I don't understand."

"I want to know what they'll be like. They're going to be *different*, I know it, they're going to feel *different*."

Eyes almost closed, he moved heavily in the creaking chair, rocking, as if searching inside himself for the feeling he wanted. Charles was looking at him, smiling, apparently used to this sort of thing. Tim was embarrassed: the lined, heavy face seemed exposed, indecent, like a poor, old man's face out in the rain.

"It's the times," Jack said, looking at him suddenly. "The looks, the styles, the feelings. Everything. They're doing something to bodies. At O.C.A. you spend your time discussing what's happening to art. I want to know what's happening to the human body. To that human body of yours."

He smiled, a little mockingly. "So what do you think, Tim?" He seemed to assume the question was far above Tim's head and then he was listening carefully, hoping Tim might give him exactly what he needed. The shameful softness came into his eyes again, and Tim said, looking away, "I just wish I had a lover." Because if he had one, he wouldn't be here.

"Well, I'm not stopping you," Jack said, turning away, suddenly tired of the emotions. "I'm not daring you."

Tim shrugged. The bar was filling up, but with Jack Durham there he looked at it all, the noisy faces, the fever and shine of beer, from inside a kind of silence. Jack Durham was strange, but he was interesting, a character, and perhaps more than just a character, too.

"I was just softening you up," Jack said, more kindly. "I like to know my models."

Suddenly, portentously, Charles yawned. A pink, wet, plush monster gaped out, saw how unplush, unpink, how very dry a place the world is, and fled.

"Hungry?" Jack said, hopefully.

"*Starving!*"

"Good," Jack said. "We're famished," he told Tim. "But I'll be seeing you around, okay?"

"Sure," Tim said, doubtfully.

"That's one thing you can count on in this town. You always see people around. Until they get rich. The Rabbit?" he asked Charles.

"Exactly. I feel like the Rabbit Deluxe."

"I'll be going too," Tim said, as the others got up. Jack had unsettled him – Jack and David between them – and now Tim didn't want to be left alone in the noisy gloom.

"Good," Jack said. "I really do like the way you walk."

They made their way out, Tim treading on the strange consciousness of Jack Durham. Outside, it was painfully bright, and a breeze was blowing.

"I'll get the taxi," Charles said, sprinting off.

"Charles loves taxis," Jack explained. "You're welcome to a lift, but we're not really going anywhere."

"No thanks." It was probably a mistake to ask, but he did ask. "So what do you mean by all that? Bodies are changing?"

Jack gave him a sharp, squinting look, his face bleak in the sunshine. "I don't know, maybe it's just me, my obsessions, ambitions, whatever. You can't call yourself an artist these days if you don't have a theory, can you?" He was answering Tim's irony.

"Only it isn't," he said, suddenly serious again. "Everything is changing, the looks, the feelings, the people. History's got you, I'm afraid; got you by the balls."

He laughed, looking at Tim from out of big, lonely eyes, while a second or two of 1974 blew against and past them.

"Hey, I got one!" Charles shouted, tugging on the door of the caught taxi. Jack looked at him, fondly.

"Isn't Charles grand? He says I can keep North America."

It was as if Jack was hoisting Tim up to see life from the viewpoint of saddened middle age for a moment or two.

"And him," he added, fondly.

PART 6

David went around for days hoping to see Chris and make it up to him. Chris hadn't appeared since Tim had, and now David desperately needed to see him to be reassured that nothing had been changed. Chris only had to appear in some favourite haunt under the Queen's Park trees, perhaps, magically, like a unicorn briefly detained, fabulous and polite – and then everything could go on as before. Tim's smile, his gay view of things, his living weight on top of you, that sweet, slippery tongue – it all had to be bricked away like some embarrassing corpse.

As if sensing he'd been trifled with, Chris refused to be seen, day after day. Had he left town? Gone to work in Africa, perhaps?

Then one morning he came bounding up the steps from the Hart House basement. He gave David a quick smile and went by, saying something about being in a hurry.

43

Anyone seeing them would have said they were friends.

The next day, scarcely stopping to think, David went into Queen's Park. There, below King Edward on his roof-green stallion, was Chris, coming towards him, the true, the only Chris. David waved from some distance. If they stopped to talk, David would listen and agree: he wouldn't say anything about gay rights in Cuba or anywhere else. He would be content with the right to stand two or three feet from Chris at an angle that kept their eyes from meeting.

Chris scowled. Something, David saw, was very wrong: something had put him in a bad mood. David was frightened: Chris didn't know he could kill him. And it was too late to warn him now.

"Hi there," Chris said, curtly, going past. David's arms froze at his sides, he stopped on the gravel path, almost turning, but unable to move. *Good*, said a small, mean killer's voice. *Good, you are going to be depressed.* He tipped himself into walking again.

Desperately, he made excuses for Chris. He had the right to be moody. David even felt sorry for him – desperately sorry. He wanted to fight his despair, shout it down, run away. He knew he couldn't: it was absolute. Chris had given it all the power.

He looked up at fat King Edward and swore he would never come into the park again, now all the damage was done. He could die of this – he was in love with that thought, and mortally afraid of it.

He headed towards the residence, barely seeing his way, and went in and up and through the blue door into his room. He ploughed everything off his bed and lay down. It was a kind of relief to feel depression pull him into its classic shape, like a fetus, like a fist.

He was curled into a ball, and his thoughts went round and round. He thought of each time he had seen Chris or imagined he had. He had kept a sort of a log – a list of dates and times and locations, with a C for Chris and a * for the false Chris's, followed by a few words: "Hi there," or "Really smiled," or "Discussed Lin Piao." He went through it in his head, rehearsing all the scenes again, each with its particular weather and flavour. The whole drama had been leading to this.

His thoughts went round and round and he began to wonder if he had to go on thinking them.

Dear Chris. I was never part of your life.

Yes, the voice yelled. Yes.

He wrote long suicide letters, almost believing them. Then he began to take pity on himself and cast about for ways of living. The voice that called for his death fell silent, contemptuous, as David began writing a different kind of letter in his head. But after all the letters were more interesting than suicide.

Dear Chris. When we saw each other in the park today I realize you may have been in a hurry, but –

But that would be absurd, to write like a hurt lover.

The tight head on the pillow went on writing letters. After several hours, he pulled

44

out his left arm and looked at his watch. He knew the doors of Chris's residence were locked at midnight. By midnight, he had to hammer out his destiny. Just before eleven he began to uncurl and let the cruel blood back into his limbs. He staggered over to the desk to type. The letter went through several tearful drafts, but finally it was enough:

> Dear Chris,
> I've enjoyed seeing you and talking about things, about politics. I'm finding that book on peasant revolutions very interesting, though I can't agree with everything it says. But I've come to see that it's time for my own revolution. There's something I think you ought to know. At least, that I want you to know. I hope it won't be too upsetting. I love you. Does this surprise you? Perhaps it does, I really don't know. Of course, it would be much better if I didn't, but there it is, I do. And of course you have the right to react in whatever way you feel is right. Please don't think, though, that you have to do or say anything about it. It's just that I wanted you to know. So really nothing very earth-shaking has occurred. After all, I'm just writing to let you know how glad I am you exist.

He signed it 'David' and put it in an envelope and set out, afraid the doors might be locked early, shutting him out forever. This courage, this exalted despair, couldn't last the night.

It had rained during the evening, and now the air was rinsed fresh. The night was black and buoyant. The mirrored sidewalks promised new clarity. He arrived ten minutes before midnight. He had never been here before, but Chris had mentioned where he lived – had even pointed to Che Guevara looking down from his window at the green quadrangle. He slipped in and up two flights of stairs. The first corridors he explored were wrong. He heard voices talking, laughing: Bob Dylan sang sneeringly through a door. He was lost and afraid to ask for help. But he had to, to save his soul. He went to a door to knock and, fatefully, saw a little card that said, in Italic letters, *Christopher Grahame Leggatt.* There was no sound from behind it, no light under the door. Who had written the card? Surely not dear Christopher himself. The middle name was like another tender part of him disclosed, like the belly peering from under his T-shirt. David laughed, not quite out loud. Everything he had done today was ridiculous and worth it. He had acted: he had said he was in love. He was stepping out from his silence into the world. Even Tim Grey, though he would never know about this, would have applauded. He stooped and shoved the letter under the door. When he straightened up, a desperate white corner still peeked out, his old life crying out to be saved. He stooped again, gave it a ruthless tap, and heard it skitter in across the hardwood floor.

Does this surprise you?

CHAPTER II: FRIENDS

Three days later, coming out of the Victoria College Library, David saw Chris walking towards the residence. He had been hoping for a meeting like this – that was why he was there – but now he wanted to hide. Chris saw him, smiled his shy smile and came over in a few loping steps to say hello. He was just about to go north, he said, to spend a week canoeing with some old friends, up in Algonquin Park. They were close to Chris's room, in sight of his window. David looked away at Che Guevara, wondering what was happening to himself.

The prospect of the trip seemed to loosen Chris up. "I've even promised them not to talk politics," Chris said, laughing at himself.

"Have you canoed before?"

"Sure, all my life."

The two pairs of eyes had a silent meeting, like children staring out from beside their parents. If Chris had got the letter, there would have to be some sign of it in his eyes. Instead, he looked away and David was sure there had been nothing.

"I was practically raised in a canoe, in the summer," Chris was saying. "They used to say I must have Indian blood. But now I've got to rush: they're picking me up in a few minutes."

"Well, be careful!" David said. "Remember what happened to Tom Thomson!"

Then he blushed, because he hadn't quite remembered himself—at least, not the theory that the painter had tipped out of his canoe while standing to take a piss. Chris whooped in delight, and the noise made them both straight, young men.

"I know what I'm doing! See you."

If he had got the letter there would have to be something now, at least, in the final moment of separation. He couldn't go without some look or special tone of voice. Chris looked away towards his room as if towards the cold, northern lakes and then back at David, still smiling, and he was off.

At first, David felt a kind of empty relief. At least, there had been no scene, no scene of any kind – because Chris acting friendly and tolerant would have been unbearable, too. Chris was still his friend. But relief gave way to the familiar feeling of helplessness. He couldn't do anything successfully. There was something about him, some fate that kept him shut up inside himself. When he wrote letters, he wrote them to silence, to nothingness. He spent the week Chris was away in a kind of grieving despair. He imagined Chris in the Ontario north, which for David was mainly childhood reading, endangered, drowning. He saw the blinding white body from the Hart House showers sinking through cold gray water, a lake of tears and silence, and he ached for all the grief of that sweet, white body. He began on a poem called 'The Letter.' He couldn't decide how he would end it, but for now he didn't want it to end. It was in the second person: he fed himself on the word 'you.'

But at the same time he was defending himself against all this, inventing a way to survive. The letter had been lost, but he had done his part. He had really acted. The love, the terror, had been so real they nearly killed him. And in spite of that, he had pushed the letter under the door, committing himself forever. Tim—still the only other person in the world who knew about the love-affair going on inside him – was present when David thought this way. He was the one person David could imagine talking to, arguing with. He felt a kind of irritation now with him for having stupidly got himself hit. Then he would remember Tim's look as he left, and despair would close over David again, and the blow and the letter became the same thing, the same deadly silence.

On the Friday of Chris's canoeing week, after spending a half-hour in the musty back rooms of a second-hand bookstore, David came out onto Queen Street West, blinking, his hands free. Several books had been left behind, to hold out until next month, when he might be able to afford them. He looked along the wide sunny street and saw Tim on a bike, pedaling fast, his head thrust out, his hips high and striving in white shorts. He was going too fast to see him, David thought with a kind of relief – and then he did see him with a dark look from under his eyebrows. David's right arm shot up, desperate for forgiveness before he disappeared.

Snatching a look backward, Tim braked abruptly. He waited as cars and two lumbering streetcars went past, while David stood at the curb, contrite and nervous.

"How've you been?" Tim called, bumping over the streetcar tracks.

"I really am terribly sorry," David said, dumping it all without ceremony.

Tim came up with a few skillful wobbles. His weight, thrown onto bare arms, made them into muscled forelegs. He stopped, putting down a foot, breathing fast. He looked uncertainly, even shyly at David, with anger standing right behind the shyness. Then Tim sat back, both feet down, just touching the handlebars with the tips of paint-spattered fingers.

"No harm done," he said, almost easily. "Maybe I was too – " he gave a wry shrug, "*eager*".

"That's good, thanks," David mumbled. He hadn't been entirely forgiven, but he was grateful for what he got.

"So where are you off to?" he said. "In such a hurry?"

Tim laughed. "I was going down to the ferry dock, to go to the Island." He looked down into the hot book of his palms, held up side by side. "I was trying to paint, and it wasn't going anywhere, so I jumped on my bike. But the Island is a stupid idea. When you're alone." He rubbed the sore hands together and looked up, with a smile. "Alone and faithful, anyway."

It took David a second to unriddle this. "Oh?" he said.

"Anyway, now I'm getting hungry. Have you had lunch?"

"No. Lunch would be great," David said, glad the unransomed books left him money enough to say this.

Tim got off his bike, a leg going up and over in a smooth, golden swoop. Tim's legs were hairless – he was that blond – and they looked almost indecently naked to David, who came from hairier stock.

They went along Queen to Spadina, Tim wheeling the bike by the saddle. He'd just bought it, he said. "I have an old one in Napier, but it's not fancy enough for Toronto. Or for Duncan, anyway."

"Duncan?"

Tim smiled. "I'll tell you all about him."

Duncan, David guessed, had a lot to do with his being forgiven, so whoever he was he owed him something. The chance, at least, to talk with Tim about the letter.

Tim took them to a small health food cafe, where they sat outside and ate things David had never heard of. David didn't know how to get started on the question of the letter. And Tim was eager to give his news.

"I've been seeing a lot of this guy," he said, modestly. "Duncan."

"Duncan?" David wasn't ready to give up on last names.

"Holland."

"What does he do?"

"Works in a travel agency."

David went after the usual facts, hoping that the way Tim spoke them would give some clues to what he really wanted to know: how you put two young men together. He stopped, afraid to ask more, and Tim smiled, complacent in his possession of a lover. He seemed to wear him like silk.

"You'll like Duncan," Tim said. This was another step in David's rehabilitation: he was going to meet Tim's boyfriend. But there was a note of warning in Tim's voice. David had to be prepared for something, but he couldn't tell what.

"Maybe you'd like to have dinner with us, tomorrow evening? And a movie afterwards, perhaps."

"Yes, that would be wonderful."

Tim pulled his knapsack up onto the table, got out a worn, red address book and a thick fountain pen, a drawing pen, he said. He uncapped the pen, and David recited his number into Tim's Toronto Mc's and Mac's.

"Duncan's a bit younger than us," Tim said, capping the pen carefully.

"Oh?"

"He's just turned twenty. And – " whatever it was, it came first in a laugh – "well, Duncan never had to tell anyone he was gay."

David took this in, and they went back to shared, eating silence. He still couldn't find the way to start talking about Chris. It was Tim who got him going.

"How's our friend Chris?"

"He's up north right now. In Algonquin Park, canoeing."

"Great – I've done that. What does Chairman Mao think, though?"

David coughed. "The exciting news is, I wrote him a letter. Before he went."

"Yes?" Tim didn't understand.

"I told him."

He coughed again, into his fist, and looked up for approval.

"Why?" Tim said.

"Why?" Tim had suggested it himself, hadn't he? "Because I had to do something."

Tim sat back and looked at him, and David relaxed, with a certain nervous pride.

"And how did he react?"

"Well, unfortunately, fate stepped in and screwed me up a little. I don't know why, but he didn't actually get it."

Tim gave him an odd look. "He didn't get it? Why not?"

"It must have – I don't know – gone astray. I shoved it under his door, like Tess of the d'Urbervilles, you know? Only there's no carpet. I heard it sliding across the floor. But afterwards he didn't say anything about it, he didn't even look different, so it must have got lost."

"How could it?" Tim said, sensibly. He didn't understand that David's universe wasn't sensible: cracks could open in it anywhere, at any moment.

"If he'd got it," David said, "it would have been bound to show. He couldn't have hid it." If he let him, Tim might make him doubt this. "But that's not the point. The point is what I did. I sat down and wrote it and delivered it."

"But if he didn't get it?" Tim said, stupidly.

"That's not my fault. The point is, it was a real breakthrough for me. It was the realest thing I've ever done: when I shoved it under the door, I was shaking."

"Why are you so sure he didn't get it? How could he not have got it?"

"I don't know, but I'm sure he didn't. I know what he's like. He couldn't hide something like that."

"Why not ask him?"

"Ask him? To his face? 'By the way, did you get a letter from me saying I –'" David just laughed.

"Maybe you could write another letter," Tim said, a little sarcastically.

"Don't you see?" David cried. "Don't you see what it means?"

He was desperate for something to impress Tim, to save himself from some oncoming feeling, humiliation or despair. The unendable poem came around him like a passionate, echoing mist, suddenly in danger of being horribly silly if he didn't act fast. And what he needed came. "It means that, some day, it will be over!"

He hadn't quite seen that himself till now, but now it made sense: writing the letter to Chris was a step toward getting free of him. Tim drew back, playing scared, as if

David was suddenly fierce, a killer.

"But you'll always be fond of him, you know," Tim said. "I still see guys from high school, and I like them. It turns out they're nice guys."

David pounced. "But you don't love people for being nice guys, do you?"

Tim laughed. And David sat back in his chair, suddenly tired, looking down at a sparrow hopping among the crumbs.

"Of course, I don't mean it," he said to the sparrow, dejectedly. "What would I do without him?"

After lunch they crossed the street to Tim's bike, chained to a railing in half-leafed shade. Tim was going back to his apartment: perhaps he could do some work after all, and Duncan was going to meet him there after work.

"Maybe he did get the letter," David admitted, as Tim squatted to untwine the plastic-coated chain. "I guess I can't really read his face – I have trouble looking at it." Tim rose and began coiling the chain around, below the saddle.

"Oh, who knows?" David said, suddenly feeling all his humiliation in a rush. He wished, he almost wished, he hadn't told Tim. But at least Tim hadn't laughed at him. He was a fool, a cripple, writing dead letters, letters to nothingness, to God. Not quite, though: at least Tim kept him from that. He looked at him sidelong, feeling the way he stood by his bike, taking the ground he stood on up into himself through legs and the set of hips and spine into himself, into Tim Grey. It was Chris he was in love with, but he couldn't help liking the way Tim stood on his feet on the ground there and then – getting on towards three in late May, 1974.

"We'll have to get you another Chris," Tim said, cheerfully.

"God forbid!"

"I mean a gay one. They exist. Curly hair, wire-rimmed glasses, political – it won't be hard at all."

"Or maybe another Duncan?" David laughed to make it clear this was a joke.

"You'll like Duncan," Tim repeated, again not quite certain. Leaning the bike against his thigh, he reached with crossed arms for the bottom of his T-shirt. He stopped for a modest moment, as if he didn't know how David would take the outburst of his chest, then went ahead.

"It's getting warmer," he said, shouldering into his knapsack.

He mounted the bike, his leg swinging over and calling up, like a conductor's baton, a larger, finer world. He got himself carefully onto the high, hard saddle, with David not quite watching, but following it all obliquely. Not lusting, starved for a sense of how things were out in the world of bare skins.

"So I'll phone tomorrow, about where to meet for dinner? It won't be expensive – don't worry."

"Okay, great. Be careful, though!"

"Why?"

"The cars," David said.

Tim laughed and gave David a sort of tap on the arm just below the shoulder and pushed off. He made his way at a wandering crawl down onto the street, then faster out into traffic, rising off his saddle to get some speed, pumping, the white shorts raised like a rabbit's scut, vulnerable among the cars. David watched him nervously, going in crouched, level flight now, afraid for his half-naked friend. At any moment, it seemed, a car could swerve and strike him and leave Tim forever silenced.

PART 2

Tim phoned and arranged to meet David at a restaurant on Yonge Street – a trendy diner. They were waiting for him, rising to pull over a second table. Duncan was an inch or two shorter than Tim. He was, David silently agreed, good-looking: pretty, going on handsome, with smoke-gray eyes and wheat-coloured hair so fine it was almost gaseous. His white shirt, the sleeves carefully rolled up almost to the shoulders, let you in on several buttons worth of tanned skin. David looked and glanced away. There was a softness like puppy fat in Duncan's looks. He did a dramatic reading from the menu, considering and relinquishing dishes regretfully, even tragically, looking across into a mirror, torn between two selves, one fat, one sexy.

"All right, it's the salad," he said, closing the menu firmly and smiling at David: the sexy self won hands down.

He'd been working on his weight when he met Tim, he explained. They were jogging around Winston Churchill Park, in opposite directions.

"He smiled," Duncan said. "And in this city, joggers don't smile, they go pounding by like the wrath of God."

"You didn't look like the usual jogger, though," Tim said.

"Well, perhaps not. But they're so *grim!*" And suddenly he was looking wide-eyed at David, giving the last word a funny, sweet twist upward. David smiled back quickly, to show he wasn't grim. In spite of Tim's warnings, he wasn't prepared for Duncan.

He worked at a travel agency, "Azure, not far from here: it's right on Bloor Street." And when David asked where he was from, he gave a thoughtful pout and said, "From the moon. Well, Sudbury—as close as you can get in this country."

Suddenly the nickel town was a fascinating place, though Duncan "*hated it—hated it.*" His father had run a hardware store, not making much, trying from time to time to beat masculinity into his soft, clumsy son. In stony school corridors echoing the word 'faggot,' he'd been "sometimes a real shit-disturber, a real gay brat," and sometimes suicidal. Only he'd always known there was Toronto, there was a bus, and one day he had got on it.

"When I got here, that was a year ago, only a year, I said, 'all right, gentlemen, stand back.'"

He looked affectionately at his Sudbury self stepping down from the bus. "I lost twenty pounds in two months – I *gave* them away."

David wanted to like Duncan, for Tim's sake. And he thought he did like him, except that he didn't know how to respond to his style – pleasured, girlish, willfully hilarious. There had been no one like Duncan back in Oak Bay, and when he'd seen boys like him in the Toronto streets he hadn't been able to look for more than a second. But here was Duncan smiling into him with knowing and shining eyes. It was as if with Duncan the only way to have a place to stand was to start dancing, and David didn't know how. He could never laugh the way Duncan did, for instance, festooning the air. If Duncan gave him a well-turned smile or a taste of long lashes, David would stiffen back and up like an old cat, afraid Duncan was about to embarrass him cruelly, mortally. But he never did, quite.

He saw how Tim was drawn in by the softness that blurred and sweetened Duncan's looks. Tim seemed a little drunk, tipsy, on the brink of toppling onto or into the V of skin. David felt the hovering of Tim's desire, and the way Duncan owned it, consulted it, moved around inside it. At times, Tim and Duncan could evoke David's feelings for Chris, but fleshed and fattened out, made silly and childish and feminine. Because at times Tim seemed to have changed, becoming sinuous and even girlish himself, caught up in Duncan's soft, funny, self-intoxicating ways, following him up in the flights of laughter. David would feel that Tim was being irresponsible, forgetting his duty to look after him. They laughed like excited children, almost overcome, scared of how excited they were getting. David would stare through the hilarity, bewildered and reproachful: sometimes he got back the reassuring look he needed, sometimes not. It was disconcerting. One minute Tim was everything you could want, masculine, intelligent, straightforward, and the next David felt he hardly recognized him. He put it down to Duncan's influence, and assured himself it was a kind of regression, more boyish than girlish. Boyish and blond, David thought, darkly.

After dinner, they all went to a movie, and David noticed about halfway through it that Duncan's hand had come to rest in Tim's crotch. He was quietly, domestically, holding on by the obvious handle. David almost looked for the police whose beat was just over his shoulder, but they left him to stew in his own guilt. He tried to forget about Duncan's hand, Tim's crotch, and get back into *L'Aventura*, but he was caught up in a grainy, badly lit film of his own, about Tim and Duncan in bed, trying to fit two young men together.

After the movie, when they went for dessert "all right, but we'll both regret it," Duncan said – it was the lovers who could recall the movie: in fact, Duncan had a memory like videotape. A troupe of his friends came up, and insisted they come dancing at Desire's, whatever that was.

Tim sent David a secret, understanding look, as if he was just remembering that David had never even been in a gay bar.

"It's getting a bit late, isn't it?" David said.

Duncan looked at his black-faced watch. "Late? They haven't opened yet."

David tried not to look stupid, knowing that Duncan and his friends had enough laughter behind their young and handsome faces to kill him, if the mood happened to take them.

"David's a real worker," Tim said. "He's got papers to write."

David gave him a grateful look. Tim promised to phone the next day, and did, late in the morning.

"I liked Duncan," David said, tentatively.

"He likes you too," Tim said.

"Really?"

"He says he's got a thing for scholarly types."

David looked down at the typewriter in front of him and the messy sheet in it. Scholarly: it was enough to get on with.

And David made a place for himself in Tim's and Duncan's affair. It wasn't always rewarding. Sometimes David felt like a heavy father, sometimes like the neglected child of a feckless marriage. Duncan made him part of a family too: he was a backward sister-brother who wasn't 'out' yet, but they'd see about that, they'd tidy him up, send him out into a world as wide as Duncan's gray-blue eyes.

Over the weeks, he became familiar with Tim's apartment, in a post-war apartment block in what Duncan classified as fringe Forest Hill. And with Duncan's, in a high-rise on Jarvis Street. He even let himself be taken up the stairs to Desire's, where he stood like a rock in a gay sea, watching Tim and Duncan dancing. Once Duncan came over, laughing, hands stretched out: when he saw the terror on David's face, he dropped them, taking pity, and stayed to talk.

David didn't ask Tim how he thought he fitted in. Part of it seemed to be that Tim liked to have someone to talk with from outside Duncan's world. He would treat David as if he was high above the moil of passion – but also a student, an anthropologist, trying to learn about it all. David didn't mind the ambiguities: he could be objective, impassive, and sneak little glances into that world of emotions when he wanted. He would be part of the gay world some day, though probably not soon. Tim's friends seemed to be all neatly coupled already. Duncan's laughter-loving friends were out of the question: too young, too pretty, too fashionable for David.

A week after his first encounter with Duncan, David met Tim for lunch. David asked, "Aren't you going to live together?" Coming from another planet, he could ask these questions. And it was a nice thought: Tim and Duncan's. He'd put them up in Forest Hill.

"Well, no," Tim said. "I don't think so." Obviously, he had thought of it.

"Why not?"

"He's kind of – dizzy, and I can't live like that. Not all the time. And he's a bit of a duchess: he has to have his own way. It would be hard to get much done if he was always around. Besides ..." He looked apologetically at David.

"Besides what?" David said, hovering, interplanetary, but worried.

"Well, who knows how long it will last? This may not be one of those feature-length love-affairs, David."

"Oh?"

Disappointment must have sounded like disapproval, because Tim moved irritably and said, "You sound like my mother!"

David quailed, then took up the challenge, wanting to know what Tim's mother could be like. "You mean she knows about Duncan?"

"No!"

"She doesn't know you're gay?"

Tim moved his shoulders from side to side in a dance of doubt. "I've never told her. I thought of telling Susan, my sister, but I decided not to. She'll never know – my mother, I mean. Not officially. Can you see me introducing Duncan to her? What a disaster!"

Tim laughed at some spectacle David couldn't see. Then, almost abruptly, he pulled himself together. "No, she'll never know. She's really heroic, when it comes to ignoring things."

He straightened and David could see his mother inside him, pulling him up. For a moment, he seemed to be suspended between two people, shifting back and forth between them. And David, embarrassed and almost frightened, gave a nervous cough.

"Oh, David," Tim said, exasperated, "What the fuck do you know about Duncan and me? It doesn't have to be marriage, does it? Anyway, this way is more fun. When the phone rings I get a hard-on."

"It must be a disappointment, sometimes, answering the phone," David said, a little hurt.

"Oh, poor David!" Tim said, reaching for his arm. "Your time will come. I can see it. Your virginity is getting very fragile. Duncan would love to hook you up with someone: he's a born match-maker. You're asking all these sneaky questions. *Next thing* – "

David stared, afraid to learn what the next thing would be, then disappointed when Tim just pulled away.

"Don't worry, David," Tim said. "He's coming. He's on his way, whoever he is."

As if, David thought, he just had to hear Tim's laughter to come running.

PART 3

David was a sort of a foreign visitor in the world of Tim and Duncan for seven weeks, scouting it out, putting intelligent questions: 'I hope I'm not being rude, but – ' Then Tim and Duncan came to an end.

A house-warming party was to be given by two friends of Tim's, Alan Connor and Michael Levy. David was invited too, though he hadn't met them yet.

"You'll love them," Duncan said. "They're dying to meet you."

David had to laugh: *dying?*

"No, really, they are. And there are going to be some great men there, David, *if* you're interested." Suddenly his eyes were sharply, alarmingly focussed on the side of David's head.

"David, excuse me for asking, but where on earth did you get your hair cut?"

"It was a long time ago," he said, weakly.

"We can see that. You've got great hair," Duncan said. "At least...but, David, you should go to Ray's very, very quickly. If you want, I'll phone him and get you in."

"Will it be expensive?"

"He's not bad, actually. Fifteen."

"Fifteen dollars! I could buy a Mahler symphony for that."

"A symphony? David, are you serious?"

David was sure that at last it was going to happen: Duncan was going to embarrass him to death. His hair was a scandal. He couldn't deny it. But somehow, he couldn't give in.

"But if I spend that much money, I'll be broke."

Duncan took a deep breath. "David, I'm sorry, but you don't understand. This is not Victoria. In this town, people look at you. They look at you and they see: either you're in shape or you aren't. Your clothes, your hair, you've got them right or you don't. They look and they *decide*. Am I right, Tim?"

Watching, half amused, half concerned, Tim gave a small shrug. "As Jack Durham says, to each his infinity."

"What?" David said, startled "Who?"

Tim was about to explain, but Duncan stepped in. "He's this totally bizarre old sleaze-artist who says he wants to take pictures of Timmy's nude body. I can't imagine why."

Tim laughed, and stuck to the matter at hand. "You know you're never going to turn David into a fashion plate, Duncan."

"Why not. I think we have got a good deal to work with."

"You sound like some lady in Rosedale, trying to cope with one of her horsey daughters."

"Well, what's wrong with that? Those ladies know their business. The daughters have just got to get off their horses and unfrump themselves."

Tim rubbed Duncan's back and whispered something in his ear. Duncan just stared straight and cold at David, who was sure that he was going to have to manage on his own. He just wasn't gay enough. It wasn't fair. How could Tim let him be judged by a clerk from a travel agency who had never been to university? By a teenager from Sudbury who was at least half a girl?

As Tim finished and pulled away, Duncan came out with sweet *roulades* of laughter.

"He's telling me not to be a bitch, David. As if he didn't know any better."

David laughed too, relieved. He could go on as before, although not without a last word from Duncan. "Believe me, David, I don't like it either, but for some people in this city you're only as good as your last haircut."

His hair was neatly trimmed when he arrived at Alan and Michael's, wringing the neck of a bottle of white wine. He was on time, so he arrived before everyone else. Michael, the shorter of two dark-haired young men, gave him a kiss. David thrust the bottle at him.

"You're our first party guest in this house," Michael said, as Alan kissed him from the other side.

They showed him around. The rooms were almost empty. David couldn't get over it: boys with a house. They took him to the kitchen to get on with their preparations. They still didn't quite know where things were, kept groping around for them and each other.

As other people arrived, David stayed safely in the kitchen, which attracted a lot of people. He got into a discussion of gay politics with someone who worked for *The Body Politic*. David tried to find out more without sounding like a policeman. "Well, Tim says," he began, "I mean, Tim Grey, he's really into gay politics." And the man from *The Body Politic* said, scathingly, "Tim Grey? The swimmer? Into politics?"

So David left, venturing into the living room. Tim and Duncan had just arrived, cheerful, shouting hellos, giving out embraces as at a ceremony where everyone won a prize. At first, David felt something was wrong. They were too cheerful, too smilingly a couple. But then as they turned the glad smiles on him "David! There you are!" he decided it was their party manner. Alan and Michael's party was on its way to being a great success.

Two women brought David into their discussion, mostly about the house and the neighbourhood. They were a couple too, Brenda and Trish. Brenda was rather fat, in her thirties, Trish his age and boyish and taut, earrings swinging in a jaunty, elegant breeze of their own. They seemed sensible and intelligent, prepared to be motherly and feminine within reason, and David kept in their lee, afraid of the growing complexities of the gay men around him. Was there a future lover for him here, he wondered. What would he do if he was that noisy?

Tim came up. Brenda and Trish were old friends and gave him hugs.

"So how are things going?" he said, smiling at him, but as if from out of the party.

"Fine," David said, bravely. "Terrific. Why don't you buy a house?"

Tim smiled as if he was proud of him, and David resolved to make him prouder. His position as spectator in gay life was beginning to be irksome: he resolved not to leave Alan and Michael's until he had found a boyfriend – a boyfriend nice enough to make Tim happy. It would have nothing to do with love, because he was still in love with Chris, but in some friendly bed he could find out how things really worked and what he thought about it. He took a deep gulp of wine to seal this decision.

An hour later, after talking with more people than he could remember, he sat on a couch in the living room to rest. In the excitement, he had drunk a lot, without noticing it: it became part of the cheerful shouting. A tall, lean, black-haired young man with a moustache and a red and green Argyle sweater came up. David had noticed him earlier, talking with Tim, who had looked across at him with a special understanding smile, as if they were discussing him. The young man introduced himself as Andrew Johnston: the 't' was important. David liked him at once, and not just because he was in the mood to like everyone: he could see they had a lot in common.

"I'm David McTavish," he said: this fact, when he stated it, usually called up a certain bother and puzzlement, but now it was fine with him. And then, remembering Tim's smile, he added impulsively, "Tim Grey's virgin."

Andrew blinked a little, sitting down on the couch. "Yes, well, Tim's a good friend of mine."

As they began talking, David liked him more and more. He liked the way his long body lounged in the sagging couch. There was something a little fussy in his manner, but that made David feel at home. Andrew was in art history; in other words, he was scholarly, as Duncan would have said, and more important, he was intelligent, up to David's ironies. He liked the fact that he was in art, that exciting, vivid world Tim had begun to evoke for him. In it but at a certain remove: art history was reassuring, because it meant art could be validated by words. Andrew had real strength, real determination with finicky edges: you could see that from the way he'd come up by himself. He was almost as diffident as David, his eyes blurring over in a frenzy of lashes when contact lasted more than a moment or two. More and more, it seemed likely he had come with Tim's blessing.

Andrew talked about his work: he was studying what he called the New York School, who were painters, it seemed. Great and famous painters. You could hear that in Andrew's voice. When Andrew had finished, had introduced himself, spread out all his Abstract Expressionist wares, and suggested they go home together. Somehow it would be possible. They would rise and take their leave and step out through Alan and Michael's door into the imagination of the other guests, a couple. David was sure by now that Andrew had come like a present from Tim: a big, warm, thoughtful present. David had to figure out for himself how to take off the red and green wrapping, but if this drunkenness wasn't enough for that, there was more drunkenness beyond. He looked at Andrew and the eyes didn't fur over, and they were blue and kind. He looked around to check on Tim.

He was in a corner with Duncan, who stood coldly surveying the room like a blond Napoleon. Tim leaned against the wall with his arms tightly folded. David looked away, not wanting to be caught with their quarrel in his eyes.

"Actually," Andrew was saying, drawing a little closer, "I'll be using Frank O'Hara a lot, including his poems."

"Who's he?" David said, not really listening.

"You must know Frank O'Hara."

"Well, I took a course on Modern Poetry last year, but we never made it past Yeats and Eliot."

Andrew laughed. "Frank O'Hara is more modern than that. He lived in New York during the fifties and sixties. He was gay, too. He worked at the Museum of Modern Art, so of course he knew everybody."

"He sounds fascinating," David said, politely. But he had to look away into the corner where Tim was now actually holding Duncan's arm to keep him from walking away.

"The fifties and sixties?" David asked, trying to do his best. "He left New York?"

Duncan pulled his arm away but didn't leave: he always had to have the last word, David thought.

"No. He was killed in 1966. In an accident on Fire Island."

"Fire Island?" The name seemed odd, a contradiction in terms.

"Yes, he was hit by a – "

But Duncan turned on his heel and walked away. Alone in the corner, Tim looked as if he had been hit, stricken and bleak and angry. David tried to call back what he had only half-heard and must have misheard.

"By a June bug?" he said, knowing he was being silly, unable to resist. You look as if Duncan punched you in the stomach, David thought. David giggled hysterically. "He must have been *awfully* frail."

"A dune buggy," Andrew said, with hardened consonants. "It was terribly bad luck: it didn't look too bad at first, but it turned out there was internal bleeding. They could not stop it."

Andrew wanted to force these details on him, almost vindictively. Perhaps if David could feel sorry for this poet cruelly bleeding to death in the sand he would be forgiven, and could save one part of Tim's plan at least. But poets do a lot of dying, and so do gay men, and David couldn't find any pity for them now, not with Tim alone in front of him, bleeding inwardly, too, in his way.

"Well, I should read him," David conceded. "He sounds really interesting." He knew this was not going to be enough to redeem him. Andrew was sitting straighter: The Argyle diamonds pulling themselves tighter, preparing for a leap.

"I think Tim's got his poems," he said, shortly.

Andrew couldn't see, but now Tim was walking out of the room, not in Duncan's direction.

"I'm afraid Tim and Duncan have just had a fight," David said, trying to sound apologetic.

He hoped Andrew might see that this was a sort of apology, but he didn't. "Really?" he said, coolly. "Worse things have happened, Lord knows."

"Why?"

"Tim Grey and Duncan Holland? It makes no sense at all: it's just Tim's got this thing for mindless blonds."

"Really?" Was that really all? David had seen Tim being happy with Duncan and that had been enough for him: the crusty duenna had proved to have a marshmallow heart and could let the lovers do whatever they wanted. But could Andrew be right? No, David thought loyally. The explanation was obvious: he was after Tim himself. That was understandable, but, but – David's mind lost its grip on the world, everything spun around, he didn't know where he was. He remembered he was in a house owned by young men, he was at a party, and Andrew Johnston with a 't' was getting up from the wallowing springs of the couch because David had offended him.

"Can I get you some wine?" Andrew said.

"Please, yes," David said, to be nice to him, though wine was the last thing he needed. As Andrew took the glass, their hands touched, and David said, wildly, staring at Andrew's chest, "You know, I'd love to take all those clothes right off."

Andrew stared and blinked. "It was the white, wasn't it?" he said, from behind his lashes, and walked away.

David laughed at himself, bitterly, complacently. He'd failed. He'd made a fool of himself. But he always did; he was at home with it. He looked around, but he couldn't see either Tim or Duncan. Except for himself, everyone in the living room was being mercilessly happy. Andrew had begun doing it, after delivering the wine with a small, forgiving smile, talking and arguing cheerfully with a stocky man with red hair and tortoise-shell glasses. Alone and tunneling farther into drunkenness, David seemed to be taking on the role no one else wanted, the part of the brooding, unhappy drunk, nursing all the dark truths parties conspire to ignore. He took a defiant gulp of the wine Andrew had brought, thinking of his modern poets, all indisputably classic, with Roland Akenside moving nimbly among them.

"Nine and forty swans? Lover by lover?" He'd waited for the class's arithmetic. "Dear me, what's going on here?"

But Yeats was right, after all: no flock is without its forty-ninth, forlorn among passionate wings.

He was halfway down his glass, even slumping a little, when someone leaned over from behind the couch, bringing the smell of vetiver. David knew what it was from sniffing around Duncan's bathroom. "So how's the mystery guest?"

Before he could answer, Duncan came around and sat close beside him.

"You've got them all wondering, you know. Who is that dark, handsome stranger? He's so mysterious, he's so *intense*, and I just can't catch his eye."

"Who is?" David said, alarmed, pulling himself together.

Duncan just produced one of his finest laughs: sweet, sovereign, cordial. It was wonderful, David thought: it deserved a Kochel number. If Duncan could laugh so freely, they couldn't still be fighting: the storm had gone past. No, he thought loyally, Andrew was wrong. Duncan wasn't mindless. Tim wasn't being silly.

"I love your laugh, Duncan," David confessed, frankly drunk. "It's a whole *Weltanschauung*."

"A what?" Duncan let out another, shorter one and said, "Well, I like your hair, even though it isn't Ray's styling. You know," and he moved confidingly closer, "you know, David, I'll bet you're so sexy."

"What! Oh, Duncan, come on."

"The world is crawling with people who ought to be virgins, David, – but you aren't one of them."

David sloshed his wine around gratefully, modestly.

"I mean, you're so *intense* – if you're like that in bed, well, we'd better watch out!" This future David could almost be seen reflected in Duncan's wide, smoke-blue eyes. David laughed at the idea, but why shouldn't Duncan be right? Duncan knew about sex, at least.

"And there are lots of gorgeous men here tonight," Duncan went on. "There's Tom Kierans, over there, sitting on the floor – and I saw how he looked at you!"

"He's nice," David said, as if he could pick and choose. "But what about Andrew Johnston – he's sort of attractive, isn't he?" Duncan would surely have been in on Tim's plan, which might after all still be feasible, if not tonight, some other night. Andrew could see that he was smart enough not to say stupid things when he was sober.

"Andrew?" Duncan gave a quick, unstylish shrug. He seemed to be searching for something cutting enough to say about Andrew, and coldness gathered in his face, thickening it like the dead fat of middle age. It was frightening: Duncan, and the universe, were about to look cold and mean. Suddenly, to prevent it, David was leaning towards him, falling against him as the old springs gave under them. With grief slopping into his heart, he toppled into Duncan's warmth – into Tim's and Duncan's mysterious, perfumed warmth – and he was saying into his ear, "Don't hurt him, be nice to him, he really loves you." He pulled himself away with stinging eyes.

Duncan stared as if he might choose not to understand. Then he said, "I'm always nice to him. As nice as he deserves."

"I'm sorry," David said. "It's not my business. I'm drunk. I didn't know you could get this drunk."

Duncan gave him a sharp, searching look, and David shrank a little. What did he see? He was too drunk to see into his own mind, but perhaps Duncan could see right through him. Suddenly he wanted to tell him all about Chris. Duncan knew the story, but he didn't understand how helplessly, hopelessly in love David was with a gorgeous guy named Chris, who was straight. That was why he was backward at parties and said stupid things, to Duncan, to Andrew. That was why he was mysterious and intense and alone here on the couch.

"I'm not kidding, David," Duncan said. "Tom Kierans has got a personality that never stops."

He got up.

"Can I get you anything?" he said, doubtfully.

"No, I think I'd better slow down. But thanks, Duncan."

He sat and sipped, knowing he shouldn't, but not caring. He'd got too drunk to care about anything, or, for that matter, to do anything tonight. For tonight at least he would be swan forty-nine, and he sat thinking about Tim and Duncan and Chris and the world he was in now. It seemed a pity now that Frank O'Hara had died just when he did: what David had said about Andrew and his clothes was true, though he'd been deliberately silly and shocking in saying it. He would like to see what Andrew's long, intelligent body, so like his own, had to say for itself.

"David! David, we're going now, if you want a lift."

He found his eyes, got them to look at Tim and Duncan at the entrance to the living room, smiling, happy, lover by lover.

"Norman Farber is taking us," Tim went on. "He says he could easily drop you off."

A deep voice corroborated this. "No problem, it's right on the way."

"Is it really that late?" David said. He was past looking at his watch.

"It's two thirty," Tim said.

"Two thirty?" He said it as if it was funny, somehow, though he didn't know more than anyone else why it should be. He looked at Tim, at Duncan, at the couple they made. Tim had his arm on Duncan's shoulder, not just affectionately—anxiously – as if he was afraid he might get away. And Duncan was content to wear the arm, for now at least. Tim was the weaker of the two, the one more in love, David saw. He was glad to see it, in a way: glad his friend, his best friend in Toronto, in the world really, was the emotional one.

"I don't know," he said, almost sleepily as if he'd forgotten the question.

"Well…" Tim seemed a little exasperated, as if he had had enough complications for that night.

"I'll stay for a bit," David said, trying to sound alert. "Help Alan and Michael tidy up this wonderful house of theirs."

"Well, all right," Tim said, doubtfully. "I'll call tomorrow, okay?"

"Sure," David said. "Good night, Tim. Good night, Duncan. Sweet dreams."

But then, as they turned, he wanted to call Tim's name and did.

"What? Yes?"

He didn't know what he'd done, or why he'd done it: he hadn't expected to be heard through all the noise. The only sensible thing he could think of to say was that he'd changed his mind, would come with them after all. And that was the last thing he wanted, to be shut up in a car with Tim and Duncan and whatever it was they felt about each other.

"Oh, I don't know," he said wearily, knowing he could claim a few seconds of patience. He was drunk, after all: pitiable and threatening, too. For all poor Tim knew, or the rest of them, he was drunk enough to say anything.

He looked around, despairingly: there was no way out of it, he would have to go with them, the useless third in a love affair of two. His eyes fixed on an Argyle sweater. For a moment he thought it was Andrew's, but it wasn't, and he remembered Andrew had already left with a group of friends. He had had a sweater like that when he was six.

It was itchy, he hated it, but it was a Christmas present from an aunt. He had to wear it when she came. Now he felt that feeling again, as if all the unfairness of the world came around him, itching him. His drunkenness seemed to be turning against him. It wanted to poison him, make him sick. He couldn't believe it: how had he got into this misery? He wanted to ask Tim. Tim ought to tell him, because after all it was Tim who had got him here. It was Tim who had broken open his jaws – made him open his mouth to say he was gay and then shoved his tongue in it, and then abandoned him, here, now, in this drunken, braying hell. He saw Tim was watching anxiously, afraid that a scene was about to be made. Duncan stood a little behind him, with other people, too. He didn't want to upset them, and saw the person in the Argyle sweater turning and leaving. Why had he been so nasty to Andrew?

"Oh, I don't know, Tim," he said, as if wise and weary of it all. "I just don't know. I mean, who the fuck is Frank O'Hara anyway?"

For a moment, it got out everything inside him: he was free of Andrew, of the party, of the problem of finding a lover, of his whole life. Tim started, then laughed uneasily.

"Are you *sure* you don't want a ride?"

"Nope," he said, smiling at him happily. He was content. He had made Tim jump. He had heard concern in his voice and seen it in his eyes. He had, for the first time in his life, let out the anger-sweet word 'fuck' without thinking, without irony. It was freedom, it was almost poetry: anyway, it was going to be his love-life for the night, and it was something like enough.

He looked at Tim and gave him a beautiful, drunken, fatuous smile. It *was* enough.

"No, Tim, I'll manage. Really. Good night."

PART 4

But when David phoned Tim's the next day, still hung over, wondering what on earth he had done, there was no answer. The day after, Tim phoned him.

Andrew, it turned out had been a sort of delusion. They hadn't been talking about him, there had been nothing special in Tim's smile.

"Not that it was such a bad idea," he added, thoughtfully. He sounded depressed.

David laughed nervously. "At least I didn't disappoint you. That was what I meant about Frank O'Hara. He's Andrew's favourite poet, apparently, and he got annoyed because I hadn't heard of him."

Tim just laughed a little.

"I can't be expected to have heard of everyone. And people are always doing that to me. Telling me to read *Dune* or *Steppenwolf* or *Atlas Shrugged*, just because it's the only book they've ever got through in their lives."

Tim didn't say anything. David began to fear he had insulted one of his favourites.

"Duncan and I have broken up," Tim said.

"Oh, Tim," David said, stunned. "Oh, I'm sorry. Forever?"

"Is that your favourite word?"

"I'm really sorry."

He paused; Tim would want to talk about it. But there was silence, while he contemplated the end of his seven-week world of Tim and Duncan. Their ramshackle house had fallen down on him. He could feel Tim's sadness over the phone, and now it bothered him that Tim was the one more in love. It was indecent: Tim without Duncan felt like an open wound.

"That's a real shame," he said.

"So you liked him?" Tim said.

What an unfair question, he thought. But maybe Tim needed advice, help in seeing Duncan clearly. "I don't know," he said. "I liked him a lot more than I expected at first. At first, I thought you liked him mainly for his looks, and I was scared of him, but then he was nice to me. But – "

"Well?"

"I don't like him for the way he treated you. I don't think he ever really appreciated you." He saw again the arm on Duncan's shoulder. What he didn't like was that Tim should be so upset. He was sure that Duncan's announcements of the break-up to his friends would be very different from Tim's: starting off sad but sensible, then getting brave and even breezy. "I mean – " he couldn't say anything about mindless blonds.

Tim let him struggle on this hook for a moment, then laughed.

"Don't worry, David. I'll live." And more important, he said he'd phone again in a couple of days. He was going up to Napier to see his mother and his sister.

That afternoon, David was walking through the Victoria College campus, by the steps of its granite castle, thinking of what had happened, what he had learned, when a familiar voice called hello. He looked up to see that for the first time he had got into Chris's presence without the stretched-out, unreal interval when he saw Chris and couldn't speak. They were both going across to the main campus, and went through the park together, talking about the news, the Watergate hearings.

David was convinced that whatever happened, Nixon would get away with it: he always did, didn't he?

"Not a chance," Chris said, delighted. "They're going to dump him."

"But why? You can't put the President in jail."

"The Watergate thing is all a charade. It's the war: they're beaten, and they've got to have a scapegoat. But they can't even admit what it's for, so they'll dump him for something else, something minor. Christ, it must happen all the time down there."

Chris's theory was too easy, too comfortable. "Do you really think things work that way?"

"Oh, they're in *bad* shape."

"Who exactly? The Americans?"

"The Americans, the capitalists. They're on the skids. I mean, think, Saigon is going to *fall*."

Chris's deceitful fellow-traveller looked sideways at good looks enhanced by glad, contented anger. He felt a sense of history: cities falling, and rulers of the world too, perhaps, the times alive with change. But none of it was really going to happen the way Chris wanted, David felt: history deceives us. And somehow David had to speak out at last.

"So do you think we ought to get ready for a revolution?"

He was afraid of what he had done as soon as he spoke. Chris looked at him sharply, as if he had been waiting for this. "You sound skeptical?"

"Well!" David said, almost cried, seeing that now he had to go on. "Do you really think there's going to be a revolution here? Do you expect the American Consulate to start barricading their building on University Avenue with concrete abutments to keep away the mad bombers from Oakville? Will we have crowds and barriers and banners and the Internationale, in *Toronto*?"

He gestured as if appealing to the trees, all good Tories, fat and self-satisfied, the park comfortably shared out among them. He'd pronounced To-ron-to in a disparaging, boondocks sneer. Locals labeled it Traw-no, or simply T.O., but he'd meant to sound arrogant and offensive. It was ludicrous to imagine "Toronto the Good", the very heartland of quiet, boring, stable Canada, as suddenly erupting into wild, burning chaos.

"It won't be like the past, no. But it's got to happen, sooner or later. And probably sooner than you think."

Chris was fierce and expectant: he seemed to smell revolution in the air.

"But why? Why would it happen?"

"Because capitalism is getting old. It's losing its grip. It isn't giving the people what they need."

"It seems to be giving them what they want, here at least."

He felt Toronto spreading out comfortably around them, middling away through all the green shades of the middle class. Reaching down to despair here and there: drunks, welfare cases, homeless madmen, but all isolated, no great open pits of misery.

"What they think they want, perhaps," Chris said, contemptuously. "What the box tells them they want. They'll wake up."

He was fierce and handsome: if the revolution could have been a kiss, David almost might have given it to him then. Instead, he shrugged, as if all Toronto, smug and self-satisfied, had risen onto his shoulders.

Irritated, Chris went on the offensive. "You're so cut off. That's what English does to you. If you aren't careful, David, you'll end up like Geoffrey Exton."

David flinched, but he savoured the sound of his name in Chris's voice, in Chris's throat and chest. Chris didn't despair of him, it seemed: he was still worth some friendly advice.

"I mean, reading all those books. Do you think Jane Austen makes a difference?

Do you think the world is going to be saved by that Methodist Pope of yours?"

"Oh – did you see him too?" Because earlier that morning, David had seen Northrop Frye stalking across the Victoria College campus, pensive and terrific, like the ghost in *Hamlet* and all the other plays at a blow.

"No, I missed him," Chris said, with a laugh.

"He's not my Pope," David protested. "I'm not one of those disciples. But you've got to admit – " He stopped. Frye really didn't have anything to do with it.

"What?" Chris said. "What do I have to admit?"

"Well, you've been to his lectures, you know what he's like. He's a *wizard*. He's irresistible."

Chris sniffed. "In his *petit bourgeois* way."

"You know what I mean. It's like he's got it all spread out in front of him. Everything. Everything ever written."

"That isn't everything."

"But you can't expect him to solve the world's problems! He's a literary critic."

Chris just handed back the syllables in a dry staccato: "A literary critic!"

"But he's a great one!" David still felt the alarm and awe of seeing Frye go by with all the books in the world behind his forehead. "He's a great man!" David said, stripped of irony.

"Boy, you've got it bad," Chris said, indulgently.

David was silent, hurt. He'd never shown Chris his real feelings about anything before, and now Chris was laughing at him. Suddenly Chris was on the attack again. "It's unreal: you're going on about him like a girl with a crush on David Bowie and people are being killed. Right now, right here on this planet. Napalmed, bombed, starved – they're dying!"

The last word came as a cry of pain and not the pain of people dying far away, Chris's. It was the most intimate sound David had ever heard from him, and he longed to know what lay behind it. But he never would: Chris had heard the weakness in his voice at once and pulled himself back.

"That's just a fact," he said curtly. "Not some myth."

They were silent for a minute, then Chris said, looking ahead, cheerfully, "King Eddie's in bad shape, isn't he?"

A white mess wrapped his head, as though a kind of ghostliness was descending on him, with a seagull perched on top of it. His horse's cock and balls had been painted bright red. But the king went riding on through blue sky as if nothing could touch him. David gave a little grin. "All right," he said, sadly, "you're right, I guess." People were dying on the planet they walked on, as they spoke. Chris was trying to do something about it, while he cared only about Chris. He loved Chris's courage, his heroism, the way he loved the curly hair.

"But maybe books make a difference, too," he said. "Sometimes."

"You'll never go through with it, you know," Chris said, as if to make up for his attack.

"With what?"

"I just don't think you've got a Ph.D. written on your forehead."

David laughed. It was sweet of Chris to prophesy about him, but he was off the mark. "That's what I'm always saying," he said. "But I'll wriggle through somehow. Like Nixon."

They were coming to the crossing where David had first noticed the smiling blond young man who had almost watched him die halfway through *Clarissa*. Now the cars gave them a chance and they were running, side by side. It was a game, a race, and David with his months on the Hart House track and his long legs, pulled ahead easily. On the other side, laughing, he saw that he really was taller and bigger than Chris. It was as if he had been stooping to hear Chris's low voice until now.

Their paths divided here, and on the brink of separation, a gap of freedom opened, a moment when he could say, almost as a joke – because clearly the letter was lost now, it was just a matter of confirming that – "Did you ever get my letter?"

He saw it arriving in the pained, shrinking look that came over Chris's face.

"Of course I got it."

Of course. Of course they were in a universe where solid things don't evaporate. Where he stood in strong sunshine, solid himself, the David McTavish who was claiming to love Chris Leggatt.

"I thought it must have got lost."

"No," Chris said, impatiently.

"Why didn't you say something?"

"Because I thought you didn't want me to." There was fear and distaste in this, and David could sympathize. Chris after all shouldn't have to deal with obscure situations like this. But he saw that Chris was in his power for a moment, being well brought up and also too kind simply to walk away. In this sunlit moment, David could say what he felt, not just shove it under a door. But what did he feel? He smiled, trying to get his eyes to meet Chris's, but looking into the lovely, normal curls.

"Well, maybe I didn't," he admitted.

Chris moved his shoulders in relief, seeing he was going to be let go.

"Anyway, thanks," David said, not clear for what. "Thanks, Chris."

"Sure," Chris said, quickly, off to a meeting. "Sure, I'll see you around."

PART 5

A few days later, Tim phoned and suggested they go to some of the galleries in Yorkville. David had said he thought he should know more about the art scene. They met at a show of Canadian high realists. Tim was subdued, nearly silent. David fell in with this, moving along past the paintings beside or behind him, looking into them sympathetically. He liked these high and magic super realists, soothed by their milky, mysterious underpainting, taken by their anxiety to tell half a story vividly. They were very Canadian, coolly Gothic, their sex and their anger reserved and gleaming. David felt right at home.

They went on to the show Tim was really interested in, of abstract expressionists. "Some real greats," Tim said, with irony and awe carefully blended. "Andrew's painters." With that, he lead David into a storm of paint.

It was easier for David to see the respect Tim gave the paintings than the paintings themselves. They took all his attention, filled his eyes. It seemed you didn't look for some point, some feeling to send you on your way: you exposed yourself for minutes to, say, a Rothko's sombre radiation.

But the paintings defeated David. They seemed clumsy or else frantic. Their colours were hard and shrill in electric light. David began to feel Tim had led him into some nihilist desert and abandoned him, except for cryptic mutterings about triangles and greens.

Finally they came to the last one – it was taller than they were, like a gate into hell, and David resolved to try one last time. He would look at this painting like Tim beside him, with steady, slow-moving eyes. He looked, and for a moment it seemed that all the oil had become liquid again, could have taken any shape it liked and was taking the shape he saw, that lyric choiring of colours. But only for a moment, he couldn't sustain it, and felt suddenly depressed. As if the painting had reached out to pierce him with colour, with chaos. He turned to Tim, still serene, entranced. Somehow a painter named Hofmann could take a healthy, intelligent twenty-two-year-old by the eyes and stand him there to take in his colours for minutes on end.

Then Tim looked away, satisfied. "What do you think?" he said, as they headed out.

"Think?" How could you think amid the shrieking colours? "I prefer Christopher Pratt."

Tim just smiled.

"That is all new to me," David said. "At least I'm trying to keep up-to-date."

"Oh, they're old masters now."

"Really?" Things seemed to move very fast in the art world. "Are there books?" David said. "Maybe if I knew what was going on..."

"Are there books? There are hundreds. If you come up to my place after lunch, I can lend you some. But where do you want to eat?"

On Yorkville, they were surrounded by restaurants. But short of money as usual, David suggested another place.

"Why not that glass-enclosed cafeteria, where we met before?"

Tim looked a little surprised.

"At least, I know the prices there. Of course, you've got to promise not to pry any more secrets out of me."

"There are more?"

"Who knows?" He didn't want to announce his news yet. Not until they were seated in the restaurant did he say, "Guess what, he did get it. The letter, I mean."

"How do you know?"

"I asked! You'd've been proud of me. I just opened my mouth and asked: it's amazing how easy that is. You have to breathe out anyway, and it might as well be words."

"So he had got it all along?"

"Yes, of course."

"But why didn't he say anything?" Now it was Tim who seemed upset by this, although in David's opinion it was really his feelings about Duncan showing through.

"Well, I discouraged him, I guess. I more or less told him not to."

"But then, how could he let you think all this time he hadn't got it?"

"You know," David said. "It's his background. He knows how to ignore things that are unpleasant. It was easier for him – for both of us."

"What a bastard!"

"No! Imagine, getting a letter like that out of the blue, when you're straight, I mean. He didn't know what to do: he was scared."

"That's no reason not to be human. To react somehow. If I said 'I love you,' you'd bat an eyelash, wouldn't you?"

David blinked. The breakup with Duncan really was confusing things. "I'll introduce you sometime," he said. "You'll see what I mean, really."

Tim didn't seem to look forward to this. "So what happens now?" he said.

David gave a little laugh. "I don't know. It's not the way it was, somehow. I find I can turn it on and off, sort of. I can think of him and say to myself, 'Wouldn't it be nice to get all in a state about him.' And say back, 'No, not just now'." He laughed. "Which is scary. I mean, it was the biggest thing in my life!"

They ate quietly for a while, and since Tim didn't seem to want to talk, David began remembering out loud.

"I remember my first weeks here, last fall. It seemed so crowded and busy I had to run to keep up. And I was planning to fall in love. How could I come all that way, driving thousands of miles, and then not fall in love? I'd made it to this huge city, and there had to be *somebody* here, in the crowds, in the subway – he didn't know it yet, but he was mine. I even went and spent some of the Canada Council's money on contact lenses, so as not to be too scholarly. So he could see me. That meant I saw it all through tearing, which didn't help."

Was he helping to distract Tim from his loss? He thought so: Tim was amused, attentive.

"But I didn't know anybody here, so that left the people I might meet in my courses. In the first two, in the first week of classes, there was no one – some real powerhouses, but no one you'd fall in love with. And then Frye's class is so big, and everybody is sort of flattening themselves out in front of the great man. That left the 'Novel and Society' on Thursday afternoon. In University College, off the quadrangle. I got there early because I'd planned to get lost and didn't. I could watch the people coming in. They were nice enough, most of them, but I kept thinking, give it time, maybe when I've got my M.A."

"And then he looked in. Obviously wondering if it was the right room, but you don't want to ask and have them all snicker and say 'of course not, this is Anglo-Saxon Religious Poetry.' I picked up my copy of *Waverley* for him to see, but he didn't notice. He was going along behind the chairs – it's a small room– pulling himself in a little, that soft little bit of a pot. And I was thinking, 'Well, he isn't that good-looking, but that's all right. He's okay. I don't feel swept away or anything, but I suppose he might do…'"

Tim was smiling sympathetically. Surprising both of them, David pulled himself up into a shaking stage hunchback and rasped at him, "*Homosexual melodrama!*"

"What?"

David laughed, delighted. "Sayings of Roland Akenside. It was when someone in his first class, just shopping I guess, he didn't come back, put up his hand in the middle of Akenside on *The Waste Land* and said 'But what about Jean Verdenal?' Apparently there's some theory that The Waste Land is really all about being in love with someone killed in the First World War. And Roland Akenside huffed and hunched and beetled and said, 'It's unthinkable, it's *inconceivable,* that one of the founding poems of the twentieth century should come out of some *mawkish homosexual melodrama!*'"

Tim winced: David had spit in his face.

"Oh, I'm sorry. Akenside does that to you." And as Tim wiped his face, "You'll meet him someday. Chris, I mean. You'll see. He wasn't a bad choice. He's okay." He sighed, with real sadness, but not much pain. "I guess it's like Duncan said. Everybody should fall for a straight boy once."

He laughed: Duncan's idea, and his manner, were coming over him. "Everyone should fall for one of those cute straight boys – they're sweet, they're adorable – with their big, brown eyes and their curls and their funny glasses and their silly politics. Everybody should," – he *was* Duncan now – "*once!*"

Tim laughed, ruefully. "One Duncan is enough, too, David."

"Sorry," David said, thoroughly pleased with himself. Being Duncan turned heads but it let you say things, too. He began on his strawberries.

Armed with a certain happiness, he felt safe in asking the big question at last. "What happened?"

Tim gave him a dark look. He had been expecting this. "We had an argument," he said, shortly.

"Not about me, I hope?"

"No. No, of course not." Tim looked surprised. "Why would we? Duncan liked you, basically."

"He did? I thought I'd die when he went after my hair."

"Well, yes, it's a good thing you gave in, or we'd never have heard the end of it. But he was flattered, because you – you, a grad student! – liked him, took him seriously, sort of."

"Mmm," David said, patronizingly fond of Duncan again for a moment. "But what did you fight about?"

Tim tried to shrug it all away. "I'd forget he was only twenty, but I was getting tired of all that style, that attitude. It really got tyrannical at times. He seemed to think he'd been born again when he got off the Sudbury bus: gay life here is a religion for him. As if wearing just the right silk shirt to the Sunday tea dance really is an accomplishment. Like a painting."

Was that the real reason? Tim hadn't quite said it was.

"Maybe I was getting too possessive," Tim admitted in a lower voice. "But what's the difference between being possessive and being in love?"

Having no idea, David shrugged and kept silent.

"But he was nice in bed, David," Tim said in a low voice, smiling at his strawberries with a bitter twist of his mouth. "He was so very nice in bed. But I'll survive."

David coughed. "I certainly hope so," he said. It was meant to be sympathetic, but an unexpected surge of emotion made it stern, almost savage. Tim looked up quickly.

"Well, I'm sorry," David said.

"What do you mean?"

"It's not for me to say, is it? But – I don't know, but you're taking it so hard! I just don't understand it, Tim."

Tim pushed his mouth into an odd, pursed smile. "Duncan told me to watch out for you."

"He did?"

"I know you must have thought Duncan was just a silly queen at times, but I miss him, David."

"Of course, but – " He didn't know how to put it, but like a fool he tried anyway. "You look as if you'd let him hit you!"

Tim blinked and scowled. "You're the one who goes in for that, David," he said, angrily.

And seeing it was true, David felt as guilty as if he had hit him again. He looked away, almost blushing.

"David, I know you're an expert on love," Tim went on, bitterly, "from Jane Austen and *Clarissa* and all those novels of yours. But I can do without advice." His voice cracked with exasperation. "What the fuck do you know about Duncan and me?"

"Nothing whatever, I suppose," David said, hastily. "I was just trying to be a friend." It was meant to be apologetic, but there was resentment in it too. He hadn't, after all, hit Tim. Not this time. And it was Duncan, Tim ought to be angry with. Was angry with, if he would only admit it. It wasn't David's fault if Tim was too possessive about someone who was so very nice in bed but liked sleeping around.

"After all," Tim said, more calmly, "it was Duncan's and my relationship, not yours."

You could say it had been David's too, his first gay love affair in a way, but he didn't want to argue. He felt suddenly depressed, tired of all of it: the affair, the odd role he had been playing, Tim's hurt right now. Really, it was time to get on with his life. That might mean people beyond Tim, people Tim didn't even know. Someday this first year in Toronto might seem just a distraction, not the real thing at all.

But for today, he had to consider his Romantic Narrative paper, put off during the last few weeks. The strong coffee he was finishing now could light up a descent into *Frankenstein*.

He sat back. They were both finished. "More galleries?" he said, a little wearily. "Back to the New York School? I kind of think they've taught me enough for today."

Tim looked at him, still annoyed, but then smiled. "Don't you remember?"

"Remember? Oh, yes." We've forgiven each other? All right, I suppose. "Yes, we were going up to your place, weren't we?"

CHAPTER III: LOVERS
Summary, 1974

PART 1

Their train was packed and hurtled them north, standing. The arms they hung by brushed against each other: polite skins, not feeling much.

"I used to *like* the subway," David complained.

He was watching a small girl with black hair– a baby, really, just contemplating life as a little girl from beside an old woman all in black. She was sucking a candy, which she would take out now and then and look at. It looked back, dark-brown and gleaming. David decided he was Tim's friend because Tim liked to have a well-read, intelligent friend like him. Today's galleries were part of bringing him into Tim's world. As for their both being gay, it was simply going to be less important. Whoever Tim found to replace Duncan, David would take less of an interest in him and in Tim's feelings about him.

The little girl popped her candy into her mouth and turned the black eyes on David. They smiled shyly.

The two friends got off at St. Clair and walked north to Tim's rundown, fiftyish yellow-brick apartment block, like hundreds of others in Toronto. From the living room you could see just over the tree-tops to yards for subway trains, then to Yonge Street and beyond it Mount Pleasant Cemetery. While Tim poured drinks in the kitchen, David looked around from a wicker chair that made splintering noises as he moved. It was pleasant to see Tim unfolding into this sunny, well-lit place, with its plants and posters and drawings, to relax and feel welcomed in it. This was the first time he had been here alone with Tim.

Tim came in, put down his gin and tonic, and sat on a Bauhaus sofa. David began wondering aloud if he could somehow afford his own apartment. Tim said he had almost gotten a place downtown, in the gay ghetto, but he preferred being up north of the escarpment, where it was clearer and cooler. It was home for him, after all. The big house he'd grown up in was only a few minutes walk to the west.

It was pleasant to have this sort of friend, intelligent and sensitive without the bristling ironies of graduate students. Tim wasn't a rival, that was part of it: he had a different career, which David asked about cautiously.

Then Tim remembered the art books. He shifted along the sofa towards a big wall unit beside it, with many heavy books on its bottom shelf. "Here's Frank O'Hara," he said, coming across a big paperback and tossing it at David.

David blinked but caught it by sheer, blind luck. He opened his eyes to see "Oh!" there was a drawing of a naked man on the cover, starting an erection.

Tim laughed, wrestling with his books. "That drawing's Larry Rivers. He was a friend of Frank O'Hara's." He grunted, pulling a paving-stone of a book out and up, onto his lap. "I suppose this one's too heavy to carry," he said, but he seemed to want to look at it himself. "I bought it and then…"

David went to sit beside him. Tim was looking at, into a painting he thought he recognized – so perhaps he was getting somewhere. Oblongs of colour stacked up against a dark ground.

"We saw that today, didn't we?"

"No. That's another Rothko."

"He does that a lot?"

"In the famous ones, yes."

"Mmm," David said. He let the painting smoulder at him from under the gloss of the paper. Tim turned the big page with care.

"I like that smell," David said. "The chemical smell of that kind of paper. It smells sharp and sweet and – rich. That's part of it, isn't it: this Art World of yours is *"rich"*.

Now Tim's eyes seemed to have been caught by dark, surging shapes that claimed to have something to do with the Spanish Civil War. They were evocative, David thought, like characters in some primitive alphabet. But perhaps that was all: perhaps you can take any shape, associate it with something important, tragic even, like the Spanish Civil War, and it will have a look of meaning and grandeur. He was beginning to wonder if he was getting impatient with these New York people, and a little jealous. Tim's art world, which David imagined around him like an aura, like a many-coloured coat, wasn't substantial enough now to satisfy him. He looked at Tim's profile, which he'd seen enough of for today, and knew he didn't want to be Tim's dry, intelligent friend. And it occurred to him that whatever he did, he was in no danger of being hit or even seriously insulted. Tim was hospitable: you could tell that from the quiet way he put down your drink, as if it was yours before he gave it to you. He might say, 'No, David,' – David could hear how he would say it – but he wouldn't throw him out.

Tim had turned the page to something like an atomic explosion seen through pink mist. Lovely, David thought, glancing at it, but just a painting, after all. Not giving himself time to think and be either stupid or wise, he put a dry kiss on Tim's cheek just below his eye.

What had happened? For a second or two, it seemed nothing had. Then Tim turned the big-eyed brown attention to his restless guest, and with it a small smile Adolf Gottlieb hadn't won. But perhaps, David thought, this was the end of it all, looking over Tim's face with a kind of farewell, photographing clarity. Perhaps Tim's hospitality didn't reach this far. He was, after all, convalescent, getting over Duncan: perhaps drama like this didn't help. Almost shaking, David leaned again and brushed at Tim' silent lips with his, inquiringly. He felt inept but determined, as if part of him knew perfectly well what it was doing. As if he had been planning something like this for a long time, but with someone he hadn't seen yet, like Tim, but not Tim himself. But here he was: Tim himself, Tim awfully silent.

"You're nice," David said. Meaning, hurry up. Be nice now.

Minor risings stirred Tim's mouth. David leaned forward, fraught with a dying kiss, and pushed his tongue in through Tim's lips, a tongue of pure despair.

He heard the heavy book close and slide down to the floor, felt arms come around his back. David pulled closer, in relief: he could collapse and let Tim take over. But then, with Tim's tongue stepping in as if into his home, David felt the dizziness he'd felt before. He had to still it, to steady himself, and keep both eyes on the situation. As if sensing his fear, Tim pulled back and began gently kissing David's face. David giggled soundlessly. His face wasn't ticklish, exactly: it was almost numb under Tim's lips, and then distantly painful beneath the numbness. The face he'd lived behind so long was a mask, carved by fear and sarcasm: why would anyone kiss it? David laughed and pulled his face away, feeling sadness cracking through it.

"Are you sure we ought to be doing this?" he said, jokingly.

"Are you, David?"

Tim's fingers were at his top shirt button. David held them, the button still clinging, half-undone, and said, "Is this why you brought me here?"

"I didn't *bring* you here."

David looked at the fingers he held, spattered as if Tim had been slashing the throats of rainbows.

"For today," Tim said, "I thought we were both wrecks, both getting over something. Aren't we? And, well, you must know as well as I do, David, we could never really be lovers."

"No, I guess not." And then, "Why not?" Not disagreeing: he wanted to hear Tim's reasons.

"I don't know. We're so different."

David let go of the fingers. "I don't think we'd be lovers either. But if we were, Mr. Grey " – David gave a ferocious, scowling smile, to show how determined a lover he would be.

Tim gave David a slightly mocking imitation of his kiss on the lips: it was like putting back something he'd borrowed. The fingers were back at the shirt button. So: Tim would grant him what he'd asked for. The way out of virginity and Chris: the way into other people, Tim and beyond. He looked down helplessly, thinking there would still be time to stop. To stop and tell Tim how much he liked him, how interesting the day had been, and get out. But Tim's hand made its way in, reaching inside David's clothed self for its core, the skinned, helpless pulp of a fiercely intelligent graduate student. David was afraid, but Tim had buttons too. He fumbled at one, and Tim reached down to help: it seemed incredibly generous, princely, for him to show you the way to his skin. David's long hands went in and through, feeling out unseen, soft terrain. Emulating Tim's, his hands moved up towards his breasts.

Suddenly Tim pulled back, quickly twisting down the buttons, throwing the shirt back and off as if he would never want a shirt again. David blinked. For years the shock of bare chests had been ambushing him from playing fields and docks: now here it was, the body's own sweet blind face right in front of him. He reached as if he was growing new arms and found himself falling into the world of the body, arriving in the rush and thud of Tim's heart. He felt something like at last, or again. He'd come in out of the bitter wilderness which went back as far as he could remember, and now he wanted to rest for a while in the sound of blood. But Tim's hands were yanking at the bottom of David's shirt.

"What's wrong?"

"Take your shirt off, you twit!"

He sat up, a twit, and realizing he liked to be called that: it dissolved away another layer of loneliness. He pulled the shirt up off over his head, wondering for an unseeing moment where he was headed, what he was doing. Then Tim was greeting him, reaching for the old scarred-over wound of his nakedness.

Tim touched his shoulder, David shivered, and Tim's hand dropped, brushing the side of his breast, then down along his side. What could the paint-flecked fingers make of this stale off-white?

"You have nice tits," Tim said.

"Tits! I haven't heard that word since high school."

Tim's fingers brushed one, then the other nipple. "Do you like that?" he said.

David shook his head.

Tim laughed, his hand moved down into the quaking pit of his belly, and David put his hand out to Tim's mile-swimming left breast, which was smooth as a boy's.

"Do you? Like that?"

"Yes – gently." The nipples erected, and David was taken, tickled by their tiny excitement.

"Like this?"

Tim arched back his eyes, giving in to David, to something that came up his spine. "Yes," he said, his eyes fading a little.

"They're not supposed to do that," David declared.

"Oh, yes they are."

David was fascinated by the huskiness in Tim's voice. His friend, strong and handsome, really was queer: A little touch and you could turn him into this sighing, heavy-shouldered odalisque.

"Lick it," Tim said, reaching into David's crotch, shaping out his penis through the cloth. David decided to do what Tim asked, experimentally tasting and kissing the little biological joke Tim took so seriously. Tim was digging in his crotch, and he was falling into a kind of curious, hungry love with Tim's breast. But it couldn't last: he realized Tim had got him, and he pulled away, saying "No, please." Tim shuddered at the touch of breath on his wet nipple, and David saw he couldn't leave that patch of skin, leaning back and mumbling into it, "Don't." Tim's hand was out to destroy him. Then he was fighting away and back, his eyes squeezing shut, and for one long instant stretching out and out he was coming, with a noise tearing out of him like rusty hinges pulled slowly open.

He lay with his mind and his mouth open, gaping. Something soft had broken his fall – a breathing bank of flesh. He gave himself a little shake, blinked, and said "Sorry!"

"Why?"

"That's what they call premature, isn't it?"

"You're twenty-two."

"I didn't even have my pants off."

"I'll lend you a pair."

"With tears in them?"

Tim laughed, and pulled him closer. "What are we going to do with you, David?"

"Lots more," he said, drowsily, not needing to deal with Tim's real question now. "Lots, lots more." He yawned, wide and wider, as if he might try sleeping inside out, like jeans being washed. "Of course," he said, making himself at home on Tim's chest, "I've got to do it to you too. Don't worry. I'm looking forward to it."

Eyes closed, he rubbed his face against Tim, into the sounds of his blood. He was seeing sunlit, green country he'd never seen before, vividly, as if it came from the miraculous time before glasses. It was so bright and green he was dreaming it.

PART 2

"Are you asleep?" Tim asked, surprised. He was, abruptly unconscious, as if he'd knocked himself out on Tim's chest. Tim was trapped in a sort of awkward, leggy pieta, without being marble, without being very maternal. But he could give David a few minutes before he had to move.

He sat looking with uncertain pride at what he'd done, or begun: this sprawling baby, crawling determinedly out into the world of sex. But Tim was a brother at best, not a mother or a father: what was he going to do with this new David at the end of the afternoon? When David had planted a kiss on his cheek, like the flag of a new, scared, but militantly expansionist nation, Tim had seen he couldn't turn him down. It would have been like hitting him back. And besides, he didn't want to. Tim had begun to notice that David was attractive in his way, and sexual, under the lifetime of repression. His way was very different from Duncan's: dark, unpredictable, a bit twisty. David even smelled dark, with the sharp smell of his body hair, which grew around his nipples and between his breasts, and stormed out from under his belt to surround his navel. He had hard muscles: you could see the months of chin-ups and push-ups in the old Hart House gym, with sidelong glances to see if Chris was around. In profile now,

David's face was eager, striking forth into the world, though too hungry and ragged to be securely attractive. It was from in front that David could be good-looking when grimness stopped pressing on his mouth, when worry evaporated from his eyes. Then their fringe of eyelashes had a sultry look, the hot, moist darkness of desire.

The night before Tim had been at Alan and Michael's, talking about the end of his affair with Duncan, about his future. They liked to play at being his family, his gay parents. He envied them, he said: he'd love to find a lover and settle down like them. He certainly didn't believe in being infatuated as he had been with Duncan's translucent skin: it had just happened.

"So tell us, what would your ideal lover be like?" Alan had asked. He was proposing a sort of game and Tim had played along. As he did, it began to seem more real than he expected, precise enough that it had begun to develop a personality, an elusive look and presence. It was as if this other lover already existed, he said, only half joking: he could sense him around, nearby – though he certainly hadn't seen him around Toronto. He would be a lot like himself, in some ways, but calmer, more sure of himself. "How old?" Alan asked. Older, perhaps, but not by very much, a year or two at most. All Tim's real lovers, so far, had been his age or younger.

"You know," Michael said, "he sounds like another you."

"What do you mean?"

"Aren't you still a bit in love with yourself, maybe?"

Among the three of them, Michael played the role of the realist, the skeptic, and he also liked teasing Tim about his looks. But Tim wasn't bothered by Michael's suggestion. "No, that's not it at all. But when I settle down, I want it to be with someone I really feel at home with. Really know. Like a brother – I don't have one, maybe that's it." Like a rather older brother, who would know himself and what he wanted better than Tim did.

That came back now, and with it the sense, the flavour of this lover who was still only inside himself. For this afternoon he was being, not having, the wise, strong older brother. It was a role he'd often found himself playing – perhaps, he thought, because his father's death made him grow up in ways most people his age didn't know about. He was content to do it again with David, he could imagine David being a friend for a long time, but not his lover, not seriously.

His legs were starting to hurt under David's weight. He leaned to lick David's shoulder, to start waking him, and to savour David and his mysteries. David held onto sleep with his eyelids. Tim tried his name, softly at first, letting himself ponder it. It was a dark name, too, dark-Scottish, dark as the grave. An old name: because this smug sleeper had several ages, with young and old selves as guardians on either side of his twenty-two. There was the bad, wise child who was leading them giddily through this seduction, and there was the ancestral, merciless David who had struck without warning. Would he appear again?

"David!" Tim said, louder, with a gentle shake.

PART 3

He opened his eyes on a golden meadow.

"Sorry," a voice was saying above him, "but it was getting uncomfortable."

Tim: the name came back, fitting him like his skin. Everything came back.

"How long was I asleep?" He got up on his elbows, yawning.

"Ten minutes, perhaps."

Now it was dreamless, flawless black: it could have been centuries.

"You should've wakened me."

"I liked watching you sleep."

David lowered himself for another few seconds of sleep, and saw, as if from outside, his old self, pulling a hand resentfully out of the raincoat pocket, making the smallest sign. He almost hadn't, he remembered: he'd still been thinking, 'just who the hell are you?'

"Here," Tim said, and his fingers were suddenly in the pit of his stomach. David laughed and rolled away, undoing his belt, then letting Tim pull the jeans down off his legs. He sat up as Tim stood, pushing his soft washed-out jeans down off his erection and stepping sideways out of them. He almost tripped, the jeans not wanting to let go, but stood, and stood, throbbing. Bashfully, David looked sideways to the left, sideways to the right, as if he couldn't look Tim's cock in the eye. He laughed, got serious, and laughed again. Here were all the animals come from the zoo at last, solemn and friendly.

He moved his hands helplessly, as if they were tied. "Please," Tim said.

David grabbed hold, greedily, as if just about to fall. Tim shook a little, shifting on his feet. Thrilled and challenged by its upward curve, David pulled down and held it. Then pulled down and let go, to watch it leap and dance for him.

"Hello there," he said, laughing, to his first stiff cock. Straining, pompous, empurpled: our hero, absurd and dear.

"Kiss me." Tim suggested from above the two of them.

What a shifty euphemism! David looked up and away with a crumpled smile: no, never, not yet.

Tim dropped between his legs. It was astonishing: Tim had been heroic...astride. Now he was suppliant, down on his knees like the cleaning woman, his tongue pushed out like a child's, against David's rising cock. David hardly felt anything, too busy seeing that everything he'd heard about homosexuals was true. He wanted to say, 'Why are you doing that?' but he was hypnotized. Hundreds of angry, ghostly tongues were busy in his head, while one of flesh moved over his cock. Then he shook a little, gave up, gave in. It was all right: it couldn't be helped. Tim was letting him see him being queer, being a cocksucker, showing him that it was awful, it was ridiculous, and it wasn't so bad. David put his hands on the bowed shoulders, as if to push him away angrily, but feeling instead a kind of blessing go out through him into Tim, forgiveness consuming anger. He imagined leaning forward to whisper the choking, hating syllables into his ear, forgivingly. Then Tim's lips closed over him like eyelids.

After a while, Tim sat back for breath and said, as if impressed, "I love your cock, David."

David opened his eyes, looking down into the swirling crown of Tim's hair. Tim looked up, and said, defiantly, "I do! Don't stare at me like that. Close your eyes."

"Why?"

"Close your eyes, you twit."

He did, and found himself inside Tim's soft, dark, poisoned mouth again. Pleasure had taken root inside him. It was spreading through him, sweet and festering. He couldn't bear it: he had to look in spite of Tim. Tim's body had put on a sheen David had never seen before: he was transfigured by the lightest sweat and the lust of the eye. David's stare focussed hypnotically on Tim's cock, as if he had never seen it before, throbbing alone under the ceiling of his belly, unloved, forlorn. It was heart-rending, like Tim's strong heart cut out and hung throbbing in a terrible loneliness. With a kind of tragic hunger, David pulled away from the sweetness threatening to erupt inside him. Tim looked up, wet-lipped and robbed.

"What's wrong?"

"Nothing. Nothing's wrong. Here. Sit up here."

It took Tim a second to understand. Then, he sat spraddle legged. David lowered himself on doubtful knees, not sure whether his lust would carry him through. Yet, after all, this must have been his goal since Tom Sparling had hung bare-chested from the tree-branch, manly twelve to his eleven. He made a fearful, lunging grab, and the red animal he caught glared out at him with furious, knowing brutality. David stuck out his tongue in a kind of anger at what it was making him do and precisely, sharply licked at the swollen throat. It dropped its sour salt onto his tongue, into his mouth, forever.

He ought, he thought, to go on like Tim, fencing and savouring. But he couldn't: he had to simplify, to get where he was going, and simply put the head of Tim's cock into his mouth.

"Be careful with your teeth," Tim requested, nervously.

David realized he couldn't answer: he was silenced, stoppled. The only conversation was in his clumsy mouthing.

"Yes," Tim said. So he was a success. But now that he was doing it, at last, he wondered why. This wasn't Tim's heart or his own that he held in his mouth. It was too hard and awkward. He didn't feel the same longing or lust he'd experienced a minute ago. Now, he was too busy. Cautiously, he drew back to look.

"What's wrong?"

"It's kind of a nice idea, but it doesn't really work. You're too big."

"Oh, sorry!" Tim said, sardonically. "You really don't have to do anything that you don't want– it's your choice."

David put it back in. It was too big, his jaws hurt, this performance could never be really satisfying, but it was nice to have a friend at his tenderest, his most urgent and passionate, so close. Inside you, or almost, just at the entrance.

And Tim above was beginning to take it seriously. "Oh, David, "he said. "Whatever you do, David, please don't stop. I mean, stop if you want to, but please don't."

Whatever it was he was giving Tim he longed to give more, more in love with the sounds above him than anything else. Tim's hands came down to move softly through his hair, as if they were delicately spreading over him whatever blessing he was giving Tim. They explored his throat, his face, his eyelids, almost hurting the last fragments of the clothed public David, the fierce little bits of plastic the Canada Council had given him to seek out a lover. David shook a little and the blind man's hands moved on, reaching for his nipples. But his jaws were aching, and however rapturous Tim got he couldn't expect David to let him put semen in his mouth. Besides, David was getting out of his depth: he was afraid he would do something wrong, his jaws would insist on biting, in revenge for their ache. He'd got involved in something too big for him, too queer or too adult. He had to get away before it all blew up in his face. Tim seemed to have no thought of letting him get away: he was just getting more anxious and rigid and thrusting – he was getting very selfish, in fact, David thought – and the bone-breaking pain in his jaws was more than enough to justify a rest.

"Oh, David," Tim said, as if taking all the grimness out of the name forever. David couldn't leave him.

But come, he thought, trying telepathy. His jaws were going to break open: he was going to die of pain in the next second, if Tim didn't get this over with *right now – Right Now*, his brain tried to radiate up at Tim, if there was any Tim beyond the animal trying to get down his throat. *Right now, or I'll die.*

Tim groaned and lifted, arching up off the bed, taking David with him, hooked, with semen splashing against the closed inner mouth of his throat: that was what he was going to die of, David thought, he would choke on poison and die.

Then Tim was dropping back as if he was the one who was dying, or as if dying didn't matter. David separated himself from Tim's cock with a mouth full of rank mucilage. It tasted as if millions of spermatozoa wanted to poison him with their embittered deaths. He looked desperately around, saw the two glasses, their ice cubes watching coldly. He almost reached for his, but he felt the groan that had opened up along Tim like the most trusting wound. He put Tim's cock between his lips again and gulped.

He fell away, leaning his head against Tim's thigh, his cheek was slippery with tears that had been squeezed out unnoticed. He watched Tim's cock relax, still keeping a knowing eye on him.

Above him, Tim laughed. David listened: laughter with a happy sighing in it. But what was in it for David?

"Thanks, David."

Thanks? He rubbed his trickled face against Tim's smooth thigh. It felt as if he hadn't talked for a long time. His hair had fallen down into his face: he rubbed it so it covered his eyes, as if he wanted to stay blind and hidden under his wet hair.

"Come on up here," Tim said.

David rubbed his face against his thigh again, as if his trying to erase his shameful face against Tim's springy muscles. He wanted to stay down here, in the house of Tim's legs, with Tim's cock that knew him so well.

"What have I done?" he said. He meant it to be ironic, but his voice was torn open, and what came out was desperate, monstrous. He coughed and tried again, but it was the same raw, bleeding voice.

"Does this mean we're lovers?"

Tim reached for his neck and throat, as if he felt the pain too. "Here, David. Come on up and be my lover for a while."

David laughed. It seemed too far up. Tim put his hand into the wet hair and gave it a gentle pull. "Up!" he whispered.

David twisted his head a little, to feel the pulling in his scalp. "Okay," he said. He crawled up, while Tim shifted around on the couch. He slid forward along toward Tim's smile, to give him a small kiss. His cock, forgotten, was pushing stiffly along Tim's thigh and belly. David gave another kiss, while his cock, as if on its own, began exploring the slither of Tim's belly.

Tim's eyes opened wide. "Yes," he said. "come on me."

"No!" David laughed. What had happened already was too much to absorb.

Tim gave them both a wriggling heave. "You're going to come all over me."

David groaned, because he saw in the squirming look in Tim's eyes that he was right. "Doesn't it ever stop?"

"No!" Tim said, joyfully sticking his tongue into David's mouth, into any excuses he might think of. He was lost. After a life in exile, his cock was home at last, rooting in a hot mess. It was, everything was, beyond his control. "No," he groaned around Tim's tongue. "No, hold me." But Tim was holding him already, hauling him up into his wide chest. David saw it was hopeless: he couldn't be expected to hold the universe together a moment longer. "*Tiiiiim!*" he cried, desperately, disappearingly, then opened into a nameless, calling shout.

PART 4

On most nights during their affair, David would "sleep over" at Tim's. Sometimes, when he really had been sleeping, he would wake out of a dreamless crevasse not knowing where he was just back in the old, high-ceilinged room of waking up, with its shimmer and flavour of emotions in the air above him. Shifting, he would feel a shape alongside him and remember that everything has – *shifted*. He would turn and draw his fingertips believingly over Tim's sleeping body, grateful life hadn't got lost after all, that here he was in bed with it.

They said they were lovers, but no one seemed to know – Tim, or David, or their gay friends what that meant in days or months or years. Being realistic, David told himself at first that he was learning how to be a lover – but not, in the end, Tim's. He could try things out on him – like calling him 'darling' now and then, to see how Tim reacted, to see exactly how silly he sounded to himself. They would have the pleasures of learning and teaching, and then, after some unspecified length of time, they would be friends with fond memories. He didn't ask, not outright, but he was sure Tim still thought the same thing. It was partly that he couldn't imagine Tim really being in love with him. When Tim grabbed and kissed him in the elevator and said "I love you," it was sheer exuberance, love of life, not of David in particular. He saw Tim enjoyed sex with him, enjoyed talking with him, was fond of him – but to be loved point-blank would have been too much for David. There was a lot to be said for keeping a bit dark and unlovable.

But he was taking a risk. Launching his fateful, little kiss, he'd expected something more fierce and frightening than pleasant, a rending intensity of feeling he had to go through to get farther along with his life. He wasn't prepared for the bottomless gratitude he felt toward Tim for having a skin, for being there in it, waiting for him.

Usually, David would sleep over, and in the morning go yawning down to the university to try to do some work. He would meet Tim again for the afternoon, and then work or read during the evenings. Tim drew or painted – in a rather desultory way, David thought. But it was summer, and Tim devoted sunny afternoons to tanning, not just for what it did to their skins, but for what the strong sunlight could show him. They would go to the park where Tim had met Duncan – it was the best place for humid days, on top of the hill, overlooking a ravine. Or they would head in the other direction to a park down in a ravine. They would separate when Tim went swimming: it was a "nude" pool, and David was afraid he'd disgrace himself in nude water with Tim in it.

Sometimes they went out to the Island, but this took most of the day, with the trip down to the waterfront and the ferry trip across the harbour, so they usually went only on weekends. There on Toronto's southernmost edge, Tim leaned back on his elbows to watch the sky and the lake and the sprawl of male flesh – at a few square feet of Spandex stretched very thin over a whole, restless beach. David gave it all a minute, and pulled a thick book out of Tim's canvas knapsack. But he couldn't read. The light from the sand burned away his reading eyes and the space of imagination inside his head.

"So don't read here," Tim said, a little disgusted. "Just look." His steady eyes were directed at the sky, sunshine and towering mist. David put his wedge of black words back into Tim's knapsack and turned to the skyscape painting itself in front of him. He tried to see it from inside Tim, to be digested and sit safely engulfed somewhere inside all the exercise, looking out through Tim's calm, strong, slow-moving brown eyes. He'd begun to see how Tim's eyes moved carefully from one thing to the next, following their lines, drawing them, painting them. In contrast, David tended to look at things in quick, scared glances, as if his eyes could be hurt by anything they touched.

He saw the clear brown eyes would look in the same way at the sky or the old ferry labouring up or a handsome chest. "Look!" could mean the glassy waves or the shifting greens of trees in the ravine or long brown legs. David understood Tim was showing him how gay men looked at each other. He was showing him the way out into the gay world, the way they both would take soon enough, forward into separate lives. David knew he ought to feel grateful for this: Tim was teaching him the ways of desire.

PART 5

It could be frustrating to be David's first lover, but it was exciting too, a challenge, an education. It let Tim go over ground he had skipped with earlier lovers. David was determined to be gay and still be the person he'd been before coming out. In contrast, Duncan had simply given up on the fat, miserable teenager he'd been: if he'd seen him coming down the street, he wouldn't have given him a second glance. Dennis had been more reflective at first, but he'd been drawn in by the style of his friends, by the sense they'd given him, for the first time in his life, of belonging to a group and sharing a view of the world. With David, Tim could connect his gay self with his past, and with his work.

But David was almost too conscious: there were times when Tim would have been happy to take time out for laughter with Duncan. David took everything seriously, including sex. Looking at the tortuous, long body that never seemed to relax, Tim would catch sight of a grim and hungry desperation. With his hard-earned muscles, he would try to pull himself into Tim, or through him to something else. His relations with Tim's blond skin, with his cock, verged on being carnivorous: at times, Tim would have to shout "Teeth!" – And David would disgorge and apologize, and begin an emotional reconciliation, like a woman cooing over a baby: "Oh, did I hurt you? Did I hurt you? You know I love you. I could eat you right up."

"Well, you had better not," Tim said.

David learned quickly enough, but behind the sentimental cock-worship there was something hungry – clutching, demanding, or weakly clinging, depending on David's mood. At times David's dark eyes stared so silently you almost forget you had learned how to talk. It was as if his eyes were deaf, so you couldn't say no to them, you could only give David what they wanted or crush him.

At times, David could get disgustingly,completely carried away and say that he didn't really care about himself at all. "It's all *you*. It's all *yours*. When you come I think, yes, this is it, we're here, we've done it. I *love* your face when you come. You look so rapt and soulful and consumed." David smiled: he'd heard himself gushing. "It's so *important* to you, Timmy."

Tim didn't want this flattery, not all of it anyway. He didn't want to be a teddy bear god: he wanted them to be equals. He would say, "I'm *gay* too, remember." Or: "I really like your body, David."

"You do?"

"You know I do. You've got a sexy body."

Propped on pillows, David kept on staring at him, not looking down at what was suddenly, nakedly in question.

"It's one of the basic reasons why we're lovers," Tim said, frankly. "You're so exciting so – dramatic."

David looked down, frowning, as if all he saw was gangling, slapstick comedy.

"I have huge feet," he said, as if they blocked the sun.

Tim laughed, not at the feet. "They aren't huge. They're long and elegant, really. They're sort of – graceful." He stroked them: poor, downtrodden feet. "I should draw them: You're very hard to draw, but if I started from the ground up…"

"I wish I had a chest like yours." He tried producing one on the spot, but no huffing and puffing could unshackle his skeleton.

"That's just all the sun from the beach you find sexy."

David stole a modest look down at what he brought to the sharing of bodies.

"But my cock is a bit – well, defective," he said, miserably. "I used to think it was because I couldn't stop masturbating."

Like David, it had to approach things at an angle. "No. Some cocks are just like that," Tim said. "I've been told," he added. "And what's wrong with that? It certainly isn't small, is it? I love your cock."

"Oh, come on," David said.

"I do! Because you think you're so clever, and it's so *dumb*!" Tim grabbed it, laughing. "Look at it!" It goggled foolishly out of his fist, straining to hear what was being said about it. It was very different from David and very much like him too.

"Why are you so nice to me and so hard on yourself?" Tim asked.

David could be hard on Tim, too, when they weren't in bed together. His soul had teeth of its own, and sometimes they grazed Tim's tender, good-hearted feelings. His sarcasm could be vicious. In certain moods, David was snobbish about all sorts of things: intelligence, class, money – Tim had too much. As well, Tim saw, he was disturbingly good at being alone: that was how he could afford to be so nasty to the human race, that over-rated club. Solitude was something he picked up and put on like his glasses, without thinking, as Tim did, how grotesque and pitiful it was that anyone needed them to see: just to see! Tim breathed seeing.

Tim admired David for his self-sufficiency, his determination, because he knew he needed something like it for himself, especially in his work. But it could be oppressive at times. While Tim worked, David would get into a muddle of paper on the carpet in Tim's living room, "writing". Tim would look in and see him pick up a sheet from his paper pond and scribble on it in a handwriting as cruelly illegible as barbed wire, then drop it back in and fish out another. The first time he did this, he handed Tim a half-sheet with a poem laboriously printed on it. "There," he said. "Abandoned."

Tim sat on the couch to read while David looked thoughtfully at a day-old newspaper. It was hard to concentrate with so much consciousness vibrating in *The Globe and Mail*, but the poem seemed to be about a teenager snatching up his little brother without warning to swing him in the air. Trying to sound authoritative, Tim said, "It's good. I like it."

"Really?" David looked doubtfully at the sheet, alive and frail in Tim's hand.

"Yes."

"It's about this teenager I saw, Italian, perhaps, or Greek Mediterranean, anyway, out off Bloor Street West. *And* you of course, I'm sure you realize that."

It hadn't occurred to him.

"So you like it?" David said.

"Yes." He looked quickly at the last lines: *Now you're taller than he is, older, /And you see you will always do this /Fly in his teenage muscles over the neighbourhood.*

"Yes, I do."

"Thanks." For one moment, David looked crassly, obscenely pleased with himself. But when Tim reached for him, he pulled away with a shiver.

"I get funny when I'm thinking hard. The world tends to disappear."

"Have I disappeared?"

David peered at him, to see. Then he put down the paper and held out his hand, speechless. Like a dog offering his paw, like a young lady needing help from a boat: paw or hand, Tim took it. David quivered a little, then used Tim's grasp to pull back into the human world.

A day or two later, while David was at the university, Tim began working on preliminary drawings for a painting. It was going to show a man mowing a lawn in a yard behind a red brick house. Now he was drawing the figure of the man walking away from the viewer, stooped a little to push the lawn mower. The cuttings rose from the blades in a pencilled cloud, falling on the fresh-cut grass between old, battered shoes.

David came quietly into the bright extra room Tim used as a studio and stood behind the drawing table, watching. He'd been with him the day before, when he'd seen an old hand mower in Forest Hill and sat down to sketch it, fascinated.

"Who is it?" David said.

"No one in particular. A man. Just someone to push the lawn mower."

He wished David hadn't come so soon. While drawing, he had possibilities not yet drawn shimmering inside his eyes, and David's stern presence threatened to drive them away. He remembered his father standing over him like this while he drew, invisible and silent, and never knowing, Tim had hoped and still hoped even now, that the real paper, the real pencil were inside himself, and unbearably sensitive. He'd kept that from his father all his life: he hadn't gone to O.C.A. until after his death. "But why can't you see his face?" David said.

Tim could feel David at work on some insight into the painting, into his soul, because he wanted to stake a claim to both. That was why he was working his way through Tim's art books. And what if David succeeded? What if he said something penetrating, something that made Tim see David's idea instead of the shadowy feelings that were all he had?

"Because his face doesn't matter. It's really going to be in the colours, if it works."

"I really like that *misterioso* feeling," David said. "Like a Colville, perhaps?"

"No, please, David, let's keep other people out of it." He wanted David to understand, to be on his side in the struggles of art of the seventies. But Tim didn't know where he stood there himself. "I want something more playful, more urbane, in that American way. Canadian painters can't seem to get it."

"Of course not, they're all straight, aren't they? Every last gloomy one of them until you came along."

"I haven't come along yet, David."

With his father behind him he had been on the verge of throwing down the pencil and shouting, or imploring, 'I can't do it with you watching!' What would have happened? His father had turned away just in time.

Now behind him, David coughed and shifted from one foot to the other, and Tim tensed. 'Maybe what you ought to do is ' But it didn't come.

Instead, David said, "I can't understand it, how you draw. It's really a miracle."

Tim laughed. "David, could I ask something? Don't stand over me when I'm working, please."

David was all understanding. "Oh, yes, of course. It's just so fascinating." He was at the door already and Tim felt that David wasn't ruthless, after all, that he wouldn't steal his soul. To apologize, he turned and said, "I love you, David."

"Of course," David repeated stupidly, giving him a doubtful or fearful stare. It was as if the forlorn, raincoated figure on the edge of Queen's Park had looked up at him at last. "I'll start on dinner now, okay?"

PART 6

One evening four weeks into the affair, Tim startled David by asking, "Would you like to come to lunch with my mother?"

"I'd love to," David said, quickly, neither scared or delighted yet, knowing he was going to be both, but not in what proportions.

"You'd be kind of an experiment, you know: the first boy-friend of mine she's ever met. Of course, that wouldn't be said. I just want to start showing her a little."

"Showing her what?"

Tim shrugged. "That it doesn't have to be so bad."

"I'll do my best."

But what did it mean for him that he would be the first boy friend asked to meet her? It seemed like a very good sign. They had been lovers for several weeks now, getting to know each other without fights, with no terrible discoveries. The affair had taken in the rhythm of the week, and perhaps, David thought, it could reach to include months, seasons. But lunch with Mrs. Grey was a test, too, whether or not Tim realized it. Tim's family was a lot better off than his, and though David could be snobbish about this with Tim, he knew his snobbery wouldn't help him when he was face to face with his lover's mother.

Waiting for them in the lobby of what Tim described as the second stuffiest hotel in Toronto, Mrs. Grey turned out to be gray-haired, elegantly dressed and younger than her age, sixty-two. She had been beautiful once, and kept the aura of it, the sweetness. She gave David an appraising look with hazel eyes as they shook hands. Then the headwaiter came to greet them, a sour-faced man with high, tight shoulders, as if some patron had once given him a crushing bear hug. He led them out into a white ballet of thick linen. In an old jacket with elbow patches, David felt awkwardly middle-middle-class and gawky and lightheaded and toppling. He felt like a hollyhock in Rosedale. But as they seated themselves, Mrs. Grey gave him a warmer smile: he'd made it into her approval. She devoted several minutes to charming him, finding out about his family, his studies.

Then she began talking with her son about 'home'. Sitting up straight in his blazer and tie, holding the wine list, Tim was a scion of the Anglo-Saxon Toronto being mothered and bearing up under it well, proudly, effectively male. They talked about Tim's younger sister Susan, Tim in an older-brotherly way that David loved. Every so often 'your father' was mentioned, and David remembered how his mother used the same phrase, which never had to reach very far – upstairs to the den, perhaps, out to the garden or the quiet shopping street. Here it went away into the past and death and left the two of them, Mrs. Grey and her one son alone and confronted.

David saw Tim's was a family very different from his, a family with an easier, more comfortable sense of what families are, which they took from around them, from their class, and from a long tradition. They had been comfortably Torontonian for generations, as unconsciously North American as the Americans – that was what his father called Ontario smugness, that making oneself at home on the continent. Old Toronto – affectionately known as Muddy York, Hogtown or the Big Smoke – complacent and self-satisfied, had acquired a discreet regality, which was absorbed into the tightness of Tim's shoulders. David liked this sense of inherent belonging and let himself sink into it. Tim had rebelled against his family's sense of things in going to O.C.A., but he hadn't broken with it: now he wore it well, like his jacket, comfortably, handsomely.

And Mrs. Grey was wonderful, David decided: by the end of the meal, helped by the amazing wine Tim had ordered, David was in a state of enthusiastic chivalry, almost more in love with her than with Tim. She was giving him her affection, and David was too enchanted to wonder whether he was being Tim's straight friend or his presentable lover. Nothing like that came up, of course, unless perhaps a certain Stephen Radcliffe was gay. Tim mentioned him once with an odd, wry smile, but got no response from his mother.

Outside the restaurant, as they were saying goodbye, Mrs. Grey asked Tim about his health. Not anxiously or fussily, but like a lady showing she can be practical too.

Tim stirred impatiently under this. Safe and warm inside Mrs. Grey's charm, David thought it was childish to be so oppressed.

"Don't worry, Mrs. Grey," he said bravely, cheerfully. "I'm looking after him!"

She gave him a frosty look, and David saw he had ruined everything. There was going to be a disaster then and there in the airless hotel lobby.

Then, not unkindly, Mrs. Grey smiled white, evenly spaced teeth in an encompassing gesture and said, "That's very good of you, David." She made it very clear he was looking after Tim as a sensible, straight friend, not as a lover. They shook hands as if nothing had happened. Tim and his mother kissed briefly, Tim stiff as a soldier off to the trenches. They went out and saw her into a cab. Watching it go, Tim loosened his tie and took a deep breath.

"Well, did you like the wine?" he said.

"I think that must be what Hugh Armitage dreams about." It had been like a long crimson sunset in his mouth: he'd never had such wine. "But what did it cost?"

"Oh, she can afford it," Tim said, with defiance and sadness and spite. "She hardly blinked." David saw he'd intercepted some message he couldn't decipher, despite Hugh's lessons.

"It seemed to go well," David said cautiously, as they waited to cross Avenue Road. Tim said nothing.

"I think she liked me," David went on. "I certainly liked her. She's wonderful."

Tim laughed. "She's got you! I knew she would. She's got you round her little finger." He seemed perversely pleased by this.

"Well, you know, I don't think she really minds your being gay," David said.

"How the fuck would you know, David?" Tim said, angrily. The light refused to change: he tore off his blue blazer as if it was on fire.

"Sometimes," Tim said quietly, "it feels as if she's just holding her breath. She thinks even a little breath might push me away into being queer forever."

The light changed, set them free.

"Because she doesn't give up, David. She still wants to get some grandchildren out of me."

"Well, and why not?" He could see it. "I would too – I mean, I'd love to have little Tims all over the place." He gestured, as if they were in the middle of the road.

"She *has* got you! And in the meantime, David, you're a nice boy, you're not really gay, just the way I'm not. We're nice boys."

"Of course," he added bitterly, "that's what Stephen Radcliffe was, until suddenly he wasn't."

"What was that, anyway? There was a real chill in the air then, wasn't there?"

"Stephen was a friend of mine – of everyone's – at school, then at Trinity too. In second year, in spring, he went home and gassed himself in one of his family's cars." Tim's voice shook a little. "The *Buick*."

"Why?"

"Why?" Tim said. "Why? You're not supposed to say that, David. There was absolutely no reason. He came from a good home, he was bright, everybody liked him. There was no problem or scandal. The most people would say was, what a thing to do to your family. Although, now that I think of it, it was only the women who said that. The men didn't say anything at all. My father certainly didn't. Even I wasn't sure what to think. I thought maybe I knew, but I couldn't – ." Tim gave a bitter shrug.

"What?"

Tim took a deep breath. "When he was alive, people would always say, 'Well, you know Stephen.' He was everyone's pet, very talkative, and skinny and beaky like a bird, and when he was there, there was no chance of getting bored. You really didn't wonder about Stephen and sex, he was barely starting a beard. Everybody would say, 'You know Stephen, 'till he killed himself, and then they buried him without saying a thing."

David was looking for something to say. After all, straight young men have problems too…

"*Of course* he was!" Tim exclaimed bitterly to people who weren't there: some people who were looked at him, but he didn't lower his voice. "*Of course* that's why! *Of course!*"

David was silent, sympathetic, but oppressed by this suicide he hadn't known: what could he do for him? "But – " he said.

"Let's go to the Island," Tim said, cutting him off.

"Like this?" David held out the jacket folded over his arm.

"I wore a bathing suit," Tim said, moving so as to evoke it under the gray flannels. "And for you – " He pulled another suit out of his jacket and waved it in the air.

"But it's past two," David said. "It'll be three-thirty, at least, when we get there."

"It couldn't be that late," Tim said, flatly.

David held out his left forearm, unanswerably. Without even looking, Tim stuffed the bathing suit into his mouth and ground it between his teeth.

They went to a movie, as if they were boycotting sunshine, then swimming. Tim was aggrieved when he turned out to be almost a minute slower than before: he'd been sure he was going faster. He needed something deeper and darker than the swimming pool. They went home for dinner, and had sex instead. David was glad to be his escape, but Mrs. Grey was still with him, on his side. He was, after all, where she wanted someone to be, unless she wanted Tim to be alone all his life. He couldn't believe that of the charming hazel eyes. He thought he was dissolving Tim's tension into himself, so they could accept her and be the two lovers they had been before.

But afterwards, he could tell Tim was still worrying about her. "She'll come around, you know," David said, cautiously.

"Why would she?"

"Because she loves you."

"Do you really think it works that way? That is so – " Tim turned onto his front, shoving his head deep into a pillow and "stupid, stupid, stupid!" came muffled through foam rubber.

"Why?" David said. "I just don't see – "

But Tim suddenly twisted, bouncing over onto his back again, laughing up at him.

"I knew it would happen if I asked you. I *knew* it."

"What do you mean?"

"She's got you round her little finger. She's *very* seductive." Tim grinned, delighted with this.

"Well, so are you, you know," David said. Tim's smile had the special inflection which said, 'I've got all your happiness right here inside me: do you want it or don't you?'"

"Am I? Well…" The smile faded, Tim put his hands behind his head, looking up at the ceiling.

"But it would take years, David. Some day, when I'm thirty-five, forty, I'll say, 'Oh, by the way, mother, I'm sure you know I'm gay don't you?' And she'll say…"

His eyes closed for a moment, then he twisted his head sideways in the locked fingers, and smiled at him.

"What *will* she say, David? You know her so well…?"

PART 7

Tim's apartment overlooked yards where, late at night, the subway trains would come trundling in and brake with long steel shrieks and blue-white sparks that lit the bedroom and its shining lovers. The humid summer had arrived, the weather Tim had promised David, without saying it would taste of him. One hot night, David took a towel and wiped the sheet of sweat off Tim's back, to watch it all come out again, bursting suddenly through his skin, thousands of beads of pure surprise. More and more they talked as if they would be together for some long time. David wiped off the wide, breathing back again and waited. The miracle happened punctually, and he leaned to lap up what he could of Tim and instead he found himself rubbing his face as if to wash it away in sweat and lose himself in darkness the TTC couldn't light up.

He had arrived in love, in a new city. From out of Tim's presence and his paths through Toronto, David had begun seeing another city, began writing it in his head. In reality, gay Toronto was a small town: its meeting places were few, faces repeated, it was banal and provincial, with the pallor of oppression. The red-brick buildings obscured the reality that hatred as well as neighbourliness and discrimination as well as friendliness could co-exist in the expanse of Metro that stretched beyond the restricted confines of the gay ghetto. For David, it seemed to hold a whole lost civilization in its ways of moving and feeling. It was an eternal city, greeting him with a kind of tacky Latinity. It had to be eternal if you could find it enduring so far to the north of things, drinking Blues and talking football and smiling to you a little secretly under the northern sky.

'*Kill Faggots!*' attacking along a wall, the police lounging by in their Custer-yellow cars, lone drifting males, gazing at him like veterans of some horrible, soft war, – it would easily cringe back into the foul, old, beaten-down nighttown, the God-beshitten Sodom David's guilt couldn't bring itself to leave. In a back lane to another bar, men, young and old, would go padding in running shoes that opened up off the pavement like stale, gray mouths, and David would feel himself freezing into depression, unable to move except inside the dead and frozen body of his guilt. They were all ghosts, walking endlessly down the buried back lanes of all the cities. Then, if he was lucky, Tim would give him a touch or a word, and he'd be back, safe, with his lover. It was as if the house of two bodies gave the plan of whole civilizations. Look at Tim and you knew gay desire sent roots far below the paper time called history: it went down and back forever, an Atlantis in the blood. David had had gay brothers as long as there had been smiles and shoulders like Tim's.

He wanted to get it down, to make it real. He wrote himself notes, scraps of dialogue, short poems. It was called Toronto but then impossible things sent you sailing off the map. Ontario opened on the sea, tasted salt and human. Young men with names like Tim and David fell in love at non-existent intersections. Poets dropped by, famous lovers: Cavafy, oblique and many-layered, Frank O'Hara, dusting off sand, Jean Verdenal, handsome and tall – all of David's gay heroes, old and new. He knew it was Tim's magic prick at work through his lonely years of reading, ordering, transfiguring everything. And his city's dizzying architecture, its high-hearted manner, its delicious language, shaped themselves along the lines of Tim's body. He knew it was partly a scheme to rebuild the solidarity with his species he'd lost so far back he could only imagine it now. He thought he could bring it off: he had generosity and room for everyone. He would make women happy: no one would wonder what they wanted, because you would see them having it. He would even figure out straight men, placate them somehow, find something safe for them to do. But it would have to be gay to be free and wise and silly enough to fill out the whole human heart. His *Toronto* had to be both classic – clearly and thoughtfully drawn – and gay as a goose.

David was ambitious: he wanted to say, "There, world". It went deeper than his feelings about Chris had been, or even his new feelings for Tim, perhaps.

He kept telling himself to hurry, to get down the words that held it. Tim, its founder and foundation, was real and solid enough, but the city wasn't. It wasn't a feeling of any sort. It was all intuitive, from off to the side of the mind. It came around you only at lucky moments, like a city in the wind.

CHAPTER IV: FIGHTING

Tim liked to go to the Y early in the afternoon when there were few swimmers, sometimes none. One afternoon, he managed a solitary, peaceful mile, and sat on the pool's edge, alone except for the guard at the other end. Another swimmer came in from the showers, tall and lavishly muscled, wearing a tan and the ghost of a bikini. He padded towards Tim's end of the pool, smiling, though Tim had never seen him before. His eyebrows formed one black line, trying to impose seriousness on a wide-open, snub-nosed face and failing.

Pulling his blue bathing cap tighter, adjusting the strap of his goggles, he stood with the pool spread trembling before him. Tim thought he wasn't a serious swimmer a weightlifter, perhaps, who only wanted to cool off after the solemn heavings and gruntings. He got the goggles right, gave Tim a squinting grin, lowered himself into the shallow water – and began putting it behind him with perfect speed.

He was a better swimmer than Tim would ever be. Tim sat watching for a few minutes, studying his way with the water. It surrendered completely: it gave him everything he wanted. As Tim got up to go, it looked as if he might settle in forever, lapping back and forth like a metronome.

Next week, the swimmer was there again, before Tim, who slipped into the next lane, almost giving in to the urge to swim faster if only for a few lengths. But the other swimmer was a lesson in not wasting energy. Again and again, Tim watched him coming towards him or pulling past, the slats of his ribs puffing wide, his legs beating finnily, trailing a fizz of bubbles Tim felt with his hand or face. Then Tim saw him leaping up away through the water ceiling. When Tim had completed his mile, the other had gone. He went to the showers. He wasn't thinking of being unfaithful to David, but the swimmer was a treat to look at.

There were several small shower rooms. The first was empty: the sound of water came from the second. The black-haired young man was covered in white lather from the neck down, and soaping on more. He had his cap off, letting out short black hair. Tim nodded and began showering on the other side of the room. The swimmer grinned and took one wide step sideways into the water, transforming himself from white soap to brown skin in a flash.

"How's it going?" he called.

"Great," Tim said over the sound of the water, suddenly nervous.

"But your arms are too straight!"

And they were in a passionate conversation on swimming, as if their laps had been a discussion all along. The swimmer leaned into the upper half of a forward crawl, water peppering his back.

"Keep them bent just a little, like this."

"Well, I'll try it next time."

"I'll be watching." The swimmer took his goggles and cap from the taps and turned them off.

"Sure," Tim said, standing right under the shower, letting it beat on his head and closing his eyes. As the swimmer walked past, Tim felt wet fingers brushing over the front of his thighs like minnows. He jumped back, staring at the broad-shouldered back on its way out, innocent, unconscious. Chlorinated water stung his eyes.

The next time they met, a few days later, the swimmer introduced himself at the pool's edge, and again Barry and Tim were discussing swimming and exercise seriously, almost professionally. It came out soon enough that Barry had a girlfriend: several, in fact. Tim wasn't surprised or disappointed. Barry began coming quite often and he would talk about "this chick I'm seeing," and Tim would nod understandingly. On some days, Barry's talk would darken to "women," until by turning to something masculine and simple, their muscles, for example, he would work his way back into a good mood. The tickling fingers hadn't meant much, Tim decided: it had been an adolescent prank. And by now what Tim desired in Barry was the stretched, perfect swimmer seen through water. The Barry who heaved himself up like a jolly sea lion was a disappointment.

Tim mentioned the friend he was trying to persuade to come to the pool. He'd finally succeeded, so Barry would be meeting him. He laughed, thinking of the two of them together, David and Barry: what would they make of each other? He hoped David would not be nervous and rude.

Barry looked at him, the single eyebrow contracting, and said, "You're gay, aren't you?"

There must have been something too free or too fond in the way Tim had talked about his shy, awkward friend.

"Yes," he said, throwing up a hasty, improvised defiance.

"That's cool. That's *all right*. It's just at first I figured you out to be straight."

Tim raised his shoulders that were almost in Barry's league.

"Well, I'm not," he said, shortly.

"That's okay with me," Barry said. "I don't get off on it myself, but I'm easy. My two best friends in high school turned gay on me, and I still see them all the time."

Then he gave Tim a dark, a questioning scowl, as if some part of him that didn't believe what he was saying was glaring out for a moment, hating Tim. Tim looked away, angry, ready to fight. Then Barry smiled, once again broad-minded and sympathetic. "Because really, you know, it takes all kinds."

David sat on the pool's edge watching Tim with clasped, chaste knees, slowly realizing he didn't have an erection and didn't have to have one. He could commit himself to the Tim-torn water as if their sweaty nights had been washed away.

When he got out, breathless after swimming longer than he ever had before, Tim was sitting on an exercise mat with a black-haired body builder, like a cliff of muscles. David saw at once how Tim was taken with him, drawn into him, as if the muscles had their own gravity. They were introduced: the friend was Barry, whom Tim seemed to know well, and had never mentioned. He and Tim sat leaning forward, hanging heavy pectorals at each other, while David was leaning back on his arms, flat-chested, and feeling like a girl among women. Tim said, politely, "You're beginning to get some real definition." Barry just scrunched the far side of his mouth.

After a few minutes he jumped up, all springy muscle with places to go. Or Debbie would have kittens, he said.

"Isn't he *gorgeous*?" Tim said, looking at his back. "It's too bad he's such a *twit*. Did you watch him swimming?"

David rocked over on one arm to speak lower.

"Is he gay?"

"No. What do you think Debbie means? He's even talking of getting married."

"He gave you some interesting looks," David said.

"He's just like that. You meet men like that at the Y, straight men but kind and even sort of fussy and maternal. Barry's a younger version. Big pussycats."

"So Debbie will have kittens?" David said, bitchily.

They pressed out some exercises, then showered and left. On the way out, Tim said, "Do you want to meet another friend?" He sounded a little nervous, but proud and possessive too.

"Another gorgeous one?"

"Hardly! I mean Jack Durham, the photographer, the philosopher."

"Oh, him." Tim had mentioned him several times, with ironic enthusiasm. "Sure, why not?"

"He's one of my *intellectual* gay friends – that's why I think you ought to like him."

"I *ought* to like him?"

Tim laughed. "That's what I'm afraid of! But give him a chance. He's a bit odd, but he's okay, he's always got something new to say. He's full of surprises."

They went up the street and looked into a big beer hall. It was almost empty, with a few men scattered among the little tables, all alone and waiting to be rescued like Crusoes, David thought, an archipelago of Crusoes. It was the look in their eyes that told you the place was not just another tavern. "No," Tim said. "He's not here. Maybe he's off with Charles somewhere, they were going to go north. Do you feel like staying for a drink?"

"It's a bit grungy, isn't it?" David's eyes were getting used to the gloom, and the loneliness was seeping in too. He didn't expect to like anyone who hung around this place.

"That's kind of the point, I think, for Jack. It's sort of classic, prehistoric, from way before Stonewall." Tim looked again, moving to see around pillars, as if Jack might be lurking in a corner. Not for the first time, David saw how he liked being the hand-somest person in a big room, even when the audience had to be imaginary, and forgave him. "Jack's got a theory that Lascaux, the caves with the paintings, were a kind of gay bar."

"He's got theories coming out of his ears," David said, impatiently.

"For me it's like having some instructor from O.C.A., but you can fight with him, really fight with him. And sort of flirt with him too, I guess. And he's always got something more up his sleeve. Last Monday, he psychoanalyzed Clement Greenberg—into tiny little pieces, *he* said."

"So who's Clement Greenberg?"

"The art critic, remember."

"Oh, yes." But David felt claustrophobic, as if he was in a cave. "Let's go. This place can't really be gay: it's so Canadian Lower Class. And there's nothing straighter than that, is there?"

"Of course there is," he answered himself, going through the door. "Canadian Middle Class."

Just outside the door, from out of his depression, David asked, in a polite tone of voice, "So you think he's gorgeous, Barry?"

Tim laughed. "David, you're jealous! It's sweet, actually, but Barry is an odd choice to be jealous about. I wouldn't mind drawing him, that's all, or doing a painting. Barry swimming is a dream. Barry out of the water is a bit of a turkey, really."

"Like a David Hockney painting?"

"Sort of, perhaps. But the light in there is different – colder."

Suddenly Tim asked, "But if he was gay – and I'm sure he isn't – would you be upset if I did get it on with him?"

"I don't know," David said quickly. "Why are you asking?"

"What do you mean, you don't know?"

"Of course I would be, but I don't know how much. If I'd really be upset."

"David, why can't you just say what you mean?"

David was silent. This was completely unfair.

"Lovers have got to be frank with each other, don't they?" Tim said.

David didn't want to say anything, frank or not. Tim was being unfair, he was being tyrannical. In a low voice, in freezing slang, David answered, "I think you are *doing a number on me.*"

"Why?"

"*Next, you'll be telling me love is communication.*"

"Well, it is, isn't it?"

For a moment David thought of saying, 'Sorry, *you just died.*' He had a lover who thought that all problems could be dissolved in a gush of frankness. David knew that if he knew anything at all he had a voiceless centre that all the honesty in the world couldn't betray. Tim was banal, like Barry, like the shabby bar and its patrons. "Why should I say what I mean?" David said, bitterly. And then, "All right, I'll be frank, I'll be sincere. You can have Barry. Enjoy."

"I think I've got my answer, David. You're upset right now."

"I'm upset because I don't want to have a stupid lover. I don't want to live in a stupid world."

"I don't want to have sex with Barry, David. I couldn't, he's straight. And I love you, I wouldn't want to hurt you."

"You don't even know who I am."

Tim looked at him with an exasperated smile. "There you're exaggerating."

They went on in hot silence. It was time for some kind of touch, David realized, because after all Tim wasn't stupid all the time. But they were on Yonge Street: they couldn't touch across its estranging pavement. So he said instead, as a kind of apology, "But he is gay, you know. Or bisexual, anyway."

But of course, David knew, Barry wasn't the real threat: that was someone Tim hadn't seen yet, someone neither of them could imagine, though David kept trying.

PART 3

Jack Durham, full of surprises, made his appearance that day after all. After dinner and an early movie, Tim and David dropped in at another bar, an almost respectable one, where some men even wore ties.

They'd just gone to get drinks when Tim said, very softly, "Look!"

Two young men dressed in black leather were cutting through the crowd with booted pride, both handsome and yellow blond.

"They're hot," Tim said.

David felt frightened, and a little sick. Their shiny leather was like the naked skin of black, animal nights. One wore a pair of handcuffs on his belt. With their self-loving smiles, they seemed to David to be saying that in the end gay sex was cruelty and hatred and death-worship, and the blackest fun in the world.

"What do they think they are doing?" David demanded.

"David! It's just a style, a game."

"You sound like a real fan of theirs," David said. He saw how Tim liked the crackle of wickedness they brought, their handsome, evil swagger.

"I've seen them around. They're lovers, they've been together for a while now."

While he talked, a big black-haired man, maybe forty David thought, came up on his other side. David knew he had seen him before somewhere.

96

"Well, if they're lovers," he said, looking at David with dark eyes, "what the fuck is love?"

Tim turned, delighted.

"Jack! What are you doing here? David, here he is at last, Jack Durham, David McTavish."

"Oh?" Jack said. "You're the boyfriend." He seemed doubtful.

"You're the photographer," David retorted. He was surprised, off-balance: he had expected someone taut and skinny, bristling with cleverness. The real Jack Durham was a lot bigger and heavier than they were, and would have been taller, but he slouched. His face was big and heavy too, lines cutting a deep mask into its soft flesh. His eyes had an empty look, as if their core was gone, or hidden. He was probably younger than he looked, David thought: there was something in the way he moved that was younger and looser and less self-assured than forty.

"Yes," Jack said. "Among other things."

"And you work in that store on Queen Street?"

"Yes. I've seen you in the store, haven't I?"

It was a second-hand book store that sold whatever it could, but with a hankering for books on art and photography. There was an almost hostile silence, and Tim said, "So you don't approve of leather, either, Jack? But you've been around. You know it's part of the scene."

Tim obviously enjoyed bringing Jack out. He was deferential, but possessive too, confident in the power of his looks.

"I guess it's not my business, is it?" He looked cautiously at the pair, lounging farther down the bar in their lithe armour. "But I think the world has got an adequate supply of pain."

His voice was deep, but a higher note came into it, sarcasm and suffering combined.

"You take things so seriously, Jack. I know it can get pretty sordid, but with them, it's not like that."

"They're good-looking, you mean. But I just think we all ought to be kind to each other, during our short time together on this earth." Jack was playing a kindly, prim old maid. And then, suddenly looking at him, he said, she said, "Don't you agree, David?"

"Of course," he said, stupidly. Stirred up by his moment of confusion, he could ask, "Why do you want to take pictures of Tim?"

Jack's eyes fixed him for a moment, seeming to ask, why are you his boyfriend? Then, in a flurry of almost maternal kindness, he was saying, "Don't be worried. All I want is some light off him. That's all – *just a little light*!"

Then he leaned closer, across Tim, putting a friendly hand on David's shoulder and saying, in a hoarse stage whisper, "It's because he looks so innocent. You see, he does not know about cruelty. He hasn't heard about the bomb – can you believe it?"

"What do you mean?" David said, protestingly. He felt this was some kind of test, and he resented it.

Jack squeezed the muscles converging on the back of David's neck. "You're so tense, David: you know, all right. You know it's up there, you're doing your best to keep it from falling on us."

For a moment, with hunched shoulders and shut eyes, Jack mimicked someone about to be hit from above.

"But not Tim. Look at him, sitting there, thinking we're safe. Pure paradise! That's what I want to – photograph, I mean."

"Jack must like you, David," Tim said, safe from bombs and sarcasm too. "You've really got him going."

"See? Isn't he perfect?" Jack said to David, in mock wonder.

"Perfect?" David pulled away, not wanting to be part of this crazy performance at least, not knowing how. "Only when he's doing the tumble turn."

Jack stood back too, and smiled, intrigued with David's answer. Then he looked across the room. "Anyway," he said, "here comes Charles."

The sight of Charles seemed to change his mood for the better. He was an Indian, with long black hair tied in a red bandanna headband and black secretive eyes and a delicate dry handshake. He was the first Canadian Indian David had spoken to in his life.

"Isn't he something?" Jack said, proudly, but with an odd, dangerous softness too. It was another test, David knew: Jack almost seemed to be looking for reasons to dislike him. "They named a whole bar after Charles."

David was tongue-tied, smiling at Charles as if he didn't speak his language, because he knew he couldn't say anything without sounding pompous and condescending, not with Jack waiting to pounce. It was unfair: he was about to dislike Jack Durham once and for all.

It was Charles who saved him. "Oh, come on, Jack," he said. "*Give us a break.*"

PART 4

A few days later, David met Jack again. He didn't believe it at first: a tall figure was coming heavily up the subway stairs by the Royal Ontario Museum, trudging up into a noon of white haze. On the second-last step it stopped and looked around to get its bearings – to get Jack Durham's bearings – and met David's guilty eyes. David thought he liked Tim's unsettling friend, he'd even given him his number when Jack said they should get together, but right now he wasn't sure he was up to dealing with him without Tim's help. David was unhappy and nervous already, without Jack Durham springing himself – and who knew what else – on him.

"Hello, there," Jack called. taking the decisive step to ground level. He was wearing a white shirt, old, baggy jeans, and skewed black ankle boots. He smiled but his face looked pale, exposed and fearful in the white light. "The trains aren't running." He looked back down the stairs, grateful to have escaped. "They keep saying 'Emergency crews are on the scene,' but they won't say what scene, what emergency."

"The usual stuck door, I suppose," David said, trying to sound reassuring.

"Sure, that's what they *want* you to think. What *you want* to think, David – that you aren't going around on bloody wheels."

"Aren't you being a little paranoid?" David protested. He could feel Jack's hysteria reaching into his chest.

"I hope not: I never want to be a *little* paranoid."

"I like the TTC! When I first got here, it was like being in a big city at last. It was London overhead, almost, or Paris."

Jack laughed. "Sorry, but on the TTC it's just Toronto or more Toronto. But, David, I'm glad we've met like this: I've been meaning to phone, but then I felt a bit shy and bashful about it. I could see you thinking, who on earth is this person?"

Looking into the big, disconcerting eyes, David didn't know how to deny it. "Well, I couldn't imagine being a model," he admitted. "And of *course* – "

"You know," Jack interrupted, "You *remind* me of someone, that's it." He looked with a doubled, comparing gaze. "But who? No one in Toronto."

Feeling no inclination to let some double out into the noon–day, David turned away with an irritated shake.

"You're stubborn, that's part of it," Jack said, miming David's or his double's stubbornness with a scowl. "Would you like to have lunch?"

"Now?"

"Is it too early to eat?"

"No, but I've got this paper..."

David stopped, helplessly: Jack was meant to imagine in a packed, frenetic schedule. But Jack Durham smiled happily, big hands pocketed and strolling leisurely through silver, a man with all the time in the world in a clock-hearted city. And suddenly David had to confess everything to him.

"The thing is, Tim wanted me to come over today, what's a lover for, he said, but I'm so behind. I've got to work on my *Frankenstein* paper, and it isn't working out. It's supposed to be on Sin and Death, but it keeps turning into Shelley and Byron. I came out for a walk to calm down, and then go back and work."

But it wasn't just *Frankenstein*: it was Tim, he was guilty about turning him down and worried too. What would Tim do, what might he feel justified in doing? They had almost had a quarrel about it yesterday at the beach. David had been thinking of descending into the steamy subway himself, and presenting himself contritely at Tim's door – even looking for him in the parks if he had to.

The thing was, Jack – but David could hardly say this to someone he barely knew – was that *David was in love, while Tim was not.*

"Maybe lunch will help," Jack said.

"Lunch?" David said, doubtfully. "But where?"

"Why not right here?" Jack said, with a swing of his shoulders towards the carved cliff-face of the museum.

"It looks like the last place on earth for lunch."

"Haven't you been there? There's a cafeteria; it's not bad. You mean, you've been here nearly a year, and you haven't been inside the ROM?"

"I've been meaning to, of course."

"Well, let me take you. You'll love it – Charles does. They don't just have, you know, civilizations, artifacts, all that human stuff. There are dinosaurs, right here on Queen's Park Crescent."

The prospect of lunch had cheered up one person, anyway. Jack led him up the steps and in through the stony rotunda to the cafeteria. With five dollars in his wallet, David was glad to see that it was quite ordinary, and then Jack kindly paid for him. The cafeteria was full of school children on field trips, with adults like themselves here and there. They sat by a window, looking out at the tomb complex of a Ming general, which Jack explained. Then he talked about the store where he worked, which he partly owned, as if to let David get used to him – to the big, unsettling eyes, which David was learning how to read.

After a while, Jack said, "You're the same age as Tim?"

"Yes. That is, I'm a month younger. We're both twenty-two." That seemed younger than it usually did, when you were confronted with the years cut deep into Jack Durham's face.

"I'm proud of you, you know. Of both of you."

"Oh?"

"I mean, because you didn't screw up as much as I did. At least not as long. I'm thirty-two – "

David tried not to look surprised.

Jack smiled, ruefully. " – And I came out at twenty-six."

"Mm." David didn't know how he was supposed to react to this. It was apologetic, even a little submissive, as if Jack was making David out to be older and wiser than he was when it came to gay things, the expert, the authority. David liked the feeling. He had seen Jack flatter Tim this way too.

"I was actually born during the war. Do you know what that means?"

"Do you remember it?"

"No, but I absorbed it. We all did, people my age. We know in our blood the basic fact of it all: Hitler nearly won. And then I had to grow up in the fifties. David, I even got *married*."

"*Really?*" But it made sense: once given the idea, you could see Jack as a family man, a big, fussy father changing diapers.

"*And* divorced," Jack added. "But you just don't know what the world was like not long ago. I mean, I can remember the first time I saw television. Can you?"

"No."

"Of course not. But I remember: going up and plunking myself down – maybe I was eight or nine – about a foot from the screen, and waiting for something to happen. In Winnipeg, that's where I'm from, people were only beginning to get them, and they didn't know what was going to happen. It was still just a kind of radio, radio that'd got radioactive and started glowing. They just didn't know."

Jack had a superior smile, as he contemplated whatever he thought TV had done to people. David was smiling too, imagining a small, serious Jack Durham peering into the television future from a foot away.

"Anyway, I'm very impressed with you and Tim and your generation, but I've been trying to understand what it was like, not so long ago."

"Do you think there's been any real change?" David said.

"Well, don't forget, until 1968, gay sex was illegal in this country."

It was something David was only vaguely aware of.

"But the real difference, if there is one, isn't Mr. Trudeau, or Stonewall. It's something else, some shift that made things like that possible. Maybe they just got bored with torturing us, who knows?"

David didn't want to get into another political discussion. He'd been in a big battle over the weekend, trying to prove that he and Tim weren't socially constructed. He preferred real experience to theory. "What was it like for you, then?"

"Well, it wasn't easy, David, really. It was impossible even being clear about it. And of course, you didn't even imagine it was going to end – if it has ended. Nobody came and said, 'don't give up, Jack, hang in there, because ten years from now they'll make queers human too'."

"But did you really know you were gay?" David said, reasonably. "It takes people a long time, sometimes, just to know that."

"Did I know?" Jack laughed. "David, if I have any vanity at all it's in thinking that I'm conscious. Of course I knew, I just never said it, not even to myself. But it was right there all the time. It was something I controlled and measured out and hovered over minute by minute. In school, I spent all my time trying to keep from focussing too intensely on any one boy. If I was getting too attached, something would step in and make me move on to someone else. So I spent my school years going through all the shades of blond, of handsome WASPs. It was like an emotional thermostat; it kept me safe till I went to university."

He smiled at David. "The University of Manitoba. Where I began to meet people more like myself, David. More like us, I mean."

"I don't understand."

"People who read Dostoyevsky and listened to Mahler and worried about the world. In Winnipeg, most of them were Jewish. A lot of them were from the north end of the city. I remember the first time I went up there, just after a snowstorm, with

Danny Moscovitz, a new friend. Snow piled high on the sides of the road, in dazzling sunshine. It was like going to Russia, I said. Have you been on the prairies?"

"Yes, but never in winter," David said.

"Then you've never been cold. What I meant by Russia was *Crime and Punishment*, but also there was the fact that Danny was a Russian Jew, Russian and Polish, with white skin and curly black hair. It was black at noon with the sun coming up off the snow. And black eyes, with a Kirghiz fold, that Asiatic fold of extra skin, like an extra bit of smiling thrown in free. I see I've got you interested."

David looked down, bashfully. He still wasn't used to this gay sharing of desire. Danny Moscovitz sounded like a sort of exotic Chris: you only had to blacken the curls, adjust the politics, paint in the little fold of flesh. And behind the image of Danny Moscovitz, something more important was happening. David was realizing that Jack was the first person he'd met in Toronto who might understand the way he thought. Tim did on rare occasions, but he didn't like to be intellectual with Tim for long: he got bored quickly. Jack was clever in a way that matched David's cleverness, and Jack was gay. If he had doubts and reservations, so did David.

"But David, before you get swept away, let me warn you, Danny was straight. Everybody was, remember, even me. But especially Danny Moscovitz! Anyway, I first saw him sitting in front of me. We were just starting on our way from Descartes to Kant, and we began talking after class. Danny had this wonderful, elegant world-weary irony. All my defenses had been against sweet, dumb Anglo-Saxons who never had to wake up in their lives. Danny was wide awake; he just cut through everything with his intelligence, with the edge of his voice. I'd been the funny one in high school, but the moment he started talking, I was a straight man, running after his jokes, waiting for them, preparing for them. But inside, I felt I'd been set free; he made everything clearer and bigger. Tell me, David, have you ever been in love with someone as intelligent as you are?"

David's eyes widened in surprise, almost shock. He managed a diplomatic answer.

"I wouldn't have had any trouble answering that question, until I met Tim."

Jack smiled, "I know what you mean, David, about Tim, but Danny was intelligent the way you are. He had the kind of brilliance you can cash in at university. He wrote a really beautiful paper on Kant's moral theory, for instance: I almost cried when I read it. And he was interested in everything – what was going on in the States, the Civil Rights movement, the beats, all the sixties things just getting started. Half his family was down there, and he had relatives in Israel too. He was interested and intelligent and he didn't feel any need to hide it – that took my breath away. I really didn't have time to wonder how much my infatuation had to do with the black eyes. Everything about him was so *real*. It was like going to Europe, to history – and falling in love with it, wonderfully, tragically. When I was getting to know him, he was editing a paper on World War II, the Eastern Front. 'That was the real war,' he said. 'It still is.' He was fighting over battles you've never heard of – but where hundreds of thousands of soldiers, millions, were killed. So even now names like Kursk or the Pripet Marshes have a certain flavour all their own for me. Say 'The Battle of Stalingrad' and I'll think, *and I never even touched Danny Moscovitz.*"

He seemed to forget where he was for a moment. Then, as he looked back at David, shyness came over him, closing his eyes. "But do you mind me telling you all this? I didn't plan to; I haven't talked about these things for years, except with Paul, but somehow, you bring it out, or back. Are you sure you're not from Winnipeg?"

"It's fascinating," David assured him, awkwardly, trying to sound as if he really meant it. And he did mean it, but Jack's shyness turned on his own, full blast. "It's always interesting to hear about other gay men, and how they came out."

Jack smiled at this little speech. "Myself, I think it's because you're a romantic too, David: I'll bet words have flavours for you too. Anyway, Danny was wonderful, and it wasn't his looks; it was the world he came from, lived in. It turned out he'd actually lost a lot of relatives in the death-camps, and that was terrible – and exciting, exhilarating, too, may God forgive me. With Danny, I was arriving somewhere – somewhere tragic, but far from South Winnipeg. I was arriving in the world."

Jack smiled to himself, shaking his head. "He had a cousin, ten years older than we were, who had nightmares about it as if she'd been there, though she hadn't – inherited nightmares. She would go crazy and suicidal now and then. It was a family problem: Hitler staging a comeback in her mind every so often. I remember one morning Danny being upset and embarrassed, but basically resigned, because 'Florence flipped out again'. She'd got in her mother's car and driven west over the prairie. That he was telling me showed I'd made it as a friend, and I was enchanted by the way he talked about it, joking and 'cool'. The times had given him the cool style for talking about your cousin fleeing the Nazis over Manitoba gravel roads, and I loved it, breathed it right in."

Jack laughed, out of some supply of ancient, skeptical laughter that evoked his friend more than anything else. Then he sipped coffee, his remembering gone silent. This didn't please David, who wanted more of handsome, brilliant Danny Moscovitz.

"So," he said, heading for the heart of the matter: "you were in love with a straight guy." This sounded more gruff and sensible than he intended. But there was something about Jack's attitude to life that made David want to step in and tidy up. Something overwrought and disorganized: Dostoyevskyan, in fact.

Jack didn't mind his tone: in fact, he seemed to like it. "Was I? Was that it?" He laughed out loud. "You should have been there, to tell me that. 'Can't you see, Jack: you've fallen for him and it's hopeless. He's straight.' *Only you couldn't have been there*. That's my point. This happened a thousand years ago."

"But did you *really* not see what was happening?"

"David! What *was* happening? Just this: Danny and I were good friends. Intellectual friends. I got his jokes, when the Yiddish words had been explained. I could sympathize intelligently, or be the *goy* who would never, never understand when that's what he wanted. And alongside that, but in another world, I was looking down his shirt and getting dizzy. I had two selves I mean, I even had a girlfriend, because you did, because Danny had girlfriends."

David drew back in disapproval. Girlfriends could complicate things horribly, he knew. Jack smiled, seeing this.

"Did you ever tell him?" David said, curtly.

"Did I tell him?" Jack laughed. "You said you'd been on the prairies?"

"I drove all the way across them, on the way here."

"Then you must know, it's a very moral landscape. It's like a big ironing board, and if you're any kind of a wrinkle, you *know* they'll iron you. I would never have thought of telling him. I mean, I thought of it all the time, but never of actually doing it. He still doesn't know, unless he's heard, but he's down in L.A. now. I hardly knew what to tell myself: it was a kind of secret to me, too, part of my mind hadn't been let in on it."

"Well, it is hard, I know," David said, relenting a little.

"Yes, it's hard," Jack said, cheerfully. "All right, imagine, David. You're in a diner with steamed-up windows on North Main Street, eating something called the Hot Dog Special, and challenging a guy with the blackest eyes in history to give an exact definition of *tsuris*. I knew, more or less, but we were taking philosophy courses, you see, we were into definitions, the nature of language."

"So what is it?"

"*Tsuris* is—Jewish grief – grief and vexation in Yiddish. But for me, it was having Danny tell me later on that evening that the trouble with Wittgenstein was that he had never had a good fuck in his life. Because he was a fag."

David jumped. "Really? I didn't know that."

Jack gave an odd shrug, looking away out the window at the stone archway of the Ming general's tomb. "Another one bites the dust. Anyway, neither did I. I'd spent months reading Wittgenstein, Early and Later, fascinated, and the moment Danny had said it, I felt that of course he was: and that was part of the reason why he fascinated me. But with Danny there I had to be clever about it. Maybe that was why he was a great philosopher. Maybe that was why he was so brilliant about the Problem of Other Minds. Danny didn't care, of course: poor Ludwig out cruising the Prater could have been all of Descartes to Kant and Danny's fifties liberalism would have had nothing to say to him."

Jack finished his coffee, and David took the last gulp of his, unwillingly.

"So what finally happened?" he said.

"Finally?" Jack seemed taken aback. "Who said there was going to be a 'finally'? Finally I had lunch in the ROM with this attractive, dark-haired young man who would have loved talking with Danny Moscovitz too... As for Winnipeg, well, I told you, I got married. Isn't that final? God knows, it's supposed to be."

But there had to be more: Jack's story had entertained him, intrigued him, taken him away from his own problems – but now Jack was leaving him hanging.

"Would you like some more coffee?" Jack said, almost apologetically. "I'll get it, I want to stretch my legs."

Jack brought back a tray between big, careful hands and unshipped two tremulous cups of black coffee. He sat down, sipped, started away without exclamation, then sipped more cautiously.

"So I got married," Jack said, casually, as if he decided to give David what he needed. "Which I still don't regret doing. On a summer's day in 1963. Kennedy was alive, Diem was, a lot of people were. Buddhist monks were burning themselves to death in Viet Nam – Danny looked at one burning on television and said, 'He sure needed a lay.'" Jack gave a little, apologetic laugh. "Anyway, for various reasons, I decided I had to forget about the excitement of being Danny Moscovitz's gentile friend. I knew that if I didn't get married then, in my twenties, in Winnipeg, I never would. And I liked her, Sharon, even loved her."

David squirmed a little. It was a sign of weakness in Jack Durham that he had got involved in marriage, something David had never even dreamed of. Jack had been so desperate he had thrown himself to the women, begging to be saved.

"I'm sorry, David," Jack smiled at him, "but it's true. We're still friends, in a way: she's out in B.C. now, married again, separated. I learned later that she figured my weakness for Danny was some kind of male thing. She was even more in the dark about straight males than I was, though she was clearer about what she wanted. She thought she knew what she had a right to expect from men, from the world: she thought she could take 1963 as a guide to what was real. So did I, of course. I thought I could do it, and it worked not badly for several years."

He paused, watching a group of school children being guided in by their teachers. And laughed. "Oh, well. Marriage would have been all right, I might even still be married, perhaps, and happily – if you were only someone else, someone in a magazine article. If you didn't have the problem of managing yourself and being yourself too. I thought I had that kind of power, pure moral will out of Immanuel Kant. At that age, you're likely to treat yourself without mercy, aren't you? People like us, anyway, David. But I don't regret it. We have a daughter, Cathy," Jack looked out the window, as if the exuberant dragons carved on the archway soothed him.

"A daughter – really?" David said, surprised, pleased, but not quite sure what he thought.

"Really," Jack said. "I have other ambitions, but so far, she's the one big thing I've done in my life – and she's a triumph." He gave David a proud, defiant smile. David looked down, both touched and embarrassed by this odd case of fatherhood.

"But we still haven't got you out, yet, Jack, have we?" David said, sounding, he realized, a bit like Duncan, but he wanted to tidy up Jack's life for him. Now he had to get Jack out of his suffocating closet before lunch was over.

"Oh, that. *That* question. So important, isn't it? Well, I guess it was Mr. Ogilvie's doing, really."

David frowned: Mr. Ogilvie sounded old and proper and grim. Some silver-haired philosophy instructor, perhaps?

"The *blue-eyed* Mr. Ogilvie, David. Another handsome boy—how many do you want, anyway? Don't you get bored with them?"

"Do you?"

Jack shrugged. "Sometimes. Anyway, as a graduate student, I would lead philosophy seminars where we would discuss important questions, like the existence of God. Sometimes God made it through the fifty minutes (God's still big on the prairies: who else could have – or would have – made them so flat?) and sometimes he didn't. The fatal seminar, towards the end of the year, was on Moral Theory. It involved a dramatic example. There was a fort surrounded by bloodthirsty Indians. That dates it, doesn't it, because they'd better not be using Charles that way now."

"When we did it, it was CIA-financed Fascists."

"Right on. Anyway, of course there was someone they wanted, somehow he'd offended the Great Spirit, and if he wasn't surrendered to them to be killed, they'd massacre every last soul in Fort Moral Theory. A hundred people, say. He won't go voluntarily. So, Mr. McTavish, what is the moral thing to do? It had worked well in other seminars, but this time it wasn't going over. It was late in the afternoon, I was tired, so were they. I was struggling just to get them to talk. Human life is sacred, isn't it, Miss Smith?"

"Mr. Ogilvie's first name was Dugald, everyone called him Dugie, and I seemed to be the only person to notice how funny, how fleshly this sounded: Dugie Ogilvie. He was tall and handsome and athletic, and he had dark colouring, brownish skin and dark brown hair, with extremely pale blue eyes, that seemed to have their own light. He's a surgeon, now, and very successful. Skillful, I'm sure, but as well, people look at his face and think, 'no harm can come to me'. He was very nice too, so he was just being his usual self in stepping in to help me out."

"Straight, I suppose?" David said, coldly. He had decided not to like him.

"Straight? David, he was what straights are *for*! Anyway, he sat there in a short-sleeved white shirt that would look silly now except for his muscles and put the case very clearly. Of course the one man had to go, to save the hundred others. But from my point of view it was too clear. I still had to get people talking, you see. So I had to say the stupid things, like, 'What if it was you, Mr. Ogilvie? What if the Indians were after you?' He would go voluntarily, he said breaking Miss Smith's heart, I'm sure. 'But what if you were on the throwing-out squad?' and he was on all sorts of teams, of course 'could you really do that? This is a completely innocent person, remember, a model citizen, the Great Spirit has got it wrong.' Mr. Ogilvie moved his arms in a way that somehow put his muscle tone into the air, made it ring a little, for his admirers, and said yes, if he had to. Nicely but very firmly: "I guess I'd let him open me up too, decide what had to go."

Jack smiled. "Would it be any different if they were all ugly, David? Or even just plain, ordinary? I wonder. Anyway, I should have turned to other people, but I was getting hypnotized. 'With your bare hands?' I said, shocked. There they were on the table in front of us, big hands, with full veins: he opened them, I looked into his eyes, and got dazzled somehow, fell into the light blue shine. I didn't hear what he was saying: yes, basically. But I had to save myself: I was falling in love, falling like down the stairs or out of a window. 'And of course you'd be right,' I said, and got up and went out of the room.

"Maybe they thought this was teaching technique, a dramatic way to end the class, which was almost over, anyway."

"What about him?" David said, still disliking Mr. Ogilvie.

"What did he think? I don't know. I'm not making up the eyes, you know. He must have been used to having people get stuck in them, like headlights. I don't know. Someday we'll have to ask the straights, won't we? What were you thinking? Though I suppose the real truth is, people don't pay each other much attention, by and large."

"And I wasn't really in love with him, except for a few days: he wasn't Danny. It's just that things started to grab at me like that. I remember this student coming into my little office, with dark hair fizzing up from under his T-shirt, and I was thinking, 'I've been doing my best, but if you're going to do that, *that*...' It was like *Death in Venice*, when Aschenbach says, 'you shouldn't smile like that. Nobody should be allowed to smile like that.' I remember reading that and thinking, exactly. Exactly. Things would seize me. I saw a blond kid doing pushups once, and I fell in love with—so precisely! – the tops of the backs of his calves. You know, just under the pit of the knee, just a little tender and moist, and my soul stuck to them like cut grass for weeks."

Jack paused, suddenly embarrassed. David was impressed, and moved too, remembering Chris. He felt grateful to Tim for not forcing him to love him that way, so far.

"I hope I'm wiser and saner now," Jack said. "At least, I think I am. Anyway, I knew I had to do something drastic. I committed a kind of substitute suicide. I was going to go to a university in the States to study philosophy – to figure Wittgenstein out at last. I wrote them a letter: I reminded them that according to Spinoza a falling stone that suddenly became conscious would believe it was falling of its own free will. I said that I'd decided not to continue my career in philosophy. I'm sure they get that letter several times a year."

David felt sick. It *was* suicide, for a graduate student.

"And two days after mailing it, I told Sharon. Oh, God, what a night! Sharon had seen something was happening, but she wasn't prepared for this. Why had I done something so crazy? I gave all sorts of reasons, everything from the Pentagon to Cathy, but they didn't work, they all died on me, and it seemed the only way to justify myself was to start telling her about the bare legs, the fizzing hair, even Danny Moscovitz. I was queer – that was the best word available." He shrugged. "And it certainly worked."

"At the same time I was wondering if I really meant it, or if I'd just made it up to hide from her, if it was some crazy obsession that a psychiatrist could remove. But something in me knew it was real, that all the straight, solid things were the obsession. That it was real to be trudging through the snow over the bridge to a friend's apartment downtown."

David could only look his sympathy. Jack shrugged. "It could have been worse, a lot worse. For her, for Cathy, for me. Well, maybe not for Cathy. She was a good mother, but you need two parents around, if only to see how the human race gets along."

"After the term was over, I didn't want to teach anymore. Who was I to teach anybody anything – especially philosophy? I 'dropped out' – because you dropped out in those days, you didn't come out. I worked at various jobs, even driving a taxi. Then I got a job in a record store that was becoming a headshop, the only one for thousands of miles, probably. I smoked a lot of dope in those days, frizzling up brain cells meant to understand what Wittgentstein meant when he said language is a form of life. Paul was working there, Paul Murchison, my ex- (but that's a debatable point) – lover. He was a vicarious draft-dodger from Minneapolis: not one himself, in love with one. He drove him up here, a lanky kid named Al, then hung around, washing the dishes, not telling anyone why. People could think it was his way of protesting the war-in-Viet-Nam. That's how you said it, one word, and not just 'the war': too frightening, I guess. He was – Lord knows, he still is! – left-wing, a downright Marxist when he gets riled. A big, talkative, hysterical Marxist who loves to cook. My favourite kind. In fact the only kind to get mixed up with. But it took us months, each of us acting as if he was the only queer on the Prairies, even though we both could see that wasn't true.

"I mean, David, it was about this time I first heard the word 'gay,' in the Stonewall sense. Someone who was smoking grass, sitting there all alone and smiling foolishly. I thought it was a new word for stoned – something you could always use then.

"Anyway, Paulie and I finally managed a desperate clinch in the back, in the smell of incense and Indian cotton, and somehow it worked. We even came out to our friends. But after a while we got tired of Winnipeg; it's no place to be gay in. We came here, though Paul wanted to go to Vancouver, where he had lived for a while. He still wants us to settle down there some day."

Jack wiped his mouth with his napkin, as if wiping away his story, ready to go.

"So," Jack said, moving to the edge of his chair. "My aunt always wondered how I'd come out, and that's how."

At first, David didn't move. Jack's story, Jack himself in a way, felt unfinished, as if he was still struggling to get formed inside David. He could see the dazzling snow-banks, the steamy diner, the crazy dust in Florence's rearview mirror, Mr. Ogilvie's baleful eyes. It was vivid but it was all only a beginning, and he wanted Jack to give him an ending, a happy ending. Was his own next decade going to be so inconclusive, so scattered? Besides, he'd listened to Jack, keeping his own life and feelings out of the way for an hour. He'd enjoyed being a bright young authority on being gay, but Jack seemed to forget, or perhaps not to have taken in, that he'd only been out for a few weeks. Now Jack had shown he was the most intelligent gay man David knew in Toronto. He probably had what was needed to be an advisor, a confidant, and David was ready to talk about coming out, about being gay, about his lover and what he was really like. About – because it was all leading to this – the quarrel they had almost had at the beach. There were all sorts of things he wanted to let out to Jack, but he didn't know how to start.

"I guess love is never what you think it is," Jack said, hesitantly, if he saw this, and was waiting for David to say something. But he couldn't, not challenged like that. Jack took another napkin from the metal box. "I've got your number, why don't I give you mine, and the address? I mean to have you and Tim over for one of Paul's dinners."

"That would be nice." David watched him write it on the napkin, bleeding a little into the soft paper. He thought of saying, off-handedly, 'Assuming we're still together, of course.'

"Paul is a wonderful cook: he thinks the *early* Marx would have approved."

He handed David the napkin, which he folded and put in his shirt pocket as they stood up.

Jack looked as if he sensed David's unhappiness, but all he said was, "Down to the dinosaurs?" David was supposed to be a kid like Charles, someone you could cheer up in a moment, with a trip to the zoo.

Jack paid for him, anyway, and they headed into the museum rotunda and downstairs around a totem pole into palaeontological depths. Monsters heaved into view, their skeletons anyway, gleaming brown-varnished bones and teeth, rearing at them against the faded skies of millions of years ago. But he could tell they weren't going to cheer him up, especially not with Jack pretending to think he should be as impressed as the schoolchildren, their wide eyes staring into the sockets.

"I loved bringing Charles here," Jack declared, looking different in the gloom: meant to enhance old bones, it gave him a bony, cruel look too. "He couldn't stay still – like that one."

A small boy was running in dizzy circles with his arms held wide, screeching like a pterodactyl.

"Being a bit older, he also saw them as challenges to his manhood. He had to convince himself he could deal with one, if he met it coming up Yonge. You'll be glad to know he did."

"Charles. What about him?"

"Now, that is another story. Charles, my *gentle two-spirited friend*. I'll tell you sometime how I met him...how I reacted to more of that racist crap."

"More of man's inhumanity to man."

"Right. Anyway, once I'd met him in that bar, he downed more beers that night than I've ever seen him take, since. He also talked more. He told me that he'd been born on the shore of Lake Superior at Batchawana in a tar paper shack. His mother was an old woman of forty-two then, already toothless and wrinkled. His father had been a young man scarred by pox who visited his village one day. He came from somewhere north – a *Cree*, I think.

When Charles was growing up he lived either with his mother or his grandmother most of the time, but when he was twelve his mother died and he moved in with his uncle. His name was George.

George was much younger than Charles' mother. Apparently, the grandmother had had many children but only George, the youngest, and his mother had lived past seventeen. Three died in a fire, the others died from illnesses of one kind or another. Everyone thought that his mother was barren until Charles was born. So she named him Surprise. George said no, she couldn't call him that, and he gave him his second name, the one he goes by, Charles. George said that it was the name of an English king, and that has always made Charles proud.

When he was nineteen George had moved into a place with his girlfriend, but she moved out a couple of years after and eventually left the reserve altogether, so George was alone. It was a nice place. He had put up siding he got from a friend at the sawmill down at Garden River and he painted it white. The windows had glass in them, not plastic, and the house had four rooms including the kitchen, with a covered walk to the outhouse.

Charles said that when he moved in he got a room all to himself. His cousins took over his mother's place. He hadn't wanted it. It was old and smelled bad and his mother hadn't bothered to fix things or let anyone else fix things. If someone offered, she had just laughed and given them a cigarette and a cup of tea.

Charles wondered a lot about his uncle George. He had never looked for another girlfriend. He kept to himself, worked on his house or did odd jobs down in the Soo. And he read a lot. He'd borrow books from the library or he'd buy paperbacks. He had some shelves in the big room he called the living room and he would put the books there. Once George taught Charles to read books, he enjoyed them, too.

When he was a kid George wanted him to go to school, and he did for a while. But he hated the bus and the way he was supposed to do one thing at a time, or the way they broke the day up into little bits where he would study one thing for thirty minutes and then switch and study something else. It seemed really dumb. He really loved reading and had a facility for math. He wasn't sure where he learned to do it – not at school, though.   Eventually, he just stopped going. They'd send the truant officer after him and he'd go again. Then he would stop and they'd threaten to take him away and he'd go back again. Charles found it really boring and the white kids were really stuck up and stupid and the rules were there just to be rules, not because there was any real purpose for them. The only reason he kept going was because he didn't want to be taken away from Batchawana. He didn't go often enough to get past grade eight, though, and he was sixteen then. He'd been in Toronto doing different jobs and collecting welfare until I met him that night, just over a year ago."

"And you've been friends ever since?"

"Yes, David, and you can take that any way you want."

David nodded, accepting Jack's explanation without comment. They walked slowly through the dinosaurs, with Jack explaining specific details that he compulsively shared.

Jack was a real fancier of dinosaurs, it seemed, and put his knowledge on display: gloating, proprietorial, the ringmaster with the sarcastic lash. "They're egg-layers, all just birds, really, big hysterical birds: that's their charm." David tried to read signs conscientiously, to search out the evolving bones and give dead-ends their due. But now he couldn't help thinking about the day before, at Hanlan's Point. Jack's story, Jack seen as an example of the odd fate of being gay, had brought the feelings back. Now the dim light let him see the sunny beach and go over it again, trying to figure out what Tim had been up to.

Watching a group at the water's edge, Tim had said thoughtfully he would love to draw them, just their legs, from the waist down. As he explained, David thought he could see what he meant: restless angles, long, full curves, their elegant interplay. He could see what Tim meant as an artist, as an admirer of long legs and well-filled swimsuits.

"That's Mark and Brian, isn't it?" David said.

"Yes. That's their crowd, sort of."

"Muscle queens," David said, coolly: it was Tim's phrase.

"You know," Tim went on, nervously, "Mark said – of course I said no right away – but he said they'd love to get it on with you and me."

"Do they do that a lot?" he asked.

"All the time."

"With you?"

"No," Tim said, indecisively.

"Not yet, you mean," he said, bitterly. He was scared: did his position give him the right to be so bitter?

Tim's eyes didn't tell him: he was looking far away, over the water. "Look, out there – see those two guys?" He pointed seaward, with a strong sexy arm and hand, like Visconti's Tadziu. "Guess what they're doing?"

There was always a scattered, stand-up party going on out in the water. David saw two sets of heads and shoulders. "You know your eyes are a lot better than mine. So far as I can see, they're just talking."

"Maybe," Tim said, with a laugh. "Or maybe they're fucking out there, under the water."

David shut his eyes as if he'd been slapped. What did it mean? He told himself that Tim was just delighted by the scandal of it, the shockingness, as with the men in leather, and that was all.

Already Tim had become a little afraid of what he was doing, and guilty about it.

"Well, I'm sorry," he said. "But it's true. People do things like that, David. Even in Toronto the Good."

"But you don't." David announced it flatly, but in a small, scared voice.

"I'm a good boy, David," Tim said, a little mockingly. "Well brought up. Just like you."

A joke shook the group by the water, sent the legs moving, composing new drawings. David was remembering something: some Western from his childhood, men with bandannas over their faces, and suddenly the swimsuits all became the Technicolour masks of bandits, of assassins.

"I can't stand that," David said, sick and terrified of what he was risking: that Tim might rebel. "I hate the thought of it."

"Fucking?"

"That's not what I meant," David said at once, to get that over with. "All this everybody having sex with everyone else. It just turns it all into a slimy mess. How can you be a *person* and live your life that way?"

Tim looked away, with a small, regretful shrug coming into his wide shoulders. "Only you will, you know," he said. "You like sex too much not to understand."

"That's a shitty thing to say."

"Why?"

"I don't like sex at all," David said, hysterically, looking away beyond everything to the misty join of lake and sky. "I don't. It stinks. It sucks. It wears me out. All I like is you." Ontario and its huge sky were being shaken by tears, rocking in them. He hated gay sex, because it made him want Tim, because it would draw Tim away.

"So what do you think?" Jack said, neglected in the dim museum.

David shrugged, still depressed. "I wish Tim was here," he answered. Tim could be enthusiastic for both of them. He would be safe from the emotions Jack dumped so freely.

"What do you mean?"

He didn't really answer. "It's all a bit fake, isn't it? I know these bones are real, under all the varnish, but it's just a circus, and they have to make you feel it's edifying somehow."

"David, you're no fun! You're meant to enjoy them. Especially the carnivores."

David pouted. He wasn't going to be cheered up by anyone on the side of the carnivores. He identified with their victims: he could feel the foul, brown teeth sink into his heart.

"This next one's my favourite, David. If you don't like her, there's no hope for you."

An *ornithomimus* towered above them, tallest of them all, like a huge ostrich.

"Isn't she a dear?" Jack said, fondly. "All those bones, and she must have thought a lady couldn't go anywhere without all of them."

David laughed reluctantly. "Why do you think it's a she?"

"Well, look!" He gestured at the tight, egg-laying pelvic girdle. "They're all females now, aren't they? That's why they're fit for school children. Bones last, teeth last, teeth are respectable – but imagine those things with pricks! *Never in Toronto!*"

With no eyes, she, he, it had to stare through every bone. And really, David thought, *ornithomimus* was long gone: "Seventy. Million. Years," – a school teacher was solemnly feeding this fact into wide eyes. Now it was just bones that wanted to fall and scatter, that had lain at rest till humans had come along and dug them up and strung them up on their own miserable restlessness, their horror of the emptiness of the universe.

"I wish Tim was here," David said again, getting desperate. Where the darkness pooled, they could have reached for each other.

"Oh, Tim," Jack said, scornful, saurian, "Tim is a mammal."

"Why do you have to take those pictures, anyway?" he said, fiercely. Jack was getting on his nerves: he was on the verge of hating him. He didn't imagine Tim being seduced now, but somehow humiliated, betrayed, made to do ugly, sadistic things by the bitchy ringmaster.

Jack stared for a moment. "I told you, I just want to peel a few split-seconds worth of light off him."

David could feel the light peeling away from Tim's defenseless skin, and suddenly he was in tears, tears from the beach, he knew, which hadn't been satisfied, even when they'd gone to Tim's and made love. "Don't you *dare* touch him," he said, hysterically. "Don't you dare or – " it was silly, but it made sense here, now, "or I'll kill you."

He laughed, shakily. Killing Jack wouldn't be very satisfying. Even killing Tim's shadowy next lover wouldn't be tragic enough. Jack was peering at him, at the tears.

"I won't," he said, distressed and baffled. "Really, David, I'm not a shit. Besides, do you really think he'd let me?"

"I don't mean that," David said, trying to pull himself together. "I mean – I don't know – just don't *hurt* him."

"I couldn't." He held out innocent, helpless hands, trying to fathom David's tears. He almost turned to go on, then found the courage to say, "I think it's something else. Don't let him hurt you, David."

"What do you mean?"

Jack just gave a shrug and shook his head, then moved on without taking leave of his favourite monster.

Groping for something to dry his tears, David found the napkin in his shirt-pocket. After a minute, he followed into a room which pretended to be under the sea, with blue-green light and mysterious watery noises. Dinosaurs swam over them with beaks like splitting pods of teeth.

"What did you mean?" David demanded, from a little behind. "Nothing, nothing in particular." Jack was flustered. "Just that the emotions are risky, David. It isn't easy being warm-blooded, is it? Here, you've got something on your cheek – ink?"

"Oh, it's your phone number," David said, with a laughing groan. Jack pulled out an old-fashioned white handkerchief, linen, crumpled but clean, and wiped off David's cheek.

"Oh, Jack," he said, fondly, being scrubbed at. "Like Charles says, you're too much."

Nobody's problems were solved, but Jack had let him have his emotions, taken them seriously, and now at least he felt better.

They went out through a dark, empty corridor and made their way back to the rotunda. It was time for Jack to go relieve a friend at the store. He could stand to take the subway now, he said, if there were no emergencies. But perhaps David would like to stay, see what the humans had made of their chance? The oriental things were really impressive. Still in danger from his emotions, David didn't want to be left alone in the gloom. They went out into the bright, white afternoon, pausing on the steps.

"You don't really mean anything do you, Jack?"

Jack looked away at Victoria College. At courts where tennis games were bouncing: green balls, white players.

"About being warm-blooded, I mean?"

"No, no, I'm sorry, I was just startled. Why do you think I might hurt Tim?"

"I guess it was the dinosaurs." David laughed. "All the teeth, and the gloom. I don't really think you would, of course. But I'm getting very fond of him, you know," he said, in a self-mocking way. "I'm not sure if we're really lovers, but I wish we were. It's my first time, you know that, don't you? And I wish it was – in the grand manner, something that will last, something foreverish."

Jack was sympathetic, too sympathetic to look this hope right in the eyes. He turned back to the tennis game.

"I know," he said. "Tim is very – "

"What?"

"Nobody's ever really looked at him and said, well, Tim Grey, *there you are*. He's never had to ask himself who he is. I think that's what I'm after in the photographs."

"I don't quite understand." Jack was on to something, but it wasn't clear.

"David, I don't know. Everyone is a mystery, so far as I can see: in fact, they're just getting more mysterious. What can I say?" He gave him a guilty look. "You know, the truth is, Socrates really wanted the handsome boys to be wise. He wanted *them* to be teaching *him*."

"That's no help!" David protested, with a short laugh. But he gave Jack a dark, disappointed frown. Jack's intelligence wasn't much use in a crunch: he was almost too tender-hearted.

But Jack liked to scowl. "You're *stubborn*, all right," he said. "Now who is it? Why don't you give in and tell me?"

David laughed out loud, feeling flattered. His double was obviously someone Jack liked. "Doubles are bad news, any English student knows that. But thanks for lunch, and the dinosaurs, and everything."

"Lunch and *tsuris*? Well, next time it's your turn. Give me a call– really, I mean it."
David pulled out the napkin, and read out the tear-stained number.

"Good: so phone me!" Jack gave a funny, tight wave – a salute in some high-strung army – and walked away in those Italian, black leather, twisted ankle boots. David watched him go, trying to understand what he felt about Jack, about Tim. But the slumped shoulders, the heavy walk, Jack Durham's whole oppressed and complicated bearing didn't tell him a thing. Jack was running heavily down the stairs into the subway, waving one last time, and then he was gone.

PART 5

That night Tim heard all about David's lunch with Jack—he thought it was all. He was glad they'd hit it off so well. David needed friends.

Two days later, Tim got a call from David. He couldn't come swimming, because he had to finish his paper or die. "Or do anything tonight, if you don't mind. My ideas are kind of elusive."

Tim went to take a parting look at his painting. He was finished for today, he thought, and he had got what he wanted. He had the right sense of motion in the man mowing his lawn, and the masses, the colours around him – house, fence, grass, sky – all worked. Then in the doorway something made him turn for one more look. Something was missing, held back, some small, essential thing. He shook himself and left. Swimming might set free whatever was coming.

As he put on his old running shoes, a lace snapped. He tied a knot, letting himself think that perhaps the painting was simply a failure. A defeat...proof he was not a painter. But he couldn't dawdle, unless he wanted to dodge the businessmen, feel them go by greased by water and fat, be scratched by their toenails.

At the front door, he couldn't find his keys and had to search the apartment till he found them in a kitchen cupboard. On his way out, he looked in at the painting again, from the door of the studio. Now the central expanse of green was too big and too flat, a lake of green, floating everything else in the painting, and making it unreal.

He walked away abruptly, closing the front door behind him. He felt that he had forgotten something. He knew he had everything he needed for his expedition, but he stood staring at nothing. *Don't dawdle* his mother would have said: he remembered how she would say that when he was thirteen and getting too big for himself. She put a bright, energetic irony into the word, and it expressed his state so well he felt he would never be able to do anything but '*dawdle*': the word was so right it impaled him.

Trying to walk through the clinging image of the painting, he went down the hall and pressed the elevator button. It came and opened, empty, and he turned and went back to the apartment, giving up on the Y, feeling trapped and miserable. He went to the painting, to confront his failure, to submit to it if he had to. Perhaps he shouldn't paint in this way. Perhaps he shouldn't paint at all. He could draw well. He had a good colour sense. He'd make a good commercial artist, and maybe that was all.

But right now, it was too late: he had to struggle. The painting had him by his pride. He kept staring at the expanse of green: he had to have something there. A stray piece of clothing perhaps? No, it had to be even more alive than that, he realized. He imagined a blue flower, almost seeing it. But then he saw that blue would echo the sky, would lock the earth and sky together, make the painting claustrophobic, choked, a failure once and for all. It had to be red, the only red in the painting: a crimson flower half-hidden in the uncut grass just in front of the blades. He could see it, giving the painting a new focus, a new balance. The man was suddenly more real: his face was turned away from the viewer, but the flower was what he was looking at. Tim thought for a moment of putting flecks of red in the cloud of grass cuttings, and knew he shouldn't, it would be fatal. There had to be only one red in the painting.

It would work, he was sure, but he didn't want to do it now. He had to get away before doubt could set in. It was too late for swimming, he was too sensitive now to be touched by anyone, except perhaps David – no, not even David, unless he was in a loving mood. No, he would go to the ravine and take in what was left of the sunshine, alone. Putting on his bathing suit and shorts, he ran down the stairs to his bike.

It had cleared since the day before, but the sun had been uncertain all day, and there were only a few people in the park, drifting towards the end of the afternoon on bright rafts. Among them, Tim saw a someone he and David had met there before. His name was Nicholas and he lived with an airline pilot. Alone on an orange towel, a forlorn, silenced chatterer, he looked up as Tim came bumping over the grass and put on a burst of surprised delight. Tim liked to be made welcome, and there was no reason not to spread his blue towel out beside the orange one. Nicholas was small and delicately made, with honey-blond hair and gray-green eyes. There was a kind of restless, clinging tenderness in the way he moved. He looked younger than his age – he was at least as old as Tim and seemed embarrassed about it. A tell-tale spot ripened in the waxy skin under the corner of his mouth, and he would reach up to soothe or worry it, then pull his hand away and smile, the spot bravely riding up on the smile.

He offered to put suntan lotion on Tim's back and did so with measured, impersonal strokes. Folding down the little spout he handed the bottle back like an altar-boy.

"*Aren't I lucky?*" said Nicholas.

PART 6

From behind David's door came the fiery twangling of his favourite Scarlatti record, then a burst of typing. David was working. Almost a good reason not to have knocked, Tim thought, knocking again and louder. The typing stopped, and the music, and David pushed a bespectacled face through the door. "Oh, it's you. Come in."

"I phoned an hour ago, but you were out," Tim said, coming through the door and reaching for David, who snatched himself away, saying, "Before I forget!" He sat and typed fiercely.

"I'm incredibly busy," he said. "I must have been in the kitchen when you phoned. But I'm glad you came."

Hard to believe this of the hunched, scowling word-pilot. Tim sat on the bed. "This is the one on *Frankenstein*?" he said, politely.

"Milton And. I told Jay I'd give it to her last week, I hope she'll understand."

"Will you have time to come swimming?"

David flung the carriage across and sat back. "It might do me good, clear my head. But I thought you went yesterday?"

"I was working hard on the painting, so I just went down to the park for an hour."

David pulled the sheet out of the typewriter and held it up. "This is probably pure drivel," he said, proudly. He looked young, fatigue thinning and paling him. "I hope it wasn't boring all alone?"

"No, actually, it wasn't, David."

David put the sheet down and looked at him with bottled eyes.

"I met someone there," Tim went on. "I mean, we got it on."

"Oh? Really?" David said. "Really?" It was his being-interested voice. "In the bushes?" His voice faltered.

"No, of course not. They have a great apartment, just off Mount Pleasant." Tim hesitated. "You remember Nicholas, don't you?"

"Nicholas? That kid?"

"He's not a kid."

David grasped the wooden chair on both sides of the seat and made it do a solemn hop to face Tim.

"We aren't married, David," Tim said, knowing as he spoke that this came too soon, too easily.

"No."

"I mean, David, I never said I would only have sex with you."

"I noticed."

"So this was bound to happen sometime, David."

"Why do you keep calling me David like that? It sounds odd."

Tim shrugged. It was almost uncannily shrewd of David to detect it. Nicholas had used David's name, saying, "it's not as if David would have to feel *threatened* at all." His clear, thin voice had summoned up someone who was as sensible about sex as they were, and Tim had let himself imagine that such a David existed.

"And why are you telling me now?"

"You've got the right to know."

"And because you want to do it again?"

"Well, not with Nicholas," Tim said looking away. "But – "

"But that leaves you a lot of room, doesn't it?" Then, quickly, as if guilty for being so nasty, "Well, all right. All right."

He lifted himself from the chair to the bed, sitting along beside Tim and putting a stiff, brotherly arm round him. He took his glasses off. It always disturbed Tim to see this plunge into near-blindness. David gazed at him with sticky, naked eyes and said, "Of course I knew this would happen."

"You don't own me, David. And I don't own you."

David lay back, pulling Tim down with him, wriggling to find room and comfort on the narrow bed. He pushed his forehead into Tim's shoulder and mumbled some words into it.

"What?"

"I own you."

But when Tim bent to kiss him, David pulled away.

"Do you still want to go to the Y?"

"Not this minute."

"I'm sorry, David, about yesterday, but it just developed. We should have had a talk before something like this happened." He heard himself sounding like an older, wiser brother, convincingly, he hoped. "We should have had some kind of arrangement – a contract."

"I suppose we should," David said. He was silent for a minute, Tim holding him, even rocking him a little. Then he felt David's teeth, suddenly biting into the skin of his throat. Tim jumped, then arched back almost comfortably, though it hurt a little and would leave a mark. The clenched quivering in David's teeth told him he was being forgiven, but that it wasn't easy.

"We don't want to be late," Tim said, laughing, nervously. "you know how you hate being bumped."

PART 7

David didn't answer, but took his teeth away and looked at their marks, filling with blood still safe and warm under the skin. Tim would just have to wait for him to get over this. Every so often, as if measuring out the time David had to forgive him, Tim would swallow. His larynx moved up and down, dropping saliva down into the inner, comfortable, treacherous Tim. David was being his understanding lover who accepted his right to have sex with others when he wanted to. It was the only role he could think of in a hurry, and he seemed to be doing everything more or less right. This was how Michael would have done it, or other friends of Tim's. He shifted suddenly, to find the shape of the David who was forgiving and the shape of the Tim who was adequately sorry. The bed had to be big enough for two sensible lovers.

"Jack Durham warned me," David said, remembering it suddenly. "At lunch."

"Jack? What did he say?"

"He said emotions are risky. And then, last night," David took an almost deep breath, "last night, I couldn't sleep, because of my paper. I had nightmares, which makes sense because *Frankenstein* began with a nightmare, about a man bending over a shape on the table, that opens its yellow eyes. I wish I had nightmares like that. *Usable* nightmares."

He stopped abruptly – he was chattering like teeth and shifted again. He still had time for the emotional adjustments they needed, though soon, all over downtown, fat trolls disguised as businessmen would be snapping shut their attache cases to go bumping into Tim. He reached down into Tim's desolated crotch with a scared, disbelieving hand. Tim squirmed a little, and said, "We're going swimming, remember?" He took David's hand and pulled it up with his, which had red streaks on it.

"Why Nicholas?"

"It doesn't matter. He's no threat, David, really."

"Oh? Maybe you thought, he's no threat to anyone, not even David. I'll try it on with him, and then we'll see."

"You know I don't think that way."

"You think some way. I know that."

"David, it really just happened. He suggested it, there was no reason to say no. I mean, I hadn't had sex for two days, except with myself. He's not very exciting in bed, if you're interested."

David looked up at the throat, swallowing glibly, and asked "Do you want me to tell you exactly what a bastard you are?"

Tim was silent for a few seconds. "Let's go," he said in a low voice. "Let's talk about it later."

"Why?"

"Because I can see if we talk about it now, you will screw *everything* up."

"All right."

David twisted quickly to get his glasses, groping among books and papers on the floor. He could feel Tim's perfect sight on his back, loathing him, as if his eyes were always falling out and having to be picked up again, sticky with dust. He found the glasses, stared at their dust defiantly, and put them on. Pulling up his leg, Tim was tying a shoelace – a broken one. He didn't wear socks with them, and there was a slight bulge of flesh over the inside of the shoe.

"You're so *soft*," David said to it, with angry longing.

"What do you mean?"

"Nicholas had you wrapped around his little finger." Tim shrugged, pulling the bow tight.

"Don't make me feel guilty," he commanded.

"All right. You don't have to feel guilty." David sat down on the chair. "I don't really feel like going swimming today," David said, scared and ashamed of what he was doing. "You go. Maybe next time – "

Tim looked at him sharply. *"Don't be like that, David."*

"Like what?"

Tim didn't say. He came and stood in front of him, stroking his hair, as if the mess of his hair was him. He seemed to say that there was still time, that everything could be made right. He moved sideways a little, with an easy shifting of his pelvis and crotch. David couldn't tell if it was conscious, if Tim was saying, this is your answer, this is the way home. It seemed possible. It didn't occur to Tim what a punch in the balls would do. "Like what?" David said again.

Tim leaned and nuzzled the top of his head. "David," he said quietly, "either you forgive me or you don't."

A small, panicky laugh leapt out of David's chest. "I can't believe you," he said, with a groan. Tim was making it absurdly easy to be miserable. "Go swimming," David said, ambivalently.

Tim stepped back. "I'll phone you tonight, okay?"

"What will you say?"

"David, I really think you should come now."

Tim was at the door, as he had been several months before. David could see him struggling inside his guilt.

"Be sure not to drown," David said.

"I'll phone."

"*Nicholas*?" David said, scathingly. "Oh, Tim!"

That sent Tim through the door. David tried to take a deep breath, and turned his chair back to the typewriter. He was grimly determined this wouldn't stop Prof. MacPherson from knowing all about "Sin and Death in *Frankenstein*" before the end of the week. But the subtle mucilage that sticks words together had dried up and crumbled. A sharp pain was driving up into his heart, as if he was having a heart attack, or working on one. He got onto the bed and began writing more or less posthumous letters to Tim, knowing he would never be able to type them. Tim was a world closer than Chris, on this side of the keys or nowhere. If he was going to tell Tim what he felt, he would have to be holding him to do it. If he was even going to know what he felt he would have to be touching him. Which he could imagine doing only with his fists, with his nails, with a knife.

He lay dying while Tim lacerated the swimming pool. About four-thirty, when Tim would have finished, the phone rang. He didn't answer it. It rang again at five, just before six, just after seven, braying impatiently, stupidly, not getting the point. David let the rings go through him like a dentist's drilling. Sometimes he thought he hadn't known Tim at all, until now. He was hollow, faithless, the hidden wound of his homosexuality had eaten out his soul, like fruit rotting from inside. That was what Jack had meant: he liked Tim for his looks, but he didn't trust him. But at other times, Tim was simply unconsciously, unarguably male, taking what he wanted, and it was David who was hurt and broken and queer, writhing around the blunt fact of Tim's and the world's masculinity. And between these two positions he would never be able to decide. He wanted to break in two along the fault line in his chest. He wanted to simplify, like his great uncle in North Vancouver, now living only in the right side of his body, like a man half-hanged, refusing even to recognize the left.

The phone rang again at nine. He almost answered it: perhaps Tim was human but it wasn't worth getting himself upset to find out. But the bed was becoming intolerable: he would have to get out of it, and having got out he would have to go somewhere. The only place he was interested in right now was Tim's apartment. And having gone to Tim's apartment, he would have to forgive him. He couldn't go there just to tell him to go to hell. He would forgive him because he couldn't live without Tim, even if he was a bastard. He got up and tried to get the pains out of his joints, out of his chest. Heading out across the street to the subway station, he felt he couldn't bear to feel the earth closing over him. He would walk all the way up the hill through the warm summer evening and arrive at Tim's door with his feelings worn out, sorry, too tired to be angry, ready for a reconciliation.

At the entrance to Tim's block, he almost pressed the buzzer for his apartment, but knew he couldn't bear the intercom's panicky squawking. He got out his keys, let himself in, took the elevator up. Rock music was coming through Tim's door. David knocked and strained to hear through the music – voices? Moans of pleasure? He knocked again, but there was no answer. He took out the two keys on their metal ring, and Tim opened the door, wearing his blue shirt, unbuttoned, and his old jeans. He was barefoot. "Oh," Tim said. "I've been phoning you, but – ." But David hadn't answered. "Jerry Ornstein's here."

"I want to talk," David said.

"Well, come in."

David almost did, but shook his head, looking down. "What's that?" Tim said, looking at David's closed hand.

As if he had to see himself, David opened his hand to show the two keys and their tooth marks on his palm.

"Were you having sex with him?"

"No!" Tim said. Then, "No, I wasn't, as a matter of fact."

"But it wouldn't matter if you were, would it?" David said. He tried to look at Tim, to apologize for this, but his eyes dropped again.

"Just come in, David, and say hello."

"Here!" he said, thrusting the keys forward.

"No!"

"*Take them!*" He thrust them at Tim so savagely that he took them, like someone grabbing a knife aimed at this belly.

"*Good-bye!*" David said. He turned and went down the hall, with Tim following. David pressed the elevator button and the doors opened at once. He strode in. Tim hesitated at the door, as if David had packed the elevator with violence. The doors started to close and Tim raised his hands to stop them. David felt a kind of grief to see them crushed, cut off: he wanted to get out of this petty misery into something really terrible. "No!" he shouted furiously, afraid Tim would get himself hurt. Tim tossed the keys through the doors as they closed: they hit David in the face, and he glimpsed Tim's scared look as he saw this.

As the elevator dropped he brushed his cheek with his finger–tips. He was free. But when the elevator opened there was Tim, panting.

"Sorry, I didn't mean to hit you," he said, trying to smile.

David said nothing. He stepped over the keys and around Tim.

"David," Tim said. David was getting tired of the way Tim kept using his name, as if he knew all about him.

"*Go to hell,*" he muttered.

"What?"

He turned back, "*GO   TO   HELL* !" Tim jumped, his eyes wide: he was actually frightened, David saw, as if he feared an assault. You're so soft, he thought, and he turned away from Tim and went out the door and down the street. At the street corner where a whiskey bottle lay smashed into moist brown teeth, he turned and looked back, in case Tim was following on silent, bare feet. The sidewalk was empty. He turned and went on to the subway, counting himself in through the turnstile, gliding smoothly down the escalator, congratulating himself. It had been like a flash of pure, electric wisdom, that thrust of the keys. He had simplified everything. He had done his best to forgive Tim, but he had found it was impossible and left. It was better than some windy, raging argument: he had cut out all the nonsense.

At Bloor and Yonge, where he had to change, he got out and walked quickly, then ran, feeling the wind of another train on his face. With just a glance for signs, he ran in through closing doors and sat down, out of breath, on the verge of emotion, but in two stops he would be home. He closed his eyes, feeling the violent speed of the train, remembering what he'd told Jack Durham: above him he could imagine London, or Paris. He opened his eyes at the second stop and saw it wasn't his stop at all: he had never been there before. He had taken the wrong train, gone east instead of west. He was too stunned, too tired to get up. He sat back as the train went on, and suddenly, crazily, they weren't even underground. The train burst into the black sky. They were shooting across a valley, and he saw a whole undreamt-of city, towers, a black river, highways and streaming cars. Then, the earth gulped him again.

He was a fool. He got eastbound mixed with westbound, just as he got left mixed with right. He took the wrong trains, he loved the wrong sex, the wrong people. Now he felt he was too helpless to get off: it wasn't worth trying. This train could take him where it liked. It could go to hell, if they weren't already there. He looked helplessly at the strange station names going past him. Suddenly, at a place called Greenwood, he bolted through closing doors.

He walked along the platform looking for stairs, and found an escalator. It was stopped. He could not bear to climb a stopped escalator: his legs wouldn't know how.

122

He stared at it, shaking, powerless. He turned away, hitting the air with his fists, and said, "*You bastard!*" so loud that people looked at him. "*You bastard!*" he said, going along the platform, looking for a real, solid, staircase. A train was coming, pushing along its plug of air, and he went back against the wall. He slumped against the tunnel wall as if he loved it, staring at the red front of the train. He could see the little box where the driver sat, waiting for the crazy and the queer to confess they couldn't live. He longed to see some righteous, monstrous face, but he couldn't make out the face until the train was close. He knew he was playing a game with himself, but he was terrified something inside him might say, 'So you think this is a game, do you?' and he would jump.

The driver was a small, young man in his late twenties, pushed along by his train, going by without knowing how close to suicide he had come, any more than David did.

The train stopped. David almost ran in to save himself, then remembered he still hadn't unravelled east and west. There were two phones on the wall. He pulled change out of his pocket: there were enough TTC tokens to kill several people, uncannily light and dry, like withered dimes, but nothing he could phone with. Then he found a dime, silver and alive, able to speak.

He phoned Tim's number, not sure he would be able to find words. Perhaps he would just hear Tim's voice, and look around inside it, to see if he could find a human being there. He couldn't do it, and hung up before the phone began to ring. But who else could he phone? Without knowing why, he pulled out his wallet. He saw that it held the napkin Jack had written his phone number on. It was blurry, almost watery. He couldn't believe it would work, lead him out of this tiled hell, but he tried.

A low voice answered, coughing.

"Hi. It's David."

"Oh, David. Yes. Good, great."

David had an attack of silence.

"Good of you to call," Jack said.

"Well, you're right about the emotions, Jack," he said, to explain himself.

"Where are you, David?" A train was coming in, noisily.

"At the Greenwood stop," he shouted.

"Out there! Why?"

"Oh – east, west," David cried despairingly. "They're practically the same word!"

"Well, that's true."

"Tim and I broke up."

"Really?"

This seemed utterly unfair. "I don't know. How would I know? Yes, damn it."

"That's too bad," Jack said, with guarded sympathy. He must have said that a thousand times before, David thought: it was part of being gay. For a second, he felt too depressed to respond.

"Yes, isn't it," he said, in a business-like tone. "But the reason I'm phoning is, can I come to your place? Now, I mean."

"Sure," Jack said, taken aback but not very much. "That would be fine. Do you know where I live? Or do you want me to come and get you?"

"Don't be silly, Jack," David said, fondly.

Jack gave him careful instructions, as if east and west might trip over each other again. David was more soothed than insulted, sinking into the sounds of Jack's voice plotting his way back through the black city to life.

"And David – "

It was as if Jack wanted to finish with something helpful, encouraging, but couldn't think of anything. He was, instead, gawping helpless and kind at the other end of the darkness. Only his response confirmed that they were still on the phone system's endless nerves: it was like all the sadness of the world, distanced, whispered, and David laughed into it.

"Jack, I love you."

"But are you hungry? I don't have much to eat here. Charles cleaned us out again. I could send out for something, pizza, Chinese food..."

David laughed, high, hysterically high, above all bodily desires. "No thanks, Jack. I'll be there soon. Sorry to get you up."

"You didn't. Soon? Good, fantastic."

David found a real staircase, ascended it, walked over and down again to the other track just as a train came. He went back up the names, reeling them in, crossing the dreamy valley, its pouring traffic, its twinkling high-rises, feeling the undercarriage banging and shaking under him, angry at its tracks. He reached Jack's station and followed his directions from it through a rain so light it was just a tingling on his face, a darkening of the sidewalks Jack had prescribed. He was only a little damp when he arrived at a red-brick, corner house, mounted creaking steps onto its leafy verandah and pressed the doorbell.

There was silence, then a welcoming shout. Jack opened the door wearing a gray sweat suit. "You made it! Come in!"

He stepped into Jack Durham's front hall. There was a mirror. It caught sight of the old fugitive he would never get away from, David McTavish glassy and pale. He looked quickly away to a wooden toboggan, standing against a wall of coats and jackets. There was a bookshelf of slumped paperbacks: on top of them a Frisbee and a baseball mitt. Even wrapped in panic, David felt the hall around him, felt old journeys and weathers brought into this house, into its particular dust and shelter.

"Welcome!" Jack said.

"Thank you, Jack." And as if realizing for the first time what a strange thing he was doing in inviting himself here, "I really mean it."

But Jack seemed to hover on the verge of some emotional attack. David shrank, afraid of being hugged. Jack wanted to flourish a little easy emotion, he saw, then relax and take in the tear-floods.

"Are you okay?" Jack said.

"Oh, God!" David looked away into a black and white photograph of a busy street: in a North American city, but looking far-off, some classic, old northeastern American city. Then there was someone on the top of the stairs – Charles? – no, a cat, watching through the banisters, calico and briefly curious.

"All I really need is a bed for the night, Jack. It's that simple."

"Come into the kitchen. Charles is sleeping." Jack led him, unwilling, down a hallway to the back of the house and switched on the kitchen light.

"Would you like something to drink? There's milk, there's orange juice, Drambuie... "

David lowered himself into a chair at the kitchen table.

"Milk, please," he said. Jack had a carton out of the refrigerator at once, and a glass down from the cupboard. David could see exactly how Jack wanted him to pour out his problems, but he was going to continue silent and stiff. Jack put the glass in front of him and said, "There you go." And when David just looked at the white cylinder, "Drink it, please." Rather than argue, David drank, cold, commonsensical milk sliding in and down.

"There," Jack said, and perhaps he would be satisfied with half a glass. David put the milk back down on the table-cloth and tensed, feeling Jack's hand on his shoulder. He'd been right, Jack wanted to push off a cliff with that sympathetic hand.

"Well," Jack said, behind him, brightly, sadly, "tragedy time!" His hand moved gently, heavily over David's back and his insides quaked and came apart. It was a huge mistake. It was going to be unbearable, but he couldn't help himself, shoving the glass to one side, pitching into tears.

"Oh Lord," Jack said. And then, "but that's all right."

"I did it," David said. "it's my fault. I gave him back the keys."

Jack moved away the glass, plonked down a box of Kleenex.

"I told him to go to hell."

Inside him an impossibly hard lump, a rock of grief, had to be broken up and worked up and out through his most tender parts.

"Why didn't he just not tell me? Why didn't he just lie? Because I *know* he thought about it."

Jack sat down at the table, got up almost at once, and moved around the kitchen, distressed and clumsy. David moved in and out of his grief, swept into bouts of jagged-edged sobbing, then retreating to think and snivel until he found some agonizing new point he had to suffer thoroughly. Each seemed to be, had to be, the worst possible thing.

"*He let him suck his cock!*" he wailed.

"The bastard!" Jack said.

"No," David groaned. That was the point, the tragedy. "No." He was cut off from

Tim's body forever, torn away. "And I thought even *touching* him was a privilege!"

He wallowed in the table-cloth, smelling of laundry and food. Jack, when he looked, seemed lost in his own kitchen, still dismayed at what his big sad hands had done, bumping into things companionably, trying to get sympathy to David through the way he leaned on the counter or the fridge. But he just didn't know what grief was. It was as though an utterly wrong-headed, terribly late and large, unbelievably stormy baby had to get born upwards—up through all the dearest, most painful membranes of his chest and throat. David didn't think they were going to make it.

Now the worst part was the scene in his room: he could see it, Tim callous and stupid, incredibly stupid.

"He said, I can't believe it, he said, '*Either you forgive me or you don't.*'"

Jack coughed angrily.

"I thought I would go deaf."

"*What a jerk!*" Jack said.

"Oh, yes." Jack had got it: Tim was a jerk. For a moment, it was beautifully simple.

And then, in the little room, he focussed on himself, stupidly superior and cold, unable to speak what he meant, or think it. "I'm such a fool, I'm so – " What was the word for it, the thing that always shut him up inside himself? "I'm such a fool." It would have to do.

"Yes, you are," Jack said, with his arm over the refrigerator.

David was too stunned by Jack's agreeing with him to say anything for a moment, and then thought of the next thing, when his helplessness had been worst, most fool-ish. "I felt like jumping in front of the train. I really did. It felt like it would be so *grati-fying.*" And that seemed to be true now: he almost regretted it, the satisfying smash he could have made out of David McTavish, the pure, bursting rage.

"Well, don't," Jack commanded him angrily.

"You don't know what it's like!"

"No," Jack said. "But yes, I do."

"He would have been *so* sorry," David said, vengefully, gloatingly. He didn't know if he was being sarcastic or not. "He would have been so bloody sorry."

"You are a fool," Jack said.

This was so unexpected David could only ignore it and go back to crying, almost forgetting it. Then he said, reminding Jack, "But he's a bastard, he's a jerk."

"You're still a fool." Jack said, still angry at him. Which was unfair, since all the emotions were supposed to be David's. He dragged himself sideways through the crumpled tablecloth, which was becoming a big, wet handkerchief.

"Well, all right, Jack," he said, after a while. "But really, I was only pretending. I wouldn't really do that."

He looked at a Jack Durham shattered, transfigured by tears.

"Don't pretend too much," Jack said, "You might believe it."

"Besides," Jack asked, "Are you sure you have broken up?"

"I THREW THE KEYS RIGHT AT HIS FACE!"

"What?"

"I mean, he gave them back to me."

"I don't follow."

David struggled, but the words were inextricable, like east and west. "I never want to see him again," he said, to get out of the struggling. "*Never!*" Insolently, Tim was standing there inside his wet eyes and staring at him, handsome as could be.

"Poor David," Jack said. David weltered a little in this sympathy, but suspiciously. Was Jack getting impatient? He might have reason. Grief is nothing if not infinite, but David was beginning to feel he would have to let go of his some time.

"What if he said he wanted you to come back?" Jack put the question in a thoughtful, hypothetical way.

"Who cares? Either I forgive him or *I don't. I don't!*"

"Poor David," Jack said. "I know how it is," he said, with sad scorn. "You've got Tim Grey's prick all mixed up with your heart." It was as if he'd been saving this to push David into his final bout of tears.

After a while, David searched himself for some new cause, but it seemed he had gone through the whole list. It was a relief, really: he looked around, raised his face out of the toast crumbs. He sniffed and sobbed, already nostalgic for the passionate, stormy world he was leaving.

He sat up and laughed a little.

"Isn't it ridiculous?" he said, leaving Jack to wonder whether he meant the universe or his sufferings on the table. He smoothed out the cloth, impressively tear-stained, like the crumpled manuscript of a poem. Jack put his hand on his shoulder again, and now he could bear it.

"You're good at it, all right," Jack said. "You're a real trouper."

"Oh, Jack." He could feel something coming: Jack had to give him a lesson. All right: it was the price of his accommodation.

"Tim goes off with another guy for a few hours, and you start playing truth games with the TTC."

"That was nothing," David said.

"Nothing?" It sounded as if Jack would let the word die in silence. "It wasn't nothing when Larry Tyler did it, let me tell you."

"Who's he?"

"A friend of Paul's and mine."

"Well, I'm sorry," he said, feeling weary and bored. He had saved himself, but he couldn't grab for others who had already leapt.

Jack moved away across the kitchen. "It's not nothing, David. Every gay man does that sooner or later."

"What do you mean?"

Jack was facing him, leaning back against the counter, holding his elbows. "Every gay man is going to be close to suicide, sooner or later." He confessed this theory angrily, miserably, looking down at the floor.

"*What?*" David said, and Jack looked up at him, eyes full of anger, or insanity.

"Christ, Jack?" David said, pleadingly. Why did he bring up these ideas. "How would you ever know?"

"I surmise, I extrapolate. I remember Larry Tyler, and others."

"But *everyone?*" He named people, to himself, since Jack didn't know them. "Duncan? Alan and Michael?" Then, "Tim?"

Jack held his hands up, as if wanting to let Tim off, but unable to do so.

"Don't be silly," David said. Then, fearfully, not quite looking at him, "You?"

"Oh, me, of course." Jack looked away.

"You've always got to have a theory, don't you? Who knows, Jack? We're both still here, aren't we? It's just your – impatience with things. And I'm certainly not doing anything like that again."

Jack looked up, his face softened and crumpled with emotions. Suddenly his eyes were angry, his voice was hard. "Face it, David, whatever else it is, it's a question of life or death. For them, for us. They know it well enough. And we come round to knowing it too, sooner or later."

Jack's eyes were full of anger and terror, looking at David and also through him to something else. David felt he was in the presence of some particular experience. Larry Tyler? No, someone closer.

"It's part of seeing this world, seeing the people who run it, deciding what you have to give them, and what you can keep, whether it's enough."

Jack said this in a low, tight voice, as if afraid others would hear, afraid he would hear too well himself. Almost forgetting what he had gone through himself, David could feel Jack's black emotion everywhere in the room.

Then Jack let go of it, with a little, bitter laugh, and David was mercifully tired again.

"Maybe you're right, Jack, maybe you're wrong, but I'm falling asleep. I'm not even sure I know what you mean, really." What happened tonight was between Tim and me. It was just a way of being miserable about it, being angry at him. I was never going to *kill*" he laughed – "poor old David: *I sort of like him.*"

"Somebody was," Jack said coldly.

David jumped. "Oh, Jack, you're crazy," he said, weakly, fearfully, trying to call back the person he wanted, the big soft young uncle who took you to the zoo. It worked: staring across the kitchen, a gray, soft, baggy runner, Jack seemed to be searching David's eyes with deep concern, looking for the opening that would let it in. David let him search for a moment, but the concern would hurt if he felt it for more than a second, and he felt sleep dropping down over his mind. He blinked and yawned.

"It's late, Jack," he said, pleadingly. "And you worry too much. I think you enjoy it. I'm sorry if I upset you. I mean, bringing all this into your house – well, you are hospitable, Jack, to put up with this." He laughed. "I'd never really do anything like that." It seemed far away now: he was home and safe, almost. He yawned again, to show how content he could be with life, if only Jack showed him to bed. "To you," he said. "Not even to Tim."

"He phoned, by the way," Jack observed.

"When?"

"Before you did."

David stared, going back, reinterpreting everything.

"*Why didn't you tell me?*"

"I wasn't sure if I should. I thought you came here to get away from all of it."

"What did he say? *How did he sound?*"

"He was worried, obviously, or he wouldn't have phoned. He said that if you got in touch, I was to phone him."

"Did you?"

"No. Not yet."

"I guess it's too late now, for tonight," David said, doubtfully, looking at his watch: it was 1:53.

"Not really."

David looked at him. "What would you do, Jack?"

Jack blinked: in fact, he squeezed his eyes shut for a moment, turning his face into a big, blind, tender mask. "I don't know, David. It's your decision."

"Do you think he's – a jerk?" It was turning into a kind of code word, as if Jack knew exactly the Tim David didn't trust.

"Only some of the time."

"I know!" David said. "That's the worst thing. Do you think we'll be lovers for a long time?"

"What do you mean by a long time?"

"Oh, years, I suppose."

"No," Jack said.

He gave Jack a murderous look that became understanding, rueful. He believed the same thing himself, or thought he did, but now it seemed unkind of Jack to say it so definitely. He didn't want to challenge Jack, in case Jack had reasons to pile on top of his own, new reasons for thinking that basically Tim and David just wouldn't work.

"All right," he said, wearily, "phone him if you must. *Please*, I mean, Jack, *for me*. And tell him not to worry. But first, could you show me to bed? I'm *tired*."

PART 8

Tim had phoned Jack only after trying David's number several times.

"By any chance, have you heard from David?" he said, angrily, as if it was Jack's fault.

"No. Sorry, Tim, no."

"I thought he might call you. He seems to think of you as an adviser on certain things. I can't get him at his place. We just had a – fight seemed too strong – "*row*" he finished irritably, realizing that that was David's word.

"Not serious, I hope?"

"Well, he gave me back his keys. And when I tried to give them back, he just stood there and let them hit him right in the face." He laughed, bitterly: "*Poor* David! Anyway, it looks as though *we're through*. Which is fine with me: right now, I am pissed off. I don't need someone like David, Jack."

"Don't you?"

"I didn't phone for advice, Jack. I just want to be sure he's all right. If he should phone later, could you tell him I called. Tell him I want to speak to him. Please." But what if David refused to call? "And, please Jack, if you hear from him, well, give me a call, okay? He was in such a state when he left here... And don't tell him I said we're through."

"Why not?"

"I wouldn't want it to be that brutal."

"All right. Of course."

Tim got into bed and turned out the lights, turning on the scenes of the evening. He remembered saying, 'Either you forgive me or you don't.' It had been cruel, perhaps, but it was logic: it was true. And David was always glad to use that sort of logic whenever it suited him. But now he was alone, alone with the rage that had told Tim to go to hell. David hadn't killed him, after all, and the only person he would ever feel really justified in attacking was himself: he would be doing it now, one way or another, Tim knew. He didn't consider the worst possible case, aware of the basic interest in life that would keep David safe through almost anything. But he could imagine the hell David would put himself through.

He phoned David's number several times, getting no answer. Just after two, his phone rang. It was Jack again.

"He's here, staying over the night," Jack said.

"Can I speak with him."

"He went to bed. He's sleeping."

"*Sleeping*!" He'd been imagining David in misery. "Where the hell was he? I kept on phoning."

"He got lost on the subway, trying to get back from your place."

"For three hours?"

"No, he phoned from the subway and said he wanted to come over here. When he did, we had a long – discussion."

"About what?" Tim demanded, defensively.

"It would be hard to sum up," Jack said, wearily.

"David can be so – " he needed a word to demolish David and protect himself from whatever they had been saying – "childish." It wasn't really enough.

"Yes, in a way," Jack said, tersely. "But anyway, if you're interested, I think you're really all right."

"Well, thank you, Jack," he said, with heavy sarcasm.

"With David, I mean. If you're interested. And he's probably a bit less 'childish' now than yesterday."

"Is he really sleeping?" Tim said. "Did you give him something?"

"No, he fell asleep right away. He was exhausted." Jack said the last word in a way which suggested how he longed to end this call.

"Sometimes I wonder if it's worth it all, Jack," Tim said.

"What?"

"All this *crap*. I like David, I love him, but why do I have to teach him about being gay? David doesn't seem to realize it, but most people just don't do things like this."

"Oh, yes they do," Jack said, angrily. "People with years of training, Tim – decades."

There was silence: they realized they were on the verge of a discussion, and they were too tired to want to start.

"Anyway," Jack said, "I think I have an inexperienced lover here for you, if you want one. I'm not sure, though: I'm not guaranteeing anything."

"Oh, God! Just tell him I'll phone in the morning. Please, Jack, and thank you for calling."

"Sure."

It sounded as if Jack was about to hang up, and Tim suddenly lost his nerve or his anger. "Are you sure he's all right, Jack?"

"Of course I am."

"Well, could I come over now? Too," he added, with a touch of sibling rivalry.

"*Now?*"

"I can't sleep, Jack, I got very nervous with David out God knows where, and – "

"Now? Oh well," Jack laughed, as if pleased with what was happening. "All right, fine," Jack said. "You've been here, haven't you – you know the back bedroom, you always see it on the way to the bathroom. I'll put a key under the mat. Because I still hope to get some sleep tonight. Please don't wake anyone, Tim, okay – please."

Pedalling or coasting down through light rain towards Jack's house, Tim felt Jack's *Now?* expanding around him in incredulous rings, as if Jack thought they were awake at some hour no one had ever waked in before. But on the bigger streets, people were still up, talking in lively voices, carrying on happy lives outside of the drama he and David had produced. He could guess from Jack's tone that David's anxiety had been noisy and intense. Yet Tim had been anxious longer, still wondering if he was making a mistake—while David slept like a log.

The house was so still he could imagine he had dreamed everything. Why was he groping in the dirt under the mat? But then the key was between his fingers. It opened the door, Tim stepped into the light of the hall, went up the stairs to the door of the back bedroom. It stuck: he gave it a quiet shove with his shoulder and opened it.

Some moonlight came through bamboo blinds. David was curled on his side on a big mattress, his wrists side by side in invisible handcuffs. There was a slight frown on his face, as if for David sleeping required concentration, like everything else. Tim thought about going back, pedalling back up the liquid, shining roads towards easier lovers. David had left room on the mattress.

PART 9

David woke from a nightmare. At first, he didn't realize he should be surprised that Tim was beside him. In the nightmare, which hadn't stopped, his father was making a scene, raging, shouting as if he wanted to destroy words, language, the world, by shouting it all to pieces. If the dream was real, Tim should have been smashed, torn to shreds, and here he was breathing, a billion operations going smoothly, layer on layer on layer, surprisingly alive. His hair was damp: David touched it and heard rain on the roof above, a light, intimate, unhurried rain reaching away into the night. A roof—Jack's roof. And it all came back. What had happened? Jack had phoned and then – was it Jack's idea for Tim to come? Anyway, it was Tim who had come: on his bike – David saw him coasting downhill to the Annex to slip himself in here, asleep and calm as if nothing had happened. As if they were roughing it, up north in a cottage, sleeping on this old mattress. Tim was showing how trusting, how simple things could be. David found Tim's hand under the sheet and pulled it up. "Are you asleep?" Of course he was, that was the point: he was saying that he didn't have to be awake. His face, his presence were enough and ended any arguments. David had agonized like a woman in labour, groaned, shed tears, called for deliverance. And the child got on his Peugeot and came gliding down from Forest Hill, unmarked, unsuffering, a well-shaped twenty-two already.

"**You shit**!" David said to his magic lover.

He remembered the things he had said on the kitchen table, he imagined throwing them at the sleeping face. Nothing he'd thought then could say what Tim was. In his dreamy turning up, Tim was as elusive as ever. He hadn't been entirely faithless yesterday: he wasn't entirely faithful now.

Tim pulled his hand away, for some venture in his dream.

PART 10

When Tim woke the room was brightly lit through the blinds. David was still curled up, handcuffed by sleep. But sleep obviously wasn't the main activity of the back bedroom. There was a ten-speed bicycle a few feet from his head, with a flat tire. Cheap metal bookshelves sagged with books. The walls were covered with tattered posters and reproductions: a Jack Bush poster, a Mapplethorpe nude, Steichen's musty skyscrapers. Tim looked at David again, and David stared at him myopically.

132

"You came back."

"Yes, I did."

David sat up quickly. So did Tim.

"Well, good morning."

"Good morning, David."

"You're *wonderful*, you know," David said, with a kind of acid rapture.

"I'm really sorry, about everything. I mean, I understand better how you feel, now, and..." Tim stopped, guiltily.

"That was a brilliant move," David said, admiringly, wistfully. "Coming here, that was magnificent. It was your idea, wasn't it, not Jack's?"

"Yes."

David put his arms around Tim's chest and pushed his face against it. They both shook as David squeezed: David must be crying, Tim thought, and tears, suddenly allowed, sprang into his eyes.

"I love you, David," he said, unexpectedly. "There's no one like you."

David mumbled something.

"What?"

David sat up and back and stared at him with dry eyes. "I said, I don't see us growing old together. Do you?"

"Well, who knows?" Tim said, embarrassed to be caught alone with his tears. "We're not growing at all, right now."

David was looking coolly at the wet cheeks. He reached out delicately to touch them, to brush tears onto his fingertips, a tribute he didn't quite believe. Tim blinked and pulled away. David's hand rose and dived into his hair. "It's dry now," he said.

Understanding, Tim stared at David, who smiled, tightening the hand a little. David hadn't been taken by surprise: he had. Above him, the long hand closed tighter, pulling out his hair.

"*Ow! David!*"

"Does that hurt?"

"*Yes.*"

"But does it hurt *enough*?" David insisted, twisting.

"*Yes! Ow! Yes it does*," Tim said, laughing in pain, reaching above himself for David's steely wrist. "Yes, *please!*"

"I-forgive-you," David said, in one fast word. He let go. "I do. Will *you* forgive *me*?"

CHAPTER V: BREAKING UP

They had had their fight, it had been terrible, and they had survived it. It gave them a new beginning, and for David at least, a mythology. His subway ride, terrible and silly, the dark house with its baleful prophet and matchmaker, Tim appearing from out of the rain, sleeping and miraculous – such things don't happen for lovers who aren't meant to last.

But more practically, David realized that most of the lasting would be up to him. He had to turn the new impetus into something enduring. He decided to treat Tim's occasional excursions with a kind of practical pity. Tim couldn't help himself: it was life, energy, masculinity brimming over. And that wasn't the real threat. The threat was someone he wouldn't meet tricking – the elusive, other Tim that David sometimes imagined as his real lover. David knew he couldn't become him, but he could figure him out, and do and say the things he would do and say. He could calm and steady himself to something like Tim's calm simplicity.

A week after their fight, Jack invited them over for dinner with Paul. Greeting them in Jack's front hall, Paul was a big surprise: a big man, to start with, with round features set on a squarish head, with deepset eyes and eyebrows that tilted down at the outsides, sorrowfully, except when his smile came and lifted everything. His manner for thresholds and front halls – or much of life, it turned out – was effusive, exclamatory. "It's *wonderful* to meet you! Jack is such a fan of yours." And behind the taciturnity David used to smuggle himself through other people's doors, he became a fan of Paul's almost at once.

Paul brought something new to Jack's house. He wasn't merely an excellent cook. He loved to feed people: he wasn't complete without something in his hand to serve you from. Food hovered over you, eager to land on your plate and be loved and eaten right up. Jack and Paul seemed very married, in spite of Charles, of whom Paul was quite fond. They saw each other several times a week: they talked and bitched and bumped into each other and shared silences like a married couple. You could see that Paul was still in love with Jack, while Jack was a fond good friend of Paul's. And at times, as if irritated by Paul's attention, Jack could become bitchy – even nasty. He brought up Paul's excursions to the bars in search of a boyfriend, which never seemed to come to anything – anxiously, wanting Paul to be happy, but with an irritated, cruel edge to his feelings too. He wouldn't mind if Paul found another Jack. By the end of the evening, full of good food and wine, David was in love with Paul. He was like a big teddy bear stuffed with anxieties: you couldn't help wanting to snatch him up and make him happy, partly perhaps because you knew he would never be quite happy enough not to need more from you. Paul was *much* nicer than Jack, who would never have said anything was (Paul had his own way of getting the best out of the word) *beautiful*. At times, when Jack was being nasty, David would be sure he was much nicer than Jack deserved.

After that dinner, David was inspired to become a cook like Paul. The colonizing of Tim's apartment, begun with books and records, continued with cookbooks and chopping knives and omelette pans, while Tim looked on with amusement. David thought of himself more and more as married, not a wife, or a husband, but committed, domestic, making himself a necessary part of someone else's life. It almost seemed time to suggest that David give up his room at the graduate residence and contribute to Tim's rent. He would ask in the fall, he thought, at the beginning of their second season. If they made it through to cooler weather, he thought, they could last for years.

At the end of August, Jack decided it was time to take his photographs and phoned Tim to arrange it. They would meet in the studio of a friend of Jack's, which he borrowed for occasions like this. The next day, after a trip to the ravine park, David went back up to the apartment while Tim biked down to the Y, to make dinner. He phoned Paul for advice about the recipe, got Jack, and surprised himself by asking if he could come to the photo session on the next day. Jack had agreed, not bothered at all. After consulting with Paul, David realized there were more things he had to buy, since he wasn't prepared to let down Paul or Julia Child with cheap substitutes. He went down to Yonge and St. Clair to get them and on his way back to the apartment, he saw Tim walking ahead of him, with wet hair shaping out his handsome skull, walking his bike. He must have a flat tire, David thought, but neither tire looked flat as he ran up beside him. He felt a bit guilty for coming to Jack's: he wouldn't if Tim didn't want him to, though he wanted to see Jack in action. Tim looked around, pleasantly startled, and explained he'd felt like walking home. He didn't want to have to think about cars. His yellow T-shirt was inside out, the seams outlining him. "And it looks funny," David said.

"Good," Tim said, and laughed.

"Jack said I could come to the photo session tomorrow."

Tim laughed. "Good. If Jack tries to rape me, you can protect me."

"That's not why!" This was unfair, really: he wasn't protective any more. "I just want to see how Jack does it."

Tim shrugged. "He focusses and presses the button, I suppose."

Tim was fascinated by photography, occasionally talked of buying a good camera. However, as a draughtsman, scornful of it, threatened by it. "The skill – and Jack is good, remember those photographs of Charles? – is hard to see."

When they got to the apartment, Tim let David open the door and went and dropped into the armchair. David stood where they might have kissed and said again, "Your shirt is inside out."

"So?" Tim gave him a foolish smile. "Maybe I feel like it."

"You sound like Duncan."

"Oh? Well, then – "

David watched him pulling it off, bare-chested, headless, then sorting out the cloth mess with a kind of happy impatience, climbing back up into it again and pushing his sleek, mysterious head through, smiling at him.

"You're going to love dinner," David said.

He did: he was ravenous. Dinner disappeared into him, down the mystery.

After clearing away dinner, David went over to Tim in the armchair and leaned down for a kiss. Tim seemed indifferent, or in a teasing mood, and turned his face away. David kissed his neck.

"I can hardly taste the chlorine tonight."

"I guess I managed to get it all off."

"I'm starting to like it, sort of: I can see you swimming."

Tim yawned: David looked down into his throat, as if the truth might be there.

"You'd think you'd swum ten miles."

"More like a *hundred*. More like a *million*."

David tried to get at Tim's mouth, and when Tim again turned away, he tried to pull his head around. Tim resisted, the resistance spread through him, through them, and they were in a wrestling match: out of the chair, rolling on the carpet. They'd wrestled before, David learning, Tim winning, but now David seemed to be struggling with something new in Tim, an inexplicable languor. David found himself winning without believing it. He was sitting in the pudding of Tim's stomach, holding back his wrists.

"I won!" he said, hoping Tim would harden under him, surge and throw him off.

"Hurray. Hurray everybody, David's won."

"Are you comfortable?"

"Sure." But he couldn't be: his head was on the wood tile of the floor. His eyes filled with languor, like footprints in soggy ground.

"Do you want a pillow?"

Tim rolled his head to say no.

"We'd better hurry, if we're going to catch that film."

"What film?"

"*The Conformist*, remember?"

Tim laughed, laughing away all the films in the world. Then he said, "Dinner was really nice, David. You're a good cook."

"I think my feminine side is coming out," David said, proudly. "My *anima*."

"Maybe we could have a big dinner," Tim said, from behind closed eyes. "I'd help. We ought to start seeing more people."

"I'll buy us an enormous pot, for spaghetti, and make a really good sauce. Italian cuisine can be very sophisticated."

"That sounds great. I'll help of course. Maybe I should buy the pot." His eyes came open and shut again like a cat's. He had forgotten they were in the middle of a battle.

"This isn't fair!" David said, suddenly.

"What isn't?"

"You didn't really fight."

"You didn't swim a million miles."

"All right, if that's how it is." David sat back, the victor. "Now what do I do?"

Tim's eyes closed and opened, seductively. "Fuck me," he said.

David laughed, right away, quickly, but it wasn't a nice joke and he didn't like it at all. He asked, being serious, "What's got into you, Tim?"

"What do you mean?"

"You're different."

"Maybe I always was," Tim said, smiling with closed eyes. "And you never knew..."

"Are you getting a cold?" David said, feeling his forehead. "That old pool must be crawling with germs."

"I don't think so, David. I'm just very tired."

"You can't sleep on the floor."

Tim said nothing, and David, still not knowing what to do, lay forward on his chest, turning his ear to hear the slow thudding of his heart, that serious swimmer.

"What's going on?" he said, from this new position.

There was no response, the heart continuing to slow.

"Are you asleep?" he said. "You can't be."

But he was. David got up off his unsatisfying conquest, and put a folded towel under his head. He found the Vitamin C, but could do nothing except take some himself. When he was through with the dishes, he looked into the living room: Tim had vanished. He was in his bed, still on his back, still asleep, as if he'd dreamt himself there.

"Tell me," David said, quietly. "You bloody well tell me." He went back to the living room and spent an hour looking through Tim's books. But paintings couldn't take him away – it had to be words: he opened a book Tim said he detested, an anthology of Ruskin on Art.

He looked up from the great Victorian half an hour later, and there was Tim at the door, with nothing on, smiling at him only a little penitently. It was as if he was saying, 'this is all the truth you are going to get.' Or, worse, 'This is all the truth you really want.'

PART 2

"Summer!" Jack Durham called down from the top of the stairs. "Summer!"

137

Elegiacally: the cool morning looked into fall like a gray window.

The studio was five flights up in an old building nearer King than Queen. Jack entertained them on the long climb up.

"Up here, summer is a rich American. He comes for a few weeks, he's blond, he's handsome, everyone starts falling in love with him, you begin to think maybe life is hot and rich and blond after all..."

Did Jack, leaning on a broom and talking foolishly, know what was happening with Tim? Surely he wouldn't be so cheerful if he did.

He ushered them in through double doors, paired in their fast breathing. The studio was well-lit and wide and bare, except for clutter along the walls, mostly stretched canvases turned away.

"I hope I won't be in the way?" David said.

"You can be wardrobe mistress," Jack said. "Of course, you don't talk, please, David. Up here at least, I do the talking, the ego is all mine."

With his hand on his upper shirt button, Tim looked to Jack, who nodded, sending fingers quickly down. Tim handed his clothes to David, who sat on a high stool clutching them, while Tim calmly braved the light of the studio. He looked around as if he didn't know he was naked, then sat on a stool just like David's to wait. Jack was fussing with cameras and lenses, suddenly professional, efficient, adult. Ready at last, he looked up at Tim with a deep scoop of looking David could never have allowed himself, at least not with anyone else around. Jack started with Tim on the stool, as if that pose was as good as any, but making adjustments. He ran forward to move Tim's foot, perched on a wooden rung. Had they had sex, David wondered, as Jack's hand touched the foot. Could Jack be the unseen lover who finally came to take Tim away? They seemed hardly to notice each other right now, but it could be the calm, unspoken understanding of married people.

"I knew it would take time," Jack said. "But now, you've been naked all your life."

He spoke in a low voice, as if the words were soothing noises rather than words.

"You're not Tim," he said, the soothing tone wrapping around Tim, the meaning of the words directed to David, to keep him occupied and under control. "You're the *human body*, now. *Now*, in the middle seventies. *And you're going to be saved.*"

As if he understood the rules, Tim seemed not to listen to Jack's desultory patter, except for requests to move, to try new poses. His mind was elsewhere, and he looked toward the camera like an animal. There were times when David was sure they were lovers, that when Jack had his pictures he would turn and claim Tim too. Then he would shift, realize he was hypnotized by Jack's words, and the spell of that belief would break.

"I knew it would take time," Jack repeated, lovingly, looking through the camera. He worked quickly and smoothly, impelled by delight and fear, as if having got his moment, he had to hurry before something broke in upon it.

"I used to be a romantic. Only a few years back, when I was coming out, with Paul, reading Marcuse and Norman O. Brown and Reich. I was very sixties, or tried to be, and I thought the body was the future. It was a whole new world opening up, my body, yours: orgasm was the only answer to the bomb. Now I know better, of course, it has no future, it's finished, or nearly. Look a bit to the left, please, Tim."

"But I'm trying to save it. Like those great photographs of Indians – I fell in love with them again, thanks to Charles. Poor body," Jack said lovingly, sadly, happily, looking into the light off Tim's. "You're so sure, so proud. You don't know you're dying. You don't know, so it's hardly real, is it?"

Jack's delight, his fear, his crazy pride were in the air; he almost looked apologetically at David sitting like the widow of a drowned man, but he didn't let their eyes engage. Jack wouldn't risk whatever he held in his eyes.

"Poor body," he said, keeping up his mood, "you don't know."

David was hypnotized, but protestingly, like someone asleep and struggling to wake. He wanted to protest on Tim's behalf against the control in Jack's voice, against the way he had tied Tim in silence to get what he wanted, the wordless, defenseless, passive 'poor body' in his mind. David sensed a veiled sadism in it.

But David didn't revolt: he could never quite find a cause. It was Jack's show, after all: his art, his painting, his writing. And Tim could take care of himself. The spell was threatened only twice. At one point, Jack had Tim sitting on the bare hardwood floor, legs crossed, leaning forward a little. David stirred, and a piece of change fell out of Tim's pants. It rolled curvingly towards its owner, hit his foot and fell spinning and shining, a fresh-minted quarter catching the light.

"Sorry." David slid off the stool to get it.

"No," Jack said. "*Stay there.*"

He took several shots and then as Tim stood for another pose, let David retrieve the quarter.

Later, Tim was standing and looking back over his shoulder and Jack's eyes were dropping into the well of his camera. A few words came out, low and fierce: German, David guessed, and German was usually a sign Jack was in a bad mood.

"*What?*" David said, startled awake.

"*The world*, David, *is the totality of facts, not of things*," Jack said. "*The world is ALL.* That is the case. Those used to be mantras of mine, when I had my affair with the early Wittgenstein. And sometimes they can still dissolve things a little for me, shake up the universe, keep it from freezing solid."

Suddenly David was sure that they weren't lovers. Tim would never let someone so complicated and sad and ponderous any nearer to his delicate skin than this. Tim's secret, whatever it was, and Jack's attempted magic, opened on totally different worlds. David shook a little, realizing this.

"I wanted poor old Ludwig to be right," Jack went on. "I wanted to believe the world can get to us clearly, completely, that it can get through to us. Like a photograph, if only photographs were what they pretend to be. Maybe it had something to do with being queer and longing to be straight – but that's what we all want, isn't it? To know the world, clear and whole."

David looked at Tim, who smiled at him for the first time. Jack was playing games with his own spell.

"But that's never how it happens is it? The poor world, it can only get to us through human beings. Through *rotten* hearts."

Tim looked at him, startled: Jack had torn it, David thought. They were all disenchanted again. But Jack just took Tim's surprise into his camera.

"Don't worry," he said. "You're safe, it's nothing, it doesn't matter."

The session took a little over an hour. Towards the end, the emotions Jack was trying to manage, to ride on, seemed to become more intense and unstable. He'd gone on for nearly an hour and no disasters had happened, nothing had broken in on his lucky time. The noise of traffic came through the window: steps came up the stairs but never as far as they were, five tall stories up. But he seemed to become discontented, jostled from within by possible miseries. It was as if he was getting tired of Tim and his body, feeling trapped inside it, wanting to break out and not knowing how.

Tim was standing facing the camera, a kouros, handsome, almost banal, perhaps.

"Point," Jack said. "At the camera, at me. Point."

Jack glowered, "There he is, yes – *accuse me!*"

Tim did, Jack took pictures, unhappily, flustered, becoming human again.

"Say something," he said, "Anything."

"What?" Tim said, his unused voice clouded, adolescent. Jack took the picture and said, "That's it. That'll do, thank God."

"We're through?"

Jack took a picture. "Yes. Thanks very much, Tim." He looked away, tired of him. "Thanks."

Infected with Jack's nervousness, David came quickly forward with the clothes.

"Aren't you cold?" He was: moving had set him shivering.

"No, it's not like drawing classes, you can move around."

He sat down at a big oak desk by the door and leaned on his arms, watching Tim descend into his corduroys, grudgingly, as if now he regretted giving him up. "That would make a nice shot," he said, enviously, mockingly. "A lover hands a lover his clothes."

Worn out by wondering what was happening, David suddenly hated his tone: it was like the exhausted, cynical end of the cruelty that flavoured everything Jack had done. Jack was being a dinosaur again.

"*You shut up!*" David said, from out of his hour of silence.

Jack bowed a little, courteously, understanding this somehow. He took a deep breath and let go of it. "Thank you for letting me have him, David." He sat back in the chair and gave them a smile so big and happy it was crass. He had got his photographs, he could grin all over his face.

PART 3

It was clearing, but still cool, as they went along Queen and up Spadina. David had suggested the restaurant where they had had lunch three months before, making up after their first botched attempt at Tim and David.

"I've come a long way since I hit you," David said, thinking that hitting him again might give the universe the shake it seemed to need.

"So have I," Tim said.

"How do you mean?" David said.

"You're exciting to live with, David. You're like Jack." Tim was still quiet, partly hypnotized: he still shone, from the gleam of Jack's lenses, from whatever was happening.

"What was it like?" David said, politely. "I couldn't imagine what you were thinking."

"Nothing, really."

"You can't think nothing."

"I just let my mind drift."

"Did you listen to what Jack was saying?"

"I've heard him talking like that before, at the bar. Sometimes it can be interesting, but mainly it's only Jack. The only difference this time was that he was sober."

He laughed, invulnerably. "Most gays, when they start getting a bit older, worry about it. It's only natural. But Jack has got to go and produce a whole theory about it: it's the world that's getting old. And he's got to be the prophet, the only one who notices.

"That's a bit unkind, isn't it? If he becomes a famous photographer, he'll have made you immortal."

"That would be nice. But he won't. I don't think that was anything more than Jack's way of going to bed with me. He's really too shy to do it any other way with someone like me. Plus, he's really in love with Charles, and faithful to him, too."

"What would happen if he did want to go to bed with you?" It was clear enough from Tim's tone – 'someone like me' – that this hadn't happened, yet.

Tim pouted thoughtfully. "It's hard to imagine him trying. Under it all, Jack's a sweetheart. You'd want to give him what he wanted, but it might be a disaster, too."

"How?"

Tim moved with cool distaste: not condescending to shudder, but going through the motions of shuddering.

"He might get too emotional. You know, he might fall in love or something."

David looked at him and laughed out loud. "I can't believe it! *He might fall in love.* You're such a fucking prima donna!"

"Well, it happens. Scott's old friend Terry had this – "

141

"Oh, I don't want to hear about it. Poor Jack. Jack may be crazy but he's human."

"Well, so am I."

"Not when you're being a duchess."

The restaurant was crowded, they got the last table, stuck in a corner of metal fence. David was afraid to talk. It was Tim who started again, looking at him with an odd, appraising frankness and saying, "Did you think I might have been in bed with Jack?"

"At times, it seemed so intimate, the way he talked, like you'd been together for years, but – "

"You were right, you know," Tim said abruptly, looking away. "Barry is gay. Bisexual, anyway."

He went on eating, as if this was all David needed.

"So?" David said, when he had caught his breath.

"What do you mean?"

"What happened?"

Tim gave the one-shoulder shrug again. "Nothing earth shaking," he said, his voice getting husky, caressing its throat. He looked quickly right into David's eyes.

"Did you go home with him?"

Tim grinned. "He was in an awful hurry."

"*You fool*. You could get caught."

"I wasn't."

"Will it be happening again?"

"Don't worry, David. Barry says he doesn't want to get hooked on me. Jesus!" He laughed freely, then subsided into smiling.

Suddenly, he yawned.

"Excuse me, I didn't get much sleep last night."

"You slept like a log."

"No, David, you did."

"*What the hell is going on?*"

This made people turn and look. Tim glared at him guiltily, angrily. "We can talk about it *later*."

But after lunch, out on Spadina Avenue, Tim said, suddenly seductive and randy, "Let's go up to your place."

"Why?"

"Why? It's close. Look, there's the bus." It was swooping heavily out of traffic to its stop, and Tim ran for it. For a split-second, David thought of letting him run off forever, then followed him. On the bus they had to stand, thrown against each other without comment. Tim was inscrutable, a body you bumped against on the bus. They got off at Bloor and started walking the two blocks east to David's building. "Do you want to have sex?" David said, coolly.

"Of course!" Tim said, gallantly. "It's what lovers are for, isn't it?"

"I guess so," David said.

He kept silent, till they were almost at the gateway, then he had to speak. "Let's not go in just now," he said. "Let's go around the block."

He just walked on, pulling Tim after him. They went silently, turning south, past Varsity Stadium. David cleared his throat and got himself speaking.

"I think – I think you just want to be able to say good-bye nicely. That's what you're up to, isn't it?" What if this wasn't true, he thought, he could be destroying his own happiness – but it was true: he could see it in Tim's surprise. "Sex like a handshake, and 'So long David' from six inches away, where you know I can't argue?"

"No!"

"I'm not stupid," David said, looking at the buildings of Trinity College, where Tim had been an undergraduate and a lot nicer, probably.

David," Tim said, fondly, and upset, and a little grateful too. "You've always got to *say* things, don't you? You can't let anything just go by."

"What do you mean?"

"I wasn't going to do anything today."

"Tomorrow? The day after? How long were you going to give me?"

"As long as you needed."

"You bastard. Because you really are. As long as I needed. You've been acting like a shit since yesterday."

Tim was trying to smile, weakly, foolishly, and it reminded him of Tim on his back on the hard floor, smiling up at him.

"*Do you want to fuck me?*" David said. The words came out almost before he thought them: he was guessing, but not able to believe in the guess.

Tim was too surprised to speak. And so was David for a moment: the wild, hysterical words had seized what he'd been groping for since yesterday.

"Well, do you?" he said, shakily, almost giggling.

"You know you don't even like to be touched there," Tim said.

David shrugged miserably.

"Do you want me to?" Tim said, intrigued for a moment, with an indefinable mixture of concern for David and desire that had nothing to do with him.

"How would I know? How the fuck would I know?" A couple of new students, actually wearing jackets and ties, looked at them curiously. "I suppose I could learn."

Tim laughed. "Last week you said you were going to learn *Sanskrit*."

"What does that mean?"

"You're a real hero, David, but it's obvious it wouldn't work."

Now Tim seemed relieved, almost glad under his concern for David's feelings. He was getting free more easily than he had expected: David had done most of the work. "You don't want me to, and, well, I just don't see you *that way*, David."

"What way?"

Tim shrugged, and didn't explain. They were going past the orange walls of Massey

College now, with fewer students passing them.

"Suddenly I'm a virgin again," David said, bitterly. "They keep inventing new things, new barriers."

"David." David heard the name of the intelligent friend he'd been before, and was doomed to become again, it seemed. "David, you knew it wouldn't last forever."

"I didn't *know* it."

Tim looked as if he might not say it and then he did. "But you did. And you'll understand some day."

"What will I understand?"

"Well, Mark Storrow was right."

"What did he have to say?"

"Fucking is sex, David. Fucking is all there is." Tim lowered his voice to protect more new innocent, undergraduates, but there was a soft, fierce exultancy in it. David looked at his profile in fear and rage. He decided he'd never liked what he thought of as Tim's masculine side: now he saw it was just coldhearted pride and lust.   "So what were we doing?"

"That's for kids, really."

"This really is disgusting," David said.

"No," Tim said firmly. "It isn't."

"I mean, discussing it like this. It's revolting."

"Try it," Tim said, flatly.

"I could just as soon fly."

"Jesus, David, you've always got to fight being happy, don't you?"

"What is all this Jesus stuff, anyway?" David said, hearing something odd in the word. "In Oak Bay, they would say it was a bit Irish – oh my God!" David saw a shower room at the Y. "That's Barry, isn't it, he says it, J – " He saw Tim's eyes going wide, and felt suddenly weak. "Oh, shit, Tim, you shit! And last night you went down to the park, didn't you? Don't you know the police could get you? Well, I hope they do."

"David, shut up." Tim was angry at last. "Just shut up. I can do what I like: I always said that. So just shut up about it."

They turned north and headed back towards the residence corner. The long block along St. George gave them some time to quiet down, but it seemed obvious they would have to separate at the corner. Tim wouldn't want to come into the little room: David didn't want him there. Halfway up the street, David said, prophetically, "Your lovers will never be able to tell you what a shit you are, Tim."

Tim said nothing.

"Not because you're so handsome. Because you're too stupid to hear."

If it was a curse, it didn't seem to take. Tim said nothing, probably all he heard was the longing: 'You're so handsome.'

"I'm sorry, David," Tim said, after this had died away. "Really sorry."

It wasn't enough. Tim's face hadn't been designed to look sorry.

"I always knew you would be. I knew exactly how sorry you'd be: *exactly this much*." He looked around at the busy corner. He looked at Tim. It was quite an ordinary scene.

"Let's say goodbye now. You can go across to the subway." He held out his hand, which Tim took.

"Are you okay?" he said, weakly.

"Oh, I'll survive," David said. "I'll survive, like some good little beaver who's read his Margaret Atwood."

"Well, phone me, all right. And I'll be phoning, too."

Too long together for a Toronto street corner, the hands fell apart.

"Well," David said, sarcastically, "I guess we've done it. We've broken up."

It was meant to be brave and philosophical, bitterly wise, but it came out as a question. Some slow, stupid part of him hadn't caught on yet: perhaps it was still possible Tim would say, 'Come on up to my place. You can sleep over.'

Tim's look showed that he understood this, too. Why couldn't he be stupid all the time?

"We're still *friends*, David," Tim said, firmly.

PART 4

The day before, Barry had been in the water when Tim came out by the pool. Tim had dived in to swim alongside him, the imaginary swimmer who existed only in the rocking blue water. After swimming, they exercised side by side. Barry talked about a new girlfriend, encouraging Tim, an honorary heterosexual, to imagine her. On their way to the showers, he sketched her "great tits" with big, cupping hands. Tim could imagine them, those generous breasts. He was getting a hard-on. Barry pointed at it, laughing out loud – there was no one else around. His cock was taking an interest too, peering out like a bleary old hound. Tim said, embarrassed, "everyone is a little bisexual."

"Little?" said Barry. He took a fast shower, then snatched his things and left.

Tim closed his eyes, and let the water pour on him for a minute or two of rest, almost asleep in the rush of the water. Out of nowhere, a slippery hand closed around his prick: Tim opened his eyes, ready to fend off a wrinkled dog-paddler: it had happened before.

"I checked," Barry said, breathing fast, grinning. "*No one!*"

Tim was terrified, breathless, understanding all at once.

"*Hey, stud,*" Barry said in his ear, "*fuck me.*"

"*Yes,*" Tim declared, at once, out loud, to the world. It was as if he had wakened in a burning building.

Barry turned away against the wall, pulling him after with his soapy hand. For a moment, Tim despaired: he looked around, almost hearing someone coming. He was just about to pull away when all at once Barry got him where he wanted him. Where it seemed he'd always wanted to be.

"Yes," Tim said, now to himself, looking around inside Barry in wary, wondering ecstasy. Under him Barry was moaning a cradle song:

"Jesus, fuck me, Tim, that's it, Jesus, Tim, *deeper –* " He listened to his name driven up through Barry by his triumphant prick and for the first time in his life it sounded unchallengeably male, calling to a sweet rage of pride in the core of his heart. He looked down over Barry's big, friendly body and saw it was all his, he owned it everywhere. He lunged forward onto the wide back and began kissing the roll of muscle along behind the shoulders as if kissing was talking with it. He tried to tell himself he didn't want what was coming, not yet: he would be happy to stay arriving here forever. With one strong arm Barry pulled him deeper, and he was gone, headlong.

He'd fallen on living, breathing ground and kissed it gratefully. He looked at the wet tiles of the wall, putting together his idea of a wall, of a room. Of the new world he'd come through to.

"*Beautiful,*" Barry said, straightening, pushing Tim up and out. Tim shuddered, his legs as uncertain as a calf's, feeling out the new ground coming up through them.

"Sorry, but around here you sure can't take your time."

Tim searched inside himself for a voice.

"But, Jesus, *you're phenomenal, man!*" Barry was grinning, the same as ever.

Tim nodded and smiled a little, stepping back into the screen of water.

"Boy did I need that!" Barry said, stretching exultantly.

"So did I," Tim said, finding a voice that said he did this all the time.

"But it's just the once, okay?" Barry was apologetic. "I can't afford to get hooked on a guy, not now, not with all my obligations. But if I were going to, Tim – "

"Sure, Barry," Tim said, comfortably, not surprised at anything. Everything had happened with a deep, sweet sureness: it would all go on safely without Barry. "Thanks," he said, regally.

"Thank *you.*" Barry was leaving again. He raised his hand and crossed his lips with his forefinger in a prim, magic gesture Tim hadn't seen for years.

Alone, he went on showering, feeling out his new estate. An obscure, unfelt distaste he hadn't wanted to understand or defy had kept him from this for years. Now he calculated the time he had lost as if every day mattered, but too deeply contented to feel any regret. He imagined David, fussing in the kitchen, dusting himself and his cookbook with flour, chopping onions with grim, averted eyes. David was suddenly dwarfed, trapped in the small, lost circle of himself, his strange ideas, his fussiness, his snobbery. It seemed as if he had been given new eyes, as if he could see that David was part of the past.

He couldn't imagine telling David about this; at least, he didn't want to. It would be nice to talk with someone, to boast, to compare. He thought of Jack, remembering that tomorrow Jack was, at last, going to take his photographs. Tim laughed out loud: Jack had been getting to know him for months, and now someone he didn't know at all was heading for the studio. He could have all the photographs he wanted, but now Jack was part of the past too. Now he realized he didn't belong to the world of the talkers, Jack and David, but with Mark and Brian and Barry, the people who knew how to take their pleasure without thinking. He could belong to them: he did, he had all along, without knowing it. Barry called him a stud, and he was – why shouldn't he be? He could go fuck the world: he could hear it under him saying, praying, 'yes, Tim, yes.'

Tim's intoxication, his stupidity, was clear-eyed, poised, delicate. Three middle-aged men came along the corridor, on their way to the next shower room: they could just as easily have come in five minutes earlier, but Tim didn't feel afraid. A loving fate deep inside him had kept him safe, and watched over him now. On his way out of the shower he turned to look back a moment. There were two empty cones of air and water standing where he and Barry had showered, like auras of desire. It had all happened as it was meant to happen.

In his wire basket he found David's dark-blue Speedo, left behind from the day he had first come, not sure he could swim without it. Tim laughed, crushing the slippery nylon in his hand, seeing David's hard, nervous, utilitarian buttocks. Tim couldn't imagine sharing what he felt now with David: if he did, David, or something in David, would try to spoil it. Would try to hit him again, though he knew enough now to be safe from it. David would have to learn about these things for himself, or else stay where he was now, a good boy forever: Tim couldn't help him. He would be nice to David, he would let him detach himself slowly, give him all the time he needed, whole weeks if necessary. He wouldn't tell him what had happened, unless he was forced to. He would just say that it was time to move on. He would do it as gently as he could: he wouldn't be any more selfish than he had to be.

But if David made him, he would tell him everything, and he would be safe and right. Whatever hysterical objections David made, whatever pain or guilt or anger he tried to use against him, the new truth of fucking would sweep everything away. In comparison with what he held inside himself, no suffering could really be serious.

PART 5

On the subway home, Tim felt miserably angry. David had seen what was coming and made it his own. He'd taken all the emotions, leaving Tim to feel nothing. To be heartless, inhuman. There'd been no need for an angry break, except that David needed one for his own wretched purposes. Tim could see him, chopping onions, bravely, tearfully, insisting 'They've got to be fine, they've got to be *minced*.' No doubt he was doing that to himself now, and to Tim. Tim moved angrily in his seat, as if bits of meanness had got stuck all over him. That, he thought, was how David wanted him to feel.

But if he was wretched now, at least he knew how to be happy, unlike David. There were times, he knew, remembering the couple he'd met in the ravine park, when you had what you wanted, when all you could want more was for it not to stop. David made everything difficult, but life didn't work that way, Tim thought, glaring at a small, pinstriped man with an attache case on his knees. You couldn't have anything, unless you took it. You couldn't feel anything, unless you felt all the strength of your desire in taking it, holding it.

But really, he thought, it wasn't just David. It was this city, this country, the little man in pinstripes. With his dour colonial Britishness, David was really more Torontonian, more Canadian, than he was. He had to get out, at least for a while. Suddenly he saw the misty towers in the Steichen poster and hungered for them as if he could taste the mist. Where had he seen them? In Jack's back bedroom, as if they'd been put there to remind him. He hadn't been to New York since a visit with his family when he was sixteen, and he didn't know anyone there well enough to invite himself to stay. He remembered talking at a party with someone who'd stayed at one of the Y's there. He'd tried to sleep while people in the next room argued about a TV they'd stolen, then wakened with a cockroach running over his face. Tim had cringed, but now the story put him in the teeming night of a big city, as if he had just arrived there. In the morning he would get up and go to the galleries and museums, as he had long ago with his mother. It would be a little magical: just walking as you walk down to Bloor Street, but walking to Matisses, walking to Vermeers. In the evening he would go down to the Village. "I met this Puerto Rican in the Village," the acquaintance at the party had said, smiling. "Luis. He couldn't really talk English, but it would only have got in the way. About three in the morning, that's not late there...it's never late there."

Tim stayed home for the rest of the day, too cramped with the meanness David had imposed on him to want to go out. The next day was cold and dull, and he felt unable to decide anything. He went swimming in the afternoon, hoping to see Barry, to talk with him, although he didn't know what he would say. Through the water he saw a distant shape that might be Barry, and began imagining himself confessing to the virginity he'd concealed, suddenly longing to do it, as if the lie of not telling him was what made him into the cold-hearted sodomite David claimed to see. It was as if he had to tell him to get his emotions back. But that was absurd: Barry would just laugh and welcome him to the club. He realized now that one reason he'd left David sleeping and gone to the park was to get free from Barry, to keep himself from getting hooked on a big, friendly clown all dressed up in muscles.

The form he'd seen came closer, the shifting water washed away Barry's shape, leaving someone quite different. He went to a bar that night, looking around, thinking, *all right, I could desire you, but I don't, do I?*, and coming home alone. Next morning, the sun was back and he tried to phone for a ticket to New York and got a reel of tape. Luis, he said to himself, as if he heard it spoken in the night air of a huge city, hissing and sweet and brown-skinned: Luis. After a while he hung up and looked out over the treetops. He didn't want to abandon this summer: he wanted to be with it to the end, which might even be today.

He bicycled down into the ravine, and sat looking at the others there, as if with one or other of them he might preserve the summer they'd been soaking up. He couldn't want any of them and lay back with his shirt over his face, trying to be happy with a skull full of sunlight. The distant roar of the city was heard from the level of the ground and he relished his own familiar smells, sharp and sweet.

He was sitting up about an hour later, when his next lover appeared, running fast. He was at some distance, on the other side of the ravine and except for his brown hair and red shorts he seemed to be snow-white. Tim sat higher to take in his striking white, his fierce energy in the drugged afternoon. The runner seemed to look back at him. The meeting of eyes, with the runner's look seeming to pierce the distance, was probably imaginary, he knew, but it sent him the excitement of running, as if he was running too, on lungs like wings. The runner went into the trees where the path began up the hill, and it looked as though he meant to go up the long hill full tilt. Tim gulped, taking in his disappearance like the effort and pain of running, pain it was a pleasure to breathe in and fight through. He imagined chasing him, running till they both had had enough, and then – male desire, David, hard male lust – grabbing for the shorts.

Several minutes later there was someone coming through the nearby trees, leaf-shadow sliding back over pale shoulders, falling away from a young man in red shorts. He had come across the ravine and the stream: one shoe and sock were wet. He stopped and leaned forward a little, getting his breathing back down to earth, and giving coltish, restorative shakes to his legs. His hair was dark-brown with orange in it, with marmalade edges in the sunshine. He came as a kind of pale and hot-pink scandal among the tanners. They had all their hoarded golds and browns, and he stepped blithely out as if to say, 'Remember skin?' He glanced up from getting his breath, caught Tim's looking effortlessly, and grinned. Tim was stricken shy and looked away.

The runner dropped on the grass a few yards away and began stretching exercises. Tim watched, afraid of how he desired him. He had an angular face, with a smile more on one side than the other not handsome, exactly, but open and winning. Tim watched the muscular exercises, and took in the smaller, softer movement inside them, the bodily inflections that took you inward, into his relations with himself. Tim was still paralyzed, as if desire had begun by gulping down his spine. He realized that Barry and the couple in the bushes had left him ignorant, helpless as a girl. He was like a kid again: he didn't know how to be in love with the desire he felt now. He didn't know how to fuck and be in love.

The runner, the athlete, shoved all fingers back through the orange-brown hair, his work-out finished.

"I just quit my job," he said, as if he was too delighted to keep it in. "I don't need the pressure. I told them to shove it and went for a run." He pushed the heels of his hands into his cheeks and eyes, grinning blindly, and Tim realized he could speak after all.

"So now you're free?"

The runner dropped his hands, rubbing them eagerly in the grass beside his thighs, and smiled right at him. Tim saw it was the smaller, reticent, inward side of the grin a lover would look to.

"You've got it: *now I'm free!*" His name was Will.

Through a day of grieving and anger, David realized that he had to get out of Raskolnikov's room, and thought of Jack Durham as he had at the Greenwood stop. He wanted to get away from his room and his life, to spend time morosely in Jack's dingy, intelligent shadow.

"It turns out I'm a virgin again, Jack," he said, wildly, leaving Jack to wonder what that meant.

"Great, you'll be company," Jack said. He was going to be at work that afternoon, but there was a key inside a stack of flowerpots at the back door, for emergencies. David arrived in a taxi with a suitcase and two shopping bags of books and records. He wrenched apart the pots and let himself in with the dirty key. He poured a glass of grapefruit juice and sat down at the kitchen table to drink it. The house breathed around him, patient, thoughtful: he wasn't much of an emergency.

When he appeared, just before dinner, Jack was tactful, even delicate. He didn't draw moral conclusions or give advice. He was in mourning too. "Charles left last week for the west," he announced downward. "Taking *Biography of a Grizzly*, which is fine, I gave it to him, and his body. To Calgary. Calgary! He'll be all right, I guess. He's staying with friends."

They made each other meals and washed the dishes together. Paul Murchison was often over, and once they went to his apartment, where he showed slides from a recent trip to California. David slept in the back room, scarcely noticing Jack's desultory sex life, creaking up the stairs, splashing in the bathroom. He wasn't disappointed that Jack's mourning wasn't celibate like his. At first he was afraid he'd be like Charles's sexless ghost in the lonely house. He didn't mind being the faithful, the inconsolable one. He wanted to live very little, like lichen on a cliff. He listened to Bruckner and Mahler and Billie Holiday. He found a bulging, water-stained paperback of *Gone With the Wind* on the floor of the closet in his room. It was more a cabbage than a book, and David began slumming his way through it, pages dropping away as he went. There was a vacuum cleaner in the closet, too. He set out to clean the house. A large gray ball behind the sofa in the living room opened to reveal of pair of Jockey shorts, which he gave to Jack in the kitchen.

"Charles never wore underwear," Jack said. "As you may have noticed. Besides, these are size 34. Who knows? Who knows?" He tossed them at the kitchen garbage and missed: David put them in. "The cock is a lonely hunter, David," Jack said, apologetically.

David surrounded himself with paper and wrote poems, thrusting them now at Jack.

Politely, Jack perused his offerings.

Inside you are naked.
You are infinite layers,
invisibly dark red,
and I know each.
To me your heart in its black river
is bare as an eye or a knife.
But you seem to forget at times how close we are.

"Dear me," Jack said, mildly.

For several days, David thought of writing *Life With Two Hearts*, a novel probably longer than *Gone With the Wind*, multifoliate, labyrinthine, would-be infinite. Someone was in love with a handsome blond and following him through a huge city, endlessly: in the meantime, instructive adventures would happen to him.

"What city?" Jack said.

"It doesn't matter. Any city. A city big enough for anything to happen."

"Give us a clue. Cleveland, Venice?"

David hadn't been to either. "*Any* city, *all* cities."

Life With Two Hearts was quite real for about a week: David emanated it darkly, wore it like a mantle, chewed its edges nervously. Then it faded.

"Who wants to read a whole novel about love?" he said. "Love is boring. It's *pastoral.*"

After a week, he got Jack to show him the photographs of Tim. He was afraid of seeing – he had to see – the voiceless, dying body Jack prophesied. In the first print Jack handed to him, Tim was sitting in a chair and looking at them. At him. It wasn't the poor body at all: it was Tim. Tim at home to you in his body. The light was natural and the colours softened. So was his nudity, with Tim expecting a meeting.

"That's because we know him," Jack said.

"*Do we?*" David said.

He was afraid to stay too long with any one photograph, with Tim seen whole and clear. He lingered over the ones with his small contribution, the shiny quarter. He thought he could see that it showed its antlered, not its crowned side. So it would say, if you could read it, 1974.

He gave them back to Jack and began talking about Tim, all the thinking that had been going through his head. Jack's intelligence brought out his.

"I think the thing is, Jack, he's somehow never been allowed to realize how complex he is. He's complicated, you know that as well as I do. He is. He's got that fascinating visual side and he's really intelligent, as well as perceptive. He's really got an inquiring mind: he's interested in anything that comes up. As well, he's emotionally very aware. It would take my breath away at times. He can be as sweet and kind as a girl – only that's only possible because he's a boy, a man. It would knock me out. I mean, I could never do it. I'm just not good at being nice. And you know I'm not imagining it, Jack:

it's not *just* that I'm in love with him, I'm clear about that."

"He's nice, all right," Jack said, with only a touch of irony, not enough to take the wind from David's sails.

"So what I'm saying is there's all of that, but it has to be sort of unreal. He isn't really allowed to think it's real. He's trained to be sort of deaf to it. I think it's something in his family, his mother, his father, perhaps, the whole family tradition. His family is part of a bigger family, they have an idea of how families should be. It was new to me, because my mother and father and I, we're just we three against the world. There's no one else like us; we're like a family of only children. Anyway, all this brainwashing has descended on him from somewhere, I don't know where, but he's deluded into thinking he's a straight Anglo-Canadian who happens to be gay. You'd think that being gay would shake him up a bit, make him think. Somehow, here in Toronto, you think you can be gay without complications, be simple and straightforward like everyone else. Like a straight, you never have to leave Forest Hill."

"You're right," Jack said: "he isn't *declasse* the way we are, Paul and I and you. Or he hasn't realized he is."

"That's a good way of putting it," David said, thoughtfully. It was strange to have Jack simply agreeing with you, but David was grateful, because he saw he was heading towards a crisis. Jack still didn't know how they had broken up, and David had to tell him.

"And then there's his work, his painting. He wants to be a painter, an artist. Before I started reading his books and talking with you and him, I used to think that painters were like writers, all strange and twisty and a lot of them queer, if only you really knew. But it turns out that, until Pop Art at least, it wasn't true. It's very physical and there's this awful machismo to it. They're all jocks, having bullfights with the canvas. And I'm sure that's hanging over him, too, Jackson Pollock in the Cedar Tavern, or Jack Bush saying, 'I can try to be as great as Matisse: he won't mind. I can knock the ball right out of the park.' We had a big discussion about what that means – as if it mattered a damn."

"Shit, Jack," he said, almost running out, then seeing there was more. "I want to write him a letter and say, 'Tim Grey, you're complicated, the world is complicated, and you're smart enough to be alive to it instead of – ' But of course I won't, he'd think I was crazy. No, he'd think I was just being David."

"But it's tragic, Jack," David laughed after stating this, but it was true. "There's whole sides to him that could just be lost, lost."

He looked at Jack and then away, because he'd squirmed long enough. It had to be dealt with – how they'd broken up. Yet, he couldn't bear to tell Jack in so many words.

"So now there's this whole fucking business," he said, as if Jack knew everything about it, and giving him a miserable look imploring him to act as if he did. Jack just blinked, mercifully. "And it's just grotesque! I mean, Jack, give us a break, eh? Now he's off to do revolting things to twits like Barry and really he's doing it all for his dumb, straight-male, Anglo-Saxon Toronto super-ego. He's doing what he thinks his father and Jackson Pollock and all the Greys before him want him to be doing – sort of. It is so *stupid*!"

Tears were coming into his eyes, into his analysis, but he couldn't help it.

"I mean, I may not have been the best lover for him in the world, but at least I'm not stupid. I brought out the other parts of him, and he needs someone like me. Not like me, maybe, but not Duncan, for Christ sake, or Barry. There's this whole Tim that could just be *lost*."

"Damn it all," he said, wiping away tears.

"But he's young, David," Jack said.

"That's no excuse," David said, hotly. "He's not that young."

"No, I mean, he's still got lots of time. You both do."

David looked at Jack, wondering what he was getting at.

"To grow up some more, I mean."

That evening he phoned Tim, but didn't get an answer. He went to a bar which Tim didn't like and went home with a black-haired man of twenty-five. Afterwards he said to Jack, "It went all right. Smoothly. He was nice. I didn't tell him and he didn't guess."

"Guess what?"

"That he was only my second."

"I suppose," David added, "*in a way, he was my first*."

Jack was meant to agree with this gloomy insight. Instead he turned into the Jack who wanted to find a boyfriend for Paul, for everyone. "He was nice? Do you think my aunt would have approved of him?"

"Maybe, Jack, but *who gives a shit about your aunt?*"

"Well, I do. For one thing, *she paid for this place.*"

This sank in for a few moments. It looked like a chance to get away from Jack's clumsy matchmaking.

"Oh? I thought she was fictitious."

"Only some of the time. And really she was a kind of cousin, Edith, an old maiden lady. I don't know why she left me some of her money. No one does. She must have known I was gay when she made the will. And she was from the Anglican side of the family. A pillar of the church."

Jack looked around at his newly-tidy living room.

"Did she just take a fancy to me? Did she really not give a damn about the church? She went twice on Sundays, and during the week too. I don't know. She was strange, old-maidenly, unworldly without enjoying it much. Who wants to be a pillar? It was as if she'd just given in, collapsed upwards, like umbrellas. I really liked her, when I was little, though. She was someone to sit with quietly, when you were in that mood."

"*Maybe* – " David began shrewdly.

"That's what Paul thinks too. This is her coming out, in other words, this scatty household. I'd like to think so: I could feel I deserved it. But anyway, are you seeing this guy again? I'm sure Edith would want you to be happy, David."

David pouted, as if he didn't know.

A few days later they went to another bar, where they stood looking over each other's shoulder like horses, shouting conversation.

"Isn't he gorgeous?" David said.

Tall, handsome, declaratively alone, smiling to himself. Jack and David were quite safe: trying to get his attention would be like scaling a skyscraper.

"Where? Oh! Yes. *But why are his clothes on?*"

They cumbered each other with self-consciousness, and in the end, rather drunk, shared a cab home. Jack was thoughtful, brooding.

At a stoplight, he asked, "Did I ever tell you why I got married?"

"No, not really."

The taxi started again, going around the curve of Queen's Park.

"It was because of Danny. Something that happened. Nothing dramatic, except to me. He came over to my apartment one day and said he wanted to go for a ride somewhere. It turned out he'd just had a fight with his girlfriend, something about 'putting out'. He was restless, so restless we ended up driving out onto the prairie. In his big old dark-green car, wallowing down in its springs, on gravel back roads. He was going fast, too fast, and his mood upset me too. I wanted to stop and relax, get out under the sky. He'd say, 'No, John, this is a *ride*, we're going for a *ride*.' Or, making fun of me, 'Do you want to look at the *crops*?' As if I was a stupid old farmer, you see. 'Don't worry, the *crops* are fine.'"

Now they were speeding by Trinity, past Massey College. It had been ten days since the break-up: David wondered what would have happened if he had been able to keep his mouth shut. He and Tim might still be together, somehow, good for weeks, months, lifetimes.

"I kept at it, joking too. When we got out of Winnipeg, people would ask us about it, wouldn't they, that famous, breathtaking prairie sky. Actually nobody ever has. But we ought to get out and take a look, I said, while we had the chance, and think of what we'd say. Danny only went faster, almost slithering off the gravel at times. 'Don't *nag*,' he said. Which, now that I think of it, rhymes with '*fag*'.

"I stopped asking, but then a tire went, we slid around, but he kept us out of the ditch. It turned out I was the one who knew about changing tires, and then I stood resting and looking around. I'd earned it, and Danny seemed to have calmed down. We were in a sea of wheat or barley or whatever: crops. Off in the distance was the only one I could be sure of, mustard. The air was full of all sorts of sweet smells, saturated. And there was the sky all right, huge and at the same time close, right there at your elbow, friendly. Danny was leaning against the car with his legs crossed like a dark James Dean. I said, 'Isn't it great?' I thought he'd be impressed too, he'd have to be, though he didn't say anything. I said, 'Isn't it just *beautiful*!' Then I knew I'd ruined it. I'd gushed and ruined it all. He looked scornfully away at the horizon with a squint, a stage squint, and I could feel a lot of irony about to hit, and he said in a corny, bitter accent, Yiddish and Nazi mixed, "Beautiful? Yes, beautiful *tank country*!"

"I don't know why that was it: it was a question of timing. I saw then that I'd never get what I wanted from Danny, whatever that was, and that I ought to make an honest man of myself. I was desperate, David, I had to do something big and decisive, and marriage is like that: so big you think you'll be different after. At least, it was then."

Jack was silent, astir with memories which he kept to himself, as they drove up into the Annex to the house. On the porch, Jack said, while fumbling at the lock, "We'll never be lovers, David."

"I guess not," David said, startled. They had certainly failed tonight.

"Of each other, I mean," Jack added, pushing the door open. He went in and through to the kitchen, David following, wondering what Jack meant, aware more than usual of Jack's big, bearish body, his strong, hairy arms. For a minute or two it seemed to David there was enough drunken clumsiness in the room to blunder dozens of lonely souls into each other's embrace.

"Would you like some milk?" Jack said.

"Good idea." David sat down to have it poured. The glass Jack handed him spilled a little between their hands.

"When I say we'll never be lovers, what I really mean is, where the hell is Charles?" He drank off some of his milk sadly. "I phoned Calgary, he's doing fine, he may even get a job. But – " he said this to the walls, to the house, to Cousin Edith, perhaps, "I miss him!"

"I know," David said. "I know."

Jack sat down, facing him across the table.

"I know that I told you about his background, but did I ever tell you how I met him?"

"At your bar?"

"Yes, except it isn't my bar, David." Jack laughed. "And it wasn't the usual bar meeting. It was last winter. I used to see this odd guy in there a lot: he was a regular. Not odd, really, to look at: short, fortyish, balding, moustache, handsome in his way. A good-looking little man, but he had that peevish look a lot of gay men get. If gay lib doesn't end that look, I won't be impressed. Anyway, he would often have some young guy, talking a lot, entertaining him, teasing him. The man's voice carried, as if he had voice training: but it was an unreal voice, as if the real one had been cut out of his throat a long time ago. It bothered me, somehow: it set my teeth on edge, it depressed me. It gave me the same feeling as those books I used to torture myself with, by Nazi Park Avenue Freudians, about injustice collectors, gays as sadists or masochists or both."

"Anyway, in early spring, he was with an Indian kid, Charles, of course, who else? I was at a distance, but the word 'brown' seemed to keep coming up. He was teasing Charles about being Indian, and the way he said 'brown' reminded you shit is brown, too. When he bought Charles some beer, he seemed to be suggesting that, being Indian, he should be careful because he was bound to wind up an alcoholic. I was in a bad mood anyway, thinking about my life, and where it was going – why was I wasting it running a store, taking a few photographs, boring people in bars with theories? Perhaps I was like everyone else there, I thought, doomed to drink themselves into old age, waiting. I went to the washroom, and as I came out, they were close to the door, in the back, near the door. The man—at least six inches shorter than Charles by the way, and me had him against the wall, and he was sort of grabbing at him. Saying, 'Come on, be nice, give us some of that brown skin.' I couldn't bear it. Charles was fending off the hands good-humouredly, but they kept coming back. Charles could have pushed him away – he could have thrown him across the room – but he was too nice. The man had bought him beer and been good to him in his way. Even the brown jokes were 'just kidding,' he said later. Charles really needed lessons on how to be mean, but I never knew where to begin.

To protect myself, really, not Charles, I said, 'Get your hands off him!' He didn't quite hear, and I said it again, louder. He pulled himself up and said, 'I don't think we need your advice. Do we, Mr. Crowchild?' It was awful: I was suddenly aware that I was a physical threat to him, and at the same time that note of nastiness in his voice hit me, or the whining underneath it like some little biting animal, a rat who could sneak in a nasty bite before you smash it. I was going to say something reasonable, this kid really didn't seem to want him. But I had to end it all at once and I just said, '*Get the hell out of h–h–h*'" Jack lost his breath, and tried again. "'Get *out* of here, *faggot!*'"

David jumped, even though Jack carefully turned his eyes down at the tablecloth, to protect bystanders.

"Sorry, David," Jack said, almost coldly. "But I did, I said it, I meant it: it just went right through me. And it worked, too, I saw it work. He stared at me with fear and hatred and walked away, out the door. With a stiff, upright walk. I could see it: pulling himself up off the ground, like someone who has been utterly humiliated, his face pushed into the dirt, who will never willingly touch the ground again. I never saw him after that, which is just as well, because although I owe him some kind of apology, I wouldn't be able to give it to him, any more than I can give Charles North America. I watched him go, hating him, because he had put all this misery into me, this unbeliev-able wretchedness – "

"Jack, why do you say these things?" David broke in.

"Well, this is the only time I've ever done this, David. If that answers your question. Maybe I shouldn't have started on this. Am I going to give you nightmares? But there's a happy ending, remember, except the happy ending has up and left now, too.

Anyway, I turned and walked away, not out, because I couldn't follow him. I didn't want to see people, I wanted to think, so it was back into the washroom, into a cubicle, where I sat down to think and shake. I had the feeling I could never say anything again, that my voice had died in my throat, that I had killed my human voice. I shook and held myself tight as if I might come apart. And then I whispered it to myself: '*faggot, faggot*.' Trying to hear what it meant, what I'd said, to him, to myself. I started crying, a little: not like you, David, but leaking at the seams.

Then someone knocked at the door. The way people do: loud, importantly, life has to go on. But I still wasn't able to talk, to move, even. I stared at his feet, impatient with piss or shit or sex, I thought, waiting to see them turn and go. I looked at the door, carved with phone numbers and messages about big dicks and blowjobs. It wasn't very solid, but I loved it, I loved all the solidity it had. Because it let me think. It let me sit still and think. What is this. What is this misery? How did it get into me? Who put it here? As if I could sit there and think about it, hard, hard, till I knew.

Then a voice said, 'It's me. You know, just now. Mr. Crowchild.'

I just sat thinking, you fool, what does it have to do with you?

He asked, not believing it, 'Hey, man, are you crying?' Jack laughed at his own foolishness. 'Come on, and I'll buy you a beer.' But I still couldn't speak, or move. I was frozen, staring like a cat at the impatience and the patience in his feet. He obviously didn't like talking to doors, but he didn't go. He said, *'It can't be that bad, man.'* Jack laughed a little more.

I just thought, 'There you're wrong.' And then, something else in me thought, and almost said, 'That's enough for now. You don't have to do it all at once, and that's enough.' It was like realizing that there is such a thing as time, that the soul, after all, lives in time, breathes time. Something you forget and remember all your life. It was as if Charles' message was, 'Come live for a while, and then come back to this.' I reached for some toilet paper to wipe my face, and the squeak of the roller felt like it came from inside me, like a mousy little birth cry. It was the best I could do: it showed Charles I was alive, responding. Then I said, 'Give me a minute, okay?' Turned out, he was a lot more generous than that.   Charles, of course, never really understood: he thought that I was just overwrought, somehow. I've talked with Paul, about this, of course. I had called another gay man faggot, meaning it, feeling it. But you're the only other person I've told: it's between you and me and Paul, unless they're right when they say the police are up in the ceiling, watching. So tell me, David, how crazy was I? How evil was I?"

David didn't want to answer. He just felt a little sick. Of course there were gay men you didn't like, you despised: why did Jack have to make this sort of fuss about it?

"I got called *'faggot'* on the street a few nights ago," he admitted.

"And?"

"I thought it was so unfair! I didn't expect it at all. I wasn't wearing any of the clothes I wore with Tim, for instance. I looked perfectly normal."

"Were you alone?"

"Yes."

"That's not normal, David."

"I was so furious it made me weak and shaky. Though there was nothing to be frightened of, really, they just drove past, shouted it out the window. But I could hardly breathe."

"*Why?*"

"I don't know why. It was my first time, I suppose."

"Why?"

David gave him a resentful look. "Because they meant it. They knew exactly how to mean it."

"But what was it – what did they mean?"

"Ask them, Jack, I don't know."

Jack smiled. "Why should they tell us?"

"It's funny," David said, thoughtfully. "It was almost friendly. They were glad to see me."

"Oh yes – *if we didn't exist, they would have to invent us.* Sometimes I wonder if they did."

"Who's side are you on, Jack?"

David hadn't had his hair cut for a while, and now it was falling into his face. Jack reached, pushed it aside, and said "Yours." They looked each other in the eyes, each knowing he was far from being the other's first choice. They were good friends, an eventful half-generation apart, fond of each other although with snobberies and grudges, and lonely and horny. What they saw was that they wouldn't go to bed together.

The next day, David was downtown to buy his next symphony and saw Tim running across Dundas with his hands in the front pockets of new jeans, smiling to himself. He didn't need a phone call from David.

That evening, Jack answered the phone, handed him the receiver. It was Tim.

"I've been meaning to phone," he said, in the voice of a good friend. "We should have lunch when I get back, but right now I'm leaving town for a while. I met this guy last week, Will. I think you'll like him. When you meet. But right now, we're going to Fire Island."

"Where?" For a moment, the name was uncanny and vivid, like red hair on a rainy day. "Oh, yes, in the States. Well, be careful."

That night, he dreamt that he was walking with Tim along the beach at Hanlan's Point and suddenly felt it stir and rise under him, like the *Ongiara* setting forth across the harbour. Tim was pointing south, towards the unseen shore, squinting a little in the breeze.

"Look!" he said to a David just about to wake up. "*Rochester!*"

As if Rochester was the name of the whole passionate world. David held the feeling inside himself, and looked around at the sunlit back bedroom, seeing that its clutter could conjure a lover in out of the night only once.

He explained to Jack and thanked him and left after lunch, saying goodbye on the porch. The air was dry and cool, lightly starched. A yellow leaf let go and fell to the ground in seconds, after a long summer. David looked at the leaves on Jack's front lawn and for a moment he wanted to stay and rake them up. He couldn't wait for the autumn clearance, for winter and clarity.

"Well," Jack said, "they say you can live without anyone's skin except your own."

"Christ, Jack. *You have to make a lesson out of it, don't you? Out of everything.*"

"I know who!" Jack said, his eyes widening.

"What?"

"You remind me of my daughter!" Jack threw his arms around David. It was hello, not good-bye. Inside the hug David felt an odd, gratuitous joy – as if a baby, not him, not his, a human baby, had just been born.

"She's ten," Jack said, standing back to look. "And she's got a mind of her own. She's *stubborn.*"

"I'd love to meet her," David said, pulling away a bit, happy to make Jack happy, but not up to impersonating little girls for long. "Goodbye, then, and thanks."

"You know, David, you're a *sweetheart,*" Jack said. And he gave him a kiss on the cheek, right there on his porch in the Annex.

"Mmm," David said, not wanting to disagree.

PART TWO: 1976 - 78

"In a world full of moral and material ruin the only comfort lies in memories of days lived intensely."

Gualtieri di San Lazzaro, *Klee, A Study of His Life and Work*, New York, 1964.

CHAPTER VI: LOVERS AGAIN
July, 1976

"David!" someone shouted two summers later. Behind him, "David!" and Jack Durham came up, loping in new red running shoes, bearing an ice cream cone like a green torch.

"I hardly recognized you." He stopped, panting in hot, thick air. Toronto was hung with haze: around them, Queen and Spadina took buildings, traffic, people away into nothingness. Jack held out the ice cream cone. "Not in those legs!"

Leaning to take a bite, David wanted to explain, but he couldn't, not even to Jack. The night before, tossing alone, he'd got up and begun cutting up his clothes with nail scissors, desperately, teethingly. He'd sliced off more and more, trying to cut out just the right, desirable David needed to draw a lover in from the mist. A lover of butchered cut-offs and long legs.

Now David just swallowed his ice cream with an unhappy grin and a shrug. Jack would understand, more or less.

"My God!" Jack said with relish, fingering air like cloth. "I don't know how we stand it. This is *just terrible!*"

"Well, yes, but – " David looked away down Queen, doubtingly.

"But?"

"It's..." But David shrugged. Jack couldn't understand. No one could. A packed streetcar folded in its doors, shutting out fever-stricken lines, and lumbered off for Roncesvalles.

"It's *triste*," David said, failing to burden the word with his state. "It's *mysterious*."

Already haze was consuming the red streetcar and its passengers.

Jack smiled, scornful and positive. "So who needs mystery?" He looked quickly, diagnostically, into David's eyes. "Are you still with Peter?"

"No." Really, the shorts made it obvious: Peter wouldn't have let him make such a spectacle of himself. "No, we decided to part a week or so after you saw us at Massey Hall."

"Mm," Jack said, sympathetically, not surprised. Then he crunched into the cone. A few yards away, upwind, a brisk, blue-suited man with the *SUN* folded into his armpit had stopped to light a cigarette. Catching some of his smoke, David coughed resentfully. There were people who thrived on this stuff, it seemed, amphibians who lapped it up. And Jack was one of them: renewed, invigorated, and an expert on how to live. David felt a mixture of irritation and hope. He hadn't seen Jack for several months, because he hadn't wanted to talk with anyone about Peter during the period of their breakup.

"So, how's *your* life been going, Jack?"

"Well, I'll introduce you."

"Oh? Great."

"You and Mr. Brezhnev."

"What?"

"It's a project of mine. I want to save the world. I'm going to say, 'Look, Mr. Secretary, Mr. President, isn't he amazing? *Think* what you'd be doing'!"

Touching on everyone's inconceivably terrible death, Jack let out a moment's solemnity, then chortled. "And they'll say, 'Oh yes, you're right, he's adorable, we just can't risk it.'" They licked ice cream off their lips. "'All this nuclear crap has got to go.'"

David laughed for the first time in days. It was a quaint, appealing idea – not the world's rescue, Jack's being in love. It hadn't happened for some time, not since Charles.

"Even you'll be impressed, David. I met him two weeks ago, on the subway. He stepped in and I was astonished. *I'm still astonished*. That's a very philosophical state to be in, Plato says."

"What's his name?"

"Jim. Jim Fields, and he's from Scarborough." Jack looked along Queen Street, as if thinking how different it was from suburban Scarborough. "All the words are useless, aren't they?" he said, suddenly. "I mean, 'good-looking, attractive, handsome' – so what, so big deal! But if you go and get carried away and say someone's *beautiful*, it just comes out sounding silly."

"I suppose. It depends."

"'Beautiful'? It's as silly as 'homosexual'. But you can't just say 'he's good-looking.' You can't just say 'he's attractive'."

"Well, it's nice to know someone's in love," David said, fondly.

"No!" Jack waved this quickly away with the tail of the ice cream cone. "That would be the obvious thing, of course, but that's not it at all. Jim's a model of mine. A friend and a model, like Tim Grey was. There is nothing in this that can't be photographed. Would you like to meet him?"

"I can't wait."

"Because I'm going to be having some kind of dinner. Paul's out west, so I don't know how it will get cooked. And I thought of asking Tim, too, if..."

"I'd like that actually. I haven't seen him since your opening."

"He may not be in the city, though – I think I heard something about Provincetown. Anyway, good, you can come. I'll be in touch about the date, because I've got to run. There's a streetcar."

"Jim runs," Jack said, holding out one of the new shoes, leather and rubber and nylon cunningly stitched. "Whatever else, we'll look back on this as a great age of footwear. I'll be phoning."

He sprinted off, David calling "good-bye" and feeling abandoned. David wanted Jack to stay – stay and tell him how to be happy.

But then at the end of the line shuffling into the car, Jack turned. Was he shouting about a bridge? David didn't want to understand Jack, who brought the sight of hope and then ran away, shouting riddles through the mist.

"*What?*"

"*Do you play bridge?*"

"*Not for years!*"

"*Jim's a great teacher!*"

Last of all, Jack pressed himself into the streetcar, which embraced him with its doors.

PART 2

Two days later, David pedalled doggedly up to the reservoir park, where there would be breezes, if any were to be had in the city. But even at that height, they could only push against the steam and droop. He went through the park, towards the steep bank overlooking the ravine, and saw someone like Tim alone at the edge, leaning back on his elbows. A silver-gray bike lay beside him. Just as David shouted, he realized the bike wasn't the one he had known, and remembered Tim was on Cape Cod.

But he turned around, saw him, and said hello.

"I see you've got a new bike." Beginning to wobble, David put down his sandalled feet.

Tim gave the downed gray bike an angry look. "This is Alan's. Mine was stolen, so they lent it to me for a while."

"You're getting red, you know," David said, as if to make up for the loss of the bike.

The pink neck and shoulders twisted, Tim peering around.

"Just because you *can't see the sun* – "

"I know!" Tim distributed a damp T-shirt over his shoulders. "But I haven't been out for weeks. Come here," he said abruptly, looking at David's cut-offs.

"Why?"

But he was setting down his bike and stepping closer. Tim reached with both hands for the fringe of the shorts, grabbed a dangling clump of cotton and pulled, clenching his teeth a little. The close air sharpened the sound of breaking threads. At twenty-four, he looked much the same, except for a certain cold determination. He was resolved to get what he wanted, and knew better how to get it. Perhaps it was the ordinary, necessary selfishness of someone living and making his living in Toronto in 1976, but David couldn't help connecting it to the last scene of their affair.

"You really butchered these jeans, didn't you?" Tim said, sarcastically. That selfishness was in his voice too, in a certain hardening of his voice. It surrounded him, and kept David safe from seeing the body he'd been in love with.

Biting his upper lip, Tim tore off a few more threads and tossed the cotton away over the sloping bank. It went a few feet and dropped in the grass.

"There," he said with satisfaction.

"You just like *tearing* things," David said, glad to have given him something to tear, and feeling invited to join him. He wriggled out of his backpack and lowered himself to the grass.

"Aren't you supposed to be travelling?"

"Who said?"

"Jack. Jack Durham."

"Oh? How did he know? In the end I couldn't go. I was up seeing my mother."

"How is she?"

"Well, actually. I don't know if *you heard* – " Tim gave him a quick look " – but she had a heart attack last winter. It wasn't a big one, and now she's better, much better."

David hadn't heard. "That's good," he said, lamely.

"That was all last winter," Tim said, putting it firmly behind him. "But I was up there for a week till the day before yesterday." He laughed. "That's why I haven't been out. But how is Jack? I haven't seen him since the winter."

"Fine. He has some kind of new boyfriend. Jack says he isn't in love, but I don't believe him."

"Hm." Tim wrinkled his nose. "You know, I think Jack makes a point of falling for each of his boyfriends differently."

"Don't we all?"

Tim's shrug almost displaced the T-shirt: he reached back to save it. "How about you? Are you still with Peter?"

"No," David said, flatly. "Not for some time."

Peter had first appeared during the winter after the break with Tim, at a student production of *The Duchess of Malfi*, pushing a long, serious face up into the light from the stage. He wasn't obviously gay, except that the girl he was with was. After that, David had noticed him around the campus. He'd appeared again in the summer, alone, at an outdoor performance of *A Midsummer Night's Dream*, kneeling in the grass of the hillside that was being used as an amphitheatre, or squatting up on the balls of his feet to see over shifting heads. As the crowd dispersed, David found himself beside him, trying to drop Shakespeare's name with just the right ironic respect. They'd gone for a drink, Peter and David and David's companion, a graduate student who, so far as anyone knew, was straight. Peter was two years younger than David, an undergraduate who wanted to be an actor. He believed that all reality lay in the way lines of Shakespeare or Webster or Chekhov were sent out from a stage. David had been taken with the idea for some time, and with Peter.

"In the end we didn't really get along," David said. "Maybe we were too much alike.

But no, that's just what an outsider would say."

He added in a lower voice, "We had some really miserable fights. I can hardly believe it now."

At first it had seemed less intense than with Tim, and safer. They were good friends who made love in a joking, apologetic way. But then there had developed an intensity of dislike that was more intimate than anything before.

"Peter was – " He wanted to get it out, but he couldn't sum up several months of thinking about what was wrong with Peter, what was wrong with himself. "Peter was *Old Toronto*," he said, as if this was a beginning. "That's what Hugh liked so much."

"Well, he wasn't so bad," Tim said. "I liked Peter."

"Really?" David said, startled. "Maybe not." He looked at Tim's chest slung down from his propped arms, seeing the pool at the Y again. "There've been others since, but they didn't work out. I was going to the bars for a while. But there aren't any bars for introverts."

"Maybe you could open one," Tim said, sitting up. "I'd look in occasionally."

"Why does it all have to be so difficult?" David demanded suddenly, passionately. "So *graceless*? I don't know if it's this city. Everyone says it's so cold. There are times when I want to take people at the bars and knock their heads together – tell them to stop wasting time, make up their minds. Be happy!"

He spoke ironically, but if Tim cared to, he could hear through to David's loneliness.

"Oh, I know," Tim said, with surprising emotion, taking up the loneliness, not the irony. "I know. And you think, it could just be *simple*."

He began to show how simple with a shrug, but the gesture expanded, longing ran out along his arms, raising them, opening his hands, the shirt dropping from his back unnoticed. For a moment, he seemed to be reaching for something in the air over the ravine, then he let his arms fall and rearranged his legs, the running shoes sole to sole. It was as if he'd given up, and was going to sit on the edge of the world, holding his ankles, with his legs winging out helplessly. David felt something like pity. It was well within the rules that he should be loverless, but surely there were rules to say that Tim – handsome, determined, capable – should never be.

"Well, put your shirt on anyway," David said.

"I guess you're right." Tim picked up the shirt, and began turning it inside out. Watching the familiar hands moving in the cloth, David took a sudden decision. For two years, they had been acquaintances, not friends. But after all, there was no reason why they shouldn't be friends again. They were both older and wiser and more selfish, after all – more prudent, at least.

"Guess who I met yesterday?" Tim began, about to head into the shirt.

But David had to speak while he had the courage. "Do you want to come down and see my apartment?"

Tim looked up at him in surprise. "Sure, I'd love to."

"You probably still picture me in that little closet at the graduate residence."

Tim was raking his hands back through his hair, and began drying them in his shirt. He scrambled up, suddenly glad to be moving, picking up Alan's bike, getting on. David got up too and tried to put on his backpack, groping behind himself into a tangle of straps. From the high, hard saddle, Tim watched him struggling: his feet were just touching the ground, his shoulders thrust to take his weight, his neck twisted around. He had stuffed the T-shirt into his shorts, his shoulders were still in danger, and somehow David couldn't remind him about it. Because the backpack was winning: for a moment, David thought hysterically, he might need Tim's help to get free of it. But his tongue was tied like his arms: in his panic he saw Tim turning into the old, familiar Tim, the body and the person he'd been tangled with two years before. For a moment, he saw who it was he had invited into a space that hadn't known him, that had been safe from him. He thought of saying, 'Of course, I don't mean sex.' But that would sound very stupid. And it would mean sex.

Then Tim thought of the shirt and put it on and the backpack dropped into place. Tim turned away, shoving off, and David followed, trying to put these fears behind him. They were older: they could handle it. The heat and, perhaps, his desperate celibacy were getting to him, but he was saner and cannier than two years ago.

They went downhill, coasting a lot of the way. It was only at the end of the journey that Tim needed directions to the shabby four-storey apartment building David had come upon a year and a half before, wedged into a street of houses. He loved it: it was the first place he had lived in on his own. He boasted of his luck in finding it, as they took the bikes down one short flight of stairs into David's apartment. They went directly through into the kitchen and put both bikes there, side by side.

"Well," Tim said looking around. "It is a lot bigger." He held his arms wide, and David felt his air sliding over them, and looked away. With a smile, Tim put on his shirt, rashly stripped off again as they coasted under trees.

"This is the bedroom," David said, stepping over to the door. "Since we're here, I mean. It's odd, having it off the kitchen like this, but I don't mind. There's another bedroom, but it's just a sort of porch. It's cold in the winter."

Tim stood in the doorway, taking it in. The desk was dishevelled with a story, 'Seeing Jim'. The legs from David's jeans hung over the back of the chair. A green garbage bag, shoved tightly into the corner, was gorged with laundry. Volumes of or on Ruskin, the subject of David's thesis, lay scattered across the floor like stepping-stones going nowhere. His favourite old Klee poster had become ragged now. Numerous other posters, among them two Turners, hid most of the jagged cracked plaster. Behind him, David looked with fresh eyes at this life of his, unmade, unpartnered, strewn about. With solemnity he glanced at Tim's neck, solar pink, sensuously liquid and intelligent as his eyes in their looking around.

"What on earth is *that*?" Tim was looking at a small door about four feet high, that opened right onto David's bed.

"The landlord had to put in a second door, for fires, so he just put that into the window-frame."

"Somebody could step right into your bed. A *dwarf* perhaps."

David laughed. "No such luck! How about a gin and tonic?"

"I thought I'd go swimming later."

"Oh. Lemonade, then?"

They went into the kitchen, and while David poured the lemonade, Tim went across to look at the view, onto crowded backyards. Again, David could see him looking eagerly, but fluently, not darting from one thing to another, but moving smoothly, connecting everything. Now anything was possible, David told himself: something in the way Tim moved in his apartment, took it into himself, had changed things. He could change the terms on which he had invited Tim here. They had after all been unspoken: really, they were only in his head, terms he had made with himself.

David came up behind, balancing two full glasses, staring at the desperate pink of Tim's neck. "Here's your drink," he said, sternly. Tim turned and took it and took a long sip and gulped, gazing at him through the tops of his eyes.

David looked away and laughed – laughed himself into the desperately roguish person he could be for about thirty seconds in bars. "So, Tim – what do you think?" he said.

"About what?"

"I'm asking myself, *should we*? Does it make sense?"

"Should we what?"

"*Have sex*, of course! But you seemed surprised?"

Tim smiled and took another sip.

"Well, maybe you're right. Maybe it's a bad idea, but I thought, we're friends we'll never be lovers again, if we ever really were – but we're old friends, after all, we can handle it..."

"You thought, here we are, *both horny*, so why not?"

"No! Not like that. Not that cynically."

Tim jingled the ice in his glass like faint laughter.

"This is getting too complicated!" David's courage, or his cynicism, was about to run out: Tim would have to help him. "*It's like a SALT treaty*."

"We can handle it, David," Tim said.

David smiled a little to the side.

"Let's take these into the bedroom," he said. And turned, leading the way. He'd got Tim, but he was still afraid to touch him.

"Of course," he added pointedly, over his shoulder, "I'm still *a bit prudish* about some things."

"Oh?" Tim said. "Of course."

They sat down side by side on the bed. Tim looked at him with an odd smile, as if he saw all of David's sneakiness and had some of his own. Then he drained the glass, throwing back his head, crunching lemonade in his throat. David took the glass, and put it by his own, making two wet rings on 'Seeing Jim'. He leaned and kissed a stranger's chilled mouth. Then he was going back in time, two years at least.

"This *could* be a mistake," he said, sitting back. Not meaning it, just for the record, in case it turned out to be mistake later.

Tim gave him a long look: David was almost afraid he would take him seriously. Then he grinned.

"*Too late, David,*" he said, and attacked.

PART 3

They made love, and then, with Tim stretched out alongside him, David thought of saying, "What are we doing?" He thought better of it, realizing that the afternoon still stretched generously in front of him. He was in love with the way Tim had recreated himself so precisely out of the past, down to the smallest detail. Tim, on the other hand, said, "You've changed, David. You're growing up."

"Well, I guess I must've got really sneaky," David said exultantly. "To've gotten you here like this."

"But what exactly are we doing?"

"That sounds like my sort of question! I don't know does it matter? Right now, this is just this afternoon, isn't it? Though there could be *other* afternoons, I suppose."

Tim didn't answer. So David talked about his apartment, proudly: it was the first place he'd ever had on his own, after all. The other people in the building, some odd and colourful, some friendly, were like discoveries, inventions of his. Then he asked about Tim's work. Tim had begun doing illustrations for a friend from O.C.A., Tony Molinaro, who'd started a graphics agency. At first, it had been almost a game, something they did for friends. But they had caught on, they were trendy, and now Tim's work took up all the time he wanted to spend working, sometimes more. He liked it, he said: he liked seeing the work he'd done looking back at him on the streets, in the papers.

David was impressed: Tim was successful, an adult making his living, while he was still just a student. But now Tim was thinking of something else. His hands moved back to David's chest, his nipples, then touring down and back, fingertips taking in the lost, dark valley between his buttocks. David let them stay for a few seconds, then pulled away, still far more than a bit prudish about some things. Soon the fingers were back, cautious, curious – as if measuring the chances of those other afternoons. David shook away from them, scared and haughty – but at some deep level knowing he was doomed, that perhaps he had intended to be doomed all along.

Certainly, Tim didn't take in the message: the third time, David had to speak. "I said I wasn't into that."

"*That's what you said, all right.*"

Tim looked at him with an insolent flickering of desire and calculation: he looked not two years, but centuries older. It was hypnotic: David opened his mouth to say no, then closed it as if Tim's arrogance left him breathless. Tim smiled and began again. David closed his eyes as if to take leave of this. It was like something else down there, not him, below his busy mind. A troll, a caveman, a gollum that never learned to speak.

"No," Tim said, bringing open David's eyes.

"What?"

"'No' is all you have to say."

"*No Tim*, you mean," David said. "Don't you?"

Tim smiled, as if he thought he'd won. "Don't go way," Tim said, getting up and stepping out into the kitchen, with nothing between his skin and David's air, David's space. Nothing at all. He came back with his bottle of suntan lotion, grinning. He sat in the bed and squeezed suntan oil onto his fingers. David looked at the whitened fingers with a kind of imaginary horror, took them to stop them, and then pushed the hand over to smear lotion on the red flooding through the skin of Tim's left shoulder.

Tim laughed implacably and squeezed out more oil.

"You don't want to be peeling," David said, like a nurse, pushing the hand back awkwardly to smear the right shoulder too. He rubbed both shoulders himself.

Tim leaned to kiss him, the bottle wheezing like a rubber toy. The idea seemed to be they could be friends at the level of mouths, while Tim set about undermining David's life from below. But he wouldn't succeed, David thought. He was so outraged he was justified in not doing anything at all, not even saying no. He wasn't going to say no, but he wasn't going to like it either. He was going to prove to Tim once and for all he didn't want it. And then, having given Tim what he wanted, have something to bargain with. He put his face on the burning ledge of Tim's shoulder, with the heavy fragrance of suntan lotion in his nostrils. It was the smell of Hanlan's Point Beach, and he saw them walking along the edge where the sand was wet and firm, while one slippery finger undid everything, turning the tight, moral, necessary knot of his will into blubbery lips. Tim's finger slipped inside for a second, like a fat worm, like death, and David quivered.

"Don't you like that?"

"*Of course not.*"

"Please let me fuck you, David."

"*Why ever would I?*"

"Do you want to go trailing around *like a little, lost boy* all your life?"

"What does that have to do with it?"

"You *want it*, David."

David stared with bleak, hard anger, trying to see what Tim meant. That he was desperate for a lover – that was all.

"Do you *want me to stop?*" Tim said, with sudden timidity.

"I don't know," David said, angrily, but flattered he could have this effect on Tim. "What am I supposed to say? I can't say I don't like you. And really, so far as I can see, everything just happens anyway."

Tim smiled: he wasn't timid anymore, David saw, physically afraid for the first time. "Then turn over on your front, okay?" Tim said.

This was so cavalier that David almost refused. Then he saw it was a chance to turn his back on everything. He thought of the times he'd turned away from Tim to sleep: it could be like that now, he could feel drowsy, etherized, a patient: when he woke up, Tim would be in his debt.

"*You'll like it, David*," Tim said, in a low, urgent voice.

"That's what *I'm afraid of*!" David said, trying to show he could joke, even in adversity. Behind him, the bottle wheezed again, hoarsely, obscenely, like an angry old man, while David tried to assemble the facts of their getting here: the heat, the exhausting nights, the decision to pedal up to the park, the decision to ask Tim back. He saw him coasting down here, and said, as if making conversation, "How do you steer like that, anyway, with no hands? I certainly can't, and all my life, I've wondered, how do they do that? It looks as if you do it with your mind, by hypnosis." Something unrecognizably huge was nosing between his buttocks. It was time to say no: he didn't want this at all.

"I forgot to ask," he said, cracking a desperate last joke. "Do you love me?"

"Oh, David, *right now* I do!" There was a clumsy groping down below, then Tim gave a little thrust, and David felt a stabbing pain that turned into a ring of agony, vibrating out and out, all through him. "*Oh, Jesus!*" he cried. "*Oh, God!*"

He scrambled away, ready to go through the wall if necessary.

"Sorry! Sorry, but *that's impossible*," he was saying, chattering. He turned around fast, huddled warily, facing Tim. "*It hurts! My God it hurts*! How do they do it? It isn't possible."

He was clenched all over, trying to control the way the pain came up through him, and looking in fear at Tim, who might try to kill him again, if he hadn't already.

"I'm really sorry, Tim, but it just isn't going to work."

"No, it's my fault, I was too fast. You just looked so tempting lying there waiting."

"No, it's mine, *I should never have let yo*u. I don't know what I was thinking." He reached for Tim, who wasn't going to attack him after all, to get out of his own painful body into Tim's. "Actually, I do but – " He was about to tell Tim he loved him: anything to protect himself.

"You just have to relax," Tim said.

"Relax!" David laughed, almost gasping. "Relax! I'm sorry, Tim, but *I'm just a tight-assed, guilt-ridden, anal-retentive Calvinist*. And thank God, if it keeps that from happening to you."

"You'll let go, David, don't worry."

"*Let go*!" David shouted loudly. "I haven't *let go* for twenty-four years. Why can't *you* let go, Tim? *NOW, Tim!*"

He held onto Tim, clinging as if to console him for his disappointment: it was much more friendly, much more what he wanted to do. Someday they could look back on this and laugh. Really it was the end, the dead end of their love-affair, and now they could be friends again. He almost laughed now at the idea. The pain was receding.

"Turn over," Tim said in his ear.

"It can *not* be done."

"I'll be really gentle this time."

"Gentle? *How many people have you said that to?*"

"Enough to know what I'm doing." He fixed him with his gaze: *don't you trust these brown eyes?* David laughed at them in fond contempt, because they trusted themselves so much.

"All right," he said. "Once more, but it's not going to work." He turned over again, and lay looking at the cut-off legs of his jeans, dangling helplessly over the back of the chair. He'd worn those jeans in the drive from Victoria: over the years they'd gone from indigo to bluish-white, more cloud than sky. Then one hot night, he'd gone and cut them up: they would never get him out of here, away from the urgent, stupid stranger behind him.

"Let me in," Tim was saying. "*Please, just let me.* You don't have to worry about anything. Think about something else. All you have to do is give in."

"*Give in?*" David couldn't believe his ears. "That's the one thing I *never* do."

"Oh, David, shut up," Tim said, fondly.

It was almost an outrage, but somehow it seemed easier to let them be the last words, let them command him. Shut up: all right. His voice faded away in his throat, he watched Tim riding here, pedalling or coasting, sitting up and back. He'd even taken off the shirt again: for a few moments he'd been speeding along blind and with his arms tied in the air over his head. He hadn't wavered: it was David who gripped the handlebars in terror. He must do it with his mind and with his crotch, David realized, by some rapport with the saddle under him David would never master.

"Just relax," Tim was saying, coaxingly. "Trust me."

"I said it would hurt, and it does."

"How much?"

"How much? It *bloody well hurts!*" Tim had no right to measure out and calculate his pain. But he heard a kind of lost whimpering in his voice, as if the pain was a private infinity no one else would ever understand.

"Here, give me a kiss," Tim said, jauntily.

It seemed like an odd thing to do in the circumstances, but he twisted round, and there was Tim's mouth, salivating pure, sweet treachery.

"Does it still hurt?"

"Of course."

"If you really want me to stop, David, I will."

"Then *stop, please.*"

"But you've got to really mean it."

"Oh, *I do, I do,*" David said, with a kind of dreamy despair closing over him, as Tim sank farther in.

"Does is still hurt?"

"Jesus, *it hurts.*"

"What does that mean?"

"*It means it hurts!*"

"David, you're not as stubborn as you think. Not nearly. Do you still want me to stop?"

"You wouldn't *anyway*, would you?"

"There," Tim said, home.

David whimpered again, trying to tell himself the worst was over, that he was still alive, unless he was bleeding to death inside.

"It's nice, David," Tim said, with an obscene softness in his voice.

"Oh, God, Tim, I don't need that."

"But it is, David, it's *heaven.*"

David groaned, overwhelmed. It was as if Tim had taken possession of all of him, his ear as well as his bowels, and could pour into him whatever Satanic fantasies he wanted. David laughed bitterly, breathlessly under Tim's weight. He was in a ridiculous, humiliating position, he was at the bottom of the world, but there was no one to know about it, except Tim. Except Tim and the person he would be when he got his body back. And perhaps he could work something out with Tim: they could do this every so often, and the rest of the time make love on David's terms.

Tim began a stealthy, soothing thrusting, but it got faster, frightening David as he sensed the determination behind it. He wasn't even meant to be touched where Tim was, he was as soft as clay there, as naked and vulnerable as a soul on Judgement Day, and Tim's gentleness was giving way to an outright attack.

"Stop, *please!*"

"What's the matter?" Tim said, as if waking up.

"Be *careful!*"

"Are you okay?"

"I don't know, *I'm not a doctor.*"

"Don't worry." Tim began kissing his neck and face with a sharp, uncanny tenderness, as if taking off little films of skin with each kiss. He began thrusting again, cautiously at first, then faster. David panicked, as he felt Tim lift off towards some brutal frenzy.

"*Oh, God, stop! You're going to kill me.*"

Tim moaned, coming to a halt. "Not really," he said, and began kissing him hungrily. David turned and met his lips, hoping to distract him. But Tim grabbed at his cock and began pounding into him. David wanted to struggle away: for a second it seemed he had the strength to do it, no matter how strong Tim was, how well-entrenched. But then he couldn't want to: something, fatalism and curiosity held him there. Having come so close, he wanted to know what it was that Tim was about to do to him, whether he lived or died. And then he didn't have any choice anymore: Tim was coming, surging into him, climbing through him, and he was terrified into coming too. It was like a soft, frightened, echo.

"Thanks," Tim said, dying and kissing the side of his neck with a cold mouth. He fell silent there. David didn't have to say anything yet. Some dogs were barking outside: he knew them, the little lapdog with the high yelp, the old spaniel with a screech in its voice like a rusty gate. They barked with the usual righteousness of dogs, but their anger seemed far away.

"Thanks," Tim said again, stirring. The hero had fought hard, died hard, and come smugly to life again. "You're wonderful, David." But David couldn't tell what he had on top of him: his renewed lover or an afternoon's used-up stranger. He moved in response, impatiently, asking a kind of wriggly question through their sweat. Tim just hugged him sleepily. The sweat between them was like a lens, magnifying touch, but it didn't let him see through to Tim's mind.

"You're getting kind of heavy," David said.

Tim put his arms under and around him and rolled them both over, so that David was on his side, looking out across his room. He squirmed impatiently.

"*Stay!*" Tim sharply spat at him. David felt a sudden terror of being trapped forever. He kicked back into Tim's legs and Tim said, "Oh, all right," and pulled out carefully. David felt glad to be free for a second, then abandoned, empty, desolate, as if Tim had pulled out his heart. He sat up and turned to look over his shoulder at what had done this to him, afraid and almost longing to see it smeared with disaster: blood or shit or both. It wasn't. He watched it, pulsing down to dream of having its will of David McTavish.

Tim opened his eyes and gave him a kiss on the nearest spot, the ticklish skin over his hip, then turned on his front as if he was going to sleep. David felt as if he could never sleep again. He had to be doing something. He swung his legs into the bathroom to take a shower, then realized he had to get rid of the horrible, tearful mess inside him. With abject literalness he collapsed on the toilet and shat Tim out, sobbing. This was where it had all been leading, this misery.

He showered and washed his hair, glad he could look clean, and went back to the bedroom, where Tim still lay face down, looking as if he was the one who had been raped and left for dead. David put on a clean T-shirt and the whorish shorts. The garbage bag slumping against the wall offered something to do. "I'll be down at the corner laundromat," he said in a low voice. Tim turned his head without raising it.

"The laundromat?" he said. "Come here, David."

David blew a mocking kiss at Tim, picked up the bag, and went out past the bikes, nuzzling each other like deer. Outside the apartment, on the first step down, he wanted to go back, but couldn't. The place had been invaded by a stranger. He felt as though he was going to topple down the stairs, but let the bag fall instead, tumbling slowly, softly to the bottom. He followed it, clutching the rail.

A new wave of panic engulfed him as he moved out into the daylight: unreal, shadowless as if all the shadows were hiding deep inside him. He didn't know if he could walk: his legs were shattered, the sidewalk, or the whole city, seemed ready to crack open beneath him. He passed a blond young man, perhaps a year or two younger than himself: his yellow hair seemed to draw its own sunshine out of the haze. He smiled saucily and David looked away, grievingly: until this afternoon, he'd thought that was what being gay meant, sunny blond smiles.

When he got to the laundromat, he discovered he'd forgotten to bring money. He had change for two washing machines, but he would have to go back to fetch more. He walked back and then went twice around the block of his building, before going in. He remembered passing the house of a boy he'd been in love with in Victoria: for a year he'd gone by, looking up at his window, while the window looked away at the sea. Now his own windows were as blank. He wondered if Tim might have left, and imagined what he would do if he had. Nothing, he decided: just live with the nothing inside himself.

Tim was in the living-room, his hair sleek, wearing the red shorts, and reading a Penguin, *Vasari's Lives of the Painters*.

"Hi," he said. "There you are."

David said nothing, looking bitterly at him, at the book.

"I won't lose your place," Tim said. His finger was stuck in it.

"It's not finished," David said. "The laundry. I needed some dimes."

He looked in the little brown, chipped pot on his dresser, where change was kept: quarters, subway tokens, nickels, pennies...no dimes. Tim reached into his knapsack and pulled out some, held them out.

David went over and held out his hand. As Tim dropped them, he pulled the hand away.

"You *bastard*!"

"Why?"

"You *raped* me!"

"Not really." Tim bent to pick up the dimes. David looked murderously at the shifting bones under the pink skin.

"*Bastard*!"

"I didn't rape you, David. You know that."

"Do you want me to say thank you for fucking me?"

"People do." Tim took David's hand from his side: it opened and he dropped in the silver.

"I'll get it back to you."

"David, come on!"

"What do you mean?"

"Well, you aren't dying, are you?"

David stepped out the door, leaving the question unanswered.

Forty minutes later, he walked back, hugging his clean clothes. Tim was still reading. David was going to go past him into the bedroom.

"Come here," Tim said, putting down the book.

David sat down on the black futon he used as a couch, staring, waiting stiffly.

"So, do you still say that I raped you?"

"Not entirely."

"What does that mean?"

"I admit I was curious."

"Is that what it was? Come here." Tim held out his hand, commandingly.

David looked at it, unfolding from the wrist, down through widening ranks of bone to the waiting fingertips. He reached and took them, and swung the hand from side to side, angrily.

"You liked it, David."

He laughed. "I'll never be that desperate." He turned the hand palm up to read it. "You liked it. That's why you're upset."

David brought the hand up and bit the heel of it, sharply.

"Only if it was you," he said. "I mean, only because it was you."

He began kissing Tim's hand and wrist and forearm, deceiving himself, he knew, imagining he could live in a house of kisses.

"*Or else there's no excuse*," he said.

PART 4

As Tim looked for things in the kitchen, with a banging of cupboard doors, the phone rang. It was Jack, inviting David to dinner on the weekend after, to meet Jim Fields.

"I found Tim Grey for you," David said, proudly. "He's here right now."

"Really," Jack said. "Really? Great!" he said, responding to the happiness in David's voice. "Stupendous! Can you bring him along on Friday? And say hello."

David stepped into the kitchen. "Hello, Tim."

"Hello?"

David looked at him through a moment of silence, silence alive with Jack's telephoned presence and difficult world view. Tim cracked an egg on the edge of the pan, dumped the yolk, stretched the glassy cords out and out.

"Jack's on the phone. Do you want to go to dinner next Friday. And meet the incredible Jim Fields?"

"Sure. I'd love to see what Jack is up to now."

While they ate, David told him more about the block. About the Buddhist monk who sat praying in his basement: you could see him sometimes on your way in. About

Mrs. Lukacs, right next door, who had told Peter and David about Hungary in 1956. She didn't mind their being gay so long as they stood and fought when the Russian tanks came up Markam Street. About Charlotte and Heather and Jan, who lived in two apartments thrown together, so they spanned the building. David had met them when Charlotte, with gruff friendliness, had helped with a bag of groceries that was tearing open. "When I went to meet them, I kept thinking it was like the Three Bears in there: Mother Bear, Mother Bear, and Mother Bear. It made me nervous and silly, but I loved it."

And so on: David's first apartment block was full of interesting people. He enjoyed his neighbours, and he found them fascinating: they were sacred, they were life. The apartment was also cheap. And there was that second bedroom – perhaps it could be a studio for Tim. It had turned out to be hard to heat in the winter, but the light was good.

After breakfast, they biked down to the ferry dock. The air had begun to open up and allow for breathing. On board the ferry, they stood restraining their bikes amid a flock of bikes. Sitting up on the locker at the front, two boys were holding an animated conversation in sign language. They signed dartingly, flashingly, like gay witches weaving a spell to pull the ferry over to the green, longed-for shore of the Island. David watched them, entranced. Of course they fucked, he decided: you could see it. It was plain as day, as if there was something about it that changed you, broke your spine like a book's. It scared him: was he like that? Could people see it? In exhilaration and fear, he kept looking at the two boy witches, their secrets snapping and fluttering like pennants in the breeze.

The *Ongiara* pushed throbbing across the harbour and shouldered companionably into the giant tires of its mooring: the bikes were unpenned and scattered. Tim and David rode to a place behind the beach and began wading through the sand.

Tim stopped and looked around, leaning Alan's bike against his thigh. It tried to slide away, skittishly: he grabbed it. "Let's smoke a joint," he said, propping it more firmly and reaching into his pocket for a little white stick. He twiddled it, mysterious and powerful, like a shaman's little magic bone.

"Sure," David said, uncertainly. Grass could have strange effects on him. But only when he was with people he didn't know, he told himself.

"It's supposed to be great stuff, Colombian," Tim said. "I had it up at home. I kept thinking I'd love to go somewhere and smoke up, but I couldn't face my mother stoned."

They shared it, Tim pulling in a last toke just before the last line of scrub trees. Fire bit at his fingertips: he dropped the roach and buried it in sand with a regretful touch of his running shoe.

"Oh, it's *good stuff* all right," David huffed.

They locked their bikes into a clump of trees, which wanted to lash David with branches and feed him leaves. David shook his head, rattling thoughts that would not come together. *I have never been this stoned*, he thought. *And it's only beginning.*

He got out of the trees into the dazzling light of the beach. Into hot music and noisy conversation. He didn't know how he'd got here, now: even the bikes seemed far away. He looked at Tim and smiled weakly, not quite meeting his eyes. It felt as if his mind was running down his face like babyhood. He followed as Tim went over to a group of friends. He was introduced and just waved and smiled benevolently, hoping they could see how stoned he was.

Tim spread his towel on the edge of the group of friends. David flapped his out on the other side and dropped onto it.   "How are you doing?" Tim asked.

David shook his head, and lay down on his front. In his peripheral vision, Tim seemed to be surrounded by blackness, and he didn't dare look right at him. "Not bad," he said, judiciously, and the words, let out, went echoing around, crazily. *Not bad*, they seemed to say for the sky and the lake: are you saying that you're *not bad*? After what *you've* done? He lay helpless, and he couldn't recognize this person who had brought him here.

"It is pretty strong," Tim said. David just stared into an eternity of sand, occasionally closing his eyes to go tumbling down the outer space inside himself. Above him the person who had led him here, who had made him lie on his front and then turned into a brutal, faceless stranger, chattered away with his friends. David would listen up into the sound of Tim's voice – into its irony, its laughter, its selfishness, echoing off the other voices. He didn't know that person at all: there was nothing there to know, it seemed, no one inside that voice.

Suddenly someone put a hand on his arm. "David?"

He turned his head to look through the black shimmering that surrounded the stranger. "Who are you?" he said, and pulled his arm away, realizing that what he said was insane.

But it wasn't. He'd asked the right, the only question. Because the stranger was nobody, emptiness. Being no one, he wouldn't be able to answer. He would say, "Who do you think?" or "You know who I am." The air was full of the breezy language that strangers talked: he just had to breathe it in and speak, and David would die or be free.

"Tim," he said.

"Really?" David said, amazed, but pretending to be joking.

"Yes, David. Really."

"You know, *I have never been this stoned.*"

"Don't worry," Tim said, "You're safe." David turned away again, as Tim moved his hand over David's back, gently, not touching it, except through the heat of his hand. David could feel the heat-shadow of Tim's hand moving through his back, loosening layers of fear that had cowered there for years, letting them go quivering away into the air.

"You're starting to come back down, David," Tim said.

He lay inside the voice, in the heart of the voice, *believing it.*

That night, himself again, just tired after a long day, he sat himself squarely down on Tim, closing his eyes and letting his mind fall away down his spine, down his guts. His mind went sinking away like water into the ground, to where Tim seemed hard as death, almost. He felt how he'd been possessed with that, the black fear of death, of carrying the fear of death inside himself. But now he saw this had nothing to do with death: he could fuck courageously. As he leaned down for a kiss, changes fell into place inside him: a shift of power, a release of charity, a new seeing. He was caught in mid-air, drunken, shuddering.

"*I love it, you,*" he murmured.

PART 5

Jack Durham opened the door into the hollow of his shoulder, confidingly. "Tim and David! Welcome!"

And he stood back to draw them into his front hall. Stepping in after Tim, David felt nervous, then at home. It was the old mess in a new phase. A bicycle burrowed into the coats. A football had dropped into an Imari bowl. Virginia Woolf's beautiful, drowned, endless face looked up at them from Volume One of her Life. And Jack was as romantic as he was: as tender-hearted as the tender new world David had landed in, unhurt, falling from a great, lonely height.

"Look at you," Jack said again, as if he couldn't get over it. "You two. It restores one's faith." Banging pipes responded through the house, lifting his eyes. "He's washing his face," Jack said, with a kind of priestly reverence. "He'll be down any moment. Let's go into the living room."

There he sat in a nervous silence, flapping a dish towel and listening behind him into the kitchen and up to the plumbing and Jim. The new running shoes stuck out in front of him, *sportif*, ready for action, but at a loss till Jim should appear. Restless, Tim explored the room. He stopped by something new on the wall, an Innuit stonecut. David knew he had seen it before, but not here: a fierce, smiling face with a tattooed chin and fat red rays around her.

"*The Woman Who Lives in the Sun,*" Tim said, delighted with the savage, merry smile. "I didn't know you had this."

"I bought it back in Winnipeg, from a friend who needed money. I got it out for Paul: he loves it. The Eskimos think the sun is a woman, and the moon is her brother. Paulie's being a good feminist these days, so he supports the idea. But I'm wondering if I should sell it and buy a red Toyota?"

He listened upward for a moment. "Jim lives in Scarborough, you see. When he told me that, I thought, no, I'll kidnap you. I can't go up there, to that eastern cultural wasteland with all those picture windows. Because that's all they do up there in 'Scarberia', stare each other normal through picture windows."

There was a sudden soft downpour on the stairs. Jack gave a tight, deprecatory grin, and a tall ash-blond youth stepped in and smiled, first at David, and said hello. His accent was rather English, southern middle-class. Turning from the red sun-woman, Tim let out a surprised little laugh. David stood up, because Tim was standing, and because the boy brought something courtly in his manner. Jack had delivered, David thought: Jim was everything he wanted for 'Seeing Jim', and more than he imagined. His big eyes were violet blue, and their curve and the curve of his eyebrows made them seem even bigger. They lifted and opened your feelings like a view of the sky.

Jack was planted firmly in the armchair. "Tim Grey, Jim Fields. And David McTavish." He flapped the towel back and forth.

"You see?" Jack said. "I told you God exists."

"You did?" Tim gave the little laugh again.

"Well, at least he left the blueprints for Jim. Are you sure you'll be comfortable in that chair, Jim?"

He had dropped deeply into a golden leather-covered Windsor chair, trying to escape being the centre of attention. It was hard to tell what he thought about being taken as a proof of the existence of God. He was diffident, but without being insecure.

"I'm fine," he said, pulling his feet back along the sides.

"I don't know how that chair got in here," Jack said, irritably. It held out the loose, elegant lines of an adolescent body not quite there yet. Without seriously desiring Jim himself, David could guess how Jack felt every line.

"It's fine, Jack, really," Jim said. You could tell that, like all Jack's friends, he had learned a certain patience.

"It could fall apart at any moment," Jack said. "Paulie's going to reglue it: he likes it for some reason."

"Oh, Jack!" Jim sprang up and resettled in a threadbare armchair in the corner, away from the light.

Jack looked at Tim and David and said, "Do you believe it, this is the young man who walked into his first gay bar and said, 'I'm gay, what do I do?' All the guys who've been there since before the flood should have risen up and chanted – " Jack did chant a little for them – " '*Lord, now lettest thou thy servant depart in peace.*'"

Jim laughed. "That's not true, Jack." He turned confidingly to David, his eyes a deeper blue now they were far away from the light. "It's just that I'd never been in a gay bar before, so I said so."

"What I'm saying is, what a portent you are. You're just not bothered at all about being gay. He really isn't!"

"Why should I be bothered? If other people don't like it, that's not my fault."

"See?" Jack said. He snapped his fingers at David. "He's what we've been waiting for. But who ever thought it would be so simple? New world, new life, gay skies forever! I guess it's partly your background," Jack said, looking towards him cautiously. He explained to Tim and David. "Jim's parents and I are the best of friends. I used to say parents are for straights, gays don't really have them. Now I sit there in

Scarborough, talking gay politics. Because they aren't suburban at all. They're both English, from well-to-do, liberal families, and their eldest son's being gay fits right in. Sort of like Bloomsbury, I thought, so I'm reading up on Virginia Woolf for background."

"Jack, it's just that they like you. You're a gentleman."

"Am I? Really?" Jack was surprised by this.

The doorbell rang. "I guess you make me one, that's all. That will be Danny and Eric." He got up. "Excuse me a moment."

So for a short while, the guests were alone, the two lovers and the paragon. For David, it was the two blonds who seemed to make a pair, skins rhyming more sinuously than their names. He felt shaggy and coarse, a churl peering into some elvish grove.

"Jack is great," Tim said in a low voice, looking at Jim as if asking a question.

Jim's eyes dropped like morning glories.

"Oh, yes, he is. *He's a whole education.*"

"Jack is really special," Tim insisted, with the authority of several years older.

"I know," Jim said, looking up. "Really, Tim, I know that."

And then Danny and Eric were being ushered: friends of Jim, Jim's age, and a couple of long standing.

After dinner, as they walked south and home through the warm night, David asked, "Why did you laugh like that when he came in?"

"Like what?"

"A funny little laugh. At first, I thought maybe you knew him already."

"I guess it was because the only thing to do when you see someone who looks like that is laugh and be happy and go on living. What else can you do? Poor Jack, if he's really in love."

"Why?"

Tim paused. "Oh, I don't know. He can take care of himself, I guess. He has a lot of experience."

A light rain was beginning. David pressed the button of Tim's umbrella, watching it blossom. He went along comparing Jack's state – unreal, very shakily sublimated, disingenuous – with his own. He wasn't in love with a face, with a platonic form – he congratulated himself on this, a bit complacently perhaps. He had been thinking of inviting Tim to move in with him for days, and now, with the apartment block beginning to shoulder its way out from among houses, he had the courage to speak.

"So why don't you move in? There is that extra room, for your work."

Above them, the stretched fabric prickled like a scalp. David was almost sure he would say yes, but he knew Tim was reluctant to leave his old apartment. Yet somehow there could be no question of David's moving there. It would be psychologically wrong. The odd apartment was himself, the body he gave to Tim: it was where they were lovers.

"Well..." and David knew at once that that meant yes. "Couldn't we get a new place, after a while? I like your place, I guess, but we're bound to grow out of it."

David was too delighted to speak, or even give him a kiss. He went on as if pondering Tim's suggestion. An old man, Chinese, went by, holding a folded newspaper over his white hair. One by one, raindrops were printing themselves in among the characters.

PART 6

The unreality of Jack's new mood had seemed to follow Tim as he walked with David down towards what was becoming their apartment. It was somehow because David was obdurately real and himself that Tim wanted to live with him, because David was so different from the hopeless love Jack might try to conjure out of a teenager's evanescent good looks. David had taken Tim's ideal, perfect lover and for now at least shaped him into David McTavish or something very much like him. The reshaping wasn't complete. That ideal lover would always be with Tim, haunting him, but David had him under control, for now. Tim didn't know how long they would be together: perhaps months, perhaps years, but probably not the long, long time David thought he wanted. That was unlikely, considering the restlessness of males, their changing desire, their unchanging need to get their own way. David seemed to see himself as being feminine, accommodating himself to Tim, shaping himself around him. But it wasn't really very convincing. Tim knew David's will was as strong as his own, at least.

They borrowed a van and went to empty Tim's apartment. It took three trips, tying the two places and the two summers together for one hot, hard-working afternoon. The two different ages, twenty-two and twenty-four.

After the second trip up to Tim's, David stood looking out over the rail yards. A subway train was heading north, banging and rattling. He looked around the apartment like a conqueror: he had laid it to waste.

But he spoke regretfully.

"And you were here all this time, two years. You know, I should have run after you down the street, shouting. When we broke up before, I mean."

"Shouting what?"

"Don't be rude!" David said, with a chortling laugh. "'Fuck me! fuck me!' down Bloor Street? Well, why not?" Then all at once he was serious. "How long will we be together this time?"

"I don't know! What a question, David!"

"And what can you spring on me, I wonder? What is there I don't know about?"

"You know, you like coming up with questions like that. It's part of your – " He couldn't find a word, and stepped over to give him a hug.

"My *terribilita*," David suggested, with a smirk. Tim's mattress was leaning against the wall, waiting to be taken down into Alan and Michael's basement. Tim shuffled them over to it and butted it with his hip till it fell and followed.

"*Prick male!*" David laughed, to show he knew what was happening. There was a price to pay for the destruction he'd wrought. "That's what the Three Bears would call you: a prick male!"

A fantasy prince. Afterward, David looked him over thoughtfully and said, "You're really the intuitive one."

It was David's way of being in love, Tim knew, to spin theories and tangle you in them, like an adoring spider. But he was intrigued. Caught. Perhaps David, *intelligent behind the love*, could see who he was, what he would become.

"Christ, David, what does that mean?"

"Well, you're like that *more of the time* than I am."

"Like what?"

"*Intuitive!*" Trying to squeeze out its meaning like juice. "It means I never really know what's going on behind those brown eyes. *You will always be a mystery to me, Mr. Grey.*"

He said this theatrically – then turned away with the certainty of truth. Getting up, he began putting his new, dark-blue jeans back on, suddenly shy. Amused, exasperated, Tim watched, taking the last of his rest before the drive south and down from Forest Hill, where he'd grown up to twenty-four.

"I wish you'd make up your mind, David. Decide who I am, *once and for all*, and just tell me."

David looked up from his new jeans, frowning.

"*No, you don't,*" he said.

CHAPTER VII: HAPPINESS
Summary, 1976 - Winter, 1976-77

PART 1

Two years before, when they'd lived in separate places, David had dreamt of a fabulous city, his feelings floating along the streets that divided them, calling up another Toronto. Now their world was domestic. They were one couple, with other couples around them. Couples like Alan and Michael, or Duncan and Scott, or Charlotte and Heather and Jan (who were several couples). But there were single figures too, who might threaten the balance of things. Paul, for instance, and Jack – unless you were foolish enough to think he was taken care of by Jim Fields. Bobby Riding – we'll get to him soon. Hugh Armitage, who met them one night at Massey Hall whereupon David, on the last step down from the second balcony, gave a wholly new twist of his long body and said, "Romantic, eh?" Hugh had been changed by what David had done to himself: he wasn't an uncle anymore. He was a spinsterish older brother, somebody for David to take under his wing. Perhaps the slapdash domesticity of their apartment could cook him up a lover. There was happiness enough in the world even for Hugh, if they could only get organized. The truth is, his own new happiness made David insensitive at times, especially with unhappy people. He was inclined to think they were being stupid.

Another single figure was Mrs. Grey. They met her for lunch two weeks after Tim moved. She looked a lot older than just the two years since David had met her. She was quite gallant and showed good spirits.

After lunch, Tim said, "She approves."

"Approves? We're pals!" David gave a possessive, remembering chuckle. "I loved it when she said, 'Well, our friend Mr. Trudeau is talking through his hat, isn't he?'"

Tim smiled, but her fragile bones, her threatened heart, were with him. In him. David thought fondly and a little guiltily of his own perdurable parents, good for decades in the enchanted microclimate of Victoria.

"It's nice," Tim said, "but it makes me realize how she's changed, too."

"*You want her still to be demanding grandchildren?*" David said.

"Sort of," Tim said. "Yes, I do. *Why not?*"

David gave him a punch on the shoulder, just like a straight boy. "You're such a *sweetheart*," he said, never more in love with him.

But it wouldn't have been complete without Bobby Riding, whom David, to his surprise, produced one Sunday afternoon in September. He had gone to Bloor Street West to do some shopping. In the news store, stooping over a stack of *New York Times*, he saw he was being watched by a black-haired teenager, who was reading *The Body Politic*. The boy smiled up eagerly, and David looked down, smiling too, but at the *Times*.

"Well, isn't that dumb?" the boy said.

David picked up the paper, which he didn't usually buy.

"I mean, the fuzz in this town," the boy went on. "They all must go to Stupid School."

He seemed to be about seventeen, with rough stubble and spattered acne. He had a big, open face, but his eyes were deep-set, with the eyebrows dipping at the outsides, giving him a worried or startled look. He had full lips and a slightly receding but determined chin. His worn denim jacket was crusted with buttons, musical and political.

"I guess so," David said, warily. "But don't underestimate them."

"Yeah, sure, I know what you mean. But they are deeply dumb."

David left it at that, heading for the cash register. David took his paper with a little shrug of thanks, and put in his plastic bag. As he left the store, the boy behind him was trying to buy *The Body Politic*, rummaging through a canvas knapsack, saying "You don't take rolling papers do you?" and "Mr. Twenty, please come out!" while the clerk looked on disdainfully.

He went inside the groceteria and began tearing out green beans by handfuls, with the boy behind him again, watching. He felt as if he was being trailed by someone else's puppy.

"There are two of you, aren't there?" he said, reading this from the beans, perhaps.

"Yes, as a matter of fact."

"I could tell from the moment I saw you." He didn't seem discomfited. "And he's blond, isn't he?"

"You've seen us around?"

"No, but I see things, sometimes. I can be psychic."

"Really?" David went on to the red potatoes.

"Try me." The boy looked at the potatoes, into them, and David wondered if he was hungry.

"Well, what colour are his eyes?"

The boy stared into David's, as if flecks from one lover's eyes might get sprinkled into the other's. "Brown," he said. "Medium brown, not dark like mine."

"Well, yes, but that's not very hard. What about his name?" For some reason, it was becoming important to show this boy he wasn't psychic, that nobody is.

"Names are hard. It's because you can't see them." The boy closed his eyes tight, leaving David wondering what to say if he got it right. He didn't want to live in a world of ouija boards and ectoplasm: the imagination had to work *ex nihilo*, or it was worthless. "No, I can't," the boy said, defeated. But opening his eyes, he seemed to see it in front of him. "M!" he said. "It begins with an M. Matthew? Mark? Mitchell?"

"*Mitchell?* No, it's Tim."

The boy looked discouraged, then cheered up. "That's got an M in it."

"I suppose. Are you hungry?" As if he'd earned a prize. "Would you like an apple?"

"You must be psychic too!"

"Who knows?" But David knew he wasn't.

David paid and they went out of the store. "Can I carry something?" the boy asked.

"Are you going south?"

"South it is."

David put the plastic grips of the bag with the Times in it onto his fingers, wondering why he was giving in. The boy took the bag and then looked down in embarrassment, as if, now that he'd succeeded, he could recognize how pushy he had been.

"Anyway," David said, forgivingly, "I'm David."

"I'm Bobby, I guess."

"You guess?"

"Call me Robert, okay? I can't be Bobby forever."

"Okay. Where do you live, Robert?"

But the touch of irony in this was too heavy. "Oh, Jesus, call me Bobby!"

"Sure, whatever. But where are you from?"

"I've got some friends I can stay with any time. That's where I keep my stuff. Last night, I was dancing."

"You mean, instead of sleeping?"

Bobby's head toppled sideways, as if the word 'sleeping' had knocked him out. Then he pulled his eyes open.

"I got some sleep this morning, in the park."

"What do you do?"

"Now, that's a real problem."

"Is your family in Toronto?"

"Yes!" Bobby said determinedly. "*My family is Gay Liberation.*"

David cleared his throat, worried about what he'd taken on. "Do you have a lover?"

"I have a circle of lovers."

"And how old are you?"

"Older than I look."

"How old do you think you look?"

"I'm eighteen," he said. "Soon. How old are you, David?"

"Twenty-four."

"How long've you and Tim been together?"

"Two months, this time."

"Two months? Two months ago - I was *rich*. What do you mean, this time?"

"We were lovers the summer before last."

"Oh really?" Bobby gazed at him as if trying to read the story, psychically, and looked all the more tired and hungry.

"Was that apple enough? Would you like some lunch?"

"That would be great," Bobby confessed. "I think I spent all my money, unless there's more somewhere." He began groping again, buttons clicking.

"You spent your last money on the BP?"

"Oh, if I'd've known, I'd've just ripped it off, but there was supposed to be a twenty. And the guy on cash was looking at me and thinking, little faggot, must be a welfare case. I couldn't take it back, could I?"

David laughed. "Of course not. Well, you're welcome to lunch."

He tried to stress lunch: he and Tim didn't want to join the circle of lovers. "That's our place up ahead. It's a dump, but I like it."

"So do I."

"But we shouldn't make any noise," David said. "Mitchell may be still sleeping."

"No," Bobby said, with a psychic look.

And Tim was there as they came through the door, in the old armchair, clad in yesterday's Globe. He pulled it closer.

"Look what I found," David said, in a tone that appealed for forbearance. "Tim Grey, this is Bobby."

"Riding," he said sideways to David. And then, shyly, as if he wasn't sponsored by David and had to start from scratch, "Hello, Tim."

"We met in the store. Since Bobby looked a little hungry, I suggested lunch. I figure someone who spends his last dime on the BP has got the right stuff."

"Would you like to read it?" he said, holding it out like a gay paperboy.

"Thanks, we've got ours."

"Come into the kitchen while I unload things." David said. "What would you like to eat?"

"Salmon sandwiches."

David made the sandwiches; Bobby took them and Tim's nightgown into the living room. The sound of laughter came into the kitchen, while David worked on dinner. Then came Bobby himself, to tell him what they were talking about and say, "What a dreamboat!" He kept moving back and forth, as if to ensure neither was lonely.

When David was finished, he went in to find Bobby sitting on the couch, asking about Tim's work. David sat on the arm of the chair and gave him a hug, trying to feel what Tim thought about this new discovery of his.

"Well, David, *he's sweet, all right*," Tim said ironically after a minute, and in quite a loud voice.

Startled, David turned to look. Bobby had fallen asleep, sliding sideways along the cushions against the wall.

They rearranged cushions and their guest more comfortably and he slept all afternoon. David woke him for a late dinner, reaching into a ball of sleep. The eyes opened, looked at him in fear, then he smiled, putting them all together again.

During dinner, he told them he'd been literally thrown out of his parents' house earlier in the summer. He drew the scar on his cheek, still red, where it had been cut by the screen door. He'd come into central Toronto, which he hardly knew, on the subway, getting out at the St. Patrick stop, being in love with a boy named Patrick. To enter Toronto, by magic: David liked the idea, but knew it couldn't work. "It looked like Toronto was all hospitals." But he'd found his way around - "my legs got so tired!" - made some friends who put him up and fed him occasionally. Then he'd been picked up in a bar by a psychologist from the States, in town for a convention. The psychologist had kept him entertained for a weekend, and given him his leftover Canadian money when he left. "It was great: I was okay for weeks."

"What are you going to do now?" Tim said.

"Well, I don't know. I should get a job, I guess."

"Do you think you'd make a good waiter? We know some guys who are opening a restaurant." Tim sounded doubtful.

"Maybe I should just go down to Grosvenor Street and kind of dangle it around," he said, with unconvincing bravado.

"We're not putting you out on the street," David said, firmly.

"Don't worry about me, I'm tough." He squeezed out cold, aiming eyes.

"Well, Bobby, *they're tougher*," Tim said, gently, surprising David, who thought he was the maternal one.

As they sat drinking tea in the kitchen after dinner, there was a knocking at the door. It was Jack, looking beset and grim in the dark little corridor.

"Hello," David said. He couldn't stop adding, "What's wrong?"

"Don't ask! Nothing at all, really."

"Well, come in."

"Jim and I had a fight," Jack said, stepping through the door. "And thank God!"

There was real pain in his voice, but it seemed to David that he was wielding it quite consciously. As David led him into the kitchen, Jack explained. "We were supposed to meet in the subway, on the platform going south. It had worked before, perfectly. And he knows I can't bear waiting. I thought I was going to be there forever. A *pillar* of the TTC!"

He was surprised and put out to see there was a guest. Bobby stared back at him, fascinated. "Well," he said knowledgeably, "it can be awfully slow on Sundays."

"Who are you?" Jack said.

Bobby jumped, then froze.

"This is Jack Durham," David said. "He's an old friend, I think. And this is Bobby Riding. We just met today."

"Well, hello," Jack said, grudgingly, then turned, saying, "Let's go into the living-room, all right?" Everyone obeyed, commanded by Jack's suffering. "So I left, I had to, I'm only human. I told him that when he phoned my place, no one can wait forever, and we're finished. He said he'd run to catch his bus and missed it. Some athlete."

Jack sat on the futon, messed by Bobby's sleep.

"It was all stupid," he admitted. "We had nothing in common. In my view, he isn't even gay. I told him that: 'You're too calm, you haven't suffered enough. Hell, you haven't suffered at all. I'm sorry, but you don't pass any of the tests. You aren't even nervous.' *It drove me crazy.*"

He looked at Bobby, who was nervous, sitting cross-legged on the floor. Jack seemed to be bothered by him, as if he couldn't decide whether to forget him or make him part of the audience.

"Anyway," he said, "I thought I'd come here, and let you commiserate. I needed someone around, to tell the truth. I hope that's all right."

"Of course it is," David said. He didn't know what else to say. It looked as though Jack wanted shocked, respectful sympathy, not advice.

"It was horrible!" Jack explained, moving big, weighed-upon shoulders. "I thought they were going to say, 'Are you an emergency?' And I'd say, 'No, on the contrary, I'm just here to meet Jim.' And they'd say, 'Jim? There is no Jim. There's plutonium and madness, but there's no Jim.' And I'd say, 'Well, maybe I mixed up the time or the life or the century or the species, but I know there is a Jim and I'm waiting till he comes.' And they'd say, 'No, you're an emergency all right, and here we are.'"

Bobby was watching in fascination. Jack seemed to be losing his grip on his sarcasm, Bobby drank the story in so seriously.

"*Where the fuck was he anyway?*" Jack said, right into his stare.

"I know," Bobby said. "I know exactly what it's like."

Jack looked as if he might laugh, but didn't. "Anyway," he said, "the signore has had a journey for nothing."

"Would you like a drink?" David asked. It was the best he could think of.

While he was getting drinks for everyone, he heard Tim raising the question of Bobby Riding's future. Jack, after all, had a certain experience of street kids. But as he came back, Bobby and Tim were carrying the conversation back and forth, while Jack said almost nothing.

Then the phone rang from the bedroom. Jack scowled, painfully, afraid.

"That's probably Joel," David said. "He wants to borrow some Xeroxes." But – he closed the door when he went into the bedroom.

"Hello, David," Jim said. "Is Jack there by any chance? He doesn't seem to be at home."

"Yes, he is."

"Is he all right?"

"Well, he's upset."

"But why? I miss a bus, and the roof falls in. I don't understand: he's never been like this before. Jack is supposed to be the wise, mature one: he's always saying he is."

"That's just some of the time."

"Do you think he'd want to speak to me?"

"Right now? I don't know."

"Maybe you should call him?"

"I will, if you want me to."

"I should have known," Jim said. "I can see them coming and I think, why do this to yourself? But Jack hid it, really - he's so *fucking* cagey."

David had never heard Jim admit he was good-looking before. It was odd how he spoke: matter-of-fact or ruthless or both.

The door opened and Bobby stuck his head in to say, "Jack wants to know who it is." He looked around the room while David answered.

"Tell him it's J – just a friend."

Bobby looked at him, very much in on the secret. "All right," he said, and closed the door carefully.

"I really like him," Jim said. "But what does he want? What can I give him? With Jack, I just don't know."

David could see Jim's point of view, but now he was all on Jack's side: Jack was unreasonable, but he was the suffering one. Jim said, into the disapproving silence, "I think if I let him eat me alive, he still wouldn't be happy. So why not just give him my love and tell him I'll phone tomorrow?"

David was suddenly tongue-tied, not wanting to agree to this. Jack might never forgive him. But he was saved: Jim said, "No, could you ask him to come to the phone, please?"

In the front room, Bobby was saying, "So what if he's a hustler, he's still got all his emotions."

"Jack," David said, "Jim wants to talk to you."

Jack gave him a black look.

"I'm sorry, Jack," David said.

"So now he exists?" Jack said. "*He exists.* Well, all right."

He got up and walked heavily towards the bedroom. The door closed.

Five minutes later, he came out, looking bleak. "Thanks for the drink," he said. "For everything. I think I'm going home." He was at the door. "Don't be a whore, Bobby Riding. You'd be a flop. You're much too nice. Thanks, David."

"So what happened?" David said, worried about letting Jack go off alone.

"What happened? We're friends again. Friends! Good night."

And he went out.

"Do you think he's all right?" David asked Tim.

"Yes, I think so. Jack can take care of himself in the end."

"I guess so," David said.

"Don't worry, Bobby. It's not like this every night," Tim said.

"I like him. I like older guys too."

"Jack wasn't at his best tonight," David said.

"Oh, I could see how he felt. I was thinking about this spring when Patrick didn't come. He said he'd meet me in the park, and he didn't show. I decided to just lie down and make him come, see him come, from his bedroom, out the back window, every step. But it didn't work - I woke up in the grass."

He yawned, and Tim said, "It is getting late." Bobby looked at the hand on David's knee, sharply, with a grim wrinkling of his chin. Then he rubbed his eyes and face. "I guess I'd better let you two get some sleep."

PART 3

The next Sunday, after breakfast, Jack arrived with a surprise: a new red Toyota, which he'd managed without giving up *The Woman Who Lives in the Sun*. Jim was off with Matthew, he explained fondly. They didn't need him today, so if Tim and David wanted they could go for a drive. And then on to the Art Gallery, where Jack was going to meet Paul.

They went exploring the area near the apartment. It was a bright September day. Jack was a little too big for the car, but, as David saw, that was part of the act. Jack was a big, benevolent uncle, ready to waft you to the show or the game or the planetarium, wherever you wanted. Sitting sideways in the back seat, in the smell of new car, sped down unfamiliar streets, David felt free to ask the real questions.

"Matthew is nice, isn't he?"

"Oh yes. I really approve of him: he's just right for Jim. They're making their own little computer together now. Isn't that sweet: there's even a language for it, called LISP. I'm going to see if they can made a gay A-bomb. Of course, they know we're too nice to drop it, don't they?"

Korean and Chinese he could hardly be expected to get, but Italian and Portuguese let themselves be guessed at. *Maria le o seu futura* said her sign. *Na palma da mao e nas cartas*.

"But what about you, Jack? Are you going to the bars these days?"

"For sex, you mean?" Jack's deep, dark eyes appeared in the rear-view mirror. "No, actually, I'm not. I find that with Jim I don't really feel the need. I mean," his hand rose from the steering wheel appealingly, "don't you get tired of all that, David? Sex, passion, fucking? The whole damn slippery *Schquirmerei*?"

"No, I can't say I do, Jack. Not lately, anyway."

"Well, maybe not, but I find that Jim takes you away from all that. Jim puts you on a very different plane."

The eyes made another appearance: darksome, searching, the U-boat captain looking for prey.

"A higher one of course?"

"I'm not against sex at all," Jack hastened to say. "I'm faithful to the sixties - no sex and you'll go weird and fascist. Before you know it, you'll be voting for Nixon. And I'm certainly not saying I'm above it. Yesterday, when I was showing Paul the car, we drove out to the Beaches and sat by the boardwalk for awhile, to watch the local studs gamboling about. It was wonderful: running out into the water, with their buttocks charging along behind. Splashing back in, with those pathetic little swimsuits clinging like – " Jack was struggling, he was going to drown unless the Muse tossed him the right word – *diphtheria*! I loved it all, but with Jim around, well..."

He peered at the signs. "Portuguese? No, it's getting Italian again."

A murky window with glitter in its depths said *oro e orologio*.

"A cousin of mine died of that, diphtheria, back before I was born. It's funny, you don't die of it anymore. You don't even hear of it."

But David still wanted him to say what he was after. "Don't you get frustrated, though? Jim's a sweetheart, he's an angel to look at, as Bobby would say. But everyone needs a boyfriend of his own."

"You don't understand, David. You're right, except that right now I can't afford to be distracted. I'm working on something. I'm going to figure it out after all these years." This was less than half a joke.

"Figure out what?"

"I've decided Jim is the source of it all. Jim is the one who got you going. You know, at ten or twelve or eight, whenever, he goes by and something says, *there he goes, start wanting.*

"But what does that mean about everything after, Jack?"

"After, everything is a shadow. A nice shadow, a human shadow, one with sexy new running shoes, but not the real thing."

"I'm glad you like the running shoes, anyway." Tim said.

"Well, okay, Socrates," David said, indulgently. "Let us know your results. Will you write a book? But they won't make any difference."

"Philosophy isn't supposed to make any difference," Jack said, indignantly. "If it does, it isn't philosophy."

"Oh Jack!" David said, safe and smug. Jack was trying to unriddle love, but he didn't know anything about it. Since Jim, he'd seemed a little stunned and sexless: there was even something virginal about the big soft nice man in the front seat.

There was a comfortable silence as they sped by a *gelateria*, admiring the Italian men, who could swagger on little chairs.

"I mean, it's all very well for youngsters like you to fuck each other silly," Jack said. "But someone's got to understand what's going on. I want to know what gay love is and if Jim isn't the place to start, where is it? I mean, David, why are *you* gay?"

"The answer's right beside you."

"No! That's not philosophy. I want to know where it comes from. What it really *is*."

"But isn't that dangerous?" Tim asked, with a nervous laugh. "Once they find out, they'll know how to stop it and..."

"And Lord knows they will," Jack finished. "But don't worry. I won't tell them. Wild horses, all the king's torturers – besides, I'll make sure it's something they can't understand, something – "

"But you're wrong, Jack," David said, impatient with all the nonsense. "Tim does not get fucked."

"Oh, well – " Jack said, hastily.

"David!" Tim laughed, girlish with dismay.

"I didn't mean – " Jack said.

"No. Our Tim does *not* get fucked," David went on, implacably. He had to show Jack he'd forgotten what love was like, though he had it right here in his little car.

"We're going to be late, aren't we?" Tim said.

"I don't want Paulie waiting," Jack said, "especially today."

"No, poor boy" David went on, drunk with power, reckless, knowing what love is. "Wisdom at one entrance quite shut out."

PART 4

Paul was waiting on the steps of the Art Gallery, waving as they went by in search of a parking spot. He'd put on more weight: he looked younger and happier in the sunshine.

"You know," David said, more to Tim than to Jack, "it turns out that Paul's a friend of Charlotte and Heather and Jan. Friends of ours in the block," he explained to Jack.

"Yes, I've met them at Paul's," Jack said, a little shortly. "They're okay, I guess."

He went past a prize parking spot without seeing it, then jammed on the brakes for a narrow one.

"In their own doctrinaire way."

"Well, I like them a lot," David said, not knowing yet what he was protesting. "It's nice to be with women and not have to be stiff and straight and masculine. When I go up to their apartment I feel like – " he was going to say 'Goldilocks' and surprised himself – "Bobby Riding."

The little car had turned into a mulish hulk, sullenly refusing to be parked, while Jack shot angry looks just past David's face.

"Have you ever tried disagreeing with them?"

"They're really into the movement, of course." David agreed.

"The movement! Breathe a word of doubt and it's like rape and pornography and child abuse all at once."

Jack threw up his hands. There was nothing for it: the car was crooked forever.

"Listen, we have got to get Paul a boyfriend. *Really*. Before his mind is completely destroyed. He's actually joined a study group of men who sit around every Sunday afternoon and discuss feminist tracts. They're doing penance for all the women they raped and murdered. Of course, most of them are gay - gay and middle-aged and a bit masochistic, in my view."

He made one last attempt to wedge the car in.

"A boyfriend?" David said. "A few minutes ago you were saying you could do without one."

"That's different, I know what I'm doing. Paul's just lost. He's lonely, so he wants to play with the girls. There, if the police don't like it, fuck 'em." He turned off the ignition, opened the door, then closed it again. "But let's not talk about this. Paul and I had a kind of fight yesterday about this, about other things. We've declared a truce, but do me a favour, please: don't mention women."

So it was Tim and David who did most of the talking. They were clever children, Jack and Paul the parents who gave them an audience. Females in wait along the walls tried to entangle them, turn them against each other – for example, when David almost said, 'Hello' a De Kooning woman smiled like a shark.

"Cheerful, isn't she?" Tim said, giving him a human grin.

But there were no disasters. Then when they were about to go, Paul said, "Let's just step into the Henry Moore Gallery."

"*I love this place,*" he said, as they followed him in among the sculptures. "It's one of my *favourite* places in Toronto." You could hear how Paul had his own Toronto, which he enjoyed a lot, but which wasn't the biggest city in his country. It was refreshing to see it that way, David thought, civilized, international. There was a new spring in Paul's step, as if the open space and the natural light Moore had prescribed brought out a desire to dance in him. And in David too. The monumental figures made you a child again, immobile but alive, attentive. Jack followed last, running shoes squeaking on the polished granite of the floor.

"I didn't really know why," Paul said, "till I realized it's because this is like the old matriarchal world. You can feel human here again. At home in the world."

He spoke to David and Tim, giving his difficult ex-lover a quick, appealing look. His arms at ease behind him, Jack pushed his mouth down thoughtfully.

"I think this is my favourite," Paul said, stopping in front of a Two Piece Reclining Figure. "She's wonderful. She's so powerful! He's put all of women's power in one sculpture." Her first piece was erect, almost perpendicular, like a watch tower with small breasts and a vestigial head. The lower part was like a rock hollowed out by the sea, but still somehow human in its curves. Paul's eyes moved with exultant longing over the clay, white with green and pink gleams – ice cream colours, David thought.

"Oh?" Jack said, a little distantly. Perhaps he thought that Paul had broken the truce: perhaps he had decided to break it himself. "Cut in two? With no hands and feet? What did Moore think he was doing? Couldn't this be cruelty to women?"

"She's certainly not a victim, Jack," Paul said. He turned to Tim. "Really – that's what he's after, I'm sure. This is what the world, the landscape felt like, when the human race was matriarchal."

Jack was trying to put his hands into the pockets of his jeans, but the hands were too big, or the jeans were too tight.

"Being here is like being back when everyone worshipped the Great Mother," Paul went on, a little nervously. "When women had power. You can feel it."

"Power!" Jack said, scornfully. "In Egypt, they worshipped cats, but cats didn't have power. Paul, you've forgotten everything you ever knew. Poor old Gramsci. Last year you were crazy about him. Now, he must be rolling in his grave."

"There's an incredible amount of sexism in left-wing thought, Jack. And *homophobia*. But power isn't just the straight male idea of power."

"But it is!" Jack said. He was scowling, on the verge of a bad mood. David began to be afraid of a real scene. "Power is saying, do what I want or you starve. Do what I want or I kill you."

Tim laughed, trying to soothe Jack. He thought he had a special gift for doing that. "When was the last time someone said that to you, Jack?"

"It isn't said out loud. It doesn't have to be. It's in the air. It's unconscious. When things are running smoothly, people don't know – they don't have to know – what they're afraid of. They don't even have to know they're afraid."

"That's just your paranoia, Jack," Paul said, rashly, staring at him.

"That's just everyone's paranoia," Jack said. "I'm just a conscience, that's all."

"You'd rather be paranoid than act," Paul said. "Than get involved. Than listen."

"Oh, Paul, all right." Jack threw up his hands, affected by the open space too. "All right - I'm cruelty, to some. I'm pornography. Ban me, take me away, shut me up!"

Jack put his hand on the bottom part of the Two Piece Reclining Figure, claiming her.

"But making isn't worshipping. Moore trying to shape this woman of his. Carve her, mold her, *have* her." Jack looked ready to pick up a hammer and show them how it was done. "All the power in it is his power. Artists aren't good-hearted little Sunday School rabbits, Paul. They are conquerors. Or mean to be."

"Am I right?" he said suddenly to Tim, as if Tim was a student of his, an apprentice. Tim smiled evasively. "I didn't think your show was like that."

Jack was taken aback. "My show? No. No, maybe not, but photography is different. It's outside the world. Like philosophy."

"The truth is, Jack," Paul wheezed a little, out of nervousness, "that you're still a fifties/sixties male. Sometimes you hide it, but you never let go of one of those ideas. You still think the world revolves around your prick."

David could imagine Charlotte saying this, but not with the intimate bitterness Paul gave it. There was a certain homage in it too, which Jack heard.

Jack smiled. "I suppose there might be a kernel of truth in that, Paul."

"A kernel? Even with your friend Jim, you can't just be another middle-aged man falling for a handsome boy. Something that happens every day of the week. Jim has to be perfect, supreme, the boy at the end of the mind, and you've got to be the one who understands it all. Who's going to do a show, write a book, whatever, and tell the rest of us what love is. We don't know, we just have to sit and wait."

Jack looked away, shamed by the hurt note in Paul's voice. But he didn't give in.

"I'm sorry, Paul. But I can't help it if I'm male. I get my energy where I can. And, Paul, it may not be fashionable to say it, but any man who can't see the world through his prick is blind!"

"That's just childish, Jack," Paul said. It certainly came strangely from someone in the middle of a platonic love-affair, David thought.

"Is it? Well, maybe." Jack looked as if he was going to accept this and be good. A group of middle-aged ladies was drawing near: not feminists, but the sort of middle-class ladies who 'support' art galleries. Jack gave them an irritated, sarcastic look and declared, "Face it, Paul, nobody, *nobody*, ever had a feminist hard-on."

Paul looked away, angrily. Hearing voices raised, the women wisely guided themselves to another corner of the room. Paul turned away, to the stone and metal landscape. The sculptures were serene, august, but alert too, stern guardians. Maybe they helped Paul, David hoped.

"If you weren't gay, Jack," Paul said, in a low voice, "you'd be a Nazi."

"Then thank heaven I'm gay, Paul." Jack said.

"Well, anyway, let's go." And Paul led them out into the bright afternoon.

Trying to make peace, Jack suggested they all go for lunch at a West Indian place he knew up in the Kensington Market area. Tim and David were more than willing: Paul agreed reluctantly.

"Sharon phoned last night," Jack said, mostly to Paul. "Cathy's coming for a short stay, before school starts. My daughter, Paul's niece," he reminded Tim and David. "She's started having periods, so I'm all pink and flustered. We didn't use bronze or marble, but she's pretty powerful, my daughter!"

"I can't wait to see her again," Paul said, with some reserve.

"Maybe we can ask over Charlotte and Heather and the other one. Show them what men are still good for."

As they came into the Market area, a lime came bouncing down the gutter to greet them like a green puppy. They didn't talk much, pushing along narrow, crowded sidewalks. They stopped by a fish store, while Jack tried to figure out where he was. An octopus hung stretching from the awning, as if it had blown there in a gale. A tuna head glared at them, bathing the wound where its body had been in bloody ice.

"I love the Market," Paul said to David, again putting them in his Toronto. "Look at those fish...smell them. It's like being by the sea."

On the sea, or under it, David thought. He gazed into the pink amethyst of squid, the red-gold of crabs like legged coins from a fairy tale. At fish ranked in savage, scaly armadas, eyes seared by the air, jaws stiffened, but still with a gleam of the sea in their scales.

"The sea!" Jack said, overhearing, coming closer, as if it was the moment, the word, for a reconciliation. "The sea! That means Spanish Banks, English Bay Beach, Vancouver! Where Paul and I are headed, when we make it out of this *wretched century*. After the pretty faces, the angels, the nonsense, Paul and I are going to live in Vancouver being weird, battered, sea-beaten, old men on the beach, staring out to sea."

To charm them, to cast a spell, to win back their affections, Jack was hunching, twisting, getting gnarled and uncanny before their eyes. Stooping, reaching for Paul's arm, reaching forward into old age, for a walk with his friend along that twenty-first-century shore.

"And you come too, if you like – come and be strange, old weather-beaten lovers, too."

Paul smiled, as if he couldn't help giving in, though he knew, they all knew, that for the rest of this century at least, Jack was going to go on being himself. David gave Tim a look, taken with Jack's play-acting, relieved and moved by Jack and Paul's making up. Tim smiled back, pleased too, but refusing to get old.

"That's the way, that's how we'll do it," Jack said, still at it. "That's how we'll go out together – *all weather and waves and sea*."

PART 5

Next weekend, Jack invited them to come and meet Cathy, once David's twin sister for a few moments two years ago on the leafy porch where they were waiting now. Opening the door on a new, proud smile, Jack led them into the kitchen.

She was playing chess with Jim, pushing back rich brown hair to consider her next move. Taking it.

"Uh oh!" Jim said, as if she had him scared. As he stepped out a pawn, Matthew leaned to whisper some chess suggestion in her ear, the yellow wings of his hair brushing her brown waves.

"No," she said in a clear, low voice, pointing to a lurking red bishop, then turning dark-brown eyes on her new visitors. Jack chuckled, seeing how surprised they were, especially David, at this glossy daughter of his. Her breasts had more than started, David had to notice. Had to face, with a kind of sweet, baffled consternation: because what was he, David McTavish, gay to the death, supposed to make of this dark-eyed victory for the heterosexuals?

She advanced an ivory knight and looked up at him with a smile, not unfriendly at all but taking his measure. David found a nervous smile to come back with. And looking up at them out of the fridge, Jack gave him a wise, triumphant smirk – –as if, being such a father, he could tell you all about life.

She was a very heterosexual girl, surrounded by handsome young men, knowing they were all gay, not sure yet what she was going to make of that. She transformed them all into a skittish harem, all a little in love with her. There was enough heterosexual maleness floating in the room for at least one lover, if only she could put him together.

Later that day, Tim and David went to see Bobby Riding in the downtown restaurant where he'd got a job as a junior waiter. He was a success. His look of a punk, pink-eared cupid made a nice contrast with the modish gray decor. He confided bread and coffee like shy, hopeful secrets: sometimes customers responded with notes and telephone numbers.

When they visited his house the following weekend – he had rented a room in a gay co-op in South Riverdale – they had to cross a living-room strewn with women's clothing. You couldn't see much of the floor.

"They were dressing up," he explained. "Rennie and his gang." Rennie was the house-mother, who scared up the rent every month. "You've just got to walk on them, that's all there is to it. They don't really mind. But watch!"

A concealed pair of heels had launched Tim on a stumbling run through the wrack of clothing.

In Bobby's room, there were records and magazines and books on the floor instead. A pair of blue vinyl-covered weights sank into his futon, dreaming of pecs and lats like the ones on the wall, which was being papered with slick male flesh. And there were pictures of singers and rock groups, David Bowie flirting with various colours of hair, and – ancient history – Andy Warhol's multiple Marilyn, dying back with her sweet little sigh. A maple tree brushed hot pink leaves against Bobby's window. David felt a pang of nostalgia for the boyhood he had never experienced.

He could follow it closely, however. Bobby had adopted them. "I like couples," he said. "You're a great couple." He'd visit to keep up, to keep them up with him, to introduce friends, to borrow records and books. David had found a fellow reader, and couldn't resist taking his education in hand. He began by lending him *Wuthering Heights*, which he wolfed, which gave him nightmares. He fell victim to what he read, so *Madame Bovary* went down like a dose of arsenic. He was still agonizing when he returned it. Bobby's imagination made David envious. He was supposed to be the creative one, but his characters wouldn't let themselves be seen. They preferred to sit in dark corners and spring clever remarks. Bobby dreamt the books he read, and when he told his own stories they shone in front of him, tales of a gay, golden city.

Bobby was an explorer, as well as a reader. When they went out, he would be likely to turn up out of nowhere, as plump and impossibly buoyant as a Pitseolak bird. In clothes that were part some fashion, part his own fancy, he'd give them an odd, mocking grin that left them to wonder who he was in his mind. At bars, as the crowds began to thin, he'd appear in the gaps, wrapped in stealthy fantasy, making his way through a tall forest where the trees were alive and male and might ask you home. Or he'd slip out under the cold, wise street lights.

David was seriously worried about him. "This isn't San Francisco, Bobby. You can't fuck in the streets!"

"We're *working on it*, David," Bobby said.

One night, they saw him dancing wildly at a disco on Yonge between Gerrard and Dundas Streets. Known as *The Strip*, that area was filled with message parlours, punks and panhandlers. Bobby pranced tempestuously to some angry English opinions. When he finally stopped, David went to ask how he was doing. He must have heard, 'What are you doing?' He gave David a big smile, so blurry it was several smiles floating together like seaweed, and held up a hand to count.

"Tommy had the greatest grass, and then we went to Michel's and – " It looked as if one hand wouldn't be enough.

"Bobby," David said, desperately. "You're – " how to put it? How to save him? "You're *intelligent!*"

It took him a few seconds to see what David was getting at. He had to focus back through each drug separately to the intelligence David wanted.

"I thought my mother was in fucking Ajax!"

Before David could wriggle out of being his mother, Bobby sank smiling back into the drugs and pulled him out onto the dance floor. He had taken David in hand, too.

During the afternoons, when Tim was at work, Bobby would bring over friends. He was generous with his friends, and with David's living room. It was as if there was a sort of gay high school pouring through it, a high school of the bars and streets. David was pleased, fascinated with the odd wisdom it taught, and also a little disappointed. On their first Sunday afternoon, Bobby had seemed to be a stray, destitute, woebegone - as soulful and introverted as David without Tim. Now he seemed to have more friends than he could keep track of, including a wide selection of advisers, mentors, and surrogate parents. David couldn't claim a monopoly on any side of him.

One of the first David met became a good friend of his. Ken McAlistair - for some reason everyone always used both names – was Bobby's "best political friend," as opposed to the ones who were "just into the gay scene." He was a student at Victoria College, intelligent, a dark Scot like David. He seemed to think, and not unreasonably, that if he hadn't been militantly gay he would have had a place in the running of the country. He had the right kind of intelligence, the right background ("Dad's a *comprador*, and good at it too") and a consuming passion for Canadian politics. He read the *Globe* as if his life depended on it. He seemed to know about all the MPs in the country. Ken had the same appetite for political gossip as Peter's lust for Caroline drama. A few years earlier, he would have gone to Ottawa and become a civil servant, on the left, working for good causes, perhaps drawn in by his fascination with power. But the gay movement had happened, and some old stubborn sense of justice had required him to come out and fight. Everyone at Victoria College knew he was gay, and wouldn't shut up till gays had their rights: he'd have to follow his beloved politics from a distance.

David , impressed with Ken McAlistair, was scared of him too. He was an *enrage*.

"If you saw the premier drowning in Toronto harbour," David said, "you wouldn't even throw him a life-preserver!"

"And you would, *you rabbit!*" (And this was the first time they'd met.) "You'd fish him out and say, 'Mr. Davis, I'm so glad to meet you, can I shake your hand, can I kiss your ass?'"

"Well, I couldn't just let him drown."

Ken McAlistair stared at him with eyes that had seen injustice.

David was frightened, but he liked him. In some ways, he resembled Chris, with a different creed, without the curls, without the love. A Chris he could quarrel with, without the pain.

Another of Bobby's friends was Sally. "I really love her," he said, with a yearning look, his chin deep in his hands at the kitchen table. "Sometimes I think she's my best friend in the world."

"But that's so fashionable!" David protested, not quite knowing why. "All over the continent, gay boys are leaning and sighing and saying, 'Oh, she's really my dearest friend in all the world.'"

"You're *jealous!*"

"No. No, I've got my *own* lesbians. Right here in the block, you'll meet them. You'll fit in beautifully, too: Bear Four."

But when David saw Sally come running across Queen Street, he almost fell in love too. He staggered and pulled himself back. She ran like a long-legged boy: unlike any other woman David had chanced to look at in his life. She wasn't webbed across between her thighs with confusion and dire secrets and misery. She was like a hand-some youth, beardless and ruthless, but with a tender spot for mixed-up gay boys like Bobby. And David.

Afterwards, he was still dizzy, infatuated.

"You know lesbians are really interesting," he said to Bobby. "I never realized. I mean, the whole idea of lesbians. I used to think they were just women who wanted to muscle in on being gay, for odd female reasons. But with Sally, with Heather and Charlotte and Jan, you begin to think maybe they're a lot better at it than we are. Less tense and scatty, more human. I wonder, maybe they're the real gays?" Bobby was watching him across a little restaurant table, with a skeptical twist in his mouth and chin. He looked south across Queen Street and back.

"You want to know what Sally would say, David?"

"What?"

"She'd tell you to *suck eggs.*"

"Why!"

"You'll learn. *Some day.*"

Rennie was elusive for a while, legendary, one of Bobby's leading authorities on the gay scene. Then he turned up at a gay dance at Trinity College: a sharp-faced, sandy-haired, fast-talking young lady in a flapper's shoulderless black frock. He pretended to be scornful about political types like Ken McAlistair, casting himself as a sort of pre-Stonewall queen. She was older than the rocks, she'd seen it all and saw through it now. Rennie was in love with clothes and styles, male and female, but he didn't take them seriously. He was scornful of friends who were so fussy and fragile they could die for a shade of blue. "That crowd at Attitude! All they do is look at each other sideways and wonder, who's the fashion victim tonight? Bobby, believe me, you aren't stylish if you're scared stylish."

You could see the difference between them when they danced. As a song began to insinuate itself into the one that held the floor began to build into a cathedral of sound, throbbing and palpable as the womb, Bobby would squeal and rush onto the dance floor. He'd dance up on the balls of his feet, twice as fast as everyone else, as if he wanted to fling himself away like roses. Rennie stepped out, dropped his cigarette and killed it with a long, loving twist of his foot, and all his dancing flowered out of that cruel twist. He put the music on like another layer of fashion: mouthing the lyrics, acting them out in gay, flashing-eyed rituals, handing the poppers around like a dizzy sacrament.

Bobby wasn't scared stylish: in fact, he wasn't stylish at all. He would never be self-possessed enough to handle the crowd at Attitude. He took being gay too passionately: it was his way of taking in the world.

One day he brought over another pair of friends, plunked them down in the living room and came into the kitchen to brief David. "They are my model friends...Richard and Richard. I was going to warn you, but I couldn't get to a phone."

What did he mean, model friends? But Bobby was pulling him into the living room, where one chestnut, one auburn, they sat reflecting great, slightly melancholy handsomeness off each other. They were in Jim Fields' league, almost, David thought: they could pitch for the Thrones or the Cherubim. Had he seen them at the bars? No, in magazines.

"They're nice enough," David said afterwards. "But do you have to buy *Toronto Life* to see them smile?"

"It's tough what they do," Bobby protested. "Do you know, they don't really think they're handsome. They'll say, 'My nose is crooked, my eyes are too big, I know I'm going to break out.' It's like they aren't sure they're really worthy, and someone's bound to notice."

For Bobby their looks were mythic. Permission to dream.

"You know, they're planning to go to New York. Maybe Milan, but probably New York. They've got it all planned: got the right contacts, got the right work in their portfolios. Imagine!"

"Imagine what?"

"I mean, to be *beautiful* like that here, in *Toronto*. To be the most incredible-ever dancers at Desire's – *okay, all right*. But to be beautiful in *New York*!"

"What's the difference?"

Bobby stared at him, round eyes getting rounder. He acted shocked.

"New York! New York is the difference!"

One Saturday, there was a knock on the door. When David opened it, he recognized only Rennie, escorting a tall, pale young lady in a blue dress. Then her heels wobbled.

"Bobby," David said, almost breathless. Bobby had been discussing it with everyone he knew, and now he'd taken the plunge into the lake of dresses and come up quite pretty, though the make-up had to be thick to cover black stubble and the screen-door scar.

"We're on our way to the dance, if you'd like to come," Bobby said, stepping demurely in.

"Tim! Come see what Bobby's done!" David was excited, almost frightened. He snatched at full, impossible breasts, grabbing wildly, like a thirteen-year-old, with hands that almost hurt when the breasts didn't squeeze like flesh. Bobby had confided the recipe: nylons stuffed with rice.

"Don't get me messed!"

"Look," David said as Tim came in. "The *lovely* Roberta Riding!"

"*Don't be a jerk!*" Bobby said, indignantly.

David looked at him, apologetically, but still scared and wild. "If you were a girl, Bobby..." Bobby's heels brought his eyes level with David's. If Bobby was a girl, or if David was, or if David was straight, or if... David didn't know what he meant, except that, thanks to Tim, he'd begun looking at women differently lately. You'd never know it, watching them step proudly out of Holt's or Creed's as if they'd conquered their clothes, not bought them, but some women at least must cling to their lovers' necks and cry for joy. Even here, even in Toronto: women David could see. There was a kind of fellow-feeling in seeing that, and it was almost desire.

"Well, I'm *not*," Bobby said, hotly. "That's the whole point. And David, you just don't *know how to be gay*."

"Do you?"

Looking in Bobby's big, dark, possibly psychic eyes, David saw that the secret of their friendship was that Bobby was really as inward, as introverted as he was, for all the adhesiveness. Perhaps Bobby saw him see it too, but then he smiled, letting a dreamy femininity come welling up into his eyes.

"Do I? Honey, get your shoes on: you're going dancing."

And he had more up his sleeve. It was the weekend after the dance, when he'd been sitting silent and *farouche* in the living room, that he coughed and announced, "I guess you know I want to fuck with you two."

David was too startled to speak. But he wasn't surprised.

"Why?" Tim said.

"Why? Or it wouldn't be complete."

"But we don't do that. We said we're *monogamous*."

"So? Because what I love is *the both of you*."

"Well – " Tim's voice wavered, amused, intrigued. David was afraid that Bobby could unbalance everything. The interchangeable sex of his world could dissolve Tim and David. It would be like going to bed with the ocean.

"How can we be friends and gay and not fuck, ever?" Bobby demanded. "To me, it's just *de rigueur*. David, sometimes I think you might as well be straight. You think that sex is a Big Deal!"

"Well, *it is, damn it*!" David said, putting his foot down. "I'm sorry, but I'd feel strongly about it. I love you, but in a very different way from that."

"You're treating me like a child!"

"Well, Bobby…" David had him there: he was remarkably young.

"I knew it! I should've made you call me Robert."

"We can start doing that now," David said, generously. He could afford to be generous, seeing he'd won, for today at least.

"No, it's too late." Bobby stared at him. "But there's one thing sure: I'm going to bed with you some day."

Mercifully, he went and fell in love with a twenty-one-year-old named Doug, who drove a delivery van. When they met him, he came swinging unlaced workboots up Church Street as if they were ankle-deep in glum, northern romance. Bobby was hurrying along beside, in the same costume of jeans and flannel shirts. Doug was gruff and long-haired and just getting over a passionate affair with acne. He moved and stood as if his masculinity was so serious a thing it weighed on him.

For a while, Bobby saw less of a lot of his friends, especially the fashionable ones, but he kept in touch with Tim and David. "*I* think he's beautiful-looking," Bobby said. "And he's just got his own way of doing everything. And of course, like he says, if I'm going to be his, it's got to be all of me."

So they were safe for a while at least.

"But you know that glue?" Rennie said, "that special gay glue they use so no one can ever tear the posters down? And you're going by years later, and you see an ad for some dance, and you try to remember what happened. Who was it that night? What was his name anyway? But there it still is: come to the dance everyone. Well, that's what *you're* like, Bobby."

PART 6

Winter came, pressing its cold sides against their windows. Instead of going to his carrell high in the university library and staring at a frozen lake and its frozen city, David would usually stay home, reading and quarrelling with John Ruskin, trying to wrestle him into some kind of shape. At times, he seemed simply impossible, a sort of hysterical Proteus, a shape-changer.

"Maybe I should just go crazy," he said to Tim. "He did." Not a high Victorian like David, Tim found it hard to be enthusiastic about Ruskin.

David did have to go out occasionally, to get more books. One evening he fought his way home through a storm, his backpack weighed down with *The Stones of Venice*, stumbling over gray-glass, crocodilian sidewalks. He hadn't bothered to put in his lenses—he had a lover, he didn't have to be pretty – and came through the door of the block into the blinding beef stew. He took his glasses off, went down half-seen stairs into a blurred apartment, and stamped his feet angrily, noisily, but all to himself, since Tim wouldn't be home yet.

"Bloody winter," he said, exactly like Glenda Jackson. "*Bloody* winter. Oh!"

Because Tim had come into view, to help him out of his primitive space suit. A deadline had been extended, and he'd got home before the storm.

And somehow, out of that winter rage, David found his way into Tim at last, stepping cautiously into the heat of his blood, afraid of what he could do to Tim – transform him, perhaps, into something slippery and nelly as his insides. Beginning to wonder if he cared, lust lifting into bliss, endorphins and encephalins choiring around him, singing that he was the hero after all, his body's, this world's long-lost saviour arriving home at last.

"What have we done?" David said, into the pink curves of Tim's ear.

"I told you this would happen, David." Tim shook them both with a laugh. "It was bound to. Thanks."

"You mean that, don't you?" David said, almost incredulous. "'Thanks'. You liked it. You're saying thanks."

"Yes," Tim said. "Something wrong with that?"

Nothing, said time. Having delivered its surprise, winter went on as before, happily. Tim didn't stop being himself, and when David saw he was safe from that, he was as proud of his conquest as any teenager - secretly, except Tim saw right through him, and couldn't help hinting furiously to Bob. To Jack, until, from the platonic clouds, even he got the point and laughed at him, fondly. But the fondness had an envious sharp edge, too. The affair with Jim was somehow, obscurely, not going well, and Jack could get quite bitchy at times, David thought. Jack had forgotten how to live happily: he needed a lesson or two.

PART 7

Bobby came over for dinner one winter afternoon, bringing a brown paper bag which held, he announced, presents from GoodWill. Rennie and Bobby bought a lot of their clothes there, tugging at whirlpools of crushed shirts and pitiful, wrung arms going down for the last time. Tim wasn't home yet, so Bobby kept the presents safely in the bag. "There's something for each of you," he said. "For *all of us*, really."

"What?" David said, suspiciously.

"You'll see."

They went into the kitchen, where David was working on dinner, and talked about Doug, from whom Bobby was recovering. "In the end," he said, sharing hard-earned wisdom, "he couldn't see you just can't be queer and still be one of the guys."

There was a loud knock on the door and David went to open it. Jack Durham stood in the little passageway, his face grim and whitened by the cold, his clothes exhaling it. Something was plainly wrong, but he stalked in almost silently.

He was taken aback at finding Bobby there before him in the kitchen. It was as if he still hadn't decided what to make of him.

"How are you, Mr. Riding?" he inquired, with more grandeur than was called for.

Bobby took a fit of silence. Then he got out, "Just fine, thanks. How about you, Mr. Durham?" Jack laughed. "All the better for being asked!"

"And how's Jim and Matthew?" Bobby went on, rashly.

"Fine - they're fine." Jack pulled up a chair to sit down at the table with Bobby. "The computer is up and running. Matthew is a wonderful idea, really: I wish I'd had him."

"But you know, Jack, sometimes I think it's Jim who's the older one. He's so sensible and rational – I mean, that's a real computer, not a toy. And you're like a kid with a crush: it's like me and Chris."

"Who's Chris?" said Bobby, because he had to know everything.

"A straight guy with *confusingly* curly hair at U. of T. I was in the process of mooning around after him when I met Tim. Jack saw him once – remember? – on College Street? You admitted he was cute."

"So what happened?" Bobby asked.

"Tim came along. I got over Chris. I guess I just outgrew him, Bobby."

There was silence except for the tender ripping of lettuce.

"My God," Jack said, hurt.

David realized he'd gone a bit too far, and shrugged.

"It really is a thankless business, isn't it Bobby?"

Bobby stared warily.

"I mean, you bring them along, you help them through their little tragedies, you lie awake nights wondering if you've done the right thing. Then they tell *you* to grow up."

"I didn't mean it that way, Jack! Really. But it is kind of frustrating to see the way you treat Jim. The way you treat yourself."

"Why?" Jack demanded. *"Why should it frustrate you?"*

"I don't think you're getting anything out of it. You aren't even taking photographs."

"How could I? I told you, Jim's really invisible. He's in another world."

"Jack, I hate that Platonic crap. You know, apparently the Greeks didn't even fuck, except between the legs. That's Plato on love: fucking between the legs and saying everything real is far, far above you. It's all just guilt, and it's no wonder you aren't happy."

"But that's not true. I am happy. I'm lucky. Hell, David, I'm *blessed*!"

There was a kind of gasp coming through the last word, as if Jack couldn't believe what he'd let out.

David began cutting up tomatoes. The day before he'd run out and down the street after the knife-grinder, armed to the teeth, like a happy murderer: now the pink-orange flesh was sliced, opened before it knew it. It seemed time to dissect Jack's problems too.

"So why don't you just go to bed with him?" David said. "Whatever he's like in bed, he can only be human." He didn't really think things are that simple, of course, but he thought Jack needed to be shaken up.

Jack looked at him in silence for a moment, taking it very seriously. Bobby looked back and forth between them.

"I mean, we know Jim wouldn't mind: he's said so. Or Matthew."

"David, really! That's just so stupid. When I told you to fuck your brains out, I didn't mean it literally. I don't *want* to go to bed with him. In fact, I don't know how to – he's just not that kind of phenomenon. There's no sex act known to man that could say what I want to say."

Suddenly, as if bothered by Bobby's staring, or wanting to make a diversion, Jack demanded, "What about you? Would you like to go to bed with him?"

"You know my politics," Bobby said, shiftily.

"With *Jim*, I mean – Jim's not politics."

Bobby laughed weakly. "You take my breath away, Jack. Wouldn't you – if you were me?"

Jack gazed at him as if helpless for a moment not to imagine being Bobby Riding. Of being Bobby in bed with Jim. Then he turned away and said, "But I'm not you, am I? That's the whole point, if you don't mind me saying so. Or part of it, anyway. And David's being – I don't know what David's being, but I can't say I like it."

There was only the sound of David's knife, chopping green onions now. The hurt in Jack's voice was making David guilty: he'd been meddlesome, and even a little pompous, perhaps. Sooner or later Jack would have to face reality, but it wasn't the time yet. He was ready to apologize, except that now it seemed Jack was amicably changing the subject.

"Some gays wear clothes from New York or Milan. Or turn up in dresses and high heels. David here wears food."

"What do you mean?" David said, happy to be teased if it meant Jack had forgiven him.

"There you are, dressed in lettuce and tomatoes. Last time it was apples and pie dough."

It was true, David thought: he enjoyed these kitchen performances.

"It's just that I like feeding people, Jack. Like Paul. I do love to see food that I made disappear into happy faces."

"Yes – and it's so domestic, David. So tranquil. You know, working on the phones – I do that for Toronto Area Gays, as David knows, my little bit for the cause – and sometimes you get people who phone and then don't say anything. There's just silence, and you don't know, it could be kids daring each other and trying not to laugh, or if you want to be paranoid it could be the police. Or it could be some guy in the suburbs who's taken a year, or forty years, to get the courage to dial and needs another few minutes to get started. So you just talk, hoping he will too."

Jack laughed sadly. "Really. We forget, but there still must be gay people who live and die without speaking to anyone. Anyway, that happened last night, and I ended up talking about you, David, you and Tim, and how nice your life was, how much I liked it. In the end, I was almost giving out your recipes."

"So did he say anything?" Bobby said.

"Not that one, last night. Maybe he'll call back. Maybe Tim and David will persuade him."

"Well, let's hope so Jack," David said.

"Some of us still go through hell, I said, but there are gays who are just happy. They just go about their lives happily. *What a triumph*!"

Jack paused, letting them fall into a quiet, domestic tableau. David was content to let their quarrel die away.

Then Jack began again, musingly, "Last fall, around the end of the warm weather, I was up in Scarborough. I drove up, and Jim was in a park, throwing around a football with some friends. They do things like that up there: it's a jock Arcadia. He was barefoot – they've never heard of broken glass. He was running, looking up at the ball, not looking where his feet were."

David looked up from the cutting board. Bobby's eyes narrowed, expecting pain.

"And you know, I could taste – the grass."

Bobby scowled a little, wondering. Jack had an odd look: for the first time he looked what he'd said he was, that hazy day on Queen Street. Astonished.

"I did! Don't you know what I mean. It was as if I could suddenly taste everything through him – the grass, the air, the sun, everything around. Time, the time I was in: I could feel it in me *so deeply I could taste it*. And I thought, you fool, you'll never photograph this."

He gave David a weak smile, guilty, and defiant too. He had taken desire like a sword out of his guts and put it bleeding on the kitchen table.

"Well, Jack," David began, "I think I know what you mean, but – "

"I wasn't asking for advice," Jack said, quickly.

"Well, if we don't look after you, who will?"

"I was boasting. I don't need looking after, David. I'm doing splendidly." He shifted uncomfortably, frightened now of what he'd let out.

"That's the trouble with married people, isn't it, Bobby?" Jack said. "They think they've got the monopoly on it. Happiness. They're the professionals, the experts.

They don't like adventurers like you and me, explorers: they can't admit we have something too."

Bobby got more and more silent, his eyes darkening.

"We all need someone else to be realistic for us at times, Jack – " David said.

"Realistic! Come on, David: what a crummy, mealy-mouthed, shitty little word!"

"I'm sorry, Jack, but – "

"David, what *gives you the right* – " Jack almost lost his breath " – *the right to tell me* – " It was as if Jack was about to dive into the cold water of his own misery. Into a real fight with David. And David, though he was frightened, didn't entirely mind. He didn't like to hear that longing could be infinite, unsatisfiable, that it had to reach for the sky. If Jack wanted to fight, David had the strength, and the happiness, to fight him.

Abruptly Bobby had begun speaking, looking down at the table, talking right through them.

"You shouldn't fight. You shouldn't. *Or it's just no good.*"

"We aren't fighting," David said quickly.

Bobby pushed on, not listening. "That's what my parents did, all the time. It would come through the wall at night, it'd go *rah-rah-rah* and that was my mom, and it'd go *wuh-wuh-wuh* and that was my dad, and then they'd both be going at it, like the fucking wall was going crazy. And I could never tell what was really happening, never." He looked up with a tight, scared imploring face, at Jack, at David, then down.

Jack and David looked at each other, warily, making a truce over his bowed head.

"All right, Bobby, we aren't going to fight."

"David and I are the best of friends, really."

But David heard a note he didn't like in Jack's voice, not just relief, exultancy, as if he thought he'd won the fight that hadn't happened: he'd made his affair with Jim bigger, more serious, in his own mind, in David's. The hopelessness of his longing was a kind of triumph.

"There!" David said, thumping the salad bowl in front of Bobby, just where he was looking. It was meant to be a sort of gift, but David was so nervous it looked like an attack. "You toss it. Please."

Bobby didn't move.

"Here," Jack said, handing him the wooden fork and spoon. Bobby took one and then the other with sluggish, bitten fingers.

"You just shouldn't fight," he said. *"Or where's the point?"*

He began on the saddest salad, and nothing more was said about Jim or love for the next few minutes. Then Jack had to leave for dinner.

David followed him to the front door. Jack got his apology in first. "I'm sorry, David. I'm a little on edge these days."

"I admit I was being *kind of officious.*"

"I don't really mind. I suppose it must seem strange. It is strange. Of course I'm in love with him but – " He shrugged. "But I can't afford to let it be just that."

Just what? David wondered. He said, "I think I understand."

"I know you do," Jack said irritably. "That's why I wish you wouldn't say *stupid* things!"

David placed a rather formal kiss on Jack's stubbly cheek. "You know we love you, Jack."

Jack laughed out loud. "We!" he said. "We! You sure got yourself married, David."

"I do like that man," Bobby announced in his Bette Davis way as David came back into the kitchen.

"You do? I mean, of course, but – "

"But what?"

"It can't go on like this. He's just going to have to get over it. Write his dialogue, take his pictures, whatever, and go find someone else. Someone who's allowed to be human."

He wasn't talking down to Bobby, exactly. He was showing him how intelligent gay men talk about each other. Bobby was more than bright enough, but with his lower-middle-class background he needed models.

Bobby pouted, fixing him with big, shrewd eyes. "Why does he bother you so much?"

"He doesn't," David said shortly. Then he looked at Bobby again. The trouble with intelligence is that it's always coming back at you.

"Oh?"

"Well, maybe he does. Because if Tim left, that's how I would be in love." He laughed, exasperated. "There's no end to you, is there, Bobby? Don't be so *damn* psychic."

David still didn't see what was coming. After dinner, Bobby pulled out the brown paper bag and from it two explosive Hawaiian shirts. "*Fuck winter*, I said. I can't stand it."

He spread out Tim's shirt across his chest, sitting beside him on the couch.

"There. Now, isn't he just incredible-looking, David?"

He hugged himself against Tim's chest, his temperate-zone colouring surreal against a backdrop of palm trees. David was spreading his shirt against himself, charitably: it was like wearing Aunt Irene's awful tie down to Christmas dinner. Then he caught the dark, sharp eye trained on him from over Tim's heart.

"Because you *know* you're my favourite couple," Bobby proclaimed. "You just can't help it."

CHAPTER VIII: FIGHTING WITH JACK
Spring to Fall, 1977

PART 1

One afternoon in April, Tim was walking south to the Y, passing the tavern where he had first met Jack Durham, two years before. A teenager with long hair hurried ahead of him, chewing into an arrowhead of pizza, boot-heels pounding like sex. A hustler, Tim thought: time for the men getting off work. On the sidewalk leading to the tavern door, two youths were tossing conversation like a slow game of catch. Another was making an exhibitionist phone call, lithe and lounging inside the glass booth. And by a detachment of newspaper boxes, a man was stooping, peering at the ground.

"Hello, Jack!" Tim said, coming up from behind.

Straightening and turning, Jack looked at him with a flushed and guilty face. Tim said, "You dropped something?"

"No. No. I was just feeling the sidewalk." He made it sound obscene. And there was misery in his voice, like a flu beginning.

"Why?"

"Why? I got to thinking, I don't know what if feels like – I've been here for years now, and I've *never let myself feel the real, solid, concrete Toronto.*"

Something must have gone wrong with Jim. Embarrassed, Tim looked down, at the dirt dropped by snow, gnawed pizza rims, the bivalves hamburgers come in, sheets of the *SUN*, restless and sensational in a light breeze. In the shadow of the boxes he caught a dull gleam and stooped, grabbing for something to make Jack happy. It was a dim quarter, Elizabeth up. With his fingertips scrabbling for it in the grit, he felt what Jack had evoked, the millions of tons under them, around them.

"Is this yours?" he said apologetically, holding it out.

"Is anything mine?" Jack answered, with irritable philosophy. But he accepted it grandly, a former millionaire not too proud to accept charity. "Yes, I dropped it trying to buy a paper. But maybe now we can get ourselves a drink?"

Jack gave a slightly desperate smile, and Tim surrendered the afternoon.

They went into the bar and sat down, looking around like strangers. It was nearly empty.

"So what've you been up to?" Tim said.

"Oh, the usual. Middle-aging nicely."

"You're not *middle-aged*!" Tim protested, loyally. "You're not *old*. You're only – what? thirty-five? thirty-six?"

"Thirty-seven? Thirty-eight? No, I'm not old. That comes later – *that's a whole other trip* – as we used to say. You don't know about middle age yet, Tim. That's when you turn into something your aunt would buy for you at Simpson's, if she were buying your body. Your body, your feelings, your opinions. Something that will last well, that will get you through twenty or thirty years without a lot of wear, it you're careful. Something practical – but not fancy, not sexy at all."

"As Charles used to say, 'You're in a good mood.'"

Jack looked around again, nostalgically. "You don't *know*," he said, with sudden passion. "You're well, you're in great shape – I haven't been sick for years, I don't know how to get cavities. But your youth is in extremis. Your youth is *dying*."

"Come on, Jack," Tim said, gently. "What's really going on?" Jack stared at him angrily. "Jim, what else?" He looked away as one of the ancient waiters made his way over, to sell them draught beer, to be tipped with sidewalk-coloured quarters.

"I could do that," Jack said, as the waiter shuffled off. "Maybe you'll come in here some day, and look up and see some old geezer with a face like an elephant's knee."

He was shaping himself into this gloomy fantasy, pulling his shoulders up, lowering his head.

"And you'll say, 'That looks almost like Jack – like Jack back from the grave to breathe down our pretty necks . But no, it couldn't be, no one's that *desperate*.'"

Tim laughed. The far-off, bony shoulders were as distant as Kilimanjaro. He was worried about Jack but he was safe from his mood: there were five years, all strong and healthy, to keep him from thirty. Which is only thirty.

"Here!" Jack said, abruptly reaching alongside Tim's head. "Stay still!" His hand was into Tim's hair, almost into his thoughts. "Got it!" There was a needle of pain, and Jack was brushing his hands over the floor.

"What are you doing?"

"Just a gray hair."

"No, it wasn't!"

"Don't worry, there was only one, and now it's gone."

Tim looked, but the scratched linoleum could soak up a downpour of gray hairs.

"You prick, Jack!"

Jack stared back at him. "*Youth!*"

"Well, it's not my fault."

"Not this time." Jack looked away and said, quietly, "Jim's left town."

"*Left town!*" It was worse than he'd imagined. "Where to?"

"The States. A big place, the States."

"You don't know *where exactly*?"

"His family didn't want to tell me, and I wasn't going to ask, to beg." The humiliation of this passed across his face. "But he was from there, the new friend. *Der Americanische Freund*. A clean break is best, he said, in a letter. I could find out, I suppose, I could worm it out of people, but he's right. He's gone, that's it. Maybe he was right, that I was getting too 'possessive'."

He growled the word, looking around as if his anger could possess everything there – possess it and shake it.

"Well, I'm sorry, Jack. Really."

"Can't be helped!" He raised his beer glass. "*Close the border, I say.*" He was doing his surly sixties nationalist. "Why did we ever let them in, in the first place? Wrecking our hockey, poisoning our rain, seducing all our handsome boys!" Jack took a deep swallow. "*Sic Peggy Atwood on them!*"

Tim took a reluctant gulp of his own. He had to do something for Jack, but he didn't want to follow him down into beery depths. And now that looked almost inescapable.

"I was going to go swimming," Tim said, cautiously. "Why don't we both go?"

"You know I never go there," Jack said, as if the idea was ridiculous. And then he admitted, "I used to swim a lot. In my youth."

"Well?"

Jack looked at him, questioning the misery inside himself. "Why not?" he said.

Twenty minutes later, a naked, heavy-set Jack was lowering himself into the water, tenderly, shrinkingly, but like a man ready to try a new element. Tim watched, cheering him on cautiously, thinking about the odd way a person's nakedness rises into his face, softening it.

Tim didn't swim a mile, because they were keeping each other company, swimming a few lengths, then stopping to talk. But then, his energy not satisfied, Tim did some splashy, passionate laps of the butterfly stroke.

"I used to do that!" Jack shouted, when Tim stopped, at the other end of the pool.

"It's hard!" Tim shouted back, panting. "*Really* hard – "

But Jack was off, throwing himself at the water, arms wide: he was thrashing and surging dolphin-like towards him. Two-thirds of the way, he stopped all at once and sank. Tim swam towards him, afraid he might be in trouble.

Jack rose, standing on the shallow bottom, gasping, streaming like a Bernini fountain. Tim stood too. Jack's face was exhausted, desperate, broken open for a second, with no energy to mask a Jack Durham, solitary beyond speech.

"My last – " he pulled in air " – last *butterfly!*"

PART 2

Two days after Tim had told him all about his meeting with Jack, David ran into him at a bookstore, pale and nervous, heading for the cash register with a long armload of books. "I've *got* to catch up with these people," he said, defensively, clearly afraid of David's condolences. "They're trying to bury me." But, "I'm fine," he insisted. "Recuperating nicely. There are bad days, of course—days you want to go down to Queen Street Mental Health and say, 'My fingers are the Ten Lost Tribes. Give us shelter.' But, no, I'm okay, I'm sitting up and taking notice. I mean *he's* a looker, isn't he?"

David felt sorry for him, but Jack and Jack's unhappiness had a working marriage, he thought: they were too insensible, they liked each other too well, to do each other lasting damage.

"Well, thank God for middle age!" Jack said, with brave, bitter cheer, heading off for a weekend with Barthes and Foucault.

A week later, on Saturday, Tim and David went to a party, taking along Bobby Riding, whose usual weekend had been cancelled by the clap. It was a big party, given by two doctors, in an endless apartment forty stories above Bloor Street. In the front hall, David was startled to see a photograph of Charles from Jack's show, naked, cross-legged, holding his long toes by handfuls. He stopped to take it in again, while Tim and Bobby went ahead. Jack couldn't have breathed a word of the poor body's danger. Charles's usually elusive eyes looked, opened, right into the camera, greeting the velvet chemicals and your gaze.

Then, breathing heavily at David's elbow, breathing dour Scotch, was the artist himself, truculently shabby in old jeans and a sweatshirt.

"Turns out he's in the Bay Area," he said.

"Charles?"

"*No! Lord Jim.*"

He lumbered by, putting a half-empty glass on a table, apparently on his way out.

After an hour, David went looking for Tim and Bobby, thinking it was time to go. He found them both, and Jack too, in what had established itself as one of the quieter rooms, a sort of study, like a smaller version of the living room with a wall of books. Everyone was silenced by a fierce quarrel between two thin, pale lovers. David knew them, since one was a student in Medieval Studies. He also knew the fight, which they had often, with varying details. Right now it concerned a scandal at a church famous for music and scandals.

"It *was* the one with the squint," the student kept saying. "It was, or, Michael, I'm leaving."

Tim was in a leather armchair, near a window that looked south over the downtown and the lake. David sat on its arm and put his arm on Tim's shoulder. The fight was making him nervous: it was crazy and a little inhuman, the pair moiling and snapping like a brace of whippets. David couldn't help remembering the fights he and Peter used to have – in bed, once for instance, reading *The Jungle Books* loudly at each other, and from that getting to something like this shrill hysteria.

Jack and Bobby were at either end of the sofa that matched and more or less faced Tim's chair. Jack was heavy-eyed and apparently lost in thought, holding a large tumbler of whiskey. Bobby was fascinated by the quarrel. He'd decided on baggy shorts and a shirt with vertical green and blue stripes. His plastic thongs kicked off, he sat with his feet pulled up in front of him, holding a glass of what David hoped was soda water, since Bobby was taking penicillin.

Abruptly, as if they'd given their audience all they could ask for, the two walked out, to fight and be unhappy somewhere else. David was just about to ask Jack if he had come in the car: he didn't look as if he should be driving. But Jack spoke up, out of his sleepy state.

"*The Moral Right!*" he said, in disgust. "*Anal retentive* moral right!"

Bobby laughed out loud, delighted. Jack looked across at him as if he hadn't noticed he was there.

"It's all overrated, isn't it, Bobby?" he said, insidiously.

Bobby Riding squirmed like a tongue.

"But isn't it?" Jack went on, his voice thickened by Scotch and sadness. "It's like a zoo, where they promise all kinds of animals, endless kinds, and it turns out they're all the same. And if you say, 'Where are the zebras, zebras must be fun, all striped?' they say, 'Here's a nice fat one, like a mushroom, imagine!' And if you say, 'What about giraffes, you said there'd be giraffes,' they say, 'Here, try a black one, black as the devil's heart, and it is big, isn't it?'"

Bobby looked scared, and intrigued.

"I mean, it's like they're just dumped – no warranties, no quality control, nothing's for sure. Like they're made out of what wasn't good enough for hot water bottles and rubber ducks. In Taiwan or Korea or Singapore. In *Formosa*. But I guess you've never heard of Formosa, Bobby, have you? But don't you just get *tired*?"

This was almost a real question, weariness and envy mixed.

"Never!" Bobby said.

"You're so young," Jack said, almost forgivingly. "But sooner or later, you're bound to ask yourself, what does it all add up to? What do gay men really *want*?"

"Each other," Bobby said.

Jack almost laughed. "Oh, sure!" He took another leaden gulp.

"Jack – " David began, but Jack didn't hear him.

"Earlier at the bar tonight, I got to talking – with a gray-haired man in leather, small, skinny, friendly. And it turned out that what he wanted, one thing anyway, was to lick boots." A kind of wondering misery went over Jack's face. "It was odd the way we were just talking about it. It was just something else that people do. So I said, 'What are you thinking when you're down there?' He didn't mind me asking at all. He said, 'I'm thinking how lucky I am.' My God – *how lucky I am*!"

Bobby had pulled himself up, suddenly seeing the depth of Jack's misery, but not shocked by it yet. Rashly, he was about to say something, and David was going to speak too, to save him. But then it was Tim who was speaking, surprising all of them.

"Don't be so hard on yourself, Jack."

Jack looked at him, with a focussing scowl. At him, up at David, then back at Tim, who was saying, "I guess we all feel that way at times. It's still not easy being gay. I guess it never will be."

David gave Tim's shoulder a squeeze. He was using on Jack the voice he used to soothe David, and David could hear the complacency in it. He loved it, but he knew it wouldn't work now.

"Probably not," Jack said, looking down.

"Jack – " David began.

"They say he's in the Bay Area," Jack said, looking up toward Bobby. "But who knows? Think of how many you could hide in the ravines here. Thousands. Or maybe they've disappeared him, like in Argentina. Slit their bellies," he winced, "and drop them in the lake." Noticing the lake, he pulled it in with a scoop of his arm.

"But why?" Bobby said, caught up in the fantasy.

"Why? They can see, too. He'd get on TV, and there'd be a revolution. People would be storming down Yonge Street, with Jim on their shoulders, shouting, Jim! Jim!" He laughed. "Life! Life!"

"Jack, come on," Tim said, still thinking his voice could make him better. David rubbed his shoulders warningly, hoping he was right. He felt this scene could go anywhere.

"Who knows, Tim?" Jack said, with a smile. "They might be disappearing all of the handsome boys. You could be in danger."

David stood up off the chair and said, "Whatever, it's getting late. So, Jack, if you brought the car, I could drive you, drive all of us. I haven't had too much to drink."

"And I have?" Jack looked at him over the glass, and took a defiant mouthful and held it.

"Let's just get home safely, okay?" David said.

Jack crunched down the throatful of whiskey and said nothing.

"It was unfair, Jack, I know," David said, weakening. "But – " He shrugged.

"What was unfair?"

"He was too much, I guess," David said, warily. "Too perfect, too young, whatever. Maybe it's really not such a bad thing he's gone."

Jack pondered this, as if he might decide to consider it good, well-meant advice and come along home.

"Besides," David said, "It's not as if he was your lover."

Jack bit his lower lip, thoughtfully.

"But he wasn't perfect," he said. "He had a scar, it turned out. On his ankle. Somehow, I didn't notice it until we finally went to bed together."

David hadn't even suspected this: no one had, it seemed. Jack had held it inside himself: now, David realized, he was opening it in front of them, like *seppuku*.

"Which turned out to be his way of saying good-bye. He'd decided to go off with his friend from the States already. He could have been quoting you, David. 'I wanted you to see I was only human.'"

"*What a stupid thing to do!*" Tim said, angrily.

"Perhaps. I don't know. He was just a kid, after all. I'd forgotten that. Anyway, this scar – may I borrow your foot, Bobby?"

Bobby had little choice: Jack took his left leg by the ankle and lifted it over. "It was here," he said, drawing it on the inside, under the ankle bone: Bobby winced, comically, pulling down his toes. David felt a flash of impatience, at Jack's tyrannical self-pity, at his big hand holding Bobby captive.

"It came from a rock under the water at his parents cottage, when he was thirteen. It was about two inches long, and really nasty – ragged and ugly. White by now, of course. But maybe you're thinking it should have been on his face, David?"

"No!"

"Oh? I did. Because I think I know what you're thinking, David. That it's time, it's past time, for Jack to *grow up.*"

The words had been rankling for months. David felt sorry, but Jack was right: he still felt they applied. Was Jack going to go on making scenes like this all his life?

Jack continued, as if rehearsing the words for the day when he would mean them. "Sooner or later you think, we were younger then, and now we're older. You think, I've changed, and so has he: we've outgrown each other. You wake up one morning and think, this is my first day after Tim. Or, this is my first day after David."

David reached for Tim again, in fear. "I don't know why you're doing this, Jack," he said.

"I'm just saying, this is how it ends. I'm prophesying. You end up old and alone." Jack seemed to be shrivelling into what he talked about, his self-pity crystallizing in his joints like arthritis. "You end up old and old and old and *left!*"

David laughed at him, but it was more a bark than a laugh.

"Jack, give us a break. We're all sorry about Jim, but my God, what could you expect? You're overdoing it, you're – " David didn't know how to clinch it, but, fatally, he saw the gray-haired masochist Jack had summoned up. "Jack, you're grovelling!"

Jack started, as if he'd been shot. David knew at once there was going to be a disaster. Jack looked at Bobby's foot, which he'd kept, as if for company. "Grovelling?" he said. "Well, maybe. Maybe a little. But then, maybe I was lucky, maybe grovelling's as close to infinity as you can get these days."

He gave David a quick look, shyness almost hiding his fury.

"You find a handsome young man – and probably it doesn't really matter which one – and if you grovel enough you make him into something. You try to make yourself zero and divide him by yourself, to get infinity. David, you're out there marching, you and Tim. To liberate yourselves, to liberate kids like Bobby here," he shook the foot gently. "But that isn't hard, he's bursting to be liberated. But what about the older ones, the ones who've got to be grown up? What about *me*? How are you going to *liberate* me?"

It sounded as if the word had stung every time he had heard it in the last few years.

"Liberate yourself, Jack. You're intelligent enough."

"But maybe I'm too old. Maybe I came too late. I remember my first TV. I can remember Formosa. Maybe I just don't belong in your new world, David. If you do," he said, suddenly changing course, "because face it, David, if you got yourself 'liberated,' it was just in the nick of time."

It was partly bitter, partly apologetic.

"Why don't I tell you? Why don't I just tell you? Men don't love each other. They hunger for that soft, feminine shimmer all young skin has got. It reminds them of their mothers, it's breast country, dear old Melanie Klein territory. And when that goes, there's nothing left."

Jack seemed to be saying this, to see if he believed it himself, to see if he dared to hear himself saying it.

"That's not true," David said. "That's just not true."

"Will you love Tim when he's old and pruny?"

"Yes!"

Jack smiled, as if he thought his smile could dissolve David's picture of a handsome old man into something soft and insignificant.

"Men – gay men, straight men – don't love each other. Boys do sometimes, but they're a different gender, really. Men are always rivals, for power, for money, for whatever's to be had. For the pride of not being humiliated too much by the men farther up. We can't love each other. It's a silly idea. I *hate* being gay."

There was silence. Jack looked as if he thought he'd won the game by kicking over the board. David, furious, was about to say, "That was always obvious."

"*Well, I don't!*" Bobby said, scared and indignant.

Jack looked at him, and gave his foot a little shake, as if it was there to remind him of something. David could feel the rage and the tenderness in Jack's hand. It seemed obscene that Bobby should be held by them, by Jack's evil despair.

"Let go of him!" David said, in a loud, deep voice that surprised everyone.

But Jack didn't comply: instead he turned to Bobby with a smile, about to speak. David jumped up.

"*Let go of him, you faggot!*"

Jack stared up at him with shock and fear. Then a kind of ironic triumph came over his face. "All right, David." He put Bobby's foot back beside its mate. "Thanks, Mr. Riding," he said.

"You *traitor!*" David was shaking, breathless. Jack had been leading towards this all the time they had known each other. David turned away in order not to look at him and walked away, too, saying, "Let's get out of here."

"But David!" Tim was following. "*He's been drinking.*" As they went through the living room, people watched, wondering. "And he's really upset, I didn't realize – he's heartbroken."

"Heartbroken my ass. I hate *masochists*. He's enjoying all this, he loves it. He's a shit."

"David, he's one of our *best friends.*"

"Yours, maybe, never mine. I saw this from the start. He never was anyone's friend. You heard him, he hates gays. Damn! Bobby!" He'd just remembered him, and spun around.

"We can't leave him there," he said, striding back. But at the entrance to the study, he stopped short. He didn't believe what he saw. Bobby had his arms around Jack's neck: his back was heaving, and Jack's hands were moving soothingly over the stripes. For a moment, David could only imagine they were doing this in order to trick him somehow.

Jack looked up as David took a few uncertain steps forward. He didn't seem surprised to see David again. "He's upset, and no wonder, it's my fault, David, I – "

David wanted to hit him: his hand actually rose in a fist. Jack was loving this scene, wearing Bobby like a tragic mantle. His eyes shone with glycerin tears.

"If you want to be called a faggot, Jack, it's not my fault. If that's what you wanted, it's got nothing to do with me."

Jack watched with a tight smile.

"Say you're sorry, Jack. You damn well say you're sorry!"

For a moment, Jack kept up the small, ironic smile. "Why?" he said. "Hitler didn't."

"*What*?" David couldn't believe his ears.

"Of course, I'm sorry, David but – "

"But?" Both hands rose, hardening into clubs. David blinked to keep from seeing Jack and his endless buts being smashed into pulp. He turned and walked out of the room. At the doorway, something made him stop and shout, "Make up your mind, Jack! Make up your bloody mind!"

He hardly knew what he meant, but he'd made up his mind: he was finished with Jack Durham.

PART 3

But he phoned Bobby the next morning to find out what had happened. Bobby had driven Jack home and walked him into the house and left him sitting in the kitchen.

"I would have stayed, but he said no. I felt so sorry for him, all alone in that house."

David pushed away anything like remorse. "I used to feel like that, Bobby. But not any more."

"David, you're being *rotten*!"

"Whatever's going on, Jack started it. Why not come over for a late breakfast?"

"I mean, if Jack wants to be all tragic about being gay, what can I do?" he said, when Bobby had arrived. Speaking just as much to Tim, who was making an omelette. "Paul got it right when he said Jack was really an old Hemingway male. He's just never gotten away from that."

David blinked, seeing Hemingway put the rifle into his old, forgetting head, and went on. "He's got the mind of a prick male, but since he's gay, he's just got to keep on

218

writing and grovelling. Maybe at the end of it all, they'll say, 'For a queer, he wasn't so bad. At least he knew how things are.' But it's all useless and stupid and I'm sick of it."

Bobby turned to Tim. "Why is your boyfriend being *such a shit*?"

"I don't know what's going on. I've never seen David like this before. So I just cook and keep my mouth shut."

David gave him a dark look. "Don't you see? He attacked everything you believe in, your whole life. He said we're *pathetic little perverts*."

"I didn't hear that one. And besides, he was upset and drunk. That wasn't really Jack."

"Oh, yes it was. It was Jack at last."

"Maybe we just shouldn't talk about it," Bobby said, grimly.

David expected that the next time he met Jack he would be frigidly polite. They'd never really liked each other: their friendship had been a rivalry – Jack's theory was right there—a battle of egos.

Next Friday, David and Tim went to a bar that had just opened. It was, for the moment anyway, a great success, roaring, shaking, sweaty. They had to go in sideways. Tim saw a friend who asked him to dance, and they rushed onto the dance floor. David went to the bar, where he saw Paul. He had always liked Paul: he was the human one.

"So, do you like this place?" he shouted, affectionately.

"Well, nobody ever called a gay bar *Kindness*, did they? Or they'd lose their shirts." Paul spoke with self-amused resignation, but he seemed sadder than that.

"Have you heard?" he said, leaning closer. "Jack's left town."

"Left town?"

"Yes. He's driving down to San Francisco."

David was too startled to react.

"I'm looking after the house. Bob Riding's got the cat."

"*Why?*" David said. Did Jack imagine finding Jim, making some reconciliation? That was ridiculous. Or was he imagining a scene like this, his friends shocked, worried, contrite?

"He just said he wanted to be in San Francisco."

Tim was right at the edge of the raised dance floor, by the brass rail that kept people from toppling off, dancing wildly, extravagantly. It had been a hard day, he'd said. Paul leaned closer. "He said to find out if you forgive him yet."

"*Do you?*" David said, brutally.

Paul blinked, with a squeeze of his eyes that made him look blind for a second. "I don't know," he said, accepting the question at face value. "For a while, I thought Jim might be a good sign. That Jack had come to some sort of turning point, that after it all he might settle down. *We* might. But Jack can never let things rest. He's talking of renting his house, maybe even selling it." He laughed. "It's like he's moving to Vancouver after all, *without me*."

David hadn't wanted this glimpse into Paul's unhappiness. Out on the steamy dance floor, Tim was tearing off his shirt, tossing his chest like one more lump into the human chowder. Remember, David thought, that's mine, my home, my rest.

Paul went on, eager to speak now. "When I heard about your fight, well, I could understand. Jack gets like that, so outrageous you could strangle him at times. It must be why we love him."

David was silent: Paul saw he'd taken a false step.

"Anyway," he said, going back to the resignation, "do you think Late Capitalism can hang on long enough for me to find a boyfriend in this hole?"

"It seems to be doing pretty well," David said. "I think I should go keep an eye on my boyfriend. There's something especially flirty in his shoulders tonight."

"I'll give them another ten minutes," Paul said. "Them, him."

But on their way out an hour later, David saw Paul still at the bar. Capitalism had put on a fresh, young face to sell him another beer, and Paul was leaning forward, talking, eager for a fast grin as his Golden was uncapped.

"Jack's driving down to San Francisco," David said to Tim.

"What?"

But David went over to Paul, put a hand on his shoulder and said, "If you're writing, give Jack my regards, okay? And good luck."

Outside, absorbing it, Tim said, "The thing about Jack is, he's ambitious."

"What do you mean?"

"His life has got to be special. It has to mean more than other people's."

"Of course," David said. He wasn't interested in any other kind of person. "But what's that got to do with San Francisco?"

"Jack is after something. Some big experience."

"A big scene with Jim, I suppose."

It turned out next morning that he had phoned Bobby just before setting off, to arrange for the cat.

"He doesn't want to *locate* Jim," Bobby explained, as if it all made sense. "Just be near him, and think about things."

"Of course", he added, from his own large supply of hope, "Jim could always turn up on his own, couldn't he? Wouldn't that be something?"

"Maybe Jack is simply stupid," David said, with a kind of grim thoughtfulness. "Maybe he was stupid all along and I didn't notice somehow. That can happen, I guess."

A postcard arrived several days later, showing the Dakota Badlands: desolate, lurid, penitential. *Dear Tim and David*, Jack printed. *Am driving to San Francisco. Slowly, to think about life on the way. Life, Jim, Hitler, everything. What were we doing, David? What's your theory? Will write. Jack.*

A few days more and a card came from San Francisco. *Dear Tim, Dear David. Made it. It's amazing here, all of it. I'm staying at cheap hotel with a Great Dane behind the desk. And still thinking, of course. Jim is in the air, and that's enough. Love, Jack.*

The card showed the city at night, with the sign of the Castro Theatre at the centre: 'Castro' in pink letters stepping down from the sky.

PART 4

It was a quiet summer. Tim spent it working, David reading and trying to get started on his thesis. Bobby went west, hitch-hiking: he got as far as Ucluluet and slept on the beach, the Pacific crashing by his ear, into his dreams, and sent them a card. Tim and David didn't go far on weekends to the parks, to Hanlan's Point, sunny, breezy, asprawl.

On several weekends, they went to a cottage rented by Alan and Michael. In August, they visited Mrs. Grey at Brian and Susan's cottage in the Haliburton lakes. It was the first time David had met Susan. Brian was away, helping some friends build an addition to their cottage. Susan seemed startled to see him, though she had known he was coming. She was a loyalist, the last, diehard believer in Tim's heterosexuality, bearing an angry female knowledge of what men are supposed to be. Two stiff gins brought out a kind of family camaraderie, in her at least – the Greys had old jokes, people and subjects they had to laugh over at every meeting. It was something David had hardly noticed in Tim, a kind of jolly, smooth-skinned, Anglo-Saxon brutality. It focussed around Susan and reached back towards Mrs. Grey. Tim and Mrs. Grey knew their parts, but they were just indulging Susan. For David, there was something very Torontonian about it. It was Canadian but not British – for that you had to consult David's different snobberies. But it wasn't quite American either, as if you could be right at home in North America, without being American.

Mrs. Grey was a little apologetic for Susan. She and David were consolidating an alliance, with David turning into a kind of craggy, male daughter – or son when Tim was being foolish.

Bobby Riding arrived back in the city just after the body of an Azorean boy was found on a roof on Yonge Street. He'd been raped by four men, then drowned in a basin.

"How could they *do that?*" Bobby said, staring, possessed by the story. "A twelve-year-old kid?"

"I don't know," David said angrily. "*I don't murder little boys.*"

He felt as if a lot of people thought he did. That night Bobby's groans woke them – he was staying with them for a while. They had to haul him up out of a nightmare, persuade him they were real. He told them hands had been pushing him down into mud. He could still feel them. Then David had nightmares.

A week later, Bobby headed east. A patriot, he wanted to put both coasts into the same summer, the same sleeping bag and worn jeans. He made it to Newfoundland, and came back in September, pleased with himself, with the Pacific and Atlantic sights and stirrings and comrades behind his eyes. He'd been in all provinces except P.E.I. and boasted of sex in every one of them, as if he'd been trying to weave the country together with his prick.

"But it's summer!" Tim kept saying, getting David out – onto his bike, down to the ferry docks, up to the kite-flying hill – until it wasn't.

In October, a letter arrived from Jack. Two photos fell out when David tore the envelope open. A tall, blond man sat on the steps of a house, wearing blue-denim bib overalls over wide, tanned and freckled shoulders. He was holding a hammer loosely between his legs and grinning, strong teeth thatched with a gold-brown moustache. He must be in his late twenties, David decided. Jack smiled proudly out of the other photograph, holding the hammer up in a sort of salute. The picture was taken from farther back, so that you could see the high front of a wooden Victorian house. The sheets of the letter were gritty between David's fingers as he walked into the kitchen.

"The house is mine," Jack wrote. "89 Homer Street. Edith has done it again. I'm renovating it with my friend and carpenter Fred. Fred came first of course, I'd been thinking about what it would be like to settle here, but as if in a book: *then, at last, in his thirty-seventh year, Durham began a new life in San Francisco*...But one afternoon in a sunny bar I met Fred and thought after a bit well, I've got the carpenter, why not find the house? A falling-down old house that needs us. And a week later we found it, a few streets up back of the Castro not it, but her, because this house is a tough old lady, full of fight and shrieking nails. The renovation will need a lot of cheerful violence, banging and smashing and plaster in our creases. We'll need power tools and torches and square shoulders and big veiny hands. Fred, as you can see, isn't beautiful – Fred's *strapping*."

"It's Jack at last," David said in the kitchen, handing Tim the photographs.

"Good, I was beginning to worry."

"That's Fred. Quite a change, isn't he? And the house, Jack owns the house."

"You'd love this city," Jack went on. "It's got intuitive air. It's a Mediterranean city, humpy and human, but on an ocean so big it's like outer space. It's like here you are at the end of the world – of the West anyway, the dear, crazy old *Abendland* – but that's all right. That's no problem. It's a chance to stop and think. Think and make up your mind. *Choose*: be reasonable or not, be happy or not.

And of course it's the Americans too. I've given in, fallen in love, the way every Canadian really wants to, and at the same time I'm always thinking, what on earth are we going to do with you people? We pre-Americans, I mean, the rest of the world: how can we tell them? Naively writing happiness into things! – and doing it so sincerely, so sweetly, you can't help feeling what it would be like to believe it yourself. We kiss in the streets, Fred and I and the rest of us. Fred calls me honey without fuss, like it says somewhere, 'Of course men can call each other honey. If that isn't self-evident, what is? And what are streets for, if not to kiss in?' Americans think they can do anything: they think they can set us free. I still can't quite believe this loosening, this breathing air in deep as if it belonged to you. Imagine: gay oxygen! Like they can say, 'Forget all that history, we've got it right at last'. At last, after all the centuries…and it was easy.

Fred's just come in, a sort of plaster blond right now, asking who I'm writing to. And I've said, 'To David and Tim, my friends up in Toronto, the ones I had a fight with, at least with David. I'm telling them how I am, and I'm working my way toward an apology.' What did we fight about? That's hard to say, I'm not sure I remember, here on Homer Street – maybe I'll tell you when I finish the letter.

Fred didn't come easily, though, looking back. It took me months to work my way round to the mere strapping possibility of him. For months, I was in a hovering state, not of looking for Jim, but of sensing him, talking with him. Writing dialogues, in which we talked about desire and life – in which he would have told me what they are, if they'd worked. He was dissolving, becoming someone I'd known long ago, when I was his age, or a little younger. For a while, I'd almost see him, every so often. At a crowded street fair they have every year on Castro, for instance: for a moment, I saw him trying to dunk Harvey Milk, the gay man who's running for city supervisor. I thought no, Jim is too soft-hearted: there was something so excited and nakedly emotional about Mr. Milk, squirming like a kid. And if it had been Jim, he wouldn't have missed, and this person did and left us, Harvey and me, safe and hanging.

David, what on earth do you mean by *only human*? If Jim had been only an angel or only a handsome animal, things would have been manageable. But he was only human in bed and everywhere else: nobody's dream, just Jim, a little solemn and being kind, really kind. It was as if he thought he had the power to heal me, renew me, make me whole again, even before I knew what the wound was going to be. *Stupid*, I thought afterward, *stupid*! But maybe it worked, slowly, over the months. Maybe it's easier to break away from something you've touched. If Jim had never materialized, had just been an image, I might still be in a sort of agony of wonder about what he was.

For a long while, piecing together thoughts like these, I was a rather odd figure around the Castro. Like a tourist who couldn't leave. Like a refugee who'd come to make new life here and couldn't get started. I was sexless, and I didn't talk much either. I'd sit in the bars staring out the window – some of them have plate glass walls, imagine that in Toronto! – starting conversations, saying where I was from, but never why I'd come. I was still finding out myself. I explored, like an anthropologist: I even went to the baths, not for sex, but to find out what was happening in this city. I was modest and middle-aged, picking my way over the people fucking in the corridors. You couldn't peel them apart to drop in some northern question. 'Tell me, is this what Kant calls *positive* liberty?' This was at the *Liberty Baths*, you see.

I sat on a bench and found myself talking to a blond boy who explained that it was his twentieth birthday, he'd arrived in the city a week before, and he wasn't leaving the baths till he'd had sex with twenty men. Not just any men: real hunks. He'd come from Ohio he was reluctant to say this, and when he let it out, it was a sort of cry, all the sorrow in the Union at once: *Ohio*… He had wavy hair like meringue, a high forehead and a Roman nose, and he sat twiddling a cigarette, wrapping himself in carcinogenic romance. He came from some old, stiffly comfortable middle class I didn't understand – his name was Craig Stanton III. He said this, laughing at 'The Third,' looking over a muscled black man in a way that made you realize how, in certain parts of Ohio at least, they *really* don't like their sons getting fucked by big black men.

I sat there, everyone's hairy northern aunt, saying things like 'Twenty, isn't that quite a few? I mean, they only give you one asshole. It isn't like lungs or kidneys. I'm from Toronto, after all, so I know about these things, limits, boundaries, fate. You can't sleep with all the men in the world.' And Craig Stanton III – and Last and Wickedest! – laughed at me and said, 'but you can *try!*' Try and rejoice in the trying, exult in it – how limitless, I thought, how imperial.

But then he turned and settled into my story – got bits of it out of me and liked it, made me feel like a mad romantic too, in my way. He believed in being in love – planned to be as soon as he'd got settled: right now he was in love with the baths, with the thought of all the men in the world. And then he gave me a little smile, and I thought why not? Why come all this way and – like Columbus – pig-headedly refuse to discover Americans? But I wasn't through with Jim yet. That took time, time and what the mathematicians call delicate cancellations. And it took Fred.

And one of the nicest things about Fred is that he's not a boy, as you can see. He's twenty-nine, he's been here five years, from Pennsylvania, part German and part Italian. Jim, and Craig, and Charles, – Tim in his blonder moments – were still on a line that led back to childhood. They were lit from behind by the glow of growth. There was something about them that took you back to childhood—you could almost slip back into the womb, if you weren't careful. But Fred, though he's younger than I am, is stuck with being out here in the real world, an adult. And I like that.

Am I growing up, David? It would be nice to hear you say so. One of the things I was thinking in the plate-glass bars is that it's odd how I've been, the last few years, a seducer of youth: the idea of youth – trying to regain my own lost youth, I suppose. I didn't expect it, or plan it. It happened partly because I discovered a sort of talent for it. I think it was that I looked at them as few parents look at their children – their gay sons, anyway. Letting them look back and talk – not talk back. I think it made them think they could find out through me who they were. Though I never did know myself: Jim, Charles, all of them, they were endless studies. Even Tim – have you figured out Tim yet, David?

Of course, David, it was never really like that with you. Tim, please don't feel left out, but David and I have something to work out – *you be the wise, calm judge*. With you, David, I was flattering and sympathetic, but you weren't waiting for me to tell you who you are. You insisted on having your own ideas about that, about everything. That's why you were more my son or daughter – but never a model, or a boyfriend.

All this is leading up to my apology. I'm sure you see that. At least I hope it is. I hope this letter won't lose its nerve and die aborning – but now I'm going to go help Fred, because it's time, and because I need more time to think. I'm still uneasy about what happened, what I did and made David do. Do I have a defense? *Is it possible I'm just a shit after all?* An interesting possibility: they exist, God knows, and maybe after all I'm one of them. Will I just get myself and you upset again, David? Why not just scrap this page, and tell you more about Fred.

Anyway, I'm going off to smash plaster. Which I promise won't be you, David, just me, just the Hitler within. Wish me well."

"*Oh, Jack!*" David said, affectionate, exasperated.

Tim looked up from earlier pages. "What's wrong?"

"Nothing. You can decide. But I'm thinking, '*Jack, why can't you just keep quiet? Do I have to go through it all again?*' I thought I forgave him months ago, and now it feels like he could ruin it all again."

He brushed grit off his hands. "I'll bet he sprinkled some in on purpose. The new-found nitty-gritty. Or is it dust and ashes?"

David shook the remaining sheets over the sink and began again.

"It's the next day," Jack wrote, refreshed. "After a morning of hard work. America, it seems, has its own ancientness, which is now coating our lungs, getting sour in our creases. I'm really learning, earning my own Gothic American past. The plumbing is iron age, 1891 patent pending. Tearing out the old wiring is like a hair-pulling match with Mr. Edison. But Edith would love this house: it's like I've found another tough old lady to be her lover. Her American.

Anyway, in the dust and noise, I've been reconstructing that evening. I'd been insanely trying to distract myself with some high-camp Parisian criticism, while think-ing, 'language is a form of *life*, dammit. At least Wittgenstein was a *serious* queer.' I gave up and went for a drive, to be with Jim, since the car was Jim's in a way. Then I remembered the party and thought, why not drop in, it might help. But after several drinks I overheard – honestly, entirely by chance – a friend of Jim's friend saying that he lived in the Bay Area. That put it all in focus, somehow. You can't see the States, but you can see the Bay Area. He wouldn't want me to go looking for him, but if I was there I wouldn't be looking, I'd just be breathing the same air, and thinking about how to live without him.

But I knew I was getting drunk, and this was probably just fantasy. I was on my way out and home when I saw you, David, peering into my past with those myopic sharp eyes. Into Charles, in nothing but the tenderest wilderness – back when everything was simple (not that it was at the time). Something in your look made me stop and tell you: confess I knew where he was. But that was fatal: it wasn't a secret anymore, it was real, outside me.

I turned around, went back in to think, not wanting to be alone. But that involved drinking more, and I realized I was getting very drunk, and on hard liquor. I hate being drunk, because my stepfather was an alcoholic, and I hated the sight of it and still do. Alcohol burns out the receptors in your body that taste humanness – yours, other people's – and I was getting like that, burned out and inhuman inside, perhaps forever. And everything at that party made it worse – the shrieking voices and the way they all become one meaningless voice, the stupid gaiety. Those two kids wrangling, so whiny and medieval and U. of T., like they thought they had hooves and tails and farted brimstone, and wasn't it clever of them? What was I doing there? What on earth, what in hell was I doing there? Because what a place it was to bring feelings to! Self-pity, of course, but someone had to do it.

Anyway, when I started in with Bobby I was just trying to get rid of some of it, with a sympathetic audience. To be shrill and bitchy and bitter, in my own bearish way. Our dear friend Mr. Riding was perfectly safe, David. Sometimes I think you think you gave birth to him, but anyone can see he did it himself. And Tim was safe too – no need for their frantic self-appointed mother to come rushing in and snatch them out of my clutches.

Maybe you should just have let me do it, say my piece, squirt a little misery into the atmosphere – that would have been that. But you had to take it seriously argue with unhappiness, with the drunk of a lifetime – stand up to the huge fact that you can't get what you want. And I thought, 'All right, it's arrived, what's between us, under our hedged and guarded friendship. It's been coming for months, years. All right, David, I have a bone to pick with you.' As my mother used to say.

A friend of Charles was beaten up one night in Allen Gardens by a bunch of thugs – post-teenage, poor, probably unemployed. That happens often enough, but this case took over my imagination for days. They were saying, '*Are you a faggot? Do you like being a faggot?*' They made him answer too. I couldn't stop seeing it. It was as if I'd been there, and been on both sides. As if I was the whole economics of it, the giving and the taking of blows. So I was terrified of their packing instinct, their separate cruelty and their shared cruelty – and at the same time I could feel the delight of finding someone you don't have to worry about, whose feelings don't weigh on you at all. Someone you can throw your misery at freely – really *give* it to him, as they say. To be free of the human face – to see a human face and smash it – the freedom of that, the easing! For a while it looked as though Charles's friend might lose an eye, and I had nightmares with that eye in them.

You get the picture, David: I was in a bad, bad mood. Thinking about that sort of thing was a kind of consolation, a misery I knew inside out that wouldn't leave me, while handsome boys come and go, or stay and get old. As if, like Ken McAlistair, I'm really in it for the politics. For the outrage.

And somehow, with you getting angry and righteous, David, I wanted to see it. I had to see it, right then, I couldn't wait. I wanted to be called a faggot, to see the snarl on your face, to hear the crackle of hatred – of the executioner's fire. To sit under a faggot's eternally shitty weather and feel what it meant. From both sides, because I was you too, feeling the freedom of hatred.

It was a terrible thing to do – something I would never do to anyone again. And I didn't set out to do it – but it came up, it grew up between us. Because we both have killers in us, I think."

"Oh? So do you think I'm a murderer?" David asked sarcastically.

Tim looked up. "Uh oh! Jack thinks you are?"

"Not quite, but it's a good thing he's a few thousand miles away."

"Only we'll never actually murder anyone, David," Jack went on, blithely. "All the people we *haven't* killed have left us with a crippling tenderness. I didn't expect you to storm out like that—I was drunk remember, I was measuring emotions with a very shaky hand. But when you did, I saw it was right, it was the disaster I longed for. And then when you came back – to rescue Bobby? Why? What on earth from? I love him – it was as if fate sent you. As if fate had done it all, to give me a message. *Make up your mind, Jack Durham!* I don't know exactly what you thought you meant, but it was magnificent. You were just the dark, bloody-minded angel I needed. *Make up your mind, Jack. Get a move on. Go to San Francisco. Meet Fred!*"

There was a blank space and a new date.

"I thought I'd better wait, spend more time in the mines of plaster, thinking. When I looked over my letter again, I thought of not sending it, or not sending certain parts. Because the letter came out different from what I expected, more ruthless, less cute. Perhaps I'm taking it all too seriously – I get drunk and miserable, and I bring out Hitler like a battered, old teddy-bear they can't get you to give up. But then, Hitler's *history*, as I heard someone say in a cafe in Yorkville.

So let it stand, let it go. I won't change it, I might make it worse. And you're tough, David, tough and not stupid. That awful fate: the late seventies and you're not stupid! And you have Tim there with you, who's not stupid either and can be wise and sweet enough to handle both of us, except when we're really angry. It's not a very graceful apology but I do apologize. Hitler didn't say he was sorry, but I do, I am: I was really being nasty that night, and not just from my misery, from my will.

Anyway, here I am, starting a new life in my thirty-seventh year in a city famous for new lives. Right now, there's only one usable room in the house, with sheets of plastic to try to keep out the dust. That's where Fred and I curl up and I think, after all, North America is an island.

But soon there will be lots of room. I want you two to come down here – come visit my blue house, made of wood – what a change after all that brown Toronto brick – made of wood like a boat, with tall, serious windows thinking about the weather, the ocean. I want you to show to Fred (and the rest of them) that we can manage happiness too, sometimes."

"Love – Jack."

It was a lame, self-conscious jig of a signature: *please love this crippled hand and its clumsy possessor, in spite of everything*.

David gave the last sheets to Tim and watched him read, smiling now and then. David watched and wondered: had Jack won him over? Tim didn't quite understand how very well David and Jack knew each other. Too well for comfort.

"Let's," Tim said, looking up from the end. "Fly down there some time. I've never been to California."

"I'd love to see it," David said. "And Jack, too, of course."

CHAPTER IX: TIM IN LOVE
Winter, 1977 - Summer, 1978

PART 1

One day in early winter, Bobby called from the bubbling depths of a bad head cold. David answered, alone and miserable himself. Tim was up in Napier, where Mrs. Grey had had another heart attack, said by everyone to be "small," as if it was only a minor offense and she promised not to do it again. There'd been no question of David's going up with Tim. Mrs. Grey's ill health and the drugs she took meant a shift of power toward Susan and her husband. It felt as if even Tim thought that David would be bad for her.

At least he could do something for Bobby. He got a bottle of Vitamin C, took several grams, then went to the kitchen for some wine. There was only one large bottle. Bearing wine, Vitamin C, and *The Diviners*, he took the streetcar across town to Rennie's. Bobby let him in, standing away from the cold, in a dressing-gown as red as the wine, and so long he was tripping over it as they crossed the living room floor, now bare except for tatty, purple blue shag.

On Bobby's futon, they began a descent into the wine bottle, talking and listening to records. After a while, Bobby reached into a sagging pocket and pulled out a pack of cards and a book, all held together by a rubber band. Tarot cards, with a book of instructions.

"A taxi-driver of Rennie's left this. He was going to tell our fortunes but he never did." Bobby laughed and groaned, reminiscently. "God, I never want to have sex again," he said, stripping off the rubber band and opening the book. "This could be fun, I suppose," he said.

"Madame Bobby? With her wicked pack of cards?" David looked fondly at his head bent over the pictures. At his nape and his ears a little naked, winter white skin contrasting with bristly black-brown hair.

"Do you want your fortune told?"

"Not really." David said.

"Why not?"

"I'm happy the way things are." He didn't want Bobby touching on delicate things like Mrs. Grey's heart, and the future it held. Yet, peering, exclaiming, flipping pages, Bobby was bent on telling fortunes. "You wouldn't have to believe anything you didn't want to."

"Only I would. I'm very credulous, especially with you—being psychic and all. Start

229

with someone else, if you have to do it, someone safe."

"Who?"

"Well" – it came out of the blue – "Jim Fields, say. He's safe, he's far away. Besides, nothing bad could happen to him, could it?" Jim was all myth by now, gone and beautiful forever.

"Well, we'll see, won't we?" Bobby said, professionally. Then, peering and turning a card around and around: "Is this guy upside down or am I wrecked?"

David took a look. "Both. He's meant to be hanged by the foot like that, upside down."

"Why?"

"I forget, actually." Looking at the cards, he saw he was drunk as Bobby, and dizzy as the Hanged Man.

Pulling his gown around him, Bobby began with Jim, who came through safely, though the cards didn't say where he was. While Bobby told fortunes, David let himself talk about his book. It was something he only discussed with Tim and Jack and Bobby, and he knew that it was a different book with each of them, for each of them, except for a certain core of longing.

"I know what you think, Bobby, but it isn't about us at all. We're completely different. I mean, they're completely different people."

"The tower again," Bobby said. "So I hope you do a lot of good, hard fucking?"

"No! *We* don't, it isn't us."

"But if it isn't about you, what is it about?"

"Oh, it's about us in that sense, of course."

"What sense?"

And looking around inside himself, David couldn't find any sense at all.

"The *real* problem," he said, trying to pull himself together, "is that I don't know how to end it. I don't really want to. Who needs a book if it's just going to end? It's like with love-affairs. If you thought they were going to end, you would never start, would you?"

"Jesus, the emperor! The frigging emperor! So what's that mean?" By now, Bobby was too drunk to find his way around the book, which was falling apart like him. "I just don't know, David, you've got to help me with this here emperor."

"Here," David said with authority. "I'll find it."

"Don't grab!" Bobby held the book back above his head, and a few leaves fell on him. "I don't know, David, I just don't know. It's getting out of hand. Everything's falling apart. Things are just going up and down like the toilet seat."

"Here," David said again, drunk enough to think he could see the future through red wine. "Let me try. Let's try Tim."

And then he held back, not in fear, but with a sudden false sobriety, and took another swallow of wine. That future could wait.

They could only get drunker: Madame Bobby, Madame David in a Sibylline mess, the wisest women in Cabbagetown, squinnying at the cards, sitting on crazy gay wombs and hatching futures. So far as they could remember afterwards, they got through everyone's drunken fortune. Everyone came to joy, to grief, but it was hard to keep track, and futures kept flying off in laughter.

PART 2

In November, early on a Thursday morning, the phone rang. Still in bed, David answered it. Susan Grey said hello, not forgetting she despised him, but with a wide, cold emptiness in her voice that went right by him.

"Is my brother there?"

He saw Tim doing the tumble turn, one hundred and seventy pounds deft as his hand.

"He's in the shower."

"I have to speak to him."

There was something *final in her tone, absolute,* and David felt with pity for her that Mrs. Grey wasn't sick, wasn't dying. She wasn't making the terrible scene he'd imagined. He carried the phone to the bathroom, untangling the long cord. He tried to shout over the noise of the shower, "The phone, it's Susan!" Tim looked out through the curtain, deaf and smiling. All his muscles, all his health, David thought, hadn't kept them from this. Tim saw the phone and turned off the water.

"It's Susan," David said, handing him the phone. He stepped quickly out of the bathroom. From the kitchen, he heard a few low words, then silence. He went back. Tim was standing in the tub, dazed, his gaze wide and shallow.

He noticed David. "I said I'd take the taxi right up."

But he didn't seem to know how to get started. David handed him his towel.

"I'll come too, of course."

"No."

"But – "

"No, *they wouldn't like it.*"

He was drying himself as if he didn't quite know where his body was. David watched, trying to find an argument. Tim suddenly dropped the towel and went into the bedroom, David following. Tim began dressing, quickly, as if something terrible would happen unless he got there in time to stop it. The thing was to do everything correctly, not to rush. He put on dark pants and white shirt. His right shoulder hadn't been dried and now came through wet cotton. He pulled a suitcase down from the shelf in the closet, opened it, tumbling summer clothes onto the floor.

"Tony!" he said suddenly. "I'll phone him."

David got the phone from the bathroom. Tim dialed and said, "Hi, Tony, I can't come in to work today." David heard Tony's voice listing all the projects they had lined up, all the frantic clients.

"I know, I know," Tim said. Quivering slightly all over, he thrust the phone at David, not looking at him, as if he was a secretary.

"Hi, Tony," David said weakly. Tim went back to packing.

"David? What is this?"

"Tim has to go home for a while, up to Napier. It's – " David's voice failed: for a moment it seemed he could be imagining everything.

"What *happened*?" he said to Tim, imploringly. "Susan didn't tell me."

Tim looked at him, surprised, in a kind of fear, and just pushed at the air, pushing David's look and question right away.

"It's Tim's mother, Tony," David said. "She's – she's very sick. No, she's – " He couldn't say it, he was strangling on it while Tim was staring at him coldly, as if wondering what he would say.

"It's happened, eh?" Tony said, letting him off. And as he went on, saying something about his father's death, David could hear that he had put on the same authority Susan had had, that for Tony he was calling from death. Tim stood up and went to the closet and pushed clothes along their metal rod with a shriek.

"Maybe I *should* come," David said, hanging up. As if the decision not to go had been his.

Tim picked up black shoes, one over his thumb, one over his fingers, and began polishing them with a red sweatshirt.

"I wish you could," he said. "But it would be impossible."

"You'll be all alone!"

"Oh no! They'll be there from all over."

"Maybe they wouldn't notice one more."

"One more what? I'm sorry, David, I just have to go up there and do what they want and get it over with. I'll phone, there's the phone in my room. Every night, I promise."

Reminded, he picked up their phone, and dialed for a cab.

"They're in control for now," he said, grimly pleased. "They've won."

Dressed and packed, he gave himself a military looking-over in the mirror, not meeting his own eyes. He might have been a young executive going off to work: he seemed to have forgotten his mother, except that David felt her all around him. There was nothing to keep her in Napier any more. It had happened too soon for him, David thought: Tim had begun to prepare for this, but not really, not seriously. It was like his life, his career: he hadn't really begun on it yet.

He turned to let David at him. "Don't worry, David. They can't really do anything to me."

David gave him a hug like a clumsy attempt at seduction, and Tim jumped and said, "Shit, my shoulder. It's still wet." He laughed at his foolishness. "Fuck it, it feels awful."

"I'm so sorry," David said, not letting her go unspoken.

"Oh, well, it'll dry," he said, almost angrily, pulling small inside David's arms. All

232

the shrewd observers, David thought, Alan and Michael, Hugh Armitage, Bobby, Jack Durham, would have said that the heart of the affair was in David. David was supposed to be the emotional one, the one who loved noisily and made a fuss, the child. Only David knew the heart of it was in Tim, that a child deep and silent inside Tim was the secret of it all.

Tim shuddered a little all over, a release of energy with no emotion colouring it. "It could have been worse, David," he said. "*It was in her sleep.*"

PART 3

Tim was in Napier for three days. On the last, Jack Durham phoned from San Francisco. "I'm not giving out comfort," Jack said, recklessly. "With death there's no bright side, none at all." Tim laughed, scared of what Jack might do to him. He knew Jack was thinking about Harvey Milk, who had just been murdered, though Jack was too bitter to say anything more than, "Oh yes, you heard, they finally shot him." It was true: there was no comfort. It was good to hear it said. Yet, Tim didn't want to think about such things so long as he was in Napier, under siege, fending off horrible condolences of people he hardly knew and pointed questions about girl friends. Jack talked about the deaths of his own parents, how he'd come to see each of them differently. He understood, far better than David, that Tim's mother had been dying bit by bit...that we were all dying a little each day, from the time of conception. David felt a deep loneliness and anxiety when Tim called, with an inability to fully understand Tim's loss. David remained the isolated, only child of living parents.

Fred came onto an extension to be introduced to Tim. They talked about the house in San Francisco, and Tim began to think about buying a house of his own, an old one like Jack's, and fixing it up by himself.

"How old are you, Tim?" Jack said, just before hanging up. "Twenty-five? That's a quarter of century."

"What does that mean, Jack?" He was still afraid Jack might try putting the blackness of death into words.

"How would I know? *It's your life.*"

Afterwards, as he moved through his mother's and his father's old house, imagining Jack's gay house, "up above the Castro," whatever exactly that meant, he felt too light to own any house, to hold it down. He came upon his brother-in-law moving with a funereal reverence, from one room to another, pushing his black Oxfords across the Oriental carpets. He observed him and thought, with hatred, he looked like a real estate agent, evaluating rooms with a cold eye. He didn't hate his sister, but he resented her choice of husband, who was now measuring his mother's house back into money. Yet, like his sister, Tim was a lot richer now.

On the way into the city, driven by some friends from Trinity, he imagined long holidays journeys through Europe. Or South America, perhaps. A friend had gone hiking in Peru. David didn't have any money: Tim would be happy to pay for both of them. He saw them inside some photograph or travel poster climbing through brilliant air to what was the name? *Machu Pichu, Lost City*.

When he got back to the apartment, he held David and let out a few tears, like the spare change beggars demand. He thought, he said, "Is this real?" Meaning being held by David, by anyone, because it was as if during the days in Napier his skin had been beaten hard and numb. Suddenly, doing it as soon as he thought of it, he knelt and pulled David's cock out of his pants, saying, "Let me, David, just be quiet and let me." It didn't matter what was going on above David's waist. Tim needed to feel overarched for a while, bestraddled and safe.

The next day he phoned Tony, who said he could get by without him for a while. But Tim wanted to be working again.

He found himself working hard: it kept him safe, most of the time. Because for a while he didn't know what his emotions were going to do with him. Panic came from nowhere, when he was on the street, or talking with clients, or just moving from one room to another in the apartment. It tried to squeeze him out of his skull, out of the world. He would wake with adrenalin slamming into his heart and bursting, as if he'd dreamt of throwing himself on her heart attack – like a soldier throwing himself on a shell. He found himself stumbling on places where she still hadn't died, like pockets of resistance in a defeated city, where she fought to the death. It would seem that the world had to be the place where they were together – or be nothing at all. Intermittently through this, he felt pleased with himself, because she could see, anyone could see, how loyal he was. He was her last supporter, the last person in the world looking at her with living eyes. It was a romance, a conjuring, calling up her moments of tenderness, and his – her coldness, his. He was showing he loved her, he was showing her he could love her. And what life she had, depended on his loving her like this.

He came down into the solid world with grief coming up out of the ground to receive him. Out on the sidewalk, tears were given up suddenly on King Street, saying *look*. And people *did* look, quickly, the tears making his face transparent, childish, feminine, as if he'd put grief on like drag.

He wondered how it would have happened if he'd been without a lover. More would have been lost, cut away. But David was almost too sympathetic at times: Tim could feel him being good to him watchfully, stalking him with comfort. David seemed to think that what was going on was just an enormous sadness. He would take some of Tim's feelings and magnify them, while others went by him unfelt.

In bed, Tim was putting himself together again from out of David, getting back what he had taught David about sex, as if he'd hidden his sex, very cleverly, in a body so different from his no one would have thought of looking there. At first, it was cautious, David approaching him as if he was wounded somewhere, or everywhere. The understanding seemed to be that they didn't want to go too deep into Tim's feelings. But

Tim was finding he could be glad to be alive. He had come through: his parents had no more deaths.

In Tony's studio overlooking Queen Street, he worked hard, but in his work he found himself keeping away from anything like emotion, drawing cleanly and coldly, keeping to the lines between things. But below all this, between his feelings and his focussing eye and hand, images welled up as if something inside him was disintegrating and floating up into colours he could almost taste. He would think that the time had come for him to try painting seriously. He would be grabbed by his ambition and the terror of it, as if it must have an answer now or leave him forever.

He decided to go to New York, alone, for a week. He didn't even want to get in touch with people he knew there. He wanted to see what was happening in the galleries and where he stood with it.

It was Bobby he told first. Bobby was scared of New York, because Richard and Richard had come to grief there. For all their plans, they'd been like deer in traffic. One was mugged and beaten, one had a bad trip that left him a bit crazy for a while, one almost died of hepatitis, one fell in love with a monster. New York was a terrible place, an evil, cruel place, Bobby now thought– loyal to his heroes, and always a patriot.

"No it isn't. It's great," Tim said, briskly. "The question is, what will David think?"

"You mean he doesn't know yet?" Bobby said, still scared, and not just of New York.

David was understanding, but he knew Tim was changing. "Just promise to come back," he said, as if it was a joke.

New York was as chilly as Toronto, with a raw wind from the ocean. Everyone seemed to be trying to get through the winter on a frenzy of activity. With Tim's eyes and feelings shrinking in the cold, the outer city faded. In order to stay indoors, he started at the Met and was there three days in a row. He was in Europe, Egypt, China, and in the end he never made it to the art world, or scene, or scenes of 1978. In the evenings he went to movies and plays. Sex didn't interest him: he was too full of what he was seeing to want to be touched.

"*Safe and sound!*" he wrote to Bobby on a postcard, a Miro, since Miro's squiggly eroticism seemed to be pure Bobby Riding. And he was safe, too, but not ready for the plunge into hope and terror that he'd come to consider. He'd acted like a good Canadian of an earlier generation, like some uncle or great-uncle of his: he'd gone to the United States to visit Europe. But it wasn't because he was afraid of America. With all his feelings still tender, he was afraid of his own ambition.

Coming in by taxi from Toronto airport, he felt the cool, quiet city spread around him, the capital of the northern towns, stretching up into Shield country. Living in downtown Toronto, he'd thought he was south, but it was a very northern south, on the fringe of the gloomy hinterland.

David, looking him over carefully, was the native, not Tim.

"*I love you, David,*" Tim said. "*You'll never change.*"

"What does *that* mean?"

Tim didn't answer, but it meant that David didn't know that life is an endless piling up of experiences, and you couldn't wait to understand them all, because there were always more coming. That, anyway, was true for him. And for his mother too, he realized all at once, shaking, and shaking for both of them, since he was holding David. It seemed he heard his mother now: "Don't mourn forever. Don't *dawdle.*"

That night he dreamt she had pushed out across the lake, doing a breast stroke, and he was trying to catch up, doing the same weary stroke. When he got close, she pushed her face through the water with eyes closed, skinned over: she was in her sleep. He woke as if at the last moment for waking and looked around in sheer misery. He pulled closer to David and thought about being a quarter of a century old, and answering Jack, telling him what that meant. Images of New York came back, as if it was a foreign country where, without knowing how, he understood the language. Not the spoken, the visual language: advertisements, clothes, paintings, sexy looks from the magazines or the streets. He knew the new balance of shapes, new lines, new shades, new postures, the sudden elegant elusions, as if he had lived there in another life. His gayness and his skill at seeing and imagining seemed to come together in that atmosphere saturated with images.

Grown up, free at last, and as dreamy a boy as Bobby Riding, he pulled closer to David's back, seeing an old brown apartment block he'd only seen in passing, and hardly noticed. It was like tens of thousands of apartment blocks, except that every brick was in New York. He saw one set of windows, high above the street, and knew he was behind them, sleeping, to wake in a country where he had lived once, and lived now, in a parallel life of anecdotes, movies, and desire.

PART 4

At first, it seemed to David that Mrs. Grey's death had brought them closer together, and made them more alike. Tim had become a temporary introvert. David didn't know what was going on in Tim, but he secretly hoped that by surviving his mother, he would inherit something essential from her, become a permanent part of Tim's world. Their relationship could be more than a long love-affair they'd had while getting to be adults.

One night, just after he'd got back from New York, Tim looked at him thoughtfully and said, "You know, sometimes I think that for you – the thing about me – is just that *I'm your first.*"

They were in bed, Tim with his head back on his arms.

"*Just?*" David said, looking at his first chest, the light-brown hair on one of his first, sweet armpits. "Christ, Timmy – *just!*"

Tim was drawing a line around it, making him look at it objectively, historically. David thought he could win on those terms.

But they were widening out, branching out – as a lot of couples do. Tim saw more of friends like Alan and Michael, Duncan and Scott, and friends from work. David began to cultivate his fellow graduate students, ones he could come out to. Some he found to be quite reasonable, under the academic savagery. More and more, Hugh Armitage "borrowed" him for the symphony or the opera. With Bobby, he dropped in a lot at the Three Bears' double apartment. He even confessed that was his name for them. Did they mind? They thought about it and no, on the whole, they liked it. Teasing them more, David asked how you became a feminist, if you were a man. He was interested, perhaps he might enlist. Did you have to pass a test? Did you swear some kind of oath? "It was simple," Charlotte said, coldly: "You just stop being an asshole." David said he'd think about it, and began reading some books Paul had given Bobby. More and more, Paul was talking of moving, probably to Vancouver.

Tim began to trick. "I wouldn't mind if only you wouldn't call it that," David remarked. He wasn't threatened by anyone Tim might pick up: he feared a deeper change, some new life which wouldn't include him.

David began a counter-affair with Ken, breaking off 'McAlistair' with an audible snap. He wanted to have somebody on his side, someone he could talk to. And he could mention to Tim that really Ken wasn't very much into sex. He was still too intellectual, too puritanical: really, gay sex was for comradeship and outraging the enemy.

One day they were in the kitchen, Tim, David, Ken. David was making a stew, and the room was full of the scent of thyme. He and Ken were talking, putting on their performance of two gay Toronto men, the political-intellectual variety. It was a noisy production, and all sorts of pompous asses, straight and gay, were being shredded if only they had known it. Tim sat silent by the window.

Then David heard himself saying, "And as for Mr. Trudeau, *he's simply talking through his hat, isn't he?*"

Mrs. Grey, surprising them. He looked at Tim, *stricken*. It was is if he'd accidentally scalded him with the stew.

Tim smiled a little.

"Our old friend Mr. Trudeau," he said. "He always does, doesn't he?"

So David was forgiven. But what did that mean for Mrs. Grey? Or for him?

Ten minutes later, Ken, standing at the window, looked out and gave a stagy shiver. Tim looked too, and smiled. "That's our neighbour, Mrs. Lukacs," he said.

David stepped over, holding a ladle of stew to be tasted when it cooled. Mrs. Lukacs was taking out her garbage. It was freezing, even the Russians would stay indoors today, but Mrs. Lukacs had stepped out in a flowered dress and a sweater, counting on the fragile layer of heat she brought. But the garbage cans were putting up a fight, banging, crashing, while winter peeled her, layer by layer.

They watched in human sympathy. "Hurry, Mrs. Lukacs, please," Ken said.

And then just before the cold was about to grab and get her, she turned and ran.

"Hurray!" said Ken, raising his glass of wine.

Tim was staring through the window, then sensing David's eyes, smiled up at him.

People die, he seemed to say: they die or leave and you go on.

Then Tim went to New York for a longer visit, to stay with friends there. There was no question of David coming: by now, he knew Tim was scouting out a life beyond his world. He kept thinking of the new truth Jack had announced on a quick visit to Toronto to sell his house. "In the end, every Canadian needs his American."

"Just because you do, Jack..."

"No, all of us, it's part of arriving here. Of setting foot on North America."

"That's *ridiculous*," David said, irritably.

"Maybe Tim is *yours*," Jack said, simply because he could never lose an argument. "He's down there in SoHo, learning how to be *your American*."

One afternoon while Tim was away, David gave up on his beloved and hated Ruskin and went across the campus to Frye's four o'clock lecture. For refreshment, for recreation. Frye would lift him up out of this ironic, late-twentieth century winter world into the sacred unity of literature. As David crossed Queen's Park, there was only a thought of twilight in the air and in the hardening white of the snow, but when he came out at six it would be night. That was part of the effect of Frye's lectures in winter: revolving the archetypes, he called darkness down, and proved that dark and light obeyed him.

Christopher Grahame Leggatt was on another path some distance away, walking towards Hart House, wrapped in thought. With a hockey stick over his shoulder and a big bag full of plastic hockey armour, he looked faring, a pilgrim, and his appearance framed David's life, let him imagine what it might have been. If he'd never met Tim, would he still be alone, right now, in this winter light, still in love with Chris? No: he didn't have the patience. Sooner or later, he would have given up. He believed in suffering, but not forever, not to the death. He and Tim would come apart without terrible scenes, without help from the TTC. Their dramatic parting had been two years ago, and that was enough.

When Tim came back, still undecided about his life, David was pleased and irritated too. It put off the day when he had to give him up, but he didn't like to have an indecisive lover. Why couldn't Tim make up his mind – did he want to be a painter or didn't he? Did he want to leave him or didn't he? They were lovers at night, new lovers: they had some of their best, darkest sex, as if now they could take sex as their master, thrusting into or onto each other as they wanted to fight through to something else. David was terrified and loved it too, turning his feelings for Tim into lust and anger.

Really, this was what he had loved, Tim's body. It was beautiful, but there were other bodies. By day, Tim seemed younger, more irresponsible – even, to put it bluntly, as David did once, quite faggotty at times.

"*Grow up, David*," Tim said angrily. "Sooner or later, David, *you'll have to forgive your boyfriends for being gay*."

David shrugged: he didn't have to *forgive* a thing.

Then they stopped having sex with each other: the anger was too strong, blocking out all other emotions. They began exploring, competing. It's an odd experience, bumping into your lover at the baths literally, coming around a corner: "Hi there!" grinning, high as a kite. And David, very stoned too, ran down a thousand dizzy flights of stairs in one second to wonder, *who are you? Where were you?*

In March, Tim announced that he wanted an apartment of his own.

"So you are staying in Toronto, then?" David said.

"I guess, yes, for a while. There's a lot happening in T.O., after all."

Tim didn't bother to look: he seemed to be waiting for the apartment to come to him. And it did. Alan phoned one day — David never quite forgave him for this – with news of the perfect place, the top two stories of a renovated house, like a house of its own up in the air. Tim went over, looked at it, and signed a check.

So, suddenly, they were packing. It was a Saturday morning. They'd got up early to go through things, dividing them up.

Tim tossed a striped cotton shirt at the pile of things to be thrown out. David snatched it out of the air.

"I love this shirt."

"That old thing?"

"Yes." He was unable to look at him. A Tim-shaped piece had been cut out of each eye.

"Well, keep it. It's yours."

"The sleeve is torn. Bobby could use it, though, if I shorten the sleeves."

He threw it into an empty cardboard box. Once started, Bobby's box began filling with clothes, records, books – became two boxes. They felt guilty because he didn't know yet, and he was coming over.

There was a knock on the door. Tim got up and opened it without looking at David.

"Hello, Bobby. It's finally happened: I'm moving out," Tim said, preemptively.

Bobby came in, taking in the devastation. He sat on the couch, still in his puffy ski jacket, arms helpless by his sides. David had a horrible feeling he would start crying and thought, grow up.

"That box is yours," David said, sternly, pointing at it. "Things we thought you can use. And I put the books you wanted to borrow in there, too."

"*Howl?*"

"Yes. And *Kaddish.*"

"Christmas!" Bobby said, grimacing.

"Let's take a rest," David said. "I'll make some tea."

"No, there isn't that much more," Tim said quickly. "And I don't want to keep Alan waiting." It was obvious he was afraid that if they stopped they would talk, and fight. Bobby would pull it out of them.

"Maybe Jack was right after all," Bobby said bitterly.

"Oh, Jack is always right," David said. "About what?"

"Men don't really love each other."

"God, Bobby," Tim said. "We do not have time for that."

Bobby gave a despairing heave of his shoulders, took off his jacket, and started repacking Tim's things in cunning, space-saving ways.

"Maybe it's not so awful. I used to think my parents should get a divorce. It would have been a relief all round."

"We're not your parents," Tim said. "We never said we were."

Bobby jammed a book into place angrily.

"Well, neither did I, mister."

When they were finished, or almost, Tim stood up, looking around, his hands on his hips. With the good looks David loved, and the good looks he hated – that seemed to say, I'm so muscled and masculine I can be a little campy and get away with it, can't I? His eyes came to rest on a large jade plant.

"Maybe you'd like to keep that," David said. "You'll need some plants."

Tim had bought it two weeks ago, as a sort of peace-offering or consolation prize. David preferred to take some green serif and nurse it up.

"No. It's yours, David. You keep it," Tim said now. An odd note came into his voice, as if he realized he was getting close to the moment when he would actually have to go – have to turn his back on David, weakly, shamefully. The silent anger they were working with might not hold out.

David stared back, bleakly. He thought he could bear Tim's being a shit, but he would hate to see Tim knowing it himself.

"Maybe Bobby would like it," David suggested. "You were saying you wanted to redecorate your room."

Bobby pulled his lower lip back into his teeth, an expression David had never seen before.

"You can trust plants, Bobby," he said. "They don't have legs. They can't walk out on you."

"You're *foisting* it on me."

"You can water it and remember us in our good days. When Tim and David were happy together on Markham Street."

What he was saying was that he could be quite nasty and still not be the real bastard.

"*I don't want your fucking jade plant!*" Bobby shrieked.

His eyes were closed tight, leaving Tim and David alone together. There were several moments of shocked silence.

"Why can't you just stay together?" The eyes were still shut tight, as in some child's game.

"You can always visit," Tim said nervously. "The Dundas car is right at the foot of the street."

Bobby looked back and forth between them, not quite meeting their eyes.

"Maybe if you just stayed together, you'd get over it."

"There's nothing to get over," Tim said. "It's just that we've changed."

"Oh God, it's just no good being gay."

"You can't blackmail me that way," Tim said. "David and I have agreed to split up."

At this, David couldn't hold back. "No, we haven't!"

"What?" Tim said, amazed and scared.

"I *never* agreed."

Tim was silent, afraid the confrontation was about to happen after all. And it was, David saw.

"You said you were leaving. I said, yes, I can see that all right, you are leaving. I didn't agree. *But what rights do I have?*"

Tim looked at him with a ducking and shrinking in his neck and shoulders, afraid David was about to push him to say whatever he needed to say to get out – to be the shit he thought they'd agreed to ignore. And seeing that physical cringing, David was afraid too: he wouldn't be able to stop himself. He wanted to see that selfish, slinking, cold-blooded Tim – to see its face before he saw its back. It would be unbearable but he longed for it, too. He had to have it.

Bobby sprang up blindly, as if he couldn't bear to keep still, then ran and, grabbing the big pot by the rim, raised it high up over him. Earth spilled, raining over his wet, desperate face, streaking it. The fleshy green leaves quivered high above him, almost dancing. They both stared at him...Samson...Atlas...about to smash their world. *Throw it down*, David thought, *smash it*. And Tim was thinking the same thing: he could sense it.

The plant quivered uncertainly, feeling doom on its leaves like a wind. Bobby's arms began trembling, as if it really was made of stone. Then he breathed in, shaking all over, pulling the pot down against his chest, taking a few blind steps back to sit heavily into an armchair. He was crying with rage, the leaves of his present brushing at his tears like little, green hands.

"All right," he growled. "We'll put it in *Bobby's box*."

"I wish there were two of you," David said in a sudden fury of insight. There were two Tims, in the same body: if only one could go and be despicable, while the other stayed to wipe away tears. He felt this like a split running down through himself, but he was unable to look up and confirm it.

"Why?" Tim said, emotional with fear but hoping no, seeing that he'd gotten away with it again. *Again*, David thought. *Again. The way he has always done* The good, kind-hearted Tim, our hero, after all, or the best our gay story can do for one, saved in the nick of time.

David glared at his eyes. "Because then I could kill them *both*!"

PART 5

Late one night, a week after moving, Tim left Alan and Michael a few steps up on the stairs to Desire's, saying he was headed for the baths. He wasn't sure, though, that he really would go through its tacky, uncanny door to the plywood labyrinth beyond. His new apartment was ready for a lover, but Tim had been restless since leaving David, not sure what to do with his freedom, almost bored with it. Perhaps it was a mistake to stay in Toronto after all.

He turned off Yonge down one of its more moonlit side streets, a street of boys and shadows. In New York, he thought nostalgically, you would be risking your life by going alone down a street like this. Not very far along it, a tall youth was leaning on a brick wall, one foot up against it, hands crossed behind his tailbone. Seeing Tim coming up, he grinned. Tim gave back a smile of friendly complicity and looked away.

"Hey, you got the time?" The voice sounded young but it was deep, pushed down and held down. The hustler wore a hooded gray sweatshirt, tight jeans, and white leather basketball boots: ordinary teenage clothes worn differently, knowingly. "'Cause I sure do."

"It's way past your bedtime." Tim said teasingly, and he stopped, not knowing why. He knew it was a mistake, but he was at loose ends. He needed to be amused.

The hustler's face was in shadow, but you saw dark hair falling over a high forehead, small, high cheekbones, a small mouth. He tilted his head back, trying to put more scorn into the snub nose than it could bring off.

"It's *never* past my bedtime."

"Well, it's getting past mine," Tim admitted.

He had lots of energy with Alan and Michael, but now he felt tired. He didn't quite know how to behave in this encounter, who to be – not a customer, not a comrade. The hustler was still lounging against the brick wall, studying him. His eyes were colourless in the dim light. They had full underlies.

"Hey, guess what?" he said, stepping forward.

"What?"

"I think I'm in love."

Tim laughed out loud and looked away. Farther down, another hustler, with a big bare chest and sweatpants and flip-flopping thongs, was walking out to talk into a car window.

"It can't be that easy," Tim said.

The boy, if he was one, chortled – down in his throat, rolling his amusement down there, possessively.

"Candy from a baby!" His smile had comic parentheses at the corners, to tuck it into the full flesh around.

Tim knew he wasn't up to this scene. He looked at the hustler in sweatpants, stepping back from the car. Some biting remarks came through the soft air. It was time, more than time, to be off...to be off.

"Well, take care of yourself," Tim said. He felt it too: brash as he was, this kid could not have an easy life, or a safe one. He obviously wasn't a middle-class hustler, doing it for fun, or to put himself through university.

"You aren't going to up and leave me! Not now!" The boy took a few steps behind him.

"'Fraid so." To apologize, to defend himself, he fell into something like the other's style. "I need my sleep."

He would go straight home, he decided, and so not have lied to him anyway. From behind he expected some bitchy throwaway line, a cute curse. The boy was loping up beside him. With an odd self-confidence, he took Tim's hand from his side, holding it in both hands. They were remarkably cold.

"Let me buy you a drink."

"A drink?"

"It's just my idea, okay?"

"You're crazy." He wasn't following any rules Tim knew. You could almost think it was his first night on the street.

"That's my problem. Come on, don't go to the *baths*."

"I really am going straight home."

"All I'm after is a drink and talk and say hello. Okay?"

Tim shrugged. He couldn't bring himself to pull away and walk away alone. It was stupid to say yes, but he would still be in control.

"Just a drink, all right. And then I'm going home."

The boy turned and ran to get a red gym bag.

"Jerry's?" he said. "It's like home base for me."

Jerry's was the bar where Bobby Riding had met Doug, lower on the social scale than even Jack's old bar. Tim had never been inside it, though it was right on Yonge Street. "Why not?" he said.

"But I'm paying, mister. Don't worry, I got it. Tonight, I got it all."

As they went back to the street, Tim could see that he was tall, taller than Tim except for a country boy's stoop. He walked pigeon-toed in the basketball boots, and jauntily, as if little charges of happiness went off under each step.

"So, what's your name, mister?"

It stopped just on the tip of his tongue. He could give another name, after all: no one would know him in Jerry's. But he'd never done that before, and why should he start now?

"Tim."

"Tim! Mine's Kelly. Glad to meet you."

He held out his right hand, and again it was oddly cool, like something left over from winter, the scaly piles of snow lurking in the shade.

"Where are you from?" Tim said.

"Where I'm from, Mister, you never heard of."

"Why do you keep calling me that? Mister?"

"Oh sorry, is it missus? No, it's because you're in there thinking *he's* just a hustler."

"Well, you are hustling, aren't you?"

"Not since I met you! I'll leave Sal and Jodie to handle the crowd tonight."

It wasn't far to Jerry's double doors, and Kelly ran forward and held one of them open for him, laughing. They went into a long narrow room, almost a corridor, with a line of tables on each side. Men and boys sat drinking and watching others who took the long walk in front of them – paraded or skulked or tramped manfully along, back and forth. Happy with the attention, Kelly strode to an empty table and dropped the gym bag with a territorial thump. He was smiling and waving to friends, showing off his catch, perhaps. Tim didn't mind. He imagined how he would explain this to Alan and Michael, or to David. But of course they would never know about it. He would pay for the drinks, or somehow make sure the kid didn't come out a loser, and leave in half an hour.

They sat, both facing outward. Kelly gave him a smile. He looked older in the light, and tired. His skin was more than winter pale: it was waxy, translucent, in spite of the dark hair. Impulsively, he dived into the sweatshirt and emerged from it in a plain white T-shirt. The armpits were bearded with sweat: his nipples peered through the thin cotton. A strange sweet smell came from him.

"Did you like the guy in the sweatpants?'

"He was okay."

"*Okay*! That was Sal. I borrowed this, he saw I was getting cold, and I said, 'Now I'm the top. You're the bottom.' He wasn't any too amused."

He ducked under the table and stuffed the sweatshirt into the bag. He sat up, and tilted back against the wall. "*Whoosh!*" he said, looking tired, and putting his hand over his left breast.

"What's that mean?" Tim said, curiously.

"Nothing, nothing, just it was hard work, getting you in here. That was my audacity for *weeks*."

Tim laughed: he didn't think so. Kelly smiled sideways, gray eyes looking over the fat ledges of flesh.

On a sudden impulse he came tilting forward and put his hand on Tim's thigh, smoothing the corduroy. The movement was more neat and fussy than sexual. He looked solemnly down into the back of his hand: long, rather womanly fingers with reddened knuckles.

"I better warn you, mister—Tim – Mister Tim! – but I could really like you. I could like you in the worst possible way."

"Really?"

"Didn't I just say so?"

"How old are you – Kelly?" It was hard for Tim to say the name as if he believed it. It must be a street name, he thought, meant to sound Irish and sexy.

"Old enough to know the difference!" Noticing the waiter, he arched back, twisting to get money out his tight pocket. He almost tore a ten, but with a magenta flourish it brought several glasses of beer down from the waiter's tray. Tim let him pay: it was a touch of reality.

"You know what to do with the change," he said gruffly.

Tim still wanted to know how old he was: it was hard to tell. Sometimes he didn't seem younger than Tim.

"How old do you have to be to know the difference?" Tim said.

"Where I come from, not very."

"Where's that?"

"If you've got to know, place called Port Albert, and you never heard of it."

"I drove through it once, long time ago. With my parents, on our way home from someone's cottage."

"Well, that's a sign, then. See any cute little kids by the side of the road?"

Tim didn't answer. He remembered it well: he'd been in the back of the car watching Garry Featherstonhaugh dive into an icy lake. And shivering with a kind of fearful lust.

They sat watching the endless parade, with Kelly trying out stories now and then.

"See that one? He's lovers with the roommate of the guy who ended up in garbage bags all along the 401 last Christmas."

"Really?"

"Think I'm a liar? I can get him over here."

"No, thanks, I believe you."

But most of the time they didn't talk, working their way down through the beer. They didn't have much to say to each other, and Tim didn't want to seem particularly interested in Kelly. He sensed that this silence was part of Kelly's job – he had to be patient with another's silence, and be entertaining when it was wanted. Tim decided Kelly was older than he'd thought, not a boy at all: his smooth skin and his comic face made him seem younger. How was Tim going to get out of this situation without being nasty? Would Kelly be insulted if some money was simply left on the table when Tim left him?

As he drank off the last of his beer, Kelly looked at it jealously.

"There's more," he said.

"No thanks. Next time, drinks'll be on me. But now, I've had too much. I'll take a taxi, I guess."

He was about to get up, but conceded a few minutes more to Kelly's hurt scowl. He coughed and delivered a sort of speech: "I've been checking you out, mister. I've been in here thinking it over. And what I say is, any time. Any time."

His face was solemn, then he tried a smile. There was something almost foolishly happy in the smile, but his eyes were sad and careful. He went on: "So why not give it a try? I got what it takes, don't worry 'bout that. So why don't we check it out?"

How often had he said things like this before? It might, after all, be the first time, Tim thought, but somehow he still couldn't believe it.

"I'm sorry," Tim said. "But I guess I made a mistake out in the lane."

"That was the smartest thing you did in your life!"

"I mean, tonight, I just wasn't cruising."

"Don't give me that! With that face, you go out the door, you're cruising."

Tim shook his head and sat forward, ready to go.

"Here!" Kelly demanded. "Give me a kiss."

"Why?"

"And see, that's why. Here."

He leaned over, Tim dodged at the last moment, not knowing why. As Kelly's lips bumped along Tim's jaw and neck, ignominiously, he breathed in a sour sweetness.

Kelly sat back, arching angrily. "That's no fair! You aren't giving me my chance."

"Well, I'm sorry," Tim said, lamely. "But next time, the drinks'll be on me, I promise."

"Next time!" He sat with his forearms flat on the table, like a dog's forelegs, sulking.

"Just stay five more minutes, okay? Five minutes's not going to break you."

Tim smiled, it was so childish. "All right, five minutes."

So he sat looking down the gloomy tunnel, the air dim with smoke, the faces shiny with beer and laughter. He could casually slip Kelly some money and say, 'Here, you need a rest.'

No one was actually counting the minutes. Soon he could feel Kelly nerving himself for another attempt.

"Here," he said, "I mean, it's only a fucking kiss."

He leaned again, and Tim thought he was safe, his getaway was secure. He'd let him have a kiss goodbye. The warm, sour smell came around him as he met the lips, and a fat tongue came pushing in, with Tim thinking, 'Kelly, whatever your name is, this is ridiculous.' Then his eyes closed and he was falling. There was nothing under him: he could have fallen away forever. He hung on to the world only by drinking and drinking the sweet mouth and tongue.

"There," Kelly said, pulling back haughtily. "*Take* your taxi."

Tim blinked and looked around. He felt like something spat out, a seed stripped and wet and raw. He looked over the plain, comic face, wondering how it could possibly be connected to what he felt.

The small mouth, the rain-gray eyes with their fat underlies, the turned-up nose, and what he still felt and tasted they had to be connected, and he didn't know how.

"I guess I will," he said, in a low voice. An impulse, not quite him, told him to get up and walk away while he could.

"What?"

"I am drunk," Tim said, foolishly, shaping over the face. That was all: he had had a lot to drink with Alan and Michael, then there had been Kelly's beers. He said, indifferently, "Maybe you'd like to come along?" Maybe after all you're going to be just another trick.

Kelly's surprise turned into a smile, pure happiness, dressed up with little tucks. He leaned for a kiss, Tim brushed his lips, pulling away in a kind of fear, breathing in his smell. It was sweet and rich, like something you could drink and go on drinking, but with a sour sharpness, like something you wanted to bite. It seemed the smell, the taste, could dissolve everything into itself, as if after it everything else would be nostalgia. He had never been so drunk, he told himself.

"So let's go," Tim said, standing up.

"Oh yeah!" He got up, slinging the red bag over his shoulder, the handles pulling his left hand back, opening the long white fingers. Tim let him go first: pigeon-toed, with the country boy's stiffness in his back.

From the taxi, Tim watched the speeding streets, familiar at first, then new as they got into his new neighbourhood. Tim wondered if he was safe, imagining what his friends would say if he was robbed or knifed. Had he closed the door to the room that was going to be his studio? He could pretend to have a roommate if he had. But no, it was foolish: Kelly was all right. He was talking about Port Albert. It was in the snowbelt, they'd had terrific storms, burying the place, snow over the windows, the doors, the roads lost. But people helped each other out, went everywhere in snowshoes, calling to each other, ten feet above the town. "It's like that there, friendly."

Holding Tim's hand, interlacing cold fingers, he called, "Hey, Mr. Taxi driver!"

The driver was hugging the wheel, thinking he'd seen this scene often enough.

"Hey, you, listen here."

"Yeah?"

"You're going to be lucky tonight. I know. Tonight, you *gotta* be."

Tim paid the driver, and led Kelly up the stairs to his part of the house. He dropped his bag with a soft, knowing thump and stepped up to him.

"Do you want a drink or anything?" Tim said. "Are you hungry?"

For an answer, Kelly shoved his tongue into his ear, and from inside the strange thunder Tim could almost think that whatever had happened in the bar was already over. He was coming down from the beer. It was a relief to sink into the soft ache of fatigue.

"You got a bedroom?" Kelly said, both eager and playing eagerness.

"Oh, I suppose. This way."

Kelly followed him, and dropped sitting onto the bed, bouncing, pulling off his shirt. Tim watched, taking in the peeled first moment of skin adjusting to the air. Kelly had a flat, hairless chest, shallow for his wide shoulders, bony ribs, small, hard pectorals. He tossed the T-shirt at Tim's eyes, and it went through his hands and hit him in the face. He caught it as it fell. How odd it would be if that white, awkward body was the one that had been waiting for him through all the others. Holding the shirt, he stepped over and sat down beside Kelly. He didn't want to kiss him yet. He reached and tickled one nipple, a tiny, pink snout.

"Yeah, that's what I need," Kelly said, eyes closing. "Make me feel queer." He lurched against Tim, and the fat tongue was there again, waddling in like a circus clown.

But as Tim's hand moved down towards his belly, he pulled away, hardening.

"Don't, man, I'm ticklish."

"I was hardly touching you."

"That's what does it. You got to touch me harder."

Tim's hand went to the buckle of his belt. It was a smooth piece of metal, which hid both ends of the leather. The moment he touched it, the stomach muscles hardened, turning the belt into a steel band. Tim's fingers clawed at it helplessly.

"How do I undo this thing?"

"You find out."

When Tim tried again, he said, "*Don't tickle me*, that's out of line." He turned over on his stomach, jerking with laughter.

"Well, undo it yourself then."

"No. You can't undo it, you can't have me."

Tim reached under him. The belly was soft for a second, then rigid muscle.

"I do a hundred sit-ups every day."

"I believe you."

Tim rolled him over like a log: he lay with his hands behind his head, grinning. "*Rape!*" he shouted happily. "*This could be rape!* Here, just give me one of those sloppy kisses."

But when Tim tried to move from the kisses to what they seemed to promise, Kelly turned hard, turned impassable. Falling away from the collar of his jeans, his belly would be as tender as a throat, as tremulous, until Tim reached.

"All right, I give up," Tim said. "You take them off."

"That's no good. You got to be man enough."

Tim sat back, in exasperated disgust. Kelly pulled himself up against the wall.

"Stalemate," Tim said. He put his hands over his face: they had the smell of him, and he put them down. He held himself still, preparing, then lunged at the soft stomach, and they were rolling wildly around the bed, Tim playing at first, then putting out his strength, getting on top. Kelly thrashed like a fish in a boat, then lay still, breathing fast.

"Boy, are you strong." It was mocking, but envious too.

"So are you," Tim said. But Kelly was clumsy, doomed to use his strength in the wrong way. "I won, so you've got to take them off."

"Why?"

"Well, what are we going to do?"

"You figure it out!"

Tim stared down into the gray eyes for the moment he would decide to break free. They didn't quite look back, wavering like water. He knelt back, putting his hands on Kelly's icy feet.

"Why are your feet so cold?"

248

Kelly scowled. "'Cause you got me so scared, mister. I'm just shaking."

He shrank, miming fear and cold, then twisted, almost getting free. Tim attacked with the last, mindless end of his energy. After a flurry, he was on top again, with Kelly face down.

"You lost twice," Tim said. "That means you have to take them off." He was making up this rule, but they needed rules badly.

"You're just not up to snuff, mister. You just don't cut the mustard."

With his face shoved deep into a pillow, he chortled in his throat, as if he had Tim down there, and had rolled him around.

Tim sat back, exhausted, eyelids drowsing down: they were deadlocked. He ought to see him to the door, give him a few dollars worth of rest, freedom, however much Tim had in his wallet. Having decided this, he opened his eyes on the white, breathing shoulders, and desire pulled him down. He leaned and began licking the nape of his neck, the line of muscle curving into the shoulder. Kelly laughed, giving morsels of himself into Tim's mouth in a kind of ticklish surrender.

"You're the worst tease I ever met," Tim said in his ear. He bit gently, then harder, Kelly laughing, scared and excited.

"Oh help!" he said, to some raucous audience. "It looks like rape. He's going right off his head."

Tim bit harder, but holding back, his jaws vibrating between desire and gentleness. He could devour him. It might be the only way to get into him.

"Help, he's going for it. This one's going to rape me."

It was permission. It was a summons. Tim sat back, ready to tear the heavy denim with his hands. He saw a pair of paper scissors he'd left on the night table and said, "Yes" to them, as if they were alive. He would give Kelly what he was calling for, crying for. He shoved Kelly's neck into the bed with his left hand to hold him and grabbed the scissors.

"Oh, God, he's doing it! Help me, he's going to kill me!" It was a kind of wild, laughing terror, but Tim's hand crushed his voice, made it hoarse, as raw and desperate as if he was being killed. Tim held the scissors for a second, shaking with the rage of lust, then threw them away and got off Kelly, off the bed.

Kelly turned around, looking worried, even afraid. Because for the first time, Tim saw, things weren't going as he expected. He sat up against the wall, moving cautiously. Tim gave him a weak smile and shook a little. For a moment, if he had had to stab Kelly to fuck him, he would have. He couldn't speak, he was panting, but he wanted to say, 'What did you do to me?' It was as if the rapist he had almost been, had been brought in by Kelly.

Kelly didn't tell him. He grinned, partly reassured but a little let down, too. He put his hand to his chest, with the same precise cupping gesture as before.

"Whoosh!" he said, and coughed, his throat still hoarse.

"I don't want to rape you!" Tim cried.

"Well, thank you! Thanks a whole lot. First time anyone's said that."

Tim sat on the corner of his bed. His eyes closed. He felt depression tugging on him. What Kelly made him desire was impossible, it didn't exist. Then, forgetting, he put his hand over his face and smelled it, him, the smell that consumed everything else in nostalgia. He bit his palm with a kind of gentle rage. He opened his eyes again to look at the electric clock: their minutes deep in the night looking at them in numbers of wet, green candy.

"It's funny," he said, in a ordinary voice, trying to make friends. "But you're nice."

Kelly snorted. "Well, so are you. Maybe *too* nice."

Tim gave up. To send him away was too much trouble. But he wanted to leave this confrontation himself. "I'm tired, okay? I'm sorry, I just want to sleep."

"Tired?" Kelly gave a wide stretch, wringing out all his sleepiness. "You sure didn't look tired a minute back."

Tim shrugged. He slid out of his jeans and got under the sheet in his under shorts. "Maybe I'm not your kind of lover," he said, resentfully. "I like to *like* the people I have sex with."

"Don't give me a lecture. You sure didn't earn the right."

"Good night," Tim said, lying back and closing his eyes.

He could feel the mattress rise and looked through his eye–lashes. Perhaps Kelly would just leave, and let him restore himself. He felt as if he had been ripped open by what had happened.

Kelly was pulling his jeans down, almost tripping.

"There you go, mister. You don't toss this one back."

Without the black jeans, he was gawky and almost girlish, except for the corny tilt of his pelvis and the lolloping cock. Big enough, but sad, vulnerable, all he had on the hungry streets.

"Wow!" Tim said, closing his eyes. "Now get into bed so we can get some sleep."

"For Christ sake, mister. *It's Saturday night!*"

Tim lay, trying to digest everything, the sour sweetness, his frustration, the fight and its rage, into sleep. And for a few seconds, he succeeded. He slept. Then he woke, feeling the bed sink.

"What did I do wrong?" Kelly was sitting with his back to him, shoulders slumped.

"Nothing, really. I'm just tired, that's all."

"I fucked up. I ruined it. My chance."

Tim didn't move. He thought of saying, 'I was never your chance.'

"Me and my big hopes, eh?" His voice was rough with tears. "But there's no point sticking round." Tim could feel him about to get up: without opening his eyes, without asking himself why, as if out of the sleep he'd hardly left, he reached for the stomach. He found a soft handful, and held it, squeezing out giggles. Then he lay, eyes still closed, as if heading back into sleep that way.

"I guess I'm not so bad," Kelly said. "Just, you have to know me."

PART 6

In the morning, he had to go. "Business. Someone I have *got* to see."

"All right. I'll make you breakfast."

"I don't eat breakfast. I can't go getting fat."

But he ate his scrambled eggs and waited over coffee. Tim picked up his left foot and put it in his lap. It was icy, and the cold went all the way up to the knee.

"You've got poor circulation," he said, cautiously.

"You think I don't know that?" Irritated, he tried to pull away, but Tim held on. He had to know what was wrong. Kelly gave in, laughing.

"Oh well, I get by. The blood gets through all right."

The foot was friendly now, waggling cheerfully. The little toe was a hunchback: the big toe was splayed, off on its own.

"So are you coming back tonight?"

"Sure. Absolutely. *Here –* " He reached for a pen and began writing on the back of a flyer Tim had drawn and designed for a play in Cabbagetown.

"You can always reach me here during the day. At least, they'll know where I am."

He handed it over: "Kelly" and a phone number, with a line wandering around them, making a big, baggy heart.

Tim reached for the pen, but Kelly held it back and proudly recited his number, memorized from the bedroom phone.

At the door, he sat down to put on his basketball shoes. His waist was like a wrist, Tim thought, drawing him.

"Why don't you wear socks? For those cold toes of yours?"

"It's sexy not to. Besides, all mine got stolen. My whole trunk did, last month, that's like everything I own."

"I'll give you some. I've got lots."

Kelly looked at him doubtfully, and Tim thought, he isn't coming back. And it would be better if he didn't, wiser, safer, happier.

"Hockey socks. They ought to be butch enough."

The smile nudged into its corners. "You're out to reform me, I can see it. Fence me in." He didn't seem to mind.

He is coming back, Tim thought with a kind of frozen joy, going to get the socks. How should he plan his life?

Kelly pulled them on with comic impatience, pleased to be given something. He stood up, wrinkling his face.

"I'll never forget you, mister. Not with these suckers on."

He stepped forward for a kiss goodbye. "Remember," he said. "Any time."

Tim imagined saying, 'I'm in love with you,' – announcing it casually, as if there was no reason not to. But he decided to hold on to that.

"What sort of business?" he asked.

"Oh come on, don't you even like me?"

"Didn't I say so? I like you."

"Well, that'll do for starters. I can work with that."

"So I'll see you tonight?"

"Or I'll be sure and phone."

He had the door open and looked down the stairs, then reached for a last kiss.

"Oh, yeah, tonight, it's gotta be."

Tim went to the front window and watched him walk away with jaunty, high-arched steps. He looked absolutely ordinary, Tim thought, but he stretched Tim's feelings down the street till he turned the corner, leaving Tim in the air. He sat down in his new, quiet living-room and looked at his new furniture. "Kelly," he said out loud, not believing it. "What a name! Kelly."

But when there was no phone call and Kelly didn't appear that evening, it seemed to be just as well. Probably he would never see him again, but he was passive, waiting, in a kind of cold wonder, believing nothing.

After he got home from work the next day, the phone rang. It would be Alan, he thought: would he tell him about his adventure? Why not?

"Hi there, Mister Tim!"

"You didn't phone."

"Hey I was busy, I forgot."

"You could have phoned, couldn't you?" His bitterness was a complete surprise to him, not to Kelly.

"That's out of line! That's not allowed. I said I was sorry, didn't I? Besides, that's not why I'm calling. I am *ploughed*!"

"Where are you?" There was music in the background: country-western.

"Some bar, and this senior citizen with forty hands is after me." He giggled as if he felt them. "I need you here, right away."

Tim said nothing, imagining a life of phone calls like this.

"Come on there, Tim. I'm not lying, I need you."

"Where are you?"

"So do you love me?"

"Just tell me where you are."

"The Senator. You coming?"

"Yes."

"Then I'm glad."

He walked, then ran down to Dundas Street and got a taxi, saying, "The Senator," wondering what on earth would happen. The driver did a U-turn, silent except for the screeching of other cars, and went across the city and a long way out Queen Street East, to a shabby area near the racetrack. The taxi stopped in front of a blank four-story hotel. It looked abandoned: then a door right at the corner opened and two long-haired men in plaid shirts came out uncertainly, blinking.

The ground floor was a tavern. Kelly was sitting with a large group, mostly young, with a few who might be considered senior citizens, and some bikers in leather jackets. When Kelly saw him coming, he waved from the excitement of the group.

"Hi there, stranger," he said. "Want to join us? I told you he'd come," he said, to the girl sitting next to him. She was the only one who paid him any attention: she shrugged with one shoulder. She had long brown hair and a long skirt: sitting with one leg sideways across her knee, she displayed calf-length socks, striped green and maroon.

"The taxi's waiting."

"Good for the taxi. Let me buy you a drink. He deserves it, doesn't he? Come out to a hole like this."

"No, thanks," Tim said. "I'm in a hurry."

"I told you," Kelly said noisily. "He's like that, he just can't control his urges."

He got up and tottered, his eyes dimming.

"So don't forget your bag there, sweets," the girl said.

"What? Yeah." He grabbed it up, swung it back, and followed Tim out, saying good-bye to anyone who cared through the long fingers pulled open against his shoulder.

He was different in the cab, pale and serious.

"You know, you really must care about me, come out to hell-and-gone like this."

"I've never been in this area before, except to drive through."

"Yeah, what a dump. I was just there to help Alexis with her business."

"The girl in the socks?"

"It's what's under the socks that counts. Girl in a business like that – talk about balls."

"What business?"

"The business of getting you high." Kelly looked at him coolly. Tim looked away, not surprised, absorbing it.

He walked heavily up the stairs of Tim's apartment, dropped the bag, took off the basketball shoes, went in the socks into the living room. He looked around quickly, taking in the things that made it different from other living rooms, like the Jack Bush on the wall. Then he groaned and lay flat and face down on the sofa. "Lord, the state I'm in! Person could take advantage of a poor boy like me, right here."

He was staying at Tim's place, at least circling around it, for nearly two weeks. When he was there, he made himself at home like an antique store cat. When Tim came home from work, Kelly would usually be in front of the TV, watching in a sort of frozen rapture, or drinking and smoking grass and listening to records: dark, fake-Satanic heavy metal, or his sad, sad ladies: "Billie, Janis, Diana." Sometimes he'd be away, because of "friends" or "business", leaving a message in a wobbly heart or star or cock-and-balls.

Tim didn't know what to do with him, about him. Kelly hadn't finished high school, and couldn't bring himself to work for low wages. "An hour, a whole hour, and then you can buy a hamburger and fries, for Christ sake!" He'd once worked as a waiter and been fired for telling a customer to clean up his plate. It looked as though the only hope was that he would get older and more sensible. He lived from day to day and, with him around, so did Tim. Overnight, he'd been surrounded by his life, his personality, his sense of time.

At first Kelly didn't go out hustling, partly out of respect for Tim. "But I gotta to make ends meet, right?"

"No you don't. I can afford things for both of us."

"Well, that's real sweet, but I'm not your squaw. But you don't want me out there, I won't go."

"I don't want you hustling. I hate the idea."

"Good, great, that's what I needed to hear."

But he was out a lot: in fact he couldn't stay still without being stunned by drugs or alcohol or television. And the people he knew were all hustlers and dope pushers and petty thieves.

One day he held out a wad of bills. "I guess you could use some help with the rent," he said, truculently.

"What did you do to get it?"

"I helped a man who had a problem."

Tim looked at him.

"Is all," Kelly said scornfully. "Look, I said, I'm not going to be your squaw."

Tim knew already that he couldn't make him stop. He couldn't make him do anything he didn't want to do. He pushed drugs because he needed something to do to keep from being bored, to feel important.

"Why don't you buy something you want. Like a bike?"

"You mean a bike that you *pedal*, don't you?" Kelly said, forgivingly. "For me, it's got to be a Harley or nothing."

"Well, put it in the bank, then. You might need it some day."

"Here," Kelly said, collapsing, as if the bills were suddenly too heavy for him. "You do it then. I got money, I spend it."

One night soon after he'd moved in, Tim pulled an icy foot against his stomach, trying to warm it, and said again, "You really do have poor circulation." Should he try to get Kelly to see a doctor?

The foot jerked: Tim held on. For a moment, it looked as if Kelly might twist away into another wild wrestling match. Instead he gave a tired laugh.

"Be thankful, eh. That's why I'm not in the Forces right now. I could be off somewhere, blasting Commies, not fucking you."

"What do you mean?"

Kelly put the cupped hand over his left breast: the gesture reminded Tim of some painting of a saint. He seemed to listen inside himself for a moment. "I got a heart murmur. The blood doesn't stay in the heart long enough to get warmed up, it just goes right through, *whoosh!*"

He listened.

"Right now it's being a good heart. They told me at the medical. Soon's I turned eighteen, I went down and said, 'Here, make a *man* out of this loosey-goosey kid!' I was going to join the Navy: I hear it gets kind of cramped on those ships."

"This was last year?" Tim still didn't know his age.

"Last year, the year before."

"Is it serious?"

"Is it serious?" He gave Tim back his words in a deep, doleful voice. "I gotta be careful."

"But you aren't!"

"What do you mean?" He pulled away, haughtily, sitting up against the wall, the tall, cold shanks in front of him.

"Well, poppers for instance."

"Oh, mister, *you aren't taking my poppers*! Besides, that's what they're for, your heart. Little old ladies snort them."

Suddenly he laughed, long legs falling helplessly apart. "But what a way to go, eh? In your arms, that's how I want it." He leaned back, looking up with a dying look that frightened Tim: it was too real.

"You're joking, but they weren't when they said you have a heart murmur."

"Oh, I just made that up. Do you see me trying to get into the Navy?"

"I can tell when you're making things up."

Kelly looked him over angrily. "Who cares anyway? *You die – you die.* I never want to be old or anywhere near old. I could handle thirty-five, maybe, thirty-five and lots of cash. But forty? No way, I'm not sticking around for forty."

"Well, I am," Tim said, suddenly talking past him, trying to remember another life beyond Kelly.

"Oh, you're rich. Rich people never let go. But you won't see me hanging on like some you see out there. Like Sal says, why'd they call it Young Street?"

"Did the doctors say if there was some kind of operation?"

"Operation? On my heart?" His face wrinkled. "I saw what they did to my mother, and that was just her guts."

Tim didn't say anything more: he could find out about Kelly's mother later. He had learned to ration himself already. And Kelly was groping around under the sheets for the poppers. "Don't nag me, okay, just be grateful. I figure it's only 'cause of my heart I'm queer." He found the little bottle, waved it triumphantly. "Want to break a little ice?"

He was half hoping Tim would grab it and start a fight, but he watched, paralyzed. Kelly unscrewed the top and snorted: one nostril, the other, the pink O of his lips. He screwed the top back on and dropped the bottle beside Tim, leaning back.

Tim reached and put his hand where Kelly had put his, feeling the blood getting through. "Oh God," Kelly said, desperately bored. Then he shoved into Tim's palm, trying to make it into something like sex. The heart slowed, stumbled, lost its rhythm, then climbed back up into heavy pounding, Kelly's eyes dimming, blood flushing up his neck into his face.

"All right, so I'm alive, wha'd you expect," Kelly said woozily. "Just don't leave a guy there *hanging*."

From then on, stories would come out of nowhere, as if he was seized by them, and had to tell them with a kind of blank, cold bravado, seeing how much Tim could stand. His mother had died of cancer, "bad cancer, in her guts." It had taken years: he'd spent much of his adolescence looking after his younger brothers and visiting her in hospital. "She was really great, she fought all the way, and it doesn't make a shit's worth of difference in the end." When she was away, his father would beat him up. "Sometimes I'd be thinking, poor guy, he misses her. And times, why not just fuck me, mister, if it's what you really want. He'd say it was for being a fag."

After she died, his father had thrown him out. "But what's he going to do? He can't even boil water. And those kids – he'll get some girlfriend in there and they'll get drunk and burn the place down. I went to my lawyer about it, to see if I could get custody. But he was up front, I'll say that, he said I didn't have a chance. I try to keep in touch: any time they run I'm there for them. I'll look after them no matter what it takes."

He looked around, suddenly connecting this to where he was. "Could you put up with some cute little brown kids?"

"Brown?" Tim was too bewildered to hold this back.

"Sure, my mother was a Cree Indian, till she married Dad."

Tim looked at Kelly's skin.

"Oh, that's my dad, the dumb Swede. His genes just barged right in and took over. But I'm half Indian, believe it or not."

Tim did believe it. Suddenly, he was a lot like Charles, trapped in a white skin, and a white lower-class fatalism.

After he'd been kicked out he'd come to Toronto and worked as a prostitute for a few weeks, then been picked up by someone named Roger, forty-five and well-off, a consulting engineer.

"He was what I needed. He showed me the ropes. He showed me the world. We went to Europe and we were going to go to Rio."

And it was true: behind the odd, plain face, there were scenes of Europe.

"Then the guy goes and dies on me. And he didn't leave me a nickel neither."

He'd gone back to the street. And there'd been other patrons, though none to equal Roger.

Listening to this, Tim felt he didn't know where he was. The sadness of Kelly's life and his rigid view of things, his code—where did he fit into them?

"Am I supposed to be like Roger?"

"You? Give me a break! Roger was a man, honey. He was banging both sides of the fence. Times I look at you and think, what am I doing, giving it to a creampuff like this one. To an artist for Christ sake, with his little pens and his little pencils. No, Roger was special. I didn't have to say, 'Oh, I love you', and all that like with you. I was just *with* him."

"So what am I?"

"You? You're just a queer friend of mine. My creampuff-artist friend who never fucked pussy in his life will somebody please tell me where I am?"

And he looked him over fondly, happily, as if all the grief had been forgotten.

"Oh well, you'll have to do," he said.

"But Roger didn't die, did he?" Tim said, softly. He was afraid of saying this, but he had to know.

"What liar told you that?"

"It's the way you talk about him."

Kelly scowled. "Then it was somebody else who died. Okay?"

A few nights later, when again Kelly had been joking about 'rape', trying to find it in Tim to fight against, Tim sat back and said, "I wish you wouldn't joke like that. It's too real. I mean, it isn't really funny, is it?"

Tim had thought the idea came from the street. He would tell stories from the street about rapes and beatings – not always from the side of the victims.

Kelly looked him over ironically, shifting moods, almost deliberately.

"You think I don't know that?"

Tim looked away. He wanted to leave: he knew what was going to happen.

"Are you saying you got raped?"

It was obvious now, it had been right there in the wild wrestling matches.

"*Did I get raped*?" It was kind of a black boasting.

"When?" Tim said, weakly. Because the story had begun, he could feel that: a look he knew by now had come into Kelly's eyes and nothing could stop it.

"You mean, the *first* time? Back at home, it was spring, I'd skipped school, I was off on my own. There was this van, in an old farmyard, five guys outside drinking beer. It was a great van, space women, big tits, like on Mars. One of them came over and said would I like a beer and a toke. You're not going to turn that down."

Kelly laughed at himself, bitterly.

"After a bit they showed me the inside. They had this sound system, carpet every-where. I kept saying, 'this is wild, but you need a woman's touch, eh, I mean, where are the chicks?' Teasing them, they liked it. Then I felt this guy's fingers picking at the back of my neck, like he saw a bug there, then he was sawing off my T-shirt with a knife."

Tim was staring, in pity, in fear of what Kelly was doing. Looking over the slightly bowed shoulders, the white soft skin, in a kind of amazement.

"Boy, what a surprise! But I'll never be *that dumb* again. You should've seen me after, on the highway, all rags and blood. I was off my head, I didn't know what I was saying. *But when I had to shit, that's when I really cried."*

He reached across and brushed Tim's tears onto his fingers, flattered, but doubtful, almost angry. You could see he'd told this story to different audiences: Tim could imagine him entertaining people at Charlie's, at the Senator: "But when I had to shit, *oh my God – !"*

"How old were you?"

"Sixteen."

"And what did they say?"

"What do you mean?"

"What do people say when they're raping a sixteen-year-old boy?" As if he had to know what language evil spoke.

Kelly looked at him strangely, the big forehead furrowed. "What do you think? They talk about what a good time they're having. What *a great piece of ass* they – " He gave Tim an angry stare, as if the sudden, surprising bitterness was Tim's doing.

Tim was shaken by sobbing. Kelly was impressed, flattered, but upset too, moving impatiently.

"This was a long time ago, you know. There's been a lot of blood under the bridge since then, I can tell you. And I was lucky, I got away, though there was one didn't want me to."

"What?"

"This fat guy kept saying, 'What if he tries telling, like that other one?' I was going to say, 'No, please, mister, I won't tell a soul.' And then I thought I heard a voice telling me, 'Ignore him. You got to ignore him– don't even hear him.' So there I was like I was stone deaf and the others were saying, 'If you want to kill some kid, do it on your own time. Nobody's going to give a shit about this little cocksucker.'"

"Oh, God, I'm sorry," Tim said, knowing it was too late.

"What do you mean you're sorry? I sure don't see you raping anybody. Jesus, if I'd've known you'd go like this on me, I'd've kept my mouth shut."

He wouldn't forgive Tim for pushing him close to tears too.

But Tim couldn't help repeating, "I'm sorry," as if he had to apologize for the world.

"Christ, what's that supposed to mean?" Then he had an idea. "Here, crybaby, this'll make you feel better."

He reached out a long leg, hooked his toes into the handle of the gym bag and swung it up onto the bed. "Here, maybe this'll make you smile." He rummaged and pulled out a knife in an Army green sheath. Tim was past being surprised.

"There's a friend, eh?" He pulled it out of the sheath and held it, not very convincingly. "Next time, it won't be me on the slab."

"You're crazy," Tim said, staring at the steel blade.

"Yeah, I know, you told me already. But with this, they gotta show *respect*."

"I want you to throw that away. *Right now. Or tomorrow."*

"And you think I'm crazy."

"But it's going to get you in trouble. What if someone gets it and uses it on you?" He could see this happening, could see the knife was hungry to slide out of the reflections into Kelly's guts. "You're a klutz, Kelly, you can't unload the dishes without dropping them. I wouldn't let you cut up vegetables with that thing."

Surprisingly, he wasn't insulted. "I need this out there. It's my courage. Besides, it's special, it's from a friend, and she died because they let her go for the Change, and this is all anyone's got left of her."

Scared, joyless laughter came up out of Tim, as if everything Kelly had ever told him was a joke.

"What?" Kelly demanded, suspiciously. "What?"

"I don't know," Tim said, wildly. "People don't carry knives. They don't OD. They don't get raped, they don't get beat – ." He ran out of breath, and sobbed. He was trying to recall the world before Kelly, who stared at him uncomprehendingly, and then smiled.

"Do you ever need an education. Here – you hold it." He held the knife out, with the handle towards Tim.

"Why?"

Kelly took his right fist, made by useless grief, pried open his fingers, put in the knife, and closed the fingers, solemnly, as if the cold weight of it would send some knowledge, some power into Tim. It did: his fingers tightened unwillingly on the steel handle and he thought of Kelly dying on these eight inches, foolishly, bitterly, in a few mean seconds. There was nothing Tim could do to stop it.

"That way," Kelly said, "you can go for their guts."

"I hope you don't give lessons like this to everyone."

"What do you mean?"

"I'm not paying you, Kelly," Tim said, in his own voice. "Or whatever your name really is. You just aren't worth it." He stepped the knifepoint forward two inches, towards the shallow bellybutton with its stretched eyelids.

"I'm not stupid! I'm showing you: this is how much I trust you. I trust you all the way. Look."

He took Tim's hand in his cold long-fingered hands, and cut a solemn cross in the air just over the skin of his chest.

"See? *Because that's how much I love you.*"

PART 7

Three weeks after their first meeting, Tim came home to find a message saying, "Gone to Ottawa."

"Ottawa?" Tim said, when Kelly phoned.

"They have to lay back too, you know. Between spending all our money."

He said he would be back the next day, but he wasn't, or the day after. Tim went out to a bar for a drink, and found himself going around to all the gay bars in Toronto, and to the streets. Another boy was standing where Kelly had been, carrot-haired and pink-cheeked, in woefully ragged cut-offs, eager to change the melting currency of lips and ass for cold, hard cash. He was short and slim. He looked small enough and shrewd enough, Tim thought with a kind of uneasy pity, to slip through the dangers, through the evil hands. Then, for a moment, Tim imagined slamming him against the bricks and fucking him brutally, and tears came into his eyes.

Tim went back to a bar he had already visited. Kelly was there, dancing with a friend, both of them showing off but not to each other, like straight girls dancing together. When Kelly saw Tim, he came dancing up to the edge of the floor and said, "There you are. Don't go away. I want to talk." He was wearing new black leather loafers: they didn't suit him, they didn't want to be danced in. A song came along that evacuated the dance floor, and Kelly sauntered over in the clunky shoes.

"So how've you been? I've got some news. See, there, that guy with all the gold around his neck." He was pointing at a middle-aged man with grizzled hair leaning against the bar. "It's solid too. That's Howard, want to meet him? He's a real gentleman. Except when he's not, of course."

"Who is he?" Tim said, understanding everything, but not believing it yet.

"I'm sorry, Tim, I like you a whole lot, but I gotta have a life. Howard's from the States, and I'm going down there with him. Florida somewheres."

"You're crazy."

"That's my business." He looked him over in a not unfriendly way. "You know, you ought to grow a beard. You look like a little boy. For a young guy, Tim, you were great, but I need an older man. I need that authority."

"*But I love you!*" It was the first time he'd said so.

"Yeah, I know, I'll give you that," Kelly said, looking away over the dance floor. "I don't have any complaints there."

Tim looked at Howard, with his gold and his hairy chest, loathing him, but with a kind of fellow-feeling too. What did he know about Kelly? The white skin, the maddening sour smell? The deaths, the beatings, the rapes and near-rapes? He wondered if only he knew, if they were all in his mind.

"How can you trust him? What do you know about him?"

Kelly looked at him thoughtfully.

"You're really upset, aren't you?"

"*Yes! Yes, I am upset.*"

"But believe me, it's better this way."

"No it isn't. Why don't you just stay. I'll look after you. I'll take you to Florida."

He grabbed for Kelly's bare, white full-fleshed arm, which snatched itself away. Kelly looked at him, measuring, judging something.

"*Kelly, I love you,*" Tim said, desperate, stripped bare, not caring that people were looking, perhaps people who knew him. He was showing Kelly that he could do anything, have anything.

"Then can you keep a secret?"

"What secret?"

"Listen, I'm going to do you a favour. I never told you, but I've got cancer."

Kelly loved TV soap opera, Tim told himself quickly. And behind him there was his mother's death, making the soap operas all real.

"Down around the base of the spine, they just can't operate down there."

"I stopped going in for the treatments. If it's going to happen, I want it to happen *fast*."

Tim knew Kelly lied as easily as he breathed. He didn't believe any of what Kelly was saying, it was insane, but he saw Kelly willing him to believe from his cold gray eyes, and he knew that he would. His energy would give out and it would be true.

"That's why I left Roger. I was feeling really shitty, and I thought, I can't put him through that. It's unbelievable, I know from my mom."

He gave a hard, little laugh.

"Turned out it was just a touch of hepatitis, but by then old Roger had fixed himself up with someone else."

"*I don't believe you!*" Tim said, terrified.

Kelly gave him a long, gray stare, that could mean pique or infinite sadness, and pouted thoughtfully.

"Maybe that's a good thing, then." He looked at the dance floor, keeping up on it.

"I just *do not believe you*, Kelly," Tim said, again, desperately, terrified of being left with this.

"Well, that makes me glad," Kelly said angrily. "Now I'm sure this is the right move. You don't have to go home crying about some liar, do you?"

He strode off towards his dancing partner, then spun around and came back, grabbing Tim's arm.

"And, mister, don't you *dare* tell anyone. I can't have this getting around."

"I love you," Tim repeated, stupidly.

"Oh, fuck off!" He walked away, Tim trying to see into the familiar stiffness in his back, the high-arched walk, like a kind of cloddish prancing. Could you see cancer at the stiffened base of the spine? He imagined following, arguing, making a scene, dragging him away. But he couldn't: if he stayed it would become true.

He went down the stairs from the bar clutching the rail like an old lady. Going up the street, he could feel it closing around him, with Kelly's personality behind it, fatalism. Kelly's black grief and anger, his crippled sense of time, his lugubrious code, the dying, beaten sweetness of his sex – they were all explained, they were all around him. He went along shaking, thinking that whether it was true or not Kelly wanted him to be like this, thrashing on grief like a knife.

For days, he couldn't focus on anything else. True or not, the cancer was what Kelly had left him. He imagined getting Kelly back and persuading him to go in for treatments and saving his life. Or if there was really no hope, he would be his friend and lover to the end, living only to help him, loyal with Kelly's idea of loyalty. He imagined Kelly on his deathbed, full of pain, saying the time had come for the knife, and he would get it without thinking: his hands would be tied, he would slip it in himself, peace, rest, love for both of them. He imagined telling Kelly that he would get married, have a son, name him after him. It would please Kelly to hear it. He imagined telling his son about his dead older brother, his real father, who had taught Tim how to be a man, a father. He lay in bed writhing as if the sheets they'd made love on could be ground into being him again, kissing and biting the pillows, pounding them for not being Kelly, pounding them into being him.

Perhaps if he'd believed in it at once, completely, trusting him without hesitation, Kelly would have stayed. Stayed to give him the rest of his life. Stayed to tell him it was just a test of love. With Kelly, anything could be true: he could do anything.

And even if it was a deliberate, malicious and casual unthinking lie, as Tim was quite sure at times, it was as pitiable as death by cancer. It was revenge for everything the world had done to him, thrust at Tim because Tim was the only person who could feel it. He was right to accept the lie, to suffer it like this, to love it and make love to it, in order to make up to Kelly for what the world had done to him.

It was a cancer in his mind, a black concentration of everything, death and rape and humiliation. "I am dying where you raped me," Kelly had told him.

At times he would get angry himself: Kelly's lie was like rape, like murder. He tried to use this anger to break free. Kelly had left the pair of black jeans, torn somehow, he'd never explained, dangling over the closet door in the bedroom. On the second day after his announcement, Tim was sitting drinking in the living room. Getting up, roaming around, looking at places where Kelly had been, remembering poses he had taken, he saw the jeans and attacked them, seeing a chance to be furious, insane – snatching them down, trying to tear them, biting them, fucking them on the bed, tearing his cock in murderous hate as if he could tear it to pieces and then, more than anything else, a desire to be reconciled, to put aside all the hatred between them.

But he's forgotten me, he thought, exhausted, lucid. It was a question of money and excitement. He doesn't have cancer. He didn't think I would care very much if he did. I will never see him again.

Then that would be the terrible thing: that the only person he had loved in his life was gone. And as he grieved and raged about that, the cancer would become true again: it was satisfying, somehow, to have Kelly's cancer inside himself, tearing him apart.

After taking three days off work, he worked late on Thursday and Friday. He arrived home after dark on Friday, having barely made a deadline. He went into the kitchen to pour himself a drink. *The bottle of Scotch was gone.* Kelly still had his keys. Tim felt a leap of joy too painful to hold in.

"Hello?" he said in a small voice.

No answer. There was no one in the living room. He went up the stairs to the bedroom. Kelly was asleep, face down with a sheet over him. The Scotch was on the night table, along with an empty glass. The red bag, blue jeans, an expensive polo shirt, the basketball shoes were scattered on the floor.

He realized he had to get the keys before he could think. He went over and picked up the jeans. His hands were shaking. The denim was alive, was skin of his, smelling of him. It seemed physically cruel to search them. He let them drop, and picked up the Scotch bottle, to pour himself a drink. To have a drink and decide how he could live.

Kelly stirred, looked sideways at him. "So where've you been?" he said, lifting onto his elbows and blinking.

"Working late."

"Better late than never, right?"

"I missed you."

Kelly looked at him over his white shoulder, thoughtfully.

"Did you, then?"

"Oh, yes. Why did you come back, Kelly?"

"You don't get rid of me that easy."

"What about Howard?"

"Oh, he was a jerk, what can I say?" And then, sadly, "He was a *rich* man." It was one word, 'richman,' full of scorn and longing for peace. "But fuck him: I threw his shoes at him, right there on Yorkville."

He held out his hand for the glass of Scotch.

"You see, Tim, I thought I could really use someone like that." He took a gulp into the stretched throat and coughed, pulling down his chin. "I thought I needed that guiding hand. I mean he said he had kids, even. Real sons." He took another gulp, cautiously, and looked around smiling. "You — you, I gotta love like a brother. Like a *kid*. A brother at times."

He offered Tim the glass. Tim took it, almost saying, 'Do you really have cancer?' He could hardly believe now that Kelly had ever said he had: at least, he seemed to have forgotten it completely.

Instead, he asked, "Is Kelly your real name?"

Kelly gave him an odd look. "What's it matter, eh, so's I come? Sure it is, it was my mother's name before she met up with Dad. And when she died, I thought, they can't cut that out."

"So what was your name before?"

"Oh, they called me a lot of things." He laid his face in the pillow, suddenly bored, reaching behind to toss the sheet aside. "Climb on in there, mister." He wriggled comfortably in the bed. "One thing I'll say, you may be queer, but you can fuck. Roger was..." He shrugged white shoulders into the pillow.

"Roger?" Tim had started to undress, though a helpless part of his mind was still trying to imagine a way out. But the only way was in – stretched out in front of him.

"Howard, I mean. They're all the same, those old guys."

"By the way, you don't really have cancer, do you?" He said it jokingly, making fun of himself for being stupid enough to ask. He was safe: Kelly was not in the mood to say yes.

"Cancer?" There was silence: then Tim saw something riding up his back. Crying? For a moment he knew it was, then it was silent laughter. "What liar told you that? *Cancer*? The stuff that's going round about me! Here, just give me one those juicy kisses."

So Kelly had decided to set them free from grief, from death, for a while at least. The kiss turned into an attack, joyous, reckless, immortal.

"Oh careful!" Kelly said, delighted. "*Careful*! It takes time for it to realize, '*Uh oh! Company*!'"

CHAPTER X: TIM LEAVES
Summer, Fall, 1978

Late one night in June, David was making his way down Yonge Street alone, hurrying through the crowd. Straight teenagers, mostly, rowdy boys in pairs or packs, demure or giggly or sharp-tongued girls, laced with gays. David's evening had been drinks with Bobby Riding and Bobby's new friend from Montreal, Gaetan. Taking David along, the two of them went around the bars shouting noisy French. "We're ramming French down their throats," Bobby said. "Somebody's got to." With Tim gone, David had decided it was time to become a Toronto gay man at last, to be as good at it as Tim. But once dressed for the part, he hadn't been able to go farther, and instead found himself involved in an odd romance with Hugh Armitage. He hadn't phoned Tim or seen him, except in bitterly imagined scenes.

But Tim was suddenly coming towards him now, Tim and a tall youth who looked like one of Bobby's rougher friends.

David thought of bolting across the street through the vans and pick-ups and muscle cars. But Tim would be bound to see him. He thought of stalking past bitterly, like Dido in the underworld, and was afraid of freezing himself in bitterness forever. If he didn't forgive Tim, at least he had to show mercy to himself. By now Tim had seen him, giving him a cold, proud smile, the smile of an old friend who'd got a lot older on his own. It was as if he was embarrassed by his companion, so embarrassed their breaking-up was of little importance. The youth was about Tim's height, blackhaired, in ragged cut-offs and big white basketball boots and a checked shirt wafting back from white sides. Getting closer, he gave David a suspicious look from a plain, snub-nosed face.

They stopped, David not knowing why. Tim introduced them, in a low voice, as if reluctant to speak.

"This is David. And this is – "

"Kelly?" David said, barely catching it. The hand he shook was cold and dry and rough.

He gave a wet, mocking grin. "Yeah. Grace just didn't sound right."

There was something babyish in his face, with its high forehead, its snub nose and pouting lips, but looking into it David saw the eyes were sad and old. Confused, embarrassed, he looked down into a bruise at the base of Kelly's neck: purple-brown, decaying, anonymous lips. Tim must be drunk or stoned, David thought, to have picked up this rather odd and dangerous kid. But he wasn't drunk, and he didn't seem stoned.

David was anxious to get away, and he thought Tim was too. But then Tim said, impulsively, "Let's stop and have coffee."

"*Coffee?*" Kelly said, scornfully.

"You have a beer, and something to eat. I want to talk with an old friend." This was obviously some sort of formula for Kelly, as if Tim already knew him well, knew his ways of speaking. And the formula had power.

"All right, sure." Kelly gave David a knowing smile, with a new, ironic respect in it.

They turned back to an outdoor cafe, went in past its metal railing and sat down, Kelly placed so he could watch the street. David saw how Tim had to keep him entertained.

"I haven't seen you around." David said.

"*Around?*"

"Well, I thought you might be at the beach last Sunday, for instance."

It was Kelly who spoke, turning away from the street. "I don't tan at all, you see, David. I just burn and burn."

David was suddenly looking into the bruise, which seemed to be irridescing as he looked. He couldn't believe it, but it must be true: Tim and this kid were some sort of couple. Kelly gave him a friendly wink, like some kind of sharer. David looked bitterly at Tim and thought, 'Your mother really is dead, isn't she!' He felt like Susan.

Tim and David talked while Kelly ate and watched the jostling parade and commented on it, even calling out to it, lips smeared with blueberry topping from his cheesecake. There'd been another letter from Homer Street, David said: Jack didn't know yet they'd separated. Should he send it along? Tim wasn't interested in seeing it, so David summarized: the house coming along, Fred enduringly wonderful, the Platonic form called Jim fading, Jack looking for ways to make money. David went on to Bobby and Gaetan, and their plan to bring Montreal *joie de vivre* to Toronto. Tim laughed: what a hope! Kelly started talking about Montreal bars, comparing them knowledgeably with Toronto's, Vancouver's, Calgary's, New York. "Toronto's the most uptight city there is," he said flatly. "Anywhere. I don't know why people tolerate it." David wanted to talk about Hugh, who now, on several occasions, saying "Can I borrow you?" had had fumbling sex with him. David was confused, partly proud, partly afraid of what he'd produced. He didn't love Hugh – 'Of course,' – he would almost have said and Hugh needed him to love him: he was afraid a wretched scene might be on its way. But he couldn't talk about that through Kelly's raucous commentary.

"Take a look at those fairies!" Kelly snorted. A knot of young gay teenagers whose taste in summer shirts was a bit flowery for Yonge Street. "These Toronto faggots, they think they've got it all taped."

Tim gave David a wry, tired smile that was already familiar. "Kelly's been around, you see." It began as an apology of sorts, but became strangely defiant. "All over the world. For example, Kelly, let's hear your story about the Wall."

"The wall? There've been a lot of walls."

"You know, Berlin. Beaver Power."

"Oh, that. Why'd you want to hear about that?"

"In case David goes to Berlin some time."

He chuckled. "Well, there are some great bars, I'll give them that. You see, David, I used to have this T-shirt that said 'Beaver Power.' With this dumb beaver on its back, all teeth and waving the flag. The real flag, I mean, the Red Ensign. So we're in Berlin, see, my friend Roger and I. Roger was my main man, at the time. So I guess you know they've got this wall, to keep the Communists back where they belong. So we want to cross over, naturally, see what it's like, only they had these Nazis running it, and they wanted me to cover it up – the flag. Can you believe it?"

He looked away, as if that was the whole story. "Will you look at the tits on her," he said, thoughtfully.

"And you told them?" Tim prompted him, almost tenderly. David looked at him in disbelief: it seemed Tim was making a fool of him, deliberately. He'd never seen Tim being malicious before: he'd always thought a bed-partner deserved a certain respect. David disliked Kelly, and feared him too, but now he felt a kind of pity for him.

"What did I tell them?"

"About coming to see their Wall?"

"Well, it figures, eh David? Who's going to come see their frigging wall if they have to put up with shit like that?"

Tim looked at David, and smiled. David looked away quickly. There was a long silence. Kelly finished off his cheesecake, then licked his fork lingeringly and said, "Time to go, eh, sweets?" He stretched energetically, the shirt falling open, white skin and rosy nipples sliding up over bone. Tumbling out of the stretch, he smiled at David, consoling, conspiratorial. Tim's lovers formed a club, it seemed.

"Nice to meet you, David," he said. "But Tim and I've got some very personal and private business."

He put his hand on top of Tim's on the table.

"I can get kind of rowdy and that, it's my upbringing, but Mister Tim here, he irons out all my wrinkles."

He sat looking at him fondly for a measured moment, then jerked back his chair with a metal shriek.

"But excuse me for a minute, gentlemen. I got to take a piss in the worst possible way."

He went into the restaurant, pigeon-toed, with an odd, stiff strutting. His buttocks dropped a lunar half-inch below the soft dazzle of the cut-offs. Tim didn't turn to watch, but he was alert without looking, as if counting his steps.

"He's giving us some time alone," he explained. "He's saying he's not afraid of you.

I think he likes you. I don't know why, but he literally snarled at Bobby yesterday."

On the surface, there was a kind of familiar contempt, as if Kelly was a pet, an animal. But under it, David could hear, there was curiosity, fascination, as if you could happily make Kelly the study of a lifetime.

"How long have you known him?"

"Six weeks, about." Tim laughed. "Kelly isn't his real name, of course. I'm still trying to find out what it is."

"What does he do?" David asked, nervously.

"Right now," Tim said, grimly, "nothing."

"Well, I guess he's okay," David said. It was the best he could offer.

Tim looked at him with a laugh held painfully in his eyes, his cheeks. Then it broke out.

"Oh no, he's not okay!" Tim sounded almost triumphant. "From your point of view, David, he's awful – what Duncan calls *scum de la scum*."

David stared.

"Tim, what on earth is going on?"

"What do you mean?" Tim said, nervously. David saw Tim had expected him to ask, and was afraid now that he had. Then he smiled again, in defiance. "I'm addicted, that's what's going on. He's in my blood, he's heroin. I just can't *live* without him."

This was packaged as a joke, but then he added, with an odd precision, "Without what he is, I mean."

"I don't understand. That Berlin thing, for instance."

"What about it?"

"If he's stupid, why show it off like that? Wasn't it a little cruel?"

"I don't think he's stupid. That's just you, David. You're as snobbish as that little shit, Duncan, in your own way. You think everyone is stupid. You think I am, right now, and I'm not. That story, that's him, that's his world, he's got his own whole way of seeing things. You were lucky to hear it, privileged. And he's always coming up with stories like that. He's – " Tim looked for a word, then shrugged. "He's *amazing*," he said calmly.

A strange look came over his face, stunned, fearful, but happy too, as if he'd been converted to some fatuous religion. Then he looked at David's bewilderment and laughed at it, cheerfully.

"Of course, I knew you'd hate it, but there you were in front of me, and it's happened, and you might as well know it. And now, I have responsibilities, too: believe it or not, he needs looking after. He's not bad, really. I know what you're thinking, but I'm grateful. It could have been someone a lot worse, crazy, a real criminal. He's got problems, God knows. Getting a job, for instance. Some health problems, too."

Tim hurried through this last statement, and looked around guiltily to see if Kelly was approaching, while David wondered what he meant, searching his memory of the white body and not finding anything.

"He's good to me, David, really," Tim said, almost consolingly. "And frankly, I don't care what my friends – people like Duncan, for instance – are thinking. I'm lucky I met him. They can all just go fuck themselves, if they want to."

He didn't quite look at David as he said this. David noticed how he was now one of Tim's friends, not a former lover.

"So this is how it ended," David said, sardonically, with a kind of veiled fury, not at Tim, exactly, at fate.

"Oh, David!" Tim gave a helpless little laugh. "You're just as bad as he is, really."

David couldn't imagine what Tim meant, and couldn't bring himself to ask.

"I was always afraid you'd fall in love – " David stopped, angry at himself, because he realized he was admitting that Tim had. "But with someone like –"

"Shut up, David," Tim said in a friendly way. "Here he comes."

Sauntering out, Kelly bumped into one of the crowded tables and said, "Oops! Pardon me," haughtily, as if the straight young couple should be thankful for a moment of startling white thighs. Tim watched it all without flinching, unembarrassable.

Kelly sat down, holding his chair between his legs, leaning forward eagerly with the open wet grin. He looked at Tim, at David, at Tim.

"So'd you miss me?"

PART 2

Just the day after his meeting with David, Tim saw him again driving his lonely face like a wedge through the summer crowds. Suddenly, Tim was overcome with nostalgia for the sane world which they had shared. He imagined phoning David, telling him everything. But the hurt, stiff way David held himself, like an old cat, expressed that he would never comprehend what was happening. Tim knew he could never really talk about it: he was trapped wordlessly inside Kelly's body, the violent world it held, the rapes and beatings, the cancer Tim could never accept. Tim would try to find out if that story was true or not.

"If I knew you'd be so fucking emotional, I'd've kept my face shut. Enjoy me while I'm here, okay? Usually guys just say, well, – you only go around once."

"So it's true?"

"You calling me a liar?"

Tim looked down, ashamed. "I just don't know."

"Well, either I am or I'm not, what can I say?" He looked away angrily. "Anyway, right now I'm feeling fine. Except for you breathing up my air."

"Why not see a doctor? Just for a physical?"

Kelly stared at him hard. "Back off, mister. Just back off. You keep nagging me, I'm walking right out of here. I do *not* have cancer, all right, are you happy? It's *gone*, it's cured, forget it. Or I'm walking right *straight out of here*."

This sounded like a way of saying he had it. But most of the time Tim was almost sure the cancer was a lie, coming from a kind of insane bravado. Whenever he saw Kelly telling a lie, he would take it gratefully as one more reason to forget about the cancer. That wasn't a simple lie, of course, like Kelly's saying he hadn't been running drugs or hustling, but a sort of nightmare which possessed him at times. It came out of a black, hate-filled darkness that floated around him. Sometimes Tim thought he could see it: if he didn't look straight at him, he saw a black aura over his skin, the white shining black somehow. How could he tell that to anyone?

It was impossible to look at him the way you looked at other people. When Tim tried to draw him, he would be blinded, not by desire or sadness he realized, but Kelly's will not to be seen. Being looked at for very long was like being beaten. He was restless and couldn't stand being still. He admitted it, and traced it down to his Indian blood. In a bar, he would seek out people he knew at various places and spend all his time striding back and forth, carrying stories, jokes, messages. Tim could never find the right, satisfactory distance from him, where he could remain in love and content without being pulled into him. No distance was safe.

If Kelly was away, Tim would imagine him on the streets, foolishly trusting in spite of everything, getting beaten, knifed, arrested and put in prison. To be raped: because when Tim tried to scare him with prison, he would say, "Are you kidding? It would be heaven, like one big backroom." If he was in the apartment, there to be touched, Tim was always somewhere along the journey through him. Before Kelly, he'd thought of sex as a series of accomplishments. Now it was a cycle, a wheel: he was to be digested through Kelly's long white body endlessly.

Everything in him had changed, so that the old Tim was someone he lived inside, and sent to work, almost believing in him there. But that old self, his old life, all his friends were provisional now, dispensable. He didn't know who he was, he didn't have the energy to ask. He knew how Kelly talked, what he would say about anything, better than his own opinions. He believed in Kelly's word, his odd code, his fatalism, more than in his own world, only holding on to it to protect them, to keep them alive. It was impossible to talk to him, or even name him. Kelly, the name, was like candy, like a delectable stretch of skin, but it couldn't be his real name, and Tim imagined that if he could ever find it they would be able to talk at last, to be friends. But they were in a nameless world, where the only way to speak was through touching. And even here Kelly never quite listened. It was as if his real self was a deaf mute, hidden deep inside the soft, beaten soft, body, and Tim was always struggling to reach him. Kelly never quite let him. Kelly loved to handle sex as a hot, hard fight he hated and loved to lose. He'd fight till he gave a little melting shudder and gave in, sweetly, happily, almost as if he could put all the fighting away, let it go in a sigh. Tim would slow and stop, almost, trying to stay where they were. Everything was all right. They were doomed, Tim knew, and everything was all right. Whatever else was true, Kelly couldn't live, they couldn't live for long. Everything was terrible and all right. He saw Kelly on the streets, clumsy and foolish in the body Tim lived through, lived in, exquisitely, desperately alive. He imagined Kelly knifed, cut open, or himself, or both of them, it didn't matter, as if they could only bleed and die into a safe, undying ocean Tim felt now inside himself.

He took and kissed the ragged feet, eternally cold, imagining the friendly home town, shining, buried in snow like the white calamity of his skin.

Kelly laughed. "Are you weird."

"I love your feet," Tim said. "They brought you. I love you." He would drop this in now and then, hoping that some day Kelly would hear it.

His face wrinkled, bothered, impatient. "But this is supposed to be sex. Get a *move* on."

Tim laughed. "You're a virgin, Kelly. You always will be."

"Get out of town! What's that supposed to mean?"

"I love you so much it scares me."

That was Kelly's way of talking, and Kelly had the answer for it.

"You scare easy, don't you?"

PART 3

Summer went by with Kelly around most of the time. Tim no longer even tried to keep up with old friends. He might have been in another city, where boys arriving from the towns like his only had to expand their scale to feel at home on Yonge Street. That was just another main drag, the old portage route north.

Once Bobby bumped into him, and they had a drink together. The one time Bobby had come to his apartment, Kelly had snapped at his attempts to be friendly, as if he'd immediately placed Bobby as a rival. Bobby had sat as frankly frightened as a scared dog for a while, then left, Tim trying to apologize at the front door, but basically not able to. He was on Kelly's side.

Now Bobby's big, silent eyes authorized a confession. Tim hinted at Kelly's past, his problems: he was frank about the hustling, the drugs. "He was raped when he was sixteen," Tim said, with a kind of off-handed bitterness. "Other times, too, by customers, by friends." He was boasting, like Kelly, caught up in his fatalism. Kelly was his hero, his leader, alone and facing pain and death, wiser, stronger, older than he was. For a moment, he thought of mentioning the cancer lie, to show Bobby how much he had been through, then he saw that if he did it might all come alive again: Kelly dying, Tim doing nothing, indifferent, not even believing it.

"It's a good thing *you* weren't a hustler. You'd be – " and suddenly there were tears in his eyes, for an imaginary Bobby, raped, beaten, murdered.

After a silence, Bobby said, "How long can you go on like this? You can't live your life this way."

"That sounds like David to me."

Bobby didn't deny it.

"I don't care. I hope it goes on forever."

But the part of Tim that wanted to survive, realized that it couldn't. He was getting exhausted, from anticipating disaster. At times, he yearned that it would happen soon, to set him free from the continual tension from waiting.

Once he got the courage to phone Jack. He needed to talk to someone to save himself, to know where he was, who he was. But when Jack answered, all of his courage evaporated. "Hello?" Jack said, while Tim sat alone in Toronto, with something like crystal shards squeezing his throat shut. "Hello?" Jack said again, his voice closing over, getting polite, getting suspicious. Tim could hear fear coming up through the California happiness he'd brought to the phone, as Jack began to think fate, the police, Hitler, had got his number on Homer Street at last. Tim hung up, to be haunted for years by unanswered hellos that seemed to come from someone trapped alone forever, like a ghost.

One morning around two he was wakened by Kelly, sneaking into bed with him. When he reached for him, as cautiously as always, Kelly yelped with pain. He had been beaten up, punched, kicked, stomped on. The attack was there, printed on his skin: his left hand was in spasm, like a claw. One of the attackers had jumped on it.

He was terrified of hospitals, but Tim got him dressed in loose clothes and called a taxi. Being driven seemed to bring out a wild hysteria: he regaled them with his story, Tim and the driver. He'd gone into a back lane, where there was supposed to be someone with a joint to share. He'd been attacked, cornered by some straight teenagers. So far as Tim could tell this episode had nothing to do with hustling or drugs: they had just wanted to beat up a queer. Telling the story, performing it almost, Kelly swung back and forth, identifying with the pack of teenagers, then remembering himself, his humiliation. "One of them was going like it was Hockey Night in Canada. 'And the crowd is going wild! They're going to kill this queer.' He was the one got my hand–jumped on my *hand*, eh?"

At the emergency entrance, Tim got out, but Kelly sat, suddenly frozen, crying motionlessly like ice melting.

"What's wrong?" Tim said, desperately.

"You know what's wrong."

"You can't just sit there forever."

"I saw what they did to my mother. I *saw* it."

"This is completely different."

Kelly sat – as if by being very still – he could become invisible. Become *nothing*.

The driver twisted round, about to speak, and Tim gave him another dollar.

"Kelly, you've got to get out. They're just going to check out your hand, your ribs..."

Kelly gave him a black look, hating the world. A look of cancer. Then he got out, a captive, a slave.

No ribs were broken. The two fingers were bound into metal splints. This was the first of Kelly's disasters that Tim had seen, and at times he would hope that it could be the last: he was there to help him through it. But what lingered from the attack was bigger than he was. As the painkillers wore off, Kelly would be seized by fear, by the humiliation of fear.

"*They could have killed me!*"

"But they didn't. They just wanted – " Tim stopped: what had they wanted?

"You don't know what it's like. Like they're saying, 'We won't kill you this time, but we could, we can if we want to, *anytime*, can't we?' That's what they make you take. It's a lot of fun to beat up a guy when there are five of you...a lot of fun." He said this bitterly, then pulled himself up, cold and thoughtful, as if he were looking down on himself on the street, ready to give himself a kick. Tim saw and felt the cowardice, the spitefulness of beatings.

"Don't think about it, Kelly, please. That's all you can do: forget it."

"Forget it!" Kelly said, with black sarcasm.

A few days later, he came home to find Kelly half-drunk, brooding. Tim sat beside him on the couch, and tried to give him a hug. He pulled away.

"No wonder," he said, sloppily. "They could smell it, me just letting you, like a squaw."

"Kelly, that's just talking. I don't treat you like a squaw, and you wouldn't let me if I tried."

"They were doing me a favour," Kelly went on, not listening. "I got to cut out all this fag stuff."

"Kelly, you're gay and you know it. And there's nothing wrong with it. Nothing."

"Don't tell me what I know. You weren't even there. Roger sure would have been. I never got beat up when I was Roger's, I know that one thing. I shouldn't have been out there like that, exposed."

"What am I supposed to do, lock you up?"

"That'd be a start. I need to have some discipline around, or I don't know where I am."

"You know if I told you not to do something, you'd go straight out and do it."

Kelly grinned.

"I can't help it, if I'm a rebel. You, you're such a pushover! I need more of a man than you'll ever be, sweetie."

"Here's some discipline. *Stay out of back lanes.*"

"Or? There's got to be an or."

"What? Am I supposed to beat you, too?"

"Roger did."

"Well, to *hell* with Roger."

Kelly stared at him coolly. "Maybe," he said. "But you aren't much better. Anyway, don't worry, 'cause I figured it out. Next time I'm going in there equipped."

"What do you mean?"

"Next time, I'm going to have a gun."

"No, you aren't!" Tim said, very quickly, trying to get rid of the idea before it could take hold.

"Who are you to tell me?"

"Where would you get a gun, anyway?" Tim said. "This is *Toronto*."

"I got connections."

"You didn't have the knife with you, did you? You wouldn't have the gun, either: where would you wear it?"

"You're right, I should have my bag with me at all times. Next time you see me going out without it, remind me."

"Listen, Kelly, you get a gun and we're through, I'm kicking you out. You want discipline, that's discipline: I'll kick you out of here."

"Only I'd be handing out the discipline, wouldn't I? I'm getting a gun, Tim, and I'm not taking it anymore – especially up the ass."

"Listen, I will take it and I will throw it in the lake."

Suddenly Kelly started to laugh. "You know, mister, I gotta love you, I don't know why. You want to know the truth about you? You want to be forty. That's the straight goods on you: forty, no matter what."

"I want you to be forty, too."

"Oh, sure. And fifty? And a hundred? All wrinkles on the wrinkles? All like this?"

He tried miming old age, and came out like a slack-jawed idiot. Tim turned away in disgusted grief.

"Don't get a gun, Kelly. That's final. You'd just shoot your stupid foot off, anyway."

Kelly looked at him, appraisingly.

"You don't think I really mean it, do you?" he said, after a minute.

"I never know what you really mean. *Never*."

Kelly looked him over ironically, with a kind of bitter longing.

"If you would have had the authority, you would know. You would know it all."

PART 4

One evening in early fall, Tim came home and found Kelly was out, leaving no message. That was all right. He needed a rest. At midnight, getting into bed, he changed his mind, got dressed again, and took a taxi downtown. He went to the bars Kelly favoured, Jack's old bar, then Jerry's, and down the nearby side streets. He found him a few yards from where they had met, leaning back against a wall, his bare arms folded, the left hand with the splints diving under, the right hand on top.

"Hi there," Tim said.

The eyes opened. "Oh, you."

"How are you doing?"

"Not bad, not bad."

"It looks kind of slow tonight." He hoped Kelly wasn't really hustling. He liked the idea more than the reality: to stand in the fragile armour of tight jeans, exposed, desired.

"You gotta give it time."

"You look kind of tired. Why not let's go home?"

Kelly took only the suggestion of tiredness, rubbing his back sleepily against the wall, as if something had softened the bricks. He was very stoned, Tim realized. He took his hand, his wrist, and found the pulse: it was slow and steady.

"So what's it all mean, mister? What's it come to in cash?"

"Let's not play games, eh?" One of Kelly's expressions, but now it didn't work.

He sagged, as if whatever he was on suddenly gave way under him. "What a night!" he said. "Oh, what a night!"

"If you're on a trip, you don't want to be out here."

"Out here?" He didn't seem to know what it meant, rubbing his back against bricks soft as a mattress. Then, boasting and complaining and grieving all at once: "God! This feels like my last night on earth."

"Let's go home, Kelly," Tim said, trying not to beg or nag.

"Kelly, Kelly!" he exclaimed, as if to shake the name off.

Then he pulled himself up for an effort at diplomacy.

"Pardon me, Tim, you gotta realize, it's like my whole life is going in front of me. This is like acid *used* to be."

"But you're not safe out here! Come home, please."

He just closed his eyes, making an exit, and a shiver, kittenish and grand, ran down the long, white, folded arms.

"I love you," Tim said to the eyelids. "Don't you know that by now?"

"You poor fool."

Was that what he really thought? For now, it was just part of the scene. "I don't even know who I'm talking to," Tim said.

Kelly's eyes drowsed open, empty, gray, bleared with his whole life. He pulled his arms tighter.

"Are you cold?" Tim said, with a kind of hope.

"Cold? I don't think so."

Tim had put on the top of a jogging suit. He unzipped it, put some money in the pockets, and took it off.

"Here, just in case," he said, though Kelly wasn't listening, his eyes closed again. Tim reached the soft jacket behind and around Kelly's waist and tied the arms. They dangled over the tight crotch, hiding what it had to offer: if Kelly ever noticed, he wouldn't like it. It would cramp his style. Tim moved the limp arms a little to the side.

"There. You're beautiful. Just in case, there's some money in the pocket."

Kelly's eyes came open.

"You leaving?"

"Not if you don't want me to."

"Maybe I'll catch you tomorrow, then."

"Okay. Give me a call. Don't be hard on Tony, if it's at work."

He gave him a small kiss on the cheek, which he took with a weary laugh, pulling away sideways, inward. Tim thought of trying to lead him to a cab, like a drunk or a sleepwalker. But he knew it wouldn't work.

"See you," he said, and walked away.

"Hey, mister!"

He spun around. "You coming?"

"I warned you."

"What? What did you warn me?"

Kelly just gave an impatient wave, as if his thought had disappeared, the scene in his mind shifted. He used an old line.

"Get yourself a lover, you hear? That's what *you* need."

"I've got one."

He wasn't surprised the next day when Kelly didn't phone. There hadn't been anything unusual about the scene the night before. Kelly liked scenes: so long as they fed his mood, they didn't have to make sense.

But his absence lengthened, soured, developed a bitter flavour of its own, day by day. Tim resisted for a week, then gave in, as if saying 'All right, Kelly,' and began looking, getting more frantic the more he looked. Kelly was everywhere, like the taste of pollution on steamy days, and nowhere. Tim began asking Kelly's friends – he'd called them friends – but they didn't know where he was, or care. They looked at Tim with contemptuous interest. This one was hooked, how had "that two-bit hustler, that liar, white as they make 'em and says he's half Indian" done it? He felt guilty for seeing how mean Kelly's world was, stripping away the heroism he had given it. But searching for him, approaching hustlers in dread of what they could say, that he was sick, he was dead, he was back in town, worrying about him through the night – it was the only way left to make love to him. It was like sleeping with a ghost shaped of unbearable anxiety, a ghost with a sour aftertaste of Kelly's skin. In bars, he would have to place himself to face the doorway in order to keep his head from turning to look every time someone came in.

He told himself he couldn't live this way. Kelly wasn't going to come back, at least he couldn't live as if he was going to. One day he got drunk and began to talk to him. "No one in his right mind would care about you Kelly. Nobody. I'm the only one, I'm the poor fool. I was your chance."

"*So come back!*"

Having started, he couldn't stop.

"You liar! Liar! How could you do that? I couldn't believe it, I couldn't believe anyone could do that. I hope you do have cancer: I hope you *die* of it!"

For a few moments, this was freedom: to defy all of Kelly's evil grief, to let him be eaten by the cancer, to see it happening. But the drunkenness gave way underneath him: now it had all been so he could cry more and beg forgiveness and masturbate, rememberingly back into him.

He was like this on and off for weeks, afraid and hoping that Kelly would turn up and make it all a waste of time. He had the locks changed, and then for weeks left the door unlocked. He went over their last encounter again and again. Had Kelly been saying goodbye? No, it was just desire to put on a scene. But perhaps Kelly would look back too and let it stand as a goodbye.

He thought he ought to get back into life, not because he wanted to, as a sort of duty to a future self who might still be alive. He could have phoned up his friends, but if he did he would have to talk about what had happened. He began going to the baths, to find out what sex had been like, to find a new friend. It would be easier to face Alan and Michael if he could say, "Bill and I – but then you haven't met Bill yet, have you?"

It didn't seem to work. There was no sex outside of Kelly: He would wonder why he was there and come and apologize.

One night a young man with a sharp face and thick glasses stood by his door, smiling. He wasn't sexy, which was exactly what Tim wanted. But with the glasses off, he became a very determined lover.

"Let me fuck you," he said.

"I don't do that, at least not recently."

But soon he was saying please in a way he never would have with David, with anyone. He realized what was happening, and there wasn't any reason not to let it out. *Please Kelly. Please* – through the plywood, down the corridors.

In October, he met David downtown one afternoon, on King and Bay by the Toronto-Dominion Centre. David in jacket and tie, tentatively pleased with himself, said he'd decided to put his thesis aside and look for a job.

"I'm going to have an income," he said. "And buy things, like real people."

He wanted Tim's approval; he was claiming to be joining Tim's world. Tim just smiled, indifferent to all of this: David was long in the past.

"So, how are you?" David said, almost too scared to ask.

"All right."

"You look a bit pale."

"That's Kelly, remember, his skin burns in twenty minutes. I spent the summer inside. During the day, anyway."

"He's still with you?"

"No, he's gone. He's left town. At least, I think he has."

But he couldn't hide his doubt, his hope, from David, and he felt a sudden flash of anger. David looked away.

And don't say anything, Tim thought. Just shut up about it.

"I'm sorry, Tim, but thank God!"

Tim stared along King and scratched his jaw.

"He wasn't good for you. Anyone could see that. He treated you like shit!"

"According to Duncan," Tim said, "he wasn't worth the time of day."

"You know what Duncan's like," David said, miserably.

"Duncan…is an *asshole*."

David looked away. "I guess you've been under a lot of strain," he said quietly.

"Strain!" He laughed: it was such a lady-like word. "It wasn't easy."

"I can imagine."

Tim laughed again: David always thought he could imagine.

But he couldn't.

"He has *cancer*, David," Tim said brutally, and a black, hating stare seized him, seized David. "He's dying of *cancer*."

For a minute, David couldn't speak. Then he said, "What?" in a small voice – not believing him, Tim saw, but believing him, seeing it was true.

Tim stared away, up the nearest of the black, metal towers. It was all true: Kelly, whoever he was, his nameless lover, had cancer, and Tim hadn't had the courage to face it. Tim had let him go off to die alone. Like everyone else in the world, he had failed him – hadn't been man enough, human enough.

He couldn't look at David again.

"I hate this city," he muttered, and walked away.

PART 5

Gaetan had taken the Turbo back to swarthy, joyous Montreal, and the next day – Bobby's twentieth birthday, but he hadn't reminded anyone – he got up late and went for a long walk in the cold air, twenty and forlorn. From downtown, he went west along Bloor past the store where he'd met David, south past the old apartment block, where Charlotte and Jan and Heather still lived. He wouldn't drop in on them today, because they wouldn't take his sadness with the right seriousness. They'd laugh a little at its solemn, male side. He decided he might be on his way to visit Tim. It was another forty minutes farther west and south to Tim's, and he might not be in, but it would only be appropriate if he wasn't. At the start of his twenties, with his lover gone, he felt like being without hope.

He leaned on Tim's doorbell as if its faraway ringing was the only thing he would get out of Tim's house. Then he heard feet on the stairs.

"*Robert!*" Tim was barefoot, in old jeans streaked with paint and an old sweater.

"I guess I'm not *Robert* anymore," he confessed. "*Gaetan est parti.*"

"Oh, no! Well, they do that, men, boys."

But Tim gave him a real hug and a kiss in the front hall and led him up the stairs consolingly. And it was consoling to have an older friend with such an elegant apartment.

278

There was no trace of Kelly. He'd heard from David that he was gone, but he didn't trust Kelly: he was evil enough, cruel enough, to come skulking back.

"Have you heard from Kelly lately?"

"No, have you?" Tim retorted, but you could see him shrink a little, in case Bobby said yes. "No, he's gone, he's left the city."

"Oh. Well, too bad."

"We know you don't mean that, Bobby. Would you like some tea?"

Bobby followed him to the door of the kitchen. Tim looked up from the kettle. "I've got some news, though. I'm going to New York, at last." He got out the mugs. "Friday. I've bought the ticket."

"*Friday*! For how long?"

"For good, I think. I'll have to come back to arrange things, but now that I've decided, I'm going right away."

"Do you have a job?"

"No, but I know people. Remember Andreas? The dancer? I'll be at his place for a while. And I'm in no hurry, really, to get a job."

"But why?"

"Why?" He picked up the kettle and shook it. "I've lived in this town all my life, Bobby. *All my life*."

"If only you hadn't met him!"

"No," Tim said simply.

There was silence as the tea was made and taken into the living room. Perhaps this was part of being twenty, of getting *old*, Bobby thought: the world turned into an airport. People left.

"Does David know yet?"

"David?" Tim looked at him. "Why would he?" For a moment it looked as though he might try to force some declaration of loyalty, but then he relented, letting Bobby off the hook. Gratitude for that gave him courage to go sit beside Tim on the sofa.

"It's my birthday today," he announced.

"Really? *Happy Birthday*! Let's see: you're twenty?"

"Yes, all of twenty." As if amused at how young he was, like Tim, not dismayed at how old.

Tim leaned and gave him a kiss on the cheek.

"Why not come with me?"

"To New York?"

"Sure. A birthday present. Andreas has the space."

"But – " In another mood, he would have jumped at the chance, but now it was too much, he couldn't take it in.

Tim laughed, seeing he wouldn't come.

"But Toronto is so small, Bobby. So mean. So kindergarten."

Gaetan in certain moods said the same thing in French. Bobby rubbed his socks in the carpet, as if to root himself there. His feet were sore. His legs were weary from walking here, through just a small part of Toronto. He saw streets and streets floating alongside his moody walk, yet they were almost nothing in the huge city that had kept him roaming and fascinated for two years. He felt afraid of Tim's assured sarcasm, of the calm way he breathed under the soft wool. Tim knew that the world was so big you could never see it at all, never even imagine it all, and being grown up he didn't mind.

"Well, *I'm* not mean," Bobby said, butting his forehead into Tim's lambswool shoulder.

"Any time you want to come down, just let me know," Tim said. "I'll give you Andreas' number. Call collect."

"Well, " Bobby asked, with roguish sadness, "How do they fuck in *New York City*?"

He wanted to be penetrated, tragically, with the fabulous, cruel city, with the world of cities people leave for, present here in Tim's body.

Afterwards, he turned from the bathroom door and said, "Tim, I've just had a flash. You've decided to stay. You've realized you can't leave. We *need* you here." It was a joke, but it might still work somehow.

"Thanks, Bobby: not a chance."

Bobby turned on the shower, then looked at himself in the mirror, to see how he felt. There was a ragged sheet of paper stuck in the frame of the mirror. He looked it over quickly, recalling David handing it to him, one winter morning on Markham Street.

COUNTING
Our arithmetic, when it climbs to three,
Soon crumbles back to two.
Always we need a third
Sympathetic, objective, a wise judge.
To say, "A is wrong here, B there
Don't quarrel, be reasonable, remember you're lovers."
To share out blame and love with little or none
for himself.

But any third dissolves.
He falls in love with A,
Or B, or both.
He see's B's viewpoint only,
Or only A's, or, very helpfully, both, and has none of
his own.
Three is soon two again, two and a little bit,
A friend here in our kitchen, sharing our wine,
Welcome of course, but not helpful at all.

Our only enduring third
  Loves no one, shares nothing, clarifies everything:
  Oddest number of all,
  One, with his infinite shadow.

David – he had to see David, now, urgently, within this hour of change. But he would not ever be able to tell either of them what he was planning, at least not for a long time.

He couldn't stay for dinner, he told Tim, but he promised to check out New York sometime. It was starting to get dark as he left and went down to catch the streetcar that went all the way across to Riverdale, David's new neighbourhood. It began to snow as he got in and sat looking out into lacy, long-eyelashed snow, thinking about his two years, and Tim and David and Gaetan and Doug and all the rest going back to St. Patrick's subway stop, thinking about his Toronto unseen beyond the snow. He had it all inside him, all of them, like the deepest tears, shaken as the heavy car shook the earth, bringing the feel of the earth up into his joints, his guts. They lurched along Dundas through downtown traffic, took a dissolving bridge over the Don Valley and turned north with a softened shriek along the valley's high rim. The streetcar found its tracks under a carpet of snow like the secret line he was drawing between Tim and David, between David and Tim.

He had only a half a block to walk to the big red-brick house. The front bay window was lit up. Bobby went in the front door, and took off his running shoes. They were wet, and soon his hair was too. On the second floor, Jerry Rosenblatt leaned a lathered face over the railing. "Hi, there, Bobby," he said. "You look like there's a blizzard on. I don't know if he's in, but give it a try."

He knocked on the door at the bottom of the stairs. There was no answer. *NO*, the door said, and that is that. Go away, go home. It was all just inside *you* anyway. Then David's voice coughed its way up out of silence and called to whoever it might be to wait.

He entered past the cream-painted door, squeezing through the short dark hall inside, emerging in the middle of David's living room. David, in his baggy gray track suit, looked startled, almost resentful. But lately David was always surprised when people appeared.

"Bobby! I haven't seen you for weeks."

He went and gave David a hug. "I've been busy, you know. But now, *Gaetan et moi*, we split up."

"Oh, I'm sorry." The hug became a squeeze, then David stood back and brushed at the water in his hair. "Really sorry. I'll get you a towel, and a Scotch?"

"Yes, please, and a little water."

"What've you been doing?" David called.

"Today? Wandering around, melancholy and disconsolate."

"Well, for Heaven's sake, Bobby, don't forget your French!"

He wasn't about to, but he let this die in the silence of the apartment. In early autumn, when he'd first visited, the room had scooped in noise through the high, open windows like huge, cupped ears. David complained, but he liked it too: you could lie on the futon couch like a witch and with shut eyes see the whole leafy neighbourhood. Now the place was deaf, a snow cave in the mountains.

David came in with the drinks and a towel over his arm.

"It's always like this when winter starts," David said, consolingly. "I've been here three years, and I think winter is the real beginning of the year around here. At first it's like the end, like death, then things start up."

Under the towel, Bobby didn't find this convincing.

"For instance, I decided last week that I wasn't going to write my novel."

Bobby looked out, a little scared. It was a bad time. He'd believed in the novel at least as much as David.

"Not that particular novel, I mean," David added hastily, before the Muses cut off his line forever.

"What's the problem?" Bobby asked nervously.

David's face crimped with many complicated answers, then angrily simplified.

"There is no problem. It's just impossible. But I know now what a novel is, Bobby. It's a box. A novel is just a glass box." He took a gulp of his drink. "A novel – is just a *damn glass box that you put things in*."

"Well, some day, David," Bobby said, loyally.

"Yes. *Some Day: A Fantasy*. They'll love it."

He went over to the bay window and mused quietly for a few moments.

"It's this city, Bobby," he said, looking out. "*Toronto*. Toronto resists romance."

He stared into the white blither. Bobby tried to speak, had to clear his throat first, then got started. "Have you heard? About Tim?"

"Tim?" He stiffened a little. "Tim Grey? No."

"He's going down to New York. To live."

David was silent, the captain on the bridge, staring out into the long winter voyage. Then he said, "Finally. He should have done it in the spring. Did he say why?"

"He said he needs a change."

"From liars? From psychopaths?"

Bobby gave a scared shrug, though David couldn't see it.

"So when's he coming back, Bobby?" David turned around, demanding this with an odd, dishonest smile.

"How would I know? He doesn't know."

"Why not just take a guess?"

Bobby looked away, thinking, 'Never, of course. Never.' But he couldn't say that, and grabbed the only thing he had to defend himself with.

"It's my birthday today, David. I'm twenty today."

"Your birthday! I'm sorry, I knew it was soon, but – well, many happy returns!"

David came and sat beside him, putting down his drink, to give him a formal kiss.

"You're growing up on us, Bobby."

"Not too fast, I hope."

"Fast enough."

David was happy for him, he could feel that in the hug, but there was something else in his arms too: David still wanted an answer.

"So when's he coming back, Bobby?" David said coaxingly. "You said you were psychic, didn't you?"

"Not any more. I guess I'm getting too old."

"So when did he tell you this news?" David said, still softly, after a second.

"A while back."

He pulled down and away into David's sweatshirt. David's long fingers were in his damp hair, hard and restless, as if they wanted to pry into his thoughts. He tried to get away, pushing into David's chest, feeling the two warmths, Tim's and David's and seeing the long winter journey he was making between them.

Suddenly, David relaxed, the long fingers soothing in his wet hair, on the back of his neck.

"So, Mr. Riding," he said in his ear, "Here you are: twenty!"

PART THREE: 1986

"Even in the most tragic...there must be some joy, some lust."

Bragg, Melvyn. *The Seventh Seal*, British Film Institute,London, England, 1993.

CHAPTER XI: TIM IS BACK
June, 1986

Smoke had lost its hold on David. He'd try to get back to Baden-Baden, but Turgenev couldn't transport him from Hanlan's Point Beach and Tim, sprawled as if he'd dropped from the sky. He looked healthy, David was glad to see: lines had begun some preliminary work on his face, his hair was drawing back a bit in front, but he looked fine. Yet, it was only his towel that kept him from looking abandoned, left for dead – and the towel was so red it could have been drenched in blood.

David stirred impatiently: he weighed on him, he cumbered him, this ex-lover wrapped in sleep and softening muscle – because it looked as though Tim had been slacking off lately. It felt as if he had broken a contract. Lovers who leave so finally, muttering, "I hate this city!" are not supposed to turn up casually on a weekday afternoon at the beach. They should know better than to come almost without warning, smiling shyly and sidelong like guilty little boys. Certainly, Tim had been like a little boy, disguised as an old young man, till he'd begun with his speedy New York style. Then, he had fallen asleep and let David look over him as if they were good friends again. That, after all, hadn't been decided.

Dropping *Smoke* into his knapsack, David scrambled up and went walking along the margin of sand, until, if he went farther, Tim would disappear behind trees. He turned, stepping into the cold water, wading on stones to the wreck of an old dock, and sat himself carefully on one of its slippery logs. He wasn't quite facing Tim, now just another casualty on Toronto's one gay beachhead. Instead, he looked south to the far-off, misty seam of lake and sky: Grand, painterly, like the infinite nine years before when Tim first brought him here, now barely international.

A lean and dripping black-haired man strode in out of the lake, smiling at him as if to say, 'sex is dark, sex is dark-haired, and it belongs to us.' For a moment, David could almost imagine agreeing, heading for darkness and freedom, leaving Tim asleep in blond sunshine. Then he looked down at his log and the stranger went by, sloshing Ontario between his legs, angry he had only water there.

What had happened to Tim in New York? At first, David had relied on Alan and Michael for periodic bulletins. But the changing addresses had been too much to keep up with. There'd been a certain consistency in the names of lovers: when David knew him, he was basically domestic, for all the fantasies of being a hero, a lord of the baths. You could hope Tim hadn't spent much time down among the parasites and viruses.

As for his work, he'd been hard at it, apparently, in the sort of things he did in Toronto, commercial art on the interesting fringes, moving closer to the centre as time went by.

By the time David finally got to New York himself, Tim had been there a year. On a business trip, David had brought a brief-case full of work, determined not to be a tourist. The plane had dropped down out of the books and movies: he'd looked at the raft of skyscrapers far below his airborne, skeptical toes and told himself the towers must be fake, or the island would capsize. But on Manhattan rock, with everyone rushing past, preoccupied and colossal, he suddenly realized he had to let it be real. Here it was at last, the world-city he'd wanted all his gay life, hugely and intimately mythic. It could swallow Tim at a gulp.

The next time, he was a tourist, a civilized provincial, setting out to conquer it for himself. He'd confined himself at first to sights and stores and galleries, unwilling to enter the parallel world of sex, despite its Bronzino stares. A young man seemed to be following him down the Guggenheim's unsettling spiral. In the Village, men creaked past in black leather, like miners about to go digging for unheard-of pleasures beneath the roots of the skyscrapers: he was horrified by their solemn, bloody-minded lust, impressed and delighted at how thoroughly they were going to hell. He'd ended up at home on the upper West side with someone he knew from the first trip, a colleague in publishing. After sex, he lay listening to the city roaring up around them unchanged, all-powerful. While you groaned and forgot and hurtled off wherever, it snuffed up your ecstasy as it sucked energy from the addicts on the street. To fuck in New York was to be part of power, David thought, a little drunk and in search of fine phrases. To sacrifice to power, to feed it.

"So, what's it like to be – " and he was going to say, 'a New York native', but the real question sprang out: "American?"

"What do you mean?"

His friend had a handsome scowl and had gone to Yale.

"Or is that a rude question?" David said hastily, afraid he'd ruined everything: he was provincial, he was boorish, he would never be asked back.

He was asked back, but from then on he went about as a citizen of the international gay nation, New York his dizziest, most towering capital.

For eight years, Tim had been living in that imperial roaring: perhaps now he was simply tired. And he might, after all, just be passing through. That was what David had told himself earlier in the day, when Bob Riding had told him – on the stairs down from Glad Day bookstore, looking up from the latest *Native*, not to give him the latest figures but to say, "Guess what? Tim's back in town, Tim Grey." And even if Tim was going to stay, it didn't have to make any difference to David's life or feelings. He had other ex-lovers in Toronto, after all, and they didn't bother him. Probably he'd soon see this meeting as one of the coincidences that crop up more and more as you get older, portentous at first, soon banal enough. Coincidences without meaning: another sign of approaching middle age.

David slipped off the dock and waded till he came out of the water by Tim, still insolubly asleep. His face pushed through the towel into the sand, as if he wanted into it: his lips pulled open in a dreaming snarl. David sat down and got his scorching watch out of his gym bag: it was getting late. He waited a few minutes, holding the watch, hoping Tim would wake up on his own. But he clung to sleep, despite the touch of David's impatient shadow, or the shirt David spread over his back.

"Tim?" David said, uncertainly. "Tim?" – louder, and suddenly unhappy at being alone with the name. Without the present Tim to hear it, it called up an older, younger one. He reached uncertainly for the round of his shoulder, and touching firm, healthy flesh, David realized he would almost certainly be the one to tell Tim about Paul Murchison's death. He couldn't let him hear of it by chance, not if he was still any sort of friend at all.

"Tim!" He pulled at his arm.

Tim shook himself, dragged himself up out of sleep. "Tide?"

"No! No, it's time to go. For me anyway, and I didn't want to leave you here."

"Good, thanks." He got up on his elbow, squeezing his eyes, biddable as a child. Then looking around, he became the cunning Tim who had sneaked up behind him. "I shouldn't be late at Alan's: we're going out for dinner."

They packed up. Tim led the way over to a bike locked into scrubby trees.

"I didn't bring mine," David said. "I don't ride it much any more. I think it's more dangerous now on the streets."

"In Toronto? I feel like I'm in the country."

David had to explain, protesting something in Tim's tone of voice. "This spring, I saw a guy on the street, face down. His bike was beside him, bent. I thought he was just knocked out, but a friend goes to his gym. It was my *first dead body*."

"Your first?" Tim gave one small laugh and said, "Fuck this," wrestling with the lock and the trees.

"I hadn't realized," David went on, still protesting against something, not quite knowing what. "You're so *exposed*. I kept thinking, there was nothing between his face and the street. Nothing."

"Except being dead!" Tim ripped the bike from the trees. "So you got to be in your thirties before you saw a corpse? That's incredible."

And David decided he couldn't tell him about Paul, not now, anyway. And perhaps he'd learn from someone else: perhaps Alan would have heard about it.

They began plodding heavily through sand: hard, uphill work, and for a few minutes they'd be African, on safari. A boy with rippling orange hair came towards them, sprinting except for the yielding sand, smiling at the comedy of burning bare feet, his crotch full, jouncing in hope or remembrance or both? The smile tilted its wing in their direction going by.

Tim looked back for a second, they both did, at the orange flaring among the leaves. "Maybe he goes for older guys," Tim said ironically. "There was a guy with hair like that in Provincetown last year," he went on, thoughtfully, turning away, lifting the bike to walk again. "Every time you saw him, you felt like you'd been dreaming about fire all night before. Then at a tea dance we got to talking. He was 'a Boston Irish boy,' he said: 'Want to fuck a Boston Irish boy?' We went over to the place he was staying at, and he was – well, he was wonderful, but you know somehow, David, well – "he laughed the short, helpless laugh David had already started to dislike – "I couldn't get it up."

"Oh!" This was thumped out of David, he was so startled.

"It wasn't drugs or anything, I really wanted to, I wanted to want to. But it just wasn't on, somehow. He was beautiful, he was perfect, but he *wasn't –* "

Tim just shrugged, a grin hooking up one side of his mouth. David was still too bewildered to say anything.

"He was very sweet about it. I said I'd rather go look at the sunset from the dunes, like Hans Hofmann, and he came along." Tim gave a dry, self-conscious laugh. "And that was just the beginning. Sex and I, well, we're not an item these days."

David slogged on silently. He resented this confession, he realized. "So why are you telling me?"

"Why not? Because that kid was almost as gorgeous. Because it's something to say on the walk to the ferry." He added, impulsively, "It's good to see you again, David."

"What the fuck does that mean?" David said, still resentful. "Of course it is," he added. "Good to see you I mean."

They reached the asphalt path, civic order coming up into their legs now, and their souls, letting David feel how Tim walked beside him, with a new quietness and lightness in his step, as if he didn't want to weigh on the world. And he talked in a new way too, in a low voice, almost talking to himself.

"Last night at one of the bars I met this young guy from Saskatoon. He was homesick, can you imagine? And telling me how it's on some big prairie river, and one bank is higher than the other, so all the bridges go sloping across at the same angle. It was sweet: he really wanted to go back to the prairies. 'People here are so cold,' he said, and I was trying not to be cold too without ending up in bed with him. And after, I was thinking, to live in Saskatoon and say, 'Well, it's small, it's nowhere, it's hell in the winter, but all the bridges slope at just this certain angle, and that's enough. That's enough for a life.'"

There was a longing in his voice, and David laughed sardonically, as if at the thought of Tim out on the prairie after SoHo.

"Did I say I gave up my sublet? In New York, that's the same as cutting your throat. Everything's in storage, that I didn't give away, all my beautiful paintings. I was thinking maybe I could get on a plane somewhere. Not to go fucking this time, like another trip to Amsterdam or Mykonos, but just to be flying. To be flying and come down somewhere and just *look*. Wander around for a year or two like an adolescent and 'find myself'. I didn't do that then, and I thought coming out was finding myself. But maybe in Kabul or wherever I'd realize there was nothing I hadn't already found, that this was it."

He held out his hands, open, empty, meaning *this*.

"Well, you couldn't do it in Kabul. The Russians invaded, remember?"

"Oh, it doesn't matter, David!" It was an exasperated cry: what did the Russians have to do with anything? "Egypt, then, where everything's been dead and dried-out for thousands of years."

There was something hypnotic in Tim's voice, as if he was weaving David into this world-weariness too, seducing him into it, or trying to.

"I'm not old," David said, trying to break the spell. "I'm not even middle-aged: it's just there's no adjective for your thirties."

"But you always had that side," Tim answered quickly, with a shy glance. "An old side, David: you were ready for it."

You might almost have thought that he, David, was the older one, the leader, the initiator. But after all these years, Tim still had his month out of the womb, exploring and making himself popular, while David had floated and dreamt.

They fell silent, getting close to the ferry dock. Far out, there was the *Ongiara*, battered, enduring, turning slowly to make the last leg of its voyage. David tried to decide what to do about Tim. Did he have to do anything? Did he owe him anything? As they got close to the water, he spoke up, nervously.

"I'm on Church Street now," he said, as if merely informing Tim of this. "I liked Riverdale, but it was too far out. It's an old building, but it's worth it to be downtown."

But Tim wasn't stupid, he could hear there was another thought in his mind. He looked at David almost meekly, as if he couldn't help wanting something. Not shelter, decision: he wanted someone to make up his mind for him, for a while at least, to save him from being disappointed in Egypt. David didn't like the look at all: it was soft and weak.

"There's a second bedroom," he went on. "The study, but I don't use it that much, and there's a single bed in it. So if you want to stay for a bit..."

"Thanks," Tim said, in a tone that left David unsure whether he was coming. "I think that's what I need, actually. Some time. Just some quiet time."

"Good, great," David said, briskly. "That's settled then?"

"Time to think, I mean," Tim explained.

They were silent as the ferry laboured up, a new load of travellers behind its metal gangway. To think, David thought: what did that mean? It sounded like a thin little word, a thin little activity. What could it do for you now, in the middle of your life? The suspended crowds, on land, on the ferry, looked across at each other and down into the watery emptiness between them, waiting to be released into their crossing destinies. Merely to *think*!—David wanted to take Tim by the shoulders and shake him.

The ferry bumped into bosomy giant tires: men roped it to stanchions.

"But are you sure, David?" Tim said, in a low voice, for the first time speaking frankly.

"Of course! We should know how to get along by now, shouldn't we?"

PART 2

Tim packed and left Alan's two days later. As he climbed the stairs into David's apartment block, David came to the door to greet him, with a dark-haired young man beside him.

"Bobby!" Tim exclaimed. "Bob, I mean," as he dropped his luggage at the top of the stairs and gave him a hug.

"But are you really twenty-seven?" he said to the stranger in his arms.

"Yes," Bob said firmly, standing back. He looked as if he'd just been dropped there, in parachute pants and a blowsy shirt, to fight some desperately fashionable war. He was thinner and taller, in part because his hair was brushcut on the sides and full on top. He had a gold stud in one earlobe.

"That's probably how old you were, when I knew you before," Bob Riding said.

"God, you're right. And you still keep track of things, don't you?" Tim added ruefully.

David had picked up Tim's two suitcases: that was their embracing. He led them down the steps and into the apartment, old and unrenovated but full of the results of years of a middle-class income. While Bob went into the kitchen to make drinks, David led Tim to "the study, your room".

"Welcome!" he said, standing at the door. "The bed is all made up, under the cover."

"Thanks, David." Their eyes met for a moment, and Tim looked down, shyly. Perhaps, he thought, he took David too much for granted.

In the living room, Tim admired prints and paintings, wondering how much of David's taste was owed to him. They talked about the apartment, about the area. The front room's bay window looked up and down Church Street, from which they'd seen Tim get out of his taxi.

"I can watch the gay scene without going out anymore," David said. "I could even cruise from here if I wanted. At least the guy across the street does. People climb in and out his window at late, romantic hours."

They turned to talk about Bob, who was going to university, taking an Arts course but with the subjects he needed for Medicine. He wasn't sure yet that he wanted to be a doctor. His intense, dependent friendliness had gone: he'd learned a new manner, more clear, more fluent. It made Tim feel both older and younger to be talking with Bob Riding as an equal.

"Are you working now?"

"No, I'm taking a course, Organic Chemistry. I was going to wait tables, but now

Jack's helping me out, Jack Durham."

"That's nice," Tim said, meaning the whole idea of pairing Jack and Bob. "How did it happen – did you go down there and visit?"

"Yes," Bob said.

"So how is Jack these days?"

Bob gave David an odd look. "Well, he's fine, really. He's planning to come up here, but he can't get himself to leave San Francisco yet. He was phoning me Friday. He keeps phoning. To make sure I'll be careful, you know? And that I'm telling everyone else." Bob gave a short laugh: he'd learned to get through his nervousness faster, gulp it all down at once. "And I am. In fact, my friends think I'm some kind of a Puritan now."

"Well, that's good," Tim said. "I can remember when our whole philosophy of sex was, 'pile in, everybody'." He gave David a remembering smile. "But that's good to hear. Hardly anyone up here seems to be taking it seriously. I got into a big fight with Alan about it he's too miserable to be having sex with anyone, but he wants to think he could still fuck his brains out if he wanted to. And I meet people in bars who say there is no epidemic as far as they're concerned."

David asked, politely, almost formally, like a lady making conversation, "Do you know people in New York with AIDS?"

"Of course," Tim laughed, suddenly far away, as if these people could never understand. "Especially, the boyfriend of someone I worked with. His name was Patrick. Quite a while ago, before anyone had heard of AIDS, he began to get odd minor problems. It was like a bad joke, one thing and then another. Then the night sweats, and diarrhea. He took up all sorts of things to get better – diet, yoga, meditation. When he was finally diagnosed, he was saying, 'I'm ready to fight it now. I've been a dizzy queen for twenty-seven years, but now I'm going to grow up.'" Tim's laughter became a shallow, tight, tense sound, restricted by thoughts of the cruelty of AIDS.

"The things he tried – did they help?" Bob asked, eagerly.

"Maybe he lasted longer, who knows? They certainly didn't help at the end." Tim gave a bitter laugh. "But if I got AIDS – " He shrugged.

David looked away down the street. It was Bob who asked, "Is that why you left New York?"

"No! No, of course not. I'd been meaning to go somewhere new for quite a while. Since I broke up with Andreas. This guy from Oregon, he's a dancer. We were together for three years."

Tim gave David a brief, apologetic look. But both Bob and David were silent, as if scared and awed as they ought to be, Tim thought. He didn't like bringing this into David's quiet apartment so soon, but he couldn't help it, having been asked.

"It's incredible what's going on right now, since the papers and TV have really got onto it. They just love it: at last we're doing something they like. I'd remember Jack, actually. Saying once, in a bad mood, 'Don't think the people at Auschwitz were killed by the German's gas. They were killed by the human beings'."

Bob flinched, and turned to David, his mouth open, about to speak. But it was David who spoke.

"I should have told you before – "

Jack? It was impossible. But he blinked, recognizing a feeling he'd been expecting for months. "Paul got it. Paul Murchison."

"Who's he?" Tim said, defiantly.

"You know," David said. "Jack's old friend. And lover." As David had understood, the last name had misled him, kept him safe for a moment. He looked around the room stunned. Now he recognized the feeling clearly: at last it had fallen really close to him, among his friends. Now there was nothing to stop it.

"And how's he doing?" Tim asked, his voice hoarse and angry.

"He died last month. Pneumocystis."

Tim looked away, with a kind of relief. "Up here?"

"No, in San Francisco. With Jack looking after him. He'd gone back to the States, to L.A. When he began to get sick, before he knew it was AIDS, he went up to San Francisco, to Jack's."

There was a broken-off silence. Tim remembered his trip to Jack's house up behind the Castro. He'd talked with a jaunty woman with a western accent, then gone to the other side of the street to admire the house. Now he imagined Paul lying behind the high windows. But he pushed the thought away, he couldn't go down with Paul step by step.

"Poor Paul," he said, looking to Bob. "And Jack. God, it must be like his worst nightmare there in San Francisco."

"But he's all right," Bob said, determinedly. "I was down there again two weeks ago. And we were both there during the winter, David and I, to visit with Paulie. And we'd phone, but two months ago, more now, Jim phoned to say that Paul was in the hospital, pneumocystis for the second time. Jim Fields, remember? Because in the middle of all this, he finally turned up. And it was Jim who kept us in touch. He phoned and told us when Paul had died, and that Jack didn't want to talk for a while. Then after two or three weeks this long letter arrived, the same letter, more or less, to each of us, about Paul, about AIDS. It was – " Bob shrugged. "Perhaps you'll read it, but anyway we tried phoning again from my place, and got through, and I went down there to see him. I was there when Cathy came."

"So is he okay, now?"

"He always was *okay*," Bob said. "It's just he wasn't really talking to people for a while."

Jack silenced: it was hard to imagine at first, but perhaps there had always been something desperate in Jack's talking, a fear of silence. Tim remembered him in the swimming pool, speechless, water streaming down, and now it was as if the gleaming water had let you see into the future, see through to Jack old and bereft and terrifying.

He closed his eyes, imagined Paul's death by pneumocystis, and Patrick's, like a long, dry drowning as the lungs died inside you. He felt a kind of fear that tried to be lucid, to see or grope its way into the nothingness of death. You couldn't of course, but sometimes, at night, or given news like this, he seemed about to succeed, about to breathe in pure, airless dread, and pulling back just in time, just before he knew what it would be.

He shook himself. He'd been teasing himself with this for months. It was a bad habit, a kind of drug: with so many friends dying, he would simply have to give it up. It wasn't the fear of dying, but of knowing death, which he couldn't bear to know, which he could hardly bear not to wonder about. He would never be able to sit by someone he knew who was dying. Patrick had never been a friend, really, but he'd been grateful for all his new styles of hope: you could pretend to believe in them. He had been grateful to him for dying unexpectedly, in a horrible rush when Tim had been out of town, not pulling him into the intimacy of his death.

He felt as if he had been in the apartment for a long time. Did he want to be here, staying with David? Did he want to be in Toronto at all? How could he be expected to know what he wanted with things like this happening? He looked up at David's Kay Graham. It was beautiful, but it wouldn't save anyone. He realized he wanted to go out and come back in again, differently.

David said, as if he understood, "I didn't make dinner. I thought I'd be lazy and take you two out. There's a good place down the street."

And so they sauntered down Church, Paul's ghost jostled them a little, as if he understood that you couldn't dwell long on agony, on death, but wanted not to be forgotten. Tim remembered Paul's way of bringing his solitude guiltily into bars and taking it out again. He was one of the best people Tim had known, but he had probably found little happiness in being gay, except with Jack, perhaps.

"It isn't fair, is it?" he said bitterly.

"What do you mean?" Bob said, not looking him in the eye.

And before Tim could answer, he went on, demanding angrily, "Because how could it be fair? How could it ever be fair?"

PART 3

It looked as though David's summer would go by bright and pale beyond air-conditioning and his work. Only his parents might change it. After years of thinking about it, they had resolved to sail around the world. They planned to stop in Toronto before flying down to a New York of ocean liners.

Tim's presence made little difference in David's life or feelings. He didn't get up until David had left for work, and he was often out when David came home. They saw each other on weekends. Six years before, the leisure and the irony had been David's, by and large. Now he was the busy one, meeting deadlines, cajoling or badgering others to meet theirs. It distressed him to see someone with no deadlines of any sort. Yet they did turn out to be reasonably good at getting along. It was convenient that David was loverless, more or less. All he had by way of a love-affair was an arrangement with a man out in the western suburbs who didn't like to come "into town." So every few days, David would get on the Queen car and trundle broodingly out to Etobicoke.

"I like the trip," he told Tim, defensively. "It's a journey, a voyage. And Craig's nice enough. I mean, Craig's really nice."

"Human warmth," Tim said. "98.6 in the dark. I guess we all need it."

But he didn't seem to. It came as a surprise to David when he had to tell people they weren't lovers – to tell old friends they weren't lovers again. Tim smiled, smug and New York as if the Gioconda belonged to the Met. And he left David trapped alone with the depressing secret of his impotence, not telling even Bob Riding. "I'm just not into sex these days," he said to Bob. "The pool at the Y is enough for me. It's so cold it's sexy. The sexiest thing in Toronto, maybe."

"Well, it's a good time to take a rest," Bob said, sagely.

But for David, the unshared secret could be as oppressive and lugubrious as the wound in *Parsifal* – as cranky and demanding as a teething infant. He hated it, as if it made him sick. His first lover was impotent: where did that leave him?

Mostly Tim would be quiet, content to watch the world go past him with a wry grin that hooked up his mouth like a stroke. But sometimes he would start talking in rattling spates.

"It's so quiet here, I can't get over it. You'd think someone had just died – Queen Victoria, maybe? Or, what's his name, the one with the ouija boards, Mackenzie King? On the streets, I have to hold back in order not to trample the locals– it's like they're walking backwards."

He talked about Toronto as if he couldn't bear it, but he loved to make fun of it too. The expansion of discrimination included both homophobia and racism.

"I was in the subway yesterday, and this man – this old Anglo type, white hair, beefy face, hairy tweeds – was trying to get directions from the Indian ticket-seller, who didn't speak the same English at all. I heard, 'But I don't want the Eaton Centre, I want *Eaton's*!' and I thought, 'Christ, Tim, are you going to die here? Where what they want is *Eaton's*?'"

David liked to have Manhattan evoked as they sat looking down modest, shabby Church Street. But like a lot of the New Yorkers David knew, Tim seemed proud of a kind of harried helplessness – proud of being the slave, the addict of empire. At times, David enjoyed the idea that the doom of being gay was especially aristocratic and grandly developed down there: what bothered him was an old friend's despair. Tim had come loose from the world. He would talk occasionally about travelling, but with a kind of slackness in his voice that wouldn't get a plane off the ground. Sometimes, he would talk about taking a portfolio of his work around to people he still knew, but he never did. He drew a lot, and drawing seemed to be the only faculty that remained wholly alive. When he got out his sketchbook and drawing pen, David could see the old Tim again, as if his arm and hand had a seeing of their own, as if the world came up through them, unaffected by whatever had darkened his life. But the old question of his ambition, of whether in the end Tim Grey was to be merely one of those who may live happily or unhappily but who accomplish nothing and (because on this issue David remained adolescent, inhuman) perish – that question hadn't been answered. For Tim or for David.

David couldn't ask what might have caused his state. Tim let out a lot of his five years in fits and starts, and David built up a chronology of two important affairs – only Andreas, the dancer, had managed to outlive their time on Markham Street a few minor ones, with cruising and the baths to tide his lust and his ego over. But so far as David could make out nothing very catastrophic had happened: nothing like that affair with Kelly. Whom they never mentioned.

"I just got burned out for a while," Tim told Bob Riding, who could pose this sort of question.

"Maybe you just don't want to grow up yet," Bob said. Because now he was all for growing up and being responsible, even if you were eighteen.

"That's not true," Tim laughed. "I wish I was fifty. I wish I was a thousand."

Bob's theory was only part of the truth, David thought. What was here now, sleeping in the study meant for his novel, the deep, formless sadness he'd invited into his apartment, must have been in Tim all along, slowly coming to the surface. It was his mother or his father or his genes: it went a long way, all the way back. It had been in the mystery David had loved in Tim, while projecting his own very different psychology into it.

Or was that too simple, too? How much was he imagining and how much was still his own state? Because he wasn't really living these summer days, either: he was just waiting, and perhaps no longer even waiting. All around him, he had a sense of the times, – "the end of the eighties," everyone said in a strange way, as if hearkening for the meaning of the phrase – formless, faceless, undeclared, unless the formlessness was all there was. He felt indifferent to things, with no special emotions for them: as if, like a lot of his acquaintances, he could wake up ordinary one morning, and make a life of it, or even a kind of religion.

Certainly, his novel had been postponed for another season, at least. Forever, perhaps, if the idea of a novel had been merely hypochondria, a malaise floating vaguely through him, like cancer he'd never quite catch. A modernist longing in the post-modern world. Perhaps it would be with him all his life, never speaking out, to sit at the foot of his deathbed, silent, attentive, faceless.

It was possible: statistically – he'd read many cherished, dreadful manuscripts – it was the likely thing. But he'd gone through Toronto with such important feelings once – with such an important heart!

On the Saturday after Tim moved in, they went shopping for clothes, with Bob coming along too. Tim didn't need any new clothes, but he seemed to feel, like the middle-class lady he partly was, that the way to see a place was to go shopping in it. It was Bob who made the comparison, but dressed as he was, he couldn't argue effectively. His clothes were meant to be gay, he said, he was trying to make a statement, but so many straight boys were dressing the same way his wardrobe was moving rapidly to the right.

They shopped diligently for an hour, even David, because, invisible in last year's shirt, he might miss the love of his life. They were between stores when a demonstration came up Yonge Street towards them, led by two big puppet heads, grinning and nodding foolishly. The nation's intelligent prime minister, the continental president.

"Oh shit!" Bob said. "The demo, and I forgot."

"There are always more demos, Bob," Tim said.

David was looking with fear and distaste at the doddering heads, especially the apple-cheeked, powerful one. "I think that's who broke up Fred and Jack," he said. "On his way to vote in 1980, Fred stopped in at a bar and Republicans in leather undid all Jack's work – all Jack's trying to save the Americans from themselves. Fred said Carter reminded him of an old Sunday school teacher of his and he just couldn't stand it. They never got over it, at least Jack didn't. He was on the phone, saying, 'He was burning police cars after the Dan White verdict, and then he votes for Reagan. Try imagining that: someone you love, the body you love, voting for *Reagan!*'"

Tim smiled as if he had similar stories to tell, but now the demonstrators were bringing along a Cruise missile made of *papier mache*. It looked like a shark they'd caught. Or like a black prick, cut off and rigid with fury about its castration. It was Charlotte who suggested that because there she was, holding high a placard to say that *"Patriarchy = Nuclear Annihilation"*. Heather was beside her: *"You Can't Embrace With Nuclear Arms"*. David waved and got Tim to wave, though Charlotte and Heather were too busy or too exalted to notice. David felt guilty and caught out like Bob, and guiltily in love with Charlotte, who kept the faith, who fought like a mother bear for her children and her lovers.

"Charlotte's looking great," Tim said, bitchily, but enviously too as she went by. "Wouldn't it be nice to be like that at sixty? Bob, let's all try to be so ravaged and weather-beaten and tragic-looking that people will think we're grand old lesbians."

David laughed, understanding this longing. Bob exclaimed, "That stinks!"

"Why?" Tim said.

"I hate it when gay men do that, patronizing lesbians."

In theory, David might have agreed, but for some reason he didn't like these attacks on Tim. Bob had already declared that Tim was completely blind and that American painting from Pollock to Johns was wallpaper for the rich. Right or wrong, he ought to see that Tim was too fragile now to be attacked. And – dear Bob – Cruise missiles had nothing to do with it, nothing to do with anything, really. It was just escapism, cheap melodrama, to imagine Toronto rising and blossoming in dust, one at last with her superior sisters, with New York and Nineveh. That wouldn't happen: the patriarchs were too cunning. They might destroy Central America and try to make sure all the gay men died of AIDS, but they weren't going to blow up their chessboard.

And then for one moment the black paint gleamed a shiny eye at him, targetting the little workshop of bright ideas roofed over by David McTavish's skull.

"Oh, Bob, do you really think it matters?" Tim said, gesturing world-wearily at the demonstrators. "Because nothing anyone does up here is going to make any difference: we get blown up or we don't, it's not up to us. Charlotte's wonderful, I really think she's great, but – well, she's a fanatic, too."

"At least, she's doing something – while all you can do is make bitchy remarks and go shopping."

But, like Tim, Bob was holding a ridiculous little shopping bag full of clothes he hoped the straight beauties of Forest Hill wouldn't dare put on for a few months at least. Tim just gave it an ironic glance.

Squeezing down his mouth, without even a 'fuck you,' Bob thrust it at David and stepped off the curb.

Tim shrugged, watching as he was carried away in the crowd. It turned out to be only a block long: Suddenly it had gone by, its clamour dying away with alarming speed. In five minutes, you knew, Cruise missiles would be out of mind, back in their garages, waiting.

"Oh, well," Tim said, sadly. "But maybe that means he doesn't think we're all going to die of AIDS."

A feeling of sadness came over David too. They'd been relying on Bob, and now they were unprepared to be alone together. They went on down the street. Then on some silent impulse, Tim turned into a side street. He stopped a short way down, by a lane, in front of a stretch of red brick wall.

"This is where I met Kelly," he explained. It was the first time the name had been spoken. "Right here. He was leaning against this wall, waiting. For customers. For me. I wonder who I was – from his point of view?" He laughed. "I can't believe it now." He raised his left hand – the shopping bag hung from his right – as if he wanted to touch the rough bricks, or push them over. Instead he turned and pointed farther down. "And the last time, too, the last time I saw him, was down there, on the other side of the lane. Toronto is *so small*! It is so fucking small."

"Did you ever hear from him again?" David asked, afraid of what Tim was bringing up.

"No. No, nothing."

"I'm sorry I was so stupid then", David said, guiltily, snatching his chance to say this.

Tim gave a helpless shrug. "Were you? You weren't, not particularly. It's nobody's fault. He just came along, and suddenly I became someone else, someone impossible for his sake. I was a completely different person with him– than with you."

He laughed.

"Sometimes I think I've been a different person with each of my lovers. With Andreas, people never guessed I was Canadian: some even thought I was a dancer. Maybe I'm too adaptable."

"Did he really have cancer?" David said, almost losing his breath.

"I told you that, didn't I?" He gave David a long, almost hostile look. "I'd forgotten, almost. At least, I hoped you had. You were the only one I ever told. It's a good thing, maybe, otherwise I might think it was all a dream."

David looked away, miserably. To know, at least to feel, your lover's body being invaded, being destroyed, cell by cell: A rare experience then...no longer.

"Did he really have cancer?" Tim repeated, objectively. "I hope not." He stood, faced with a wall of brick in a brown brick city. "I hope he was lying, lying a lie from start to finish." He gave David a quick look, as if afraid he might not believe this. "I do."

"I couldn't tell anyone at the time," he went on. "While he was around. It was like being in a dream, not being able to wake up. I remember I phoned up Jack once and couldn't say a thing when I heard him answer. That's why I didn't keep in touch with him – with you, too. I should have kept up afterward, but how could you get started? Hi, it's me, back from – "

Impulsively he reached and touched the bricks, running his fingers over them. "He's dead," he said, with odd clarity. "He couldn't have lived this long. Not with his luck – ." He stood back. "Or maybe not, who knows?" he said, and turned away abruptly, back toward Yonge.

"I'm sorry," David said, helplessly. "I didn't understand. And of course I was jealous – upset that you were so much in love with *him* and – " David stopped. There was no point in going into it now.

"And not with you? Oh, David, you can't compare! It's unfair to everyone." Tim laughed, as they came back to the street, heading back toward David's. "It was a different world. I remember Jack saying, 'Hello? Hello?' and his voice changing, and I didn't want to hear that, Jack getting alone and scared, and still I couldn't talk. Oh well. I suppose by now Jack has changed completely. Five years – San Francisco – they take being gay so seriously out there, they think they invented it..."

He seemed to want David to tell him Jack was someone else now, someone he didn't know.

"You didn't read the letter?" David asked, hopefully.

"No, David, and I'm not going to. I took one look and put it back in your drawer. I'm sorry but I just don't need that, someone going on and on about his lover dying of AIDS. Bob's right, at least when he says it's going to be a long war."

"Good, I'm glad," David said. "After I got it out for you, I began hoping you would not read it. It was Bob's idea, mainly. He says it's because of that letter that he and Jack are lovers, whatever that means. He can be ruthless these days: he just forgets people have feelings at times."

"He's in shock," Tim said understandingly, surprising David. "You see a lot in New York. We all are, I guess."

PART 4

As his parents' visit drew near, David began writing sentences in his notebook. Protective Spells.

Parents are for children, like toys.

The day before they arrived, he reread the letter his mother had written to clarify their plans: the hotel they would stay at, not wanting to put anyone out, and the friends they'd visit. Around him gathered all the family assumptions, his unspoken world of which the other world lived in ignorance.

Every family is a lost civilization.

No spell could save him. He closed the notebook and set out for Etobicoke.

Just before three, he woke abruptly, insomnia staring him in the face. Craig lay curled beside him like a lesson in sleep, while his ramshackle air-conditioner roared and shook. David burrowed down under the sheet and tried using Craig's thighs as earmuffs, but he knew they wouldn't work. He imagined crossing the city on the all-night streetcar, getting into his own bed, the only place in the world where he could sleep now – he tried to dream this.

His insomnia wouldn't be moved. He got up and went looking for something to write with. Craig treated pens and pencils like cigarette butts. On the kitchen table, he daubed out apologies in lime-green Magic Marker: insomnia again, he had to go, he'd phone in the morning. Craig would understand: this had happened before.

Leaving a kiss, he went out on the street. It was empty: for ten minutes there was not one car. Then the Long Branch streetcar slipped over a rise, glided along to stop in front of him, a frumpy, red, iron-skirted streetcar saying I'm at least as real as you are. Get on.

The silent driver's only passenger, he sat watching old motels go by like toy villages, gas stations with stucco battlements and ivy. It was an old Anglo-Saxon lower-middle-class neighbourhood, where British and Indian names were equally aboriginal and quaint. The lake, unseen but shaping their journey, sent a nocturnal coolness through his window. Another streetcar waited for him at the Humber Loop, a long box of brightness with a scattering of passengers, some awake. They went faster, the car speeding, seeming to lift from its tracks, flying then grinding back down, earthbound after all. The lake came into view on the far side of expressways, and David began to remember this area, or something like it, from long go. He'd always known that he'd been in Toronto with his parents when he was very young. But now for the first time he felt it, saw bits of it. There'd been a woman who lived close to the lake, and they'd gone to see it, a misty blue plain. They'd been standing among trees, and she had told him

300

every tree was a soldier killed in the war. One of them had some connection to her. Who was she? She hadn't been mentioned in his mother's letter. The trees had been big ones: it must have been the First War.

Now they were on Queen Street, hundreds of red-brick houses pushing storefronts up to the sidewalk. A man in a summer suit got on, carrying an old, cloth-covered suitcase. "Can you let me off at Cedar Street? I'm not familiar with Toronto." His voice was loud and friendly, a daylight voice that made David realize how close to sleep he was. The man might have been a salesman, his suitcase full of hopeful health products: he was from Ontario's Toronto, the small town's big city. "Like I say, I'm not familiar with Toronto. I only know if I see the Paradise Hotel I've gone too far." That was where he'd dreamt himself, David realized: the Canada lost on the maps, the small, comfortable principality north of feelings, where everyone is friendly, neighbourly, where no one is passionate.

His parents came through the door of Canadian Pacific, the Tory airline, slightly smaller, trimmer, more seaworthy versions of themselves. They were a little drawn after the long flight, but still brisk, with an air of adventure about them. They obviously fancied themselves as circumnavigators. They were still young old people, he was relieved to see: his father balder and leaner, his mother with gray-tipped hair and a little stouter, but not dangerously so.

With their luggage tugging down his arms, David felt a pang of alarm. As if something was up, as if there might be a message from underneath the world. 'We're sorry, David, we wanted to spare you, we know you'll understand.'

His father came over and insisted on carrying a suitcase, the heavier one.

He would never understand them, just become them.

They had dinner with David and some old friends, two couples their age. When they spoke of Hugh Armitage, drowned three years ago in the Bahamas, David took his part in weaving poor Hugh into memory for a minute or two. Secretly, he feared that Hugh was one of the big failures of his life, although there was no evidence he hadn't honestly drowned.

The next morning, he and his father went for a walk. It was cool when they started: Mr. McTavish wore a tweed jacket and brought an umbrella. After years, David saw again his father's restless feel for terrain: faced with a large city, he had to trace out the shape of the earth underneath it. Striding along, he was alert, feral, dangerous, and David was suddenly like him: they were spies, scouting out enemy positions. This shared restlessness helped them avoid each other's eyes.

In the end, they went all the way to the harbourfront, driven by some racial instinct to go south and stare across watery spaces towards a lost continent. But there were no snow-capped Washington mountains to look at there, just the trees of the Island. David's night journey on the Queen Street car came back, and the woman and her soldier trees. Were they a dream?

"Good night!" his father said, mildly. "Do you remember that? You were very small."

He explained she was a distant relative: she had died years ago, a spinster.

"It was her brother who died in the war?"

"Yes, it was." His father was intrigued, as if wondering what else he could recall. "At Vimy."

Vimy Ridge: meaning, and you think it's the 1980's.

The rest of the day his parents had consecrated to old friends. The next day, the day of their flight to New York, they had lunch with David and Bob Riding.

Bob was a gamble, and a success: in fact, he made the occasion. He didn't have any doubts about going around the world, not even with a shipload of grayheads. He let Mr. and Mrs. McTavish be adventurous elderly children, something David could hardly be expected to countenance. David was nervously proud of what he'd come up with. He was trying to show how far he'd come since leaving Victoria. *I went to Toronto and look what I found: a nice young man with an earring!*

"Well," his father said in the taxi, afterwards, "He seems a fine young chap."

A bit of a girl, of course, David thought for him, without active resentment.

"Yes, he is," his mother said. "I like Bob."

And suddenly David was relieved – infinitely relieved and tickled.

"Oh, that's nothing! Everyone likes him – there are no points for liking Bob Riding!"

A few yards of the city went by speechless. He'd never spoken to them so freely before.

"Is he your lover?" his mother said, kindly, handling the word with skill. It was if they were fighting a duel of astonishments.

"No," David said. "No, I don't really have a lover now."

Another reason not to get stuck in Australia. To meet my lover, you have got to come back.

They'd allowed too much time for getting to the airport, so now they could stop off at David's apartment, which they'd visited only briefly before, as if afraid to intrude. Tim happened to be in, and came out to say hello.

"Tim Grey," David said. "He was my roommate when I was on Markham Street, remember? Tim's visiting from New York."

They shook hands, apparently unaware that what they were doing was impossible. And Tim might never have lost his courage or his soul or whatever it was he'd lost: he was everything they needed for a difficult moment, wide-smiling, frank, all gay complications almost hidden behind his broad shoulders. David could leave them to make tea. From the voices coming down the hall you could imagine a courtly, peaceful world. A Canadian world. But they were all marginal, David felt suddenly, Tim and himself as much as his parents: they meant nothing in a world neither Canadian nor gay.

"So," he heard his mother saying, "Jean Dalziel is your cousin? You know, dear, just up from the Lockarts."

Alone in the kitchen, wreathed in *bergamot*, David laughed, not quite out loud. Mountain ranges, prairies, the thousands of miles of rock, bare, glaciated rock – they were all as nothing to his mother's knowledge of Canadian connections.

In the taxi to the airport, David thought about coming home from around the world. About being married.

It was his night at the gay phone line. It was a busy night, and a bit crazy, as if the full moon shone in the wires.

Hi, guy. Where are the bars in this town?

You a queer? A real queer? How about that! I never talked to no queer before.

I've turned thirteen, I'm splitting, I'm tired of Dad always beating on me, it's not fair. This friend of mine he says he's got crabs. And they just won't go away.

I have these swellings, and my doctor would throw me out of the office if I told him I'm gay.

You know you're going to burn, don't you? That's what faggot means, it's in the Bible.

How can I tell my wife? And my kids? I love my kids more than anything.

All this, and then silence. Silence.

Perhaps kids on a dare, holding in their laughter better than most. Perhaps someone wanting to listen in outrage at the sounds of a faggot actually talking, breathing. Perhaps someone drowning like Hugh, silent, unable to talk yet, listening to hear if David could be human.

He couldn't say, "Who is this, please?" to someone who hadn't learned how to talk. So he did a friendly, shaky monologue about the phone line, about the other things his group did. Almost losing his breath, he chatted into the silence he had come from himself a long time ago, which he usually forgot, which now stretched all around him.

He stopped, and almost heard laughter, or the clickings of recording equipment. But it really was silence. And he couldn't go on like this all night. There were other people phoning.

"I should probably hang up now, okay? But call again. Tonight – or tomorrow night. Or whenever you feel like it. But call back soon, okay?"

He paused, hopefully.

"Because you've *got* to speak. *You've got to.*"

When he got home, Tim was watching the news. He looked away from a legless man in a wheelchair and said something. But the man on TV spoke louder, in a thick Middle-Eastern accent. "I saw my blood before I heard the voice of the explosion."

Tim aimed the remote control and the TV world disappeared into silent oblivion. "Jack's coming."

"Oh," David said. "Good." Not wanting to feel anything about it now: the day had been long enough.

"Bob phoned after you left. He arrives late tomorrow. Jack made his mind up all of a sudden. We'll go over there for dinner the day after, okay?"

He was looking into the gray screen. "It's been a long time, hasn't it? The last time I saw Jack, you were shouting at each other. I've forgotten why. Something about making up your mind. Something about Hitler."

"That is a long time."

"I've been sitting here wondering what he'll be like now."

David shrugged, unreassuringly.

Tim gave a nervous laugh. "It's like AIDS arriving," he said, still smiling, but with irritation in his voice. "Catching up with me. Bob is bad enough, with those figures of his, but – "

"I just don't know," David said, answering the real question. "I don't know what Jack will be like now."

And besides, he thought, they had always been friends with Jack in different ways.

"I really liked your parents," Tim said, suddenly, as if changing the subject. Enviously, perhaps.

"Yes. Yes, they're nice parents, aren't they?" David said, happily, and sorry he didn't have any to spare for Tim.

"I mean, considering," he added, fondly, not quite knowing what he meant.

PART 5

David slept badly, then slept in, getting up just before eleven, predisposed to dislike the day already.

"Let me take you out to dinner tonight," his guest said, coming around one side of the paper in the kitchen.

"Great," David said, uncertainly. For a moment it seemed some announcement trembled in the pages of the Globe.

"That restaurant Alan was mentioning? And maybe, after, we can try out that new bar, 105?"

"Sure," David said, still expecting something. Tim went back to his paper corner.

And at dinner he didn't talk much, as if he had got tired of making fun of things and had nothing else to say. David found himself exploring his parents, turning over the proprietorial, slightly bewildered perceptions of an only child. Tim's continuing silence drew David into talking about himself –his dissatisfaction with his life, the novel that wouldn't come.

"At this point, any novel would do!" David laughed. "Or almost any."

And suddenly he gave Tim's smug, handsome face a bitter looking-over. Tim just smiled, and David longed to give him some kind of shove, out of his home, perhaps – anywhere, back into life.

The closest he got was in telling him about Chris Leggatt.

"So who's he?"

"Who's he? Your rival! The U. of T. Maoist, remember? He came canvassing for the

New Democrats in the provincial election. It was good to see him, but a bit awkward in the timing. His party had just ratted on gay rights. And there'd been the bath raids, and the big demonstration. On the steps of the legislature, I had to hold Bob Riding back. I was afraid he was going to throw himself at all those fat-faced policemen and try to explode, like a gay bomb. I felt a bit superior, way ahead of Chris, sort of. I'd seen those smug faces: I saw they could be killers, just like in Chile. Anyway, we had a good talk, he'd come quite a way on women, on gays. He was trying, anyway. Because there are so many people you know who give a big sigh of relief about now and say 'Thank God, we can all stop pretending not to be ordinary'. But Chris hadn't: he was thinking of going down there to work. I suppose Nicaragua's kind of a comedown from China, but it's close and friendly and he was learning the language. I never brought up Cuba. All the machismo appealed to him, of course: he'd have loved to storm the presidential palace. But who wouldn't?"

Tim pushed his mouth down, doubtfully.

"I was proud of him, really. I mean, I was an idiot to be mooning around like that, but if I was going to do it, I didn't choose so badly. I mean, he'd *survived.*"

Tim looked at him and smiled ruefully. He could see David was telling him to survive, to have courage, to storm palaces.

"Let's not be late for 105. They say it's packed on Sundays."

The disco was a long way south, so they took a cab. They got in just before a line-up started forming. The music was tyrannically loud, the floor was shaking, the air was thick, smoke laced with sweat. David hadn't been in a crowd like this for months. But he had to follow as Tim pushed through to the bar, two more gay men eager to merge with the gay mass.

Waiting for their drinks, David stood looking into a sea of silent-film faces, their voices sheared away by the music. He was in over his head: the crowd gave out one huge shriek of all their emotions at once.

His eyes came to rest on a man sitting on top of two cigarette machines, his arms around his knees. He was about David's age, with brown hair and moustache, balding just a little, but good-looking, in shape. He wore a polo shirt, designer jeans, deck shoes with no socks. He seemed at ease there, at home, surveying the crowd, tossing down remarks to his friends. So far as David could tell, he had it all just right: he'd mastered being gay in Toronto in the 1980's, taken it all in, and was giving back a carefully worked out response. He was looking around for his next moves, what to wear and say and do tomorrow. He was an accomplishment, a small self-possessed triumph, and with a sudden rush of strangeness David understood that he didn't understand him at all: he was an absolute mystery, a Sphinx.

Tim was paying for the drinks. He shoved back the sleeves of his rugby shirt, handed David his drink and picked up his own. He was like the man on the cigarette machines, taking it all in, not resenting it when people shoved by and almost spilled his drink. That was part of what he'd come here for: the honest sense of excited human mass without the heterosexual threat. David hated it, tried to glare it away, stiffening resentfully when people pushed him, but Tim merged, yielded, one with the crowd.

David leaned close to Tim's ear and said, "I don't understand gay men." It was the only way to assert himself in this welter of souls. "I don't understand a single person here."

Mouths and ears switched.

"What's there to understand? They're just people. People who're gay."

In disgust with this feeble answer, David looked away. A teenager, androgynous for a season in the Boy George style, was telling a story to his friends – acting it so intensely, so frantically, he seemed to be clawing his way up off the ground, to be treading air. No, he didn't understand it, David thought, and nobody did.

"Maybe I just don't understand people then," David said, defiantly.

Tim tipped his head to one side. Tim thought he understood people, because he knew how to be one of them, to get along with them, to charm them when he needed to. That wasn't what David meant. He looked at the man again, now dangling one deck shoe and a bare ankle over the edge, still inscrutable. Always, he realized, he'd seen the gay world only through the eyes of his lover, whoever that lover was. Now he was blind.

In the DJ's darkened glass booth, long brown fingers came down into the light over a turntable, caressing it. A new song infiltrated the reigning one, and Tim said, "So let's dance?"

"*That* is not the answer."

Tim gave a little mocking smile, declaring loyalty to the crowd, to the dance.

"There's Todd," David said. A brainless friend of Bob's. "Why not ask him?"

But Tim went out alone by one of the speakers, dancing with all his body and dancing in his head, too, David saw, secretly, desperately, trying to pull some force up from the throbbing floor or out of the noisy air.

But when he came back, sweating and breathing fast, he said, "Music is so dull these days. I want to *push* it, make it go faster."

Soon he left David with the eighty-dollar rugby shirt they had bought the day of the demonstration against Cruise testing. David watched and wondered if Bob was right when he said, "It's here, already, it's got to be, in the baths, in all the bars." He watched, imagining the worst, seeing it, with a kind of craving gloom. Imagine, imagine and break your heart: the dance goes on, but tomorrow, perhaps, or the next day, the dancer gets his diagnosis. How sad, how terrible, how magnificent. But David shook himself and decided that whatever the virus was doing, what was happening now was what usually happened these days when David found himself alone in a bar. He drank too much and went cruising for metaphors, for a fine and lonely sadness.

After half an hour, David went out into the seething noise of the dance floor, trying to pick his way through without either bumping people or dancing with them, and thrust Tim's shirt at his slippery chest. He pointed to the door he was about to go through, expecting Tim to wave him goodbye. Tim got meekly into the shirt and followed him.

The staring, upturned faces on the stairs thought they were going very early. What had they found in fabulous 105, what were they taking away? Smoke in their clothes, sadness. Tim hadn't looked happy, David thought, but perhaps he'd looked as if he sensed happiness somewhere. David should simply have left him to be foolish without being sternly watched – perhaps to find a friend.

They walked toward the subway, hoping to see a taxi. They didn't, and descended unwillingly into the station. The platform was as crowded as if it were rush hour: something must have held up the trains. Tim walked along the platform. Some West Indian kids with a huge radio were playing the song he had just been dancing to. To get round them, they had to go along the edge.

"Careful!" David said from behind, afraid of seeing Tim fall. Sometimes the drink on the shelf by the dance floor had seemed to be Tim's partner. And he wasn't quite sober himself. They were coming to a noisy group of teenagers. Tim went along the edge again, stumbled, went running for a few steps, then jumped as if to save himself from falling. Tim wide-armed in the air, Tim landing and stumbling along the concrete bed of the tracks – David couldn't believe it.

He ran up beside him – Tim was about four feet below – and held out his hand. "Here," he said, commandingly.

Tim looked up but didn't stop walking along toward the tunnel their train would come out of. "You know, I've never been down here before," he said, with a teasing smile.

"Come on, get out of there."

"It feels kind of restful somehow."

"Well, I'm sure it's illegal."

"Oh, I'll get out, don't worry."

There was a stirring of wind around them. Before he realized that it came from the train on the other tracks, David shouted, "Get out of there!"

"Lovers' quarrel," a hoarse young voice said. David looked up at some teenagers in black Heavy Metal T-shirts. "You never know what queers'll do," another of them said knowingly.

"You come down here and say that," Tim called in his New York voice, delighted at the chance of a scene.

"That's all right, sweetheart, you just stay put," the tallest one said, the original speaker, with long blond hair and a cross dangling from his ear. Tim smiled up as if he'd argue, then lost interest, shrugged and walked on.

"Why are you doing this?" David shouted desperately, over the noise of the train bursting from its tunnel.

Tim stopped. He was saying something. Look? He held up his left arm, the wind pulling at his hair, his clothes. And for a moment, just as he pulled the sleeve back, *look!* David almost saw what he meant: purple lesions in the skin of his arm. Something he'd seen in San Francisco, but not in Toronto, not till now. Then, seeing that there was nothing wrong with Tim's arm, that Tim had gone crazy, he jumped in after him.

"Get out of here!" he shouted over the noise of the train. "Because I've had enough." He grabbed Tim and pulled, as if he could throw him out.

"I'm sorry, David," Tim said, with a scared smirk. "That was really a bit shitty."

But there was a cold look in his eyes, as if he was angry that David had understood him so quickly, so seriously. He pulled away and ripping sounds came from the shirt. David let go, following him, walking along the concrete bottom of the city. He could feel it under them, around them, the weight of Toronto, of the whole concrete world. He looked at the people lined above them, some disturbed, wondering what to do, others ignoring them. He felt another wave of anger at Tim. It was treason, letting out fear like that. What if the crowd had understood?

"Please, Tim," he said in a low voice. "Let's get out of here."

Tim stopped, looked at him, angry and blank and shaken, stepped over to the platform where there was room and jumped. For a moment, David was alone with all the people who had died here at the bottom of Toronto. Then, he tried jumping too. His first attempt failed, he scraped his leg, his hand. Then he did it: it was like hauling yourself out of a dry pool, without the lift of water, just Tim giving an ineffectual pull.

"What the hell did you think you were doing?" David said, getting up.

"I'm sorry, that was childish, I know. I did it without thinking."

He was repentant, but still shaken and angry at how real David had made it. How real it had become between them.

"Then *think*. Don't do things like that."

"Think...right..."

The train was coming, very fast, making up for lost time. Tim took an uncertain step forward. David went behind him, put his arms around him, and walked him back against the tiled wall.

"You're being ridiculous, David," Tim said, embarrassed.

"Good," David said. "It makes me feel better."

The train went past, stopped, opened its doors. David let go, they went in last and stood by the door. The car was packed.

"You've got blood on your face," Tim said. "Grease and blood."

"Oh, who cares?" David said, impatiently. "It's just my hand."

"Here," Tim said, trying to make up for what he'd done. Pulling the cuff of the ruined shirt down over his palm, he began wiping David's face.

David turned his face to the side, as the train went into the tunnel, turning the windows into shadowy mirrors. He saw himself, a blood-smeared face Tim was trying to clean up, and the crowd around, some of them curious.

The guest showered first. After showering too, David came out to find Tim waiting for him in the hall.

"I'm sorry, David. I want to apologize. I've been on edge all day. It's Jack coming, I think. When Bob phoned last night, I wanted to go out to the airport, take any plane they had."

"But why do you have to *joke* about it?"

Wearing David's Japanese gown, Tim held his arms out wide, elegant and helpless.

"You don't have it!" David said, flatly. "You are not going to get it!"

"Well, thank you, David," Tim said, sardonically.

"You damn well do not have AIDS!" David took him by the shoulders to shake this into him, and Tim let himself be shaken like a child, but with a look of bleak, untouchable skepticism. David gave up, let go, just staring at him bitterly.

"So how do you know?" Tim said. "Can you see it in my face?"

He spoke ironically, but with a painful note of hope, as if he thought maybe David had something up his sleeve, some way to convince him he was safe. It was unbearable to see: Tim afraid, weak, unresisting, not sure life wanted him any longer. David blinked, and it was as if he saw Paul dying, Jack's pitiless words forcing him to see it. Before he knew what he was doing, he'd started telling it.

"When Paul died, he barely had a face. He had herpes all over it. And the retinitis – he was *blind*!"

He couldn't stop it: he was only a witness, the truth coming through him. Tim stared, then he turned away, holding his hands like someone staggering through smoke. He shook his head, fast, several times. "*Paul!*" he said, disbelievingly.

"I'm sorry," David said, miserably.

"And I was afraid of Jack!"

"I'm sorry, I just wanted to – I couldn't bear it if you got sick." He broke off. Perhaps the only thing left to do was say good night and go down the hall to bed. David's fear, the violence it aroused, had outdone Tim's. He took Tim's hand and gave it a little tug. He felt too weak to do anything more. Tim just stood, still in shock, and let himself be tugged at. David stepped close and put his arms around him – empty arms, no hope in them. He rubbed his cheek against Tim's face.

"I'm sorry," he said, "Don't think about it, that's all you can do. Forget it."

"It's all right, David."

David absorbed this. He was forgiven, it seemed, enough to ask his question after a minute or two.

"Why are you such a wreck?" he said, as if he was joking.

"Am I? Maybe. You want me to be on my way, don't you?"

"No," David said. "Of course not. Not if you don't want to."

"But you're right, I know it, I've got to do something. Stop *dawdling*."

"I'm not going to throw you out," David said, putting a dry kiss on his cheek. Tim laughed as if tickled, and David kissed him again.

"That's nice," Tim said, meeting his lips briefly. "You still think sex is the answer, don't you?"

"No!" David said, stepping back. The kisses had been friendly, reparative. "Did I ever?"

"Oh, David, not you too!" Tim smiled, pulling him towards the door of his room.

"What's happening?" David said, following uncertainly.

Tim pulled them in and sat them down, side by side on the single bed, and kissed him again. But he couldn't be up to much: the Japanese gown, too beautiful for David to ever wear, fell open on the limpest of penises.

"You really are a wreck," David said, questioningly. "What are we going to do with you?"

"Just this is nice," Tim said.

David reached for the sorry cock, melting, drooling away like a Dali watch.

"What did you do to it, Tim? I used to love this thing."

Tim laughed, sounding almost proud of what he'd done: Castrated David's first, best lover.

"I remember when this told me what to do," David said, still protesting.

He stopped, as if desperate to revive it, this poor drowned youth. But Tim was denying himself: He'd pulled it all back up his spine to some secret, silent part of his head and now sat smiling down at him.

"I'm sorry, I guess I'm just taking some kind of rest, that's all."

David sat back.

"But you fuck me, okay?" Tim said, almost apologetically.

David started, stared at him, not understanding.

"Why?"

"God, that's the first time anyone's asked that."

He bent down to David's lonely, uninvited erection.

"But do you really mean it?" There was something wrong, almost incestuous in the idea. They were sisters by now. David wanted to leave. But he had to leave Tim with a reason.

"Do I mean it?" Tim leaned and yanked his jeans over by one narrow ankle. He took his wallet, pulled out a strip of condoms and waved it above them, like a flag. "With love from Bobby Riding!"

He seemed almost as wild as when he'd been running along between the subway tracks.

"But what would we be doing?"

"What do you think?"

"I mean, between us."

"Oh, David! Don't ask things like that." Petulantly, Tim looked away.

Distrusting his strange mood more and more, David wanted to get away. But at the same time he couldn't bear to leave Tim alone like this, hopeless, crazy, castrated forever.

David found himself arriving in Tim again, bewildered, not knowing where he was or why he was there, his prudent rubber distancing him, like the six years.

"All right?" he said.

"Great," Tim said, looking up at him with cool, untrusting curiosity, like a child on the operating table. David felt suddenly abandoned, sinking, loneliness pouring in like an icy sea.

"But what do you want?" David said, desperately.

"What do I want? I don't know. I remember this guy in the baths in New York. He said he wanted to be fucked like Blanche Doubois – *unenduringly.*"

"I'm not sure I like this," David said. "I feel – used."

"Used? – I haven't heard that word in years. David, just shut up and fuck like everyone else. Just fuck your brains out. I'm tired of them."

David looked away from Tim's face. To his feet, held high and helpless, like big, rabbity ears, he thought with cruel fondness: pink ears pathetically hearkening for cosmic vibrations. He'd once loved them for the fine way, stepping, they'd put the ground in its place, and now they were abject, like hands up in a Western, surrender proclaimed, surrender for all to see.

"Don't do this to me," he said. "I feel –"

"David, grow up. Jesus, you still think sex has to be a big deal. Truth, beauty, religion. Sex is sex, just shut up and fuck me."

David closed his eyes. Perhaps what Tim was demanding gave him the way out – to forget who he was, who Tim was, to thrust off into whatever frenzy he could find in the rubber stretched over his heart, over all his senses, death beginning everywhere.

But even that didn't work. It was as if Tim had strangled his sex too – had turned even his durable, dogged lust into this joyless gallop at nothingness. He couldn't forgive Tim for that. Whatever had happened to him in New York, or, beneath all the cities, deep in his soul, it couldn't excuse this. David couldn't forgive him or come.

He opened his eyes: Tim was gazing at him, looking bored and tired, as if nothing much had happened. His cock rolled helpless and lifeless as a death squad corpse. All David had accomplished was to shove them up into the corner, so that Tim's head was twisted a little. His odd, wistful gaze seemed to hang in the air between them, as if his soul was floating around outside him, wishing to find a home, not knowing how.

David took a kind of angry pity and closed his eyes and tried again to give Tim something he seemed to think he wanted. Then, he thought, he would have paid the full price for everything Tim had done for him: they would be even.

Nothing worked. He couldn't break and give Tim the cold satisfaction of seeing him come alone.

"I *can't,*" he said, bitterly. "I can't come."

"Yes, you can," Tim said, with a fake, laughing snarl. "I *know* you can. Come – come in me. I want to see it."

It was a kind of taunting, hateful sex-talk he'd picked up somewhere, and by now David agreed with the hatred in it: he hated sex, which betrays people and kills them as it killed Paul. And all the others. Which breaks them open and makes them hope and destroys them. Tim wanted him to accept that and let go, go falling hopelessly.

"I can't," he said to the wall, staring at the old paper a few inches from his face.

"Please?" Tim seemed to be trying a different voice, begging but mocking too, the voice crooked inside his neck. "Please, David, I want you to come, please." It was still taunting, but like a little girl's wheedling, too.

But by now, it was really all between the wall and David. He banged it with his fist. "I can't. You won't let me."

But who was there to talk to? He banged silently, obstinately, with both fists, as if he wanted out through the plaster. There was more chance of that than of coming. "I *hate* you!" he growled. "Let go of me!" Distantly, he noticed pain in his hands and wrists. He would have to be sensible and stop, or else pitch into a rage where he couldn't feel anything: he felt himself balancing in between.

"Come down here," Tim said, speaking in his own voice, more or less, and reaching for him.

"You let go of me!" David said, raging at the wall.

"David, here, please."

It was too late, David thought: he was past listening to anyone. He hit the wall and the pain was satisfying, as if he could drink it down wrists like throats. The pain was honest, was alive, more human than anything else in the room. But then hands caught at his wrists, getting one, then the other. David froze, feeling Tim's fingers closing round him. By now he was wedged into the corner. "Let go!" he cried, terrified the rubber would split, or his heart, or the sky, spilling death. "Let go," helplessly, and then "Hold me," and he was fighting coming, his breath hissing in and out, a tiny thread about to break.

He came to rest with his head tipped into the corner. His eyes came open for a second, closing on an image of Tim's face far below, distorted and unreadable. He took a breath and said through closed eyelids, "There, I came. Is that what you wanted?"

Tim didn't answer.

"To hell with you, Tim," David said, tears stabbing into his eyes. "And get out of here. *Get out of my house.*"

"You haven't changed, have you?" There was longing in this, or envy.

He felt Tim take his clenched right hand, open it, soothe it, palm and fingers. Both battered hands ached, especially the one Tim had in his, pain running up deep into the long bones of his arms. Why had he done that to them? It had been insane, useless. He hit his left fist against the wall one last time, bitterly, testingly, to feel just how crazy he'd been, and said, "I still love you."

He opened his eyes. Tim would have to go now.

Tim took the left hand, pulled it down, opened it.

"I'm lucky, then," he said.

PART 7

Half an hour later, Tim was lying with his head on David's belly in David's double bed. David was doing most of the talking, about a trip through Europe which they might take in a few months. Tim turned away, looking down along David's long legs, hiding an awkward secret. An erection had stolen up on him under the sheet. He didn't know whether he wanted it, now or ever: it felt as if there was a savage pain hovering somewhere close, attracted by it, waiting for the moment to attack.

What he had, whatever it was he had, this dangerous gift or promise, might melt as he spoke, any threat, any shadow of cruelty or sarcasm could tear out its heart, but he knew that if he didn't take up the challenge, he might be lost forever. It wouldn't be real until David learned about it, after all: it was a gift from him, to him.

He broke in upon David's Venice with a scared, comic yelp.

"I've got some news, David. I think."

He stopped to survey David's puzzled face, to see where he stood. Why did he speak, he wondered. Why not take David's hand down to his crotch? There was a reason, but he didn't quite know what it was.

"It's, I'm – well, *back*."

At once, before David could do anything, Tim scrambled up, to defend himself. The way he moved, keeping himself swaddled, gave him away. A doubtful smile came over David's face.

"Really?"

"I don't know! Yes, really."

"Thank God, Tim. I knew you weren't really impotent."

"But I am, I was, and now – "

Before Tim could think how to say how scared he was, he saw David's hand, about to reach. In a fear he didn't understand, he grabbed David's wrist and held it rigidly in both hands.

"*Ow!*" David said. Tim knew the wrist was sore from David's assault on the wall, on his friend's despair, but he was terrified of the long, cunning, dark-haired hand, an animal that could devour him at a gulp. They stared at each other, equally surprised.

"I know it's ridiculous, David, but I don't want to be touched. I don't know why, but I'm very fragile." He laughed girlishly. "Really. It feels like I could *die* if anything went wrong and spoiled it."

"All right," David said, accepting this. At thirty-one he was learning how to wait on things he didn't understand.

Tim let go of David's hand, but kept a wary eye on it.

"You always were a mystery to me, Timmy. It's why I love you." Suddenly David laughed, in outright, pure delight. "Can't I just see it, though?" he asked, with a happy smirk.

It was as if they were six and playing a game. Or playing a game of being six. Tim had to think about everything slowly, ploddingly, as if he was just learning to think.

"Please," David implored.

"All right." It was a game, but if the least cruelty came into David's voice or eyes, he didn't know what he would do. He tugged at the sheet wound round him, got free of it, moved it aside uncertainly.

His luck held up. David gazed with cherishing eyes. Gazed as if at the whole tenderness of the heart, just born, new to the world. Horribly, agonizingly exposed, and ready to live.

"Tim! Welcome back!"

Tim laughed, and then said, "But I'm so scared!" I don't know why, it's crazy, but – *don't laugh*, David, or I'll kill you."

This had a desperate truth, which David could see in his eyes. Then it set them both giggling.

"No, it's beautiful, Tim, really. It's *so* – " David didn't have a word for it, and then he did: "*Happy!*"

"But it's like anything, anyone could hurt me."

"Not me, never me," David said, solemnly.

"Oh?" I know you, David.

Silently, David shook his head.

On impulse, in a terror he couldn't believe, Tim reached and took David's hand. "Carefully," he said. "*Carefully!*" He lifted and guided it, almost losing his verve, over to his only life. David's delicate, spidery fingers closed around him, barely tightening. Tim couldn't get his breath. For a moment he was dying, his throat closing with David's hand. Then he breathed out and in, letting go of David's wrist. He leaned, pulling David's head over to his. He began kissing the dark head gratefully and desperately. He had to love David enough to prevent him from killing him.

CHAPTER XII: JACK'S LETTER

PART 1

David brought Tim's elegant printing a few inches from his eyes.
I've gone out for a walk, and I'll be back soon.
If you wake up, I love you and don't worry, just go back to sleep.
Tim.
David put on his glasses to read it again. The printing didn't give anything away. Don't worry! Walking meant thinking: it meant doubt. David got out of bed and went into the kitchen for a glass of milk. White sheets spilled face down over the table: Jack's letter from San Francisco.

"No," David cried, weakly. "*No!*" he shouted into the empty apartment. Tim was out in the night with Paul's death in his eyes, with Jack's rage in his soul. David grabbed the pages and banged them on the table, hopelessly, furiously. Tim could be changed forever by this: everything that had happened tonight could be destroyed. He banged the sheaf of paper again, harder, in rage at Jack for what he'd done, furious at himself for letting it happen.

He went to the front room and peered out the bay window. On the street, there were a few prostitutes, no one else. He almost decided to go out, simply to be out in the night with him, but Tim might come back and find him gone. All he could do was wait.

David looked at the top sheet – the little note Jack had written to explain why he had written this to him and to Bob. To thank him for being himself and for letting him speak this way. *You mean, for being almost as crazy as you, Jack*, he thought. He sat down by the front window, despairing, feeling Jack had finally got him – trapped him inside his paranoia forever.

He tried to imagine exactly what Tim had been through, what he was remembering now. The street was empty: he might have to wait for hours – he might have to wait for the rest of his life.

With nothing else to do, he began the letter again, trying to follow Tim through it.

Dear Bob, Dear David,

It might make sense to wait for months, for years, perhaps, before trying to get this down. It's only a few weeks since he died, only a few miles off, across the bay. I'm in Jim's apartment, while Jim works in the next room and keeps an eye on me. But I want to make an attempt now, before it changes in my mind. Before other things come in between: who knows if I have years, or months? I used to think I'd live out a quiet, unhappy life, and watch the millenium arrive on some kind of improved television.

How *quickly* it happened – you have to start with that. I'd followed the story from the beginning, more or less. From 'GRID.' But who could believe, accept, not laugh at 'gay-related immune deficiency'? Cancer you could catch, but only if you were gay. Life couldn't be that shitty: it had to be the government and the doctors lying about us again, trying to take us over again: Reagan was president, what did you expect? When it kept up, when it was noticed other groups got it, I began to think it was more serious, but it would still be containable. I'd lived all my life under the protection of antibiotics: death wasn't something you caught like a cold. Then overnight I had in my house, in my best friend, something that can kill more of us than Hitler.

It was July last year. Cathy had visited in June, along with Mike, the summer's boyfriend. I'd suggested to Paul that he come up to see them, but he wasn't feeling well. He thought it was some kind of flu that he couldn't shake off.

That night, I went out to dinner with a couple I know here, then we went to see *Anna Karenina*. I walked home alone, seeing a lot of men on the way, but content with my life as it was. All I wanted, all I was cruising for that evening was the sense of freedom this city gave me, freedom and hope fulfilled. I had never really entered the sex life of the city: by and large, I enjoyed it vicariously, imagining what it would have been like to arrive here in my twenties. It was good, it was very good, to see those boys and young men getting something, having something. They were overdoing it, but human beings, especially young men always do: it's their nature. If they hadn't been overdoing it, they wouldn't really have been doing it at all. Anyone who doesn't know that is less than alive.

On the steps of my house, someone was sitting with an overnight bag beside him. Paul, come to visit, I saw: good, wonderful! He looked younger and thinner – like his own younger brother. As he saw me and got up, though, he seemed weary. Strangely nervous, too, almost shaky, almost as if we were in the middle of a quarrel and he was afraid I'd make a scene. Perhaps, I thought, he was running from some fight in L.A.

We said hello, hugged. I said something about his taking off weight, appreciably. "It must be stress," he said. That was usually his excuse for putting *on* weight. He explained that he'd flown up on impulse. He'd done that before, though never without getting in touch – of course, he had his own key. "I've been phoning," he said. I was glad to see him, glad to have him visit. We were good friends, best friends, but guardedly, because I knew Paul still hoped for more than I could give him. I'd often told him he ought to move up to San Francisco: it was more his sort of place, although Paul had made a comfortable life inside the L.A. chaos. He believed in his job, teaching adult Hispanics. He was American – at home in this country in a way I could never be, could never quite understand.

It had been a strenuous journey, he admitted: he was extremely tired. You could see that in the way he pulled himself up the stairs. He didn't want a drink: he even looked a little sick when I offered one. We talked for a few minutes about Cathy, then went to

bed – Paul in the guest room, under *The Woman Who Lives in the Sun*. I still imagined
– it seemed to be tacit between us – some kind of emotional disaster had happened in
L.A. which Paul didn't want to talk about.

About three, I woke up, as I often do, and went to the kitchen. Paul's door was open,
and I heard a strange, light voice. For a moment, I wondered if Paul had brought
someone in off the street. It wasn't the voice of Paul talking in his sleep, which he used
to do. I looked in: Paul was looking at me out of hot, hollow eyes. At first I didn't make
out what he was saying or if it was to me. It was, "I'm sorry, Jack. I thought it would let
go, maybe. I thought maybe it was just L.A." I felt his hot forehead, took his pulse. It
was very fast but thin and remote, like news of something very important happening
a long way away. "Foolish," Paul was saying, half to himself, "But I've noticed it affects
your thinking." It – the way he said "it" was the strangest thing of all, as if he'd been
thinking only of it for days. As if it stood over him, a towering fever god, and he lay flat
on his back at its feet.

I was frightened. I hadn't seen or touched high fever since Cathy was little. I wanted
to go straight to the hospital. But Paul said there was no need, it came and went. And
after a while the fever broke, and Paul started pouring sweat as if he wanted to get rid
of all the water inside him. He kept shivering and saying he was sorry, humiliated by
his weakness, by the sweat drenching the sheets. "I shouldn't be here, Jack, I know. Oh
God, what a mess."

In the morning, he was very tired, but not actively sick. In the light you saw grayish
pallor. Paul said the fevers came in the night and they'd been coming on and off, for
several weeks. He'd made an appointment with this doctor, for the day before he'd
come to San Francisco. He'd set out for the doctor's feeling sick, aching and nauseous,
and "Somehow, I had a kind of horror of him. I got in a panic, it seemed like I'd never
trusted him, that I couldn't stand him." He went into a phone booth to phone some
friends, two gay women, not knowing what he was going to say. They weren't home.
He phoned me, but I was out too. But that made him think of coming up here.
"Maybe it was something in the air, pollution. Or maybe just travelling would shake it
off. Maybe it was some kind of psychological thing." He'd gone home, packed the bag,
taken a taxi to the airport, flown up here standby. When he phoned from the airport, I
was still out. He took a taxi to my house, almost let himself in, then sat on the steps to
wait for me. He felt guilty about coming: in a way that was part of the sickness. "I know
it can't be catching, Jack, really – no one else has anything like this."

I was a little worried about catching it, of course, but not seriously. No one dies of
fever anymore – this whole night scene was like something out of the past, before
antibiotics. Out of your childhood and history books: Florence Nightingale, Typhoid
Mary, a kind of dark, hollow-eyed romance we couldn't really understand anymore.

I phoned my doctor, Tom Nielsen, who's gay and has a mostly gay practice. We
were lucky and got in that day. He explored glands, took blood samples, urine. He
couldn't tell Paul what it was, he said, but told him to rest for a week. And he warned

me to be careful about hygiene, in case it was something catching. He asked if we were lovers. "Not for a long, long time," Paul said. "Well, anyway, Paul," he said, "no sex till I see you again, okay? I'm sorry. You probably don't really feel like it anyway."

During that week, Paul seemed to be getting better: the fevers weren't as high, the nightsweats were less. When we went back, Tom said that he still didn't know what Paul had, but there were some unusual readings from the blood tests. He wanted to do more tests, just to be sure.

I suppose we could have chosen to be worried. I remember thinking of GRID, not as something Paul could have, just as a sign that sometimes terrible things could actually happen. Two years ago someone I knew had died – actually died, at twenty-two of hepatitis-B. I wrote about meeting him in the baths in a letter, a kid from Ohio. And his death was unusual, unbelievable, tragic, terrible bad luck. As for Paul, he was tired of being sick, grateful he was getting better.

But of course we were worried when Tom's receptionist phoned to make an appointment for a third visit. We walked over. Paul was that strong. Tom came in, smiling, shaking hands. He's a tall, thin long-faced man with corn-silk hair. He's from somewhere on the prairies. I forget where. A bit younger than us: mid-thirties. He said that the tests were back, and that some of the blood readings still weren't quite normal. In particular, he'd done a T-cell ratio, and the ratio was down. The T-cell ratio is the closest thing there is to a test for pre-AIDS. I understood, suddenly, not believing it. "What does that mean?" Paul asked. I was looking at him as if he was smaller, farther away, hoping it was just my fear, my old distrust of the world.

"Well – " Tom said, about to explain. And Paul said, quickly, with a laugh, to ward it off, make it impossible, "It doesn't have anything to do with this gay thing does it, GRID?"

I don't remember exactly what Tom said, just my shock at realizing he was saying yes. He was explaining that Paul showed no signs of the diseases that are the markers of GRID, or AIDS, as it was starting to be called. But Paul might have something like a milder form of the real disease that underlies all the others. The signs were the T-cell ratio, the swollen lymph nodes, the period of fevers and sweats he'd been through. Paul was probably fighting off whatever the real disease was. Because it was pretty clear by then that there was some specific communicable disease, and a lot of people were passing it along without getting it themselves. And Tom had patients like Paul who felt quite sick but never got what was called AIDS – never got KS or pneumocystis or other really serious things. What Paul had was being called ARC, AIDS-related complex, though Tom didn't like the term very much.

"But," Tom said, "though you are almost certainly getting better, some people with ARC, a small proportion, do get AIDS."

"A small proportion?" Paul said. "How small?"

"It's too soon to say exactly. Five percent, ten percent."

Paul looked at me with a kind of smile, floating over shock. As if saying the odds weren't that bad. But five minutes ago he hadn't been bargaining for his life.

"But the important thing is you're fighting it off, the virus, whatever it is, right now. You've got to take care of yourself, to do everything to help yourself win."

There was silence, Paul looking like a good student absorbing his lesson so far, but no doubt just stunned, as I was. I looked at Tom when he didn't see I was looking, and understood that he'd seen more than a few patients with AIDS already. He gave me an appealing look: he needed help with Paul. Later on we heard about a gay man who tried to kill himself after his doctor had told him that he did not have AIDS or even ARC. He shot himself, through the mouth, and survived – a very lucky man, obviously. He said the thought that he could have had AIDS had been too much, he could not bear it, he couldn't put up with it. I can understand, and so, I suspect, can you. For a lot of people here what's happening isn't part of the world they've been living in. It just pushes all that aside. It's the fear, seizing you, the *knowledge* that the straights were right after all, that the gay self you thought you had put together and got living happily – it felt like happiness, didn't it? – was illusion, was false. I remember a straight friend, that is I thought he was a friend, back in Toronto, losing his temper and saying, "I've put up with this gay stuff for years now, but we both know that it's all just crap, don't we?" For some people, AIDS is reality saying that.

"So what makes the difference?" Paul said. "Why some and not others?" Poor Paul: *Why me, if I get it? Or if I don't? What is it about ME?*

No one knew. There were dozens of theories – hundreds probably. "But it's all so new." I can still hear Tom saying *new*. For a moment, he wasn't a doctor, he was scared, awed. On the whole, Paul and I liked having a doctor who was gay and feeling and afraid of death, who didn't brandish it the way other doctors we met later did – as if they owned it. Some people want the cold, white-coated gaze that goes right through your body, our life, but we didn't. Later on, there were doctors like that who may have done Paul some good – who tried, if only because saving Paul's life would have been like a hole-in-one, but thank God Tom wasn't one of them. Of course we both fell in love with our doctor: it was inevitable, love coming out of terror, helplessness. Tom was great, though how he'll get through what will happen if the numbers go on as they are, I don't know.

Anyway his advice was sensible stuff, just right for Paul. We were all from the prairies, remember, we know how cold the world can get. Avoid all drugs which Paul did anyway, partly because of his asthma. Eat well: a balanced diet, vitamin pills if you liked, nothing extreme. People can do crazy, desperate things. One of the men with AIDS Paul knew had spent a welfare cheque on vitamins and given himself Vitamin A poisoning. Tom didn't prescribe any preventative drugs: they might do more harm than good.

But then he told us what to watch for, "just in case." The purple lesions of KS, the dry cough of PCP, thrush, diarrhea. "Don't get anxious about it, please," Tom said. "It's not going to happen, this is just – in case."

"And as for sex – " he went on.

"Oh that doesn't matter!" Paul said. "Not these days."

"But Jack ought to know this too. We all do now."

Of course I'd heard it before, but I couldn't believe it. Sex had to leave the dear ocean that was its home, it had to live or die on dry land, in the desert. And me without a lover, I thought, and how could I ever find one now, groping through all that fear and fuss and wretchedness? It was selfish to think like this with Paul sick, but it seemed that if Tom was right – sex was dying cruelly, miserably.

"But does anybody really do all that?" I said, incredulous, sarcastic. How much did he think he could ask?

"Well, I do," Tom said, almost angrily. "And the sooner we all do, the fewer of us will – *Paul was there* – get sick."

I thought, how many? How many will that be? And I saw Tom had been asking himself this question, in terms of his practice, his friends. I think, though I'm guessing here, that Paul was realizing that perhaps the future he thought he'd only been afraid of, was going to go ahead and happen anyway.

Walking home, Paul was quiet. Then he said, "Well, I've got my work cut out for me." Work: a favourite word of his. He wasn't like the people who see ARC or AIDS as a challenge to be dealt with by some brand or other of positive thinking. Paul was forty, intelligent, a realist. We adopted a sort of deliberate optimism. There was no question of Paul's actually getting it, but everything we did was based on the possibility he could: Paul resting, taking it easy, avoiding crowded places, eating well. He managed to get a leave of absence from the school where he taught, to stay with me. Like most people in his condition, he took pleasure in being able to be good to himself, as if it was really all his own idea. For some, it's as if all their lives they'd been mistreating their bodies, and now there's a joyful reconciliation: together at last! Of course, Paul always had been careful about his health, because of his asthma and his allergies, and fortunately this had meant buying good medical insurance. And of course, he always took pleasure in looking after people – even himself, once the rest of us were sitting around fed and smiling.

One of the many good things about Tom was his refusal to entertain much speculation about the causes of ARC and AIDS. There might be contributing factors, he said, but the cause was some communicable agent, like a virus: it was a disease like any other. Between us, Paul and I had the sense to fight off the psychological or life-style theories on our own. They could have darkened things, if Paul had had a doctor who was pushing one of them. And even when they aren't explicitly anti-gay, they let a lot of guilt and self-hatred creep in. For instance, "*being gay is a stress in and of itself.*"

But I admit to weak moments when I was depressed, in shock. And one theory or another of the dozens floating around would come and seize me. I didn't believe it exactly, but I feared it so lucidly, so intently, that the fear was like belief. Paul was somehow sick because he was gay. And the whole experiment – Paul and I in the Indian cotton, Stonewall – was a failure, a dead end. I'd remember the feeling, the flavour even, of being alone in the sixties – alone, and reading some book or article by some Fascist Freudian on homosexuality. Dr. X would put his refusal to see me as human right at the centre of his theory, right in my soul. And reading as if at last I'd found that one book that opened onto my world, I'd feel my emptiness and his inhumanity come together, lock together: being gay, being Jack Durham *was* being loveless, lifeless, hopeless—and suicidal, why not? And now all those theories are back: forget about viruses, gays are dying because they can't live, can't connect with life. Paul didn't quite fit the pattern of the gay man, addicted to sex, with thousands of partners – but by their nature those theories are infinitely adjustable. You could think that perhaps Paul was sick of all the people he didn't go home with: loneliness, frustration, guilt had worn down his immune system.

I would shake off the feeling, go and find Paul in the back yard, reading Doris Lessing or Virginia Woolf's diaries. For all the theories, I had human eyes to see that he was human too. And I'd feel ashamed of myself.

We'd try to separate real medical news out of the evil nonsense. At this point, with Paul looking better and stronger, you could almost forget at times that it wasn't merely a fascinating puzzle, a murder mystery with hundreds of bodies. You could understand the researchers' careerist fascination: they'd been given a completely new disease, a new world of 'rare' diseases – rare and precious, lesions like rubies. I got caught up in it, too. It would seem the pattern was right there, and I could be the one to figure it out. What did Africa have to do with it, and Haiti? Was Paul sick of some African fever – "Oh God, like *Heart of Darkness*?" he said. "I never liked that book."

We didn't quite explain when you were here, but it was during this period that Paul and I became lovers again. With Tom's approval, following his guidelines like a recipe from Julia Child, making love like good burglars, without leaving traces. It happened because it was the obvious thing to do. The only thing we could do, really, old lovers with the threat of death in the house. Perhaps you'll say we were scared into love and sex, that the fear of death swept us off of our feet – you will see that happening, even in Toronto. But it didn't feel like that, not all the time. It was more that the situation dissolved a lot of reservations on both sides. It made me see Paul differently – it forced me to be more what Paul saw in me. I really admired, loved, wanted the Paul you saw now that he was up against it, the combined courage and fear and fussiness and good sense he brought to the struggle.

And, though it's hard to remember now, we weren't really afraid of death, or thought we weren't. It was a joke, when we looked each other over for the skin blemishes that could mean KS, cancer: we agreed I would never have to say, "Well, actually, Paul, there is something here on your back..." But it couldn't be sex like before – whatever that was. We weren't play-warriors, capturing, conquering, play-killing each other. We had to be realistic: the toy guns could kill. Imagine: Paul's fat, sweet, teddy-bear cock could kill you – and, who knows, perhaps I had the same problem: I could push him over into 'frank, full-blown AIDS.' I see now that there were still macho fantasies in our sex – we were defying death, taunting it. And I was making up for the guilt I'd felt for leaving Paul, for being the more loved of the two. I wasn't being irresponsible anymore: I was proving how serious I was. And there was a kind of possessive pride, too: Paul was like my child, and I was going to nurse him through to a new life. As well, we were both grabbing at an opportunity to be serious, to be honest. The gay styles – or rather, this shitty Reaganite time zone we're stuck in – give you so many ways not to be – but now we could say *this is real, this is real love*. Paul's condition was saying, *you're both forty, you know you're not immortal, it's time to make up your minds, head for the centre of things, be serious at last*. The story was going to be that Paul's T-cell ratio would hit some kind of bottom and turn around. Love, good food, hope, a new fortyish openness to life, would coax the T-helper cells back from wherever they had gone and then we would be together for good, for the rest of our lives. Irregularly, I suppose, messily, because we knew the good-looking men wouldn't disappear but whatever happened, it would all be put in its place by the struggle we were in now. This would be our testing period, our heroic age, intense enough to build the rest of our lives on. Everyone needs a story.

When Paul began coughing, a dry cough without a cold, without a reason, we couldn't believe it. We didn't quite hear it at first. Then, frantically pretending not to panic, we phoned Tom and went over to see him.

Paul's first stay in the hospital seems like something easy now, a trial run. When I was with him or with Tom, I was rational enough. In shock: Paul had AIDS, that name staring, shouting insanely at you everywhere now – as if it knew exactly what it meant, and knew that nobody else did. But he still wasn't going to die of it. He'd pull through now, and then we'd figure out how to attack the underlying problem. But I'd be different. I felt tricked. When I'd let myself fear before, I'd feared things you could see, KS or thrush or yeast infections. While it had been spreading deep inside, painless, invisible. We'd failed – I'd failed: I'd been trying to send love deep inside Paul, to radiate it down to wherever the decision was taken, in the bone marrow or the thymus gland. The love I'd given hadn't been good enough. AIDS had been stronger, deeper, more serious.

Away from Paul, or on my way to him through the hospital – God, that *straight* place, that bloody temple of straightness—stories would float around me about the savagery to AIDS patients: people abandoned, left unfed, wallowing in shit, not given the drugs they needed, called faggot, told they deserved to die. What were we doing here, I'd think. What was going on behind the masks? When a nurse thrust in a needle, did the thrust mean *live* or *die, you queer*? Which were the ones who thought the real disease was being gay, the treatment was death?

Paul got reasonably good care, thanks to Tom. Sometimes I would find his food left outside and take it in. He had the advantage that he didn't look horribly sick: he didn't look gay. He still reminded people of a favourite school teacher. He talked Spanish with the Hispanic nurses and orderlies, when they had the courage to be talked to.

And Tom is well-liked and has some authority, though you realized how the hierarchy of the place towered above us when specialists came down from on high to have a look at Paul.

I suppose all this was a way of avoiding the real fear. That the pneumocystis would not be stopped, his lungs would dry up inside him and he'd have to do an impossible thing – reach for nothingness, grab for it. And get it, hold it deep inside himself, be it. I tried to make up formulas like this: they'd work for a second, get the fear, the impossibility, then just become words. I'd wonder if Paul had known it all, unconsciously, in his bones, in his blood, when he sat on my doorstep, afraid to let himself in, waiting to be invited. Had he chosen to bring me his death? If he had, he'd made a terrible choice. I had no idea what to do – what to say or feel, how to conduct myself. I don't think I've ever said much about my parents, but I didn't have Paul's deathbed experiences. Mine both died over the phone. With Paul, I could only imagine speechless, abject shame. You're dying, and I have nothing I can say about it.

In fact, the drugs, along with whatever Paul had of an immune system, killed the parasites in his lungs. Most of them anyway. When he came home, you could see how he was changed. In bed, with *The Woman Who Lives in The Sun* smiling wickedly down on him, he was thinner, quieter, more inward. He was back to the sort of holiday life he'd been living before, picking up Virginia's diaries where he'd left off, somewhere in the twenties. As he got stronger, he seemed to be developing – so we both did, it became the house religion – a kind of cult of the moment, a sort of middle-aged hedonism. The world had been given back, but not securely – Paul's grip was literally weaker. It was partly that he had less energy to fill out his movements, to push himself into the next moment. He had to linger over himself, trying to weave himself back together. And he did, on the surface anyway: he still had resources, he still had some of the subtle stuff you call health. He began to get stronger, though perhaps it was more a question of directing what strength he had in the right way. He was looking good, and you could forget his life was up in the air.

We began having sex again, one afternoon. At my suggestion. Paul said, as if he'd been expecting it, "But are you sure? You've got to be sure, Jack, or I won't." He was afraid I was being blackmailed by his sickness. But I wasn't merely trying to be generous, courageous – I wanted what we had, and sex was an essential part of that still. It was the only way to hold Paul, to tell him that he wasn't supposed to believe the doctors and the papers and the TV, that he wasn't supposed to die.

I remember that first night, lying beside Paul. Someone was running along the street, shouting, "Hey, wait up, you jerk, I love you." I could hear Paul's heart, the usual rush of blood, and inside it, the T-4 cells fighting for life, fighting and dying silently. *Hey, wait up, because my voice can put all these sweet edges on life – can fill streets with them*! In dying the way Paul did, anyway, slowly, without neurological symptoms you come closer and closer to yourself, to the particular person you are, to what is going to die. So do the people around.

But outside, beyond, AIDS was beginning to get more and more attention in the media. I know you read the gay newspapers, you watch the news, American and Canadian, but as you saw when you were here, it's different when you're surrounded. When you can turn on the television to see them dreaming our deaths. "It's like a snuff movie!" Paul said, once, and he was right: they're eager to watch people dying of sex, if they feel safe themselves. Sometimes I'd think I should stop reading the newspapers and get rid of the television set. But we couldn't have done that: we had to know all the news, though it was mostly false. We had to know what they were up to. It was fighting AIDS. Getting outraged and frightened and depressed is struggling. It feels as if it makes a difference.

"It's just amazing," one specialist said on a local news program, smiling – not smiling broadly, but cheerful. "There's never been anything like it. They disintegrate. They just fall apart."

They.

"One of our cases had internal KS lesions all the way from his anus to his mouth. And there are some really interesting brain lesions too. We're getting psychiatric onsets, classic dementia. One of our guys we had to strap down – seems he couldn't stand the colour in his room!"

I'd gone and put my arms around Paul, who was frozen, eyes wide open. *They*: it pushed us to the brink of the world, over it.

We'd sit looking at our catastrophe on television – seeing how TV's cold, flat corporate eye turned the crowd on us. The straight world was right beside us, inside us, we'd try to understand what they were thinking, what judgement they were forming. It looked as if gays had become bored with their new freedom, and traded that freedom for the old desperate, self-pitying carnival, which now in the eighties could be shared by T.V. Once again we're doomed and sick, just like in the fifties – sick but camping it up, making it into tacky tragedy. Suddenly, the clowns have become hunger artists. Political gays who want to get something done – to warn people, to get money for research, just look hopelessly out of date. As if, politically, gays are fucked. Dead without knowing it yet, because either we all already have it, or we won't be able to help ourselves from getting it. There'll be shots of gay men in the streets, saying no, they aren't going to change, it won't spoil their party. And you feel, from TV producers, a kind of gloating, an affection of hatred for these people for being such good, such easy television. Then the camera goes on to show what awaits these fools: polymorphous death, the purple stigmata of KS, the savage wasting – not *Camille* or *Traviata*, Belsen. At Shanti, they get more calls from the media than from real people. And what they want are the gruesome cases: they will track down people in the final stages. "You want publicity, don't you? You *need* publicity."

On one program, while Paul was in the hospital, a man with AIDS was being interviewed. Twenty-five, looking almost healthy, but thin, with a dull, gray shine. He talked about how he was going to defeat it, how carefully he lived. "I have no intention of dying," he said, looking into the camera. Hoping, you could tell, that this declaration made his chances more real.

Usually they send women to interview gay men, but this time it was a young man, built like a football player, with a sort of burly liberalism.

"But with the figures?" he said. "Aren't you being unrealistic?"

The gay man's eyes went wide, as if to say, what do you want? But they'd got tired of gay men bravely declaring they were going to fight and live. That was last month.

"I know it's serious, but I've got a chance. I'm doing everything I should."

"But look at the figures. You've had it over a year, and the two-year figure is close to one hundred percent death."

The camera stared into the gay man's eyes, for the moment when he would give in, agree, accept. Take it. *What do you want? To see you die, of course.* I blinked before the moment came, if it did. Not in pity or shame: in pure fear. God is dead: everything is permitted, everything is television.

The gay man said, desperately, "There's got to be a first time, doesn't there?" Something everyone with AIDS, including Paul, has to hope. Has to, being human, until 'the figures' close over them. They cut to an oncologist.

Sometimes, I could feel them as if they sat inside me, the TV viewers, the newspaper readers, considering their verdict. It can feel like an unspoken trial, where some of the executions are being carried out already. In Texas, I think it is, they want to televise the electric chair – transmit the moment of death, while the crowd in the living room leans forward, breathes it in, says *yes, yes*. Do we deserve to die? Talk shows discuss this question.

For a lot of people, of course, the answer is obvious. For some it's God's justice, and gay men lie dying under that, believing it: this death, *every bit of it*, comes from God. The government shouldn't get in God's way by funding research. Not that the government needs the Gods' advice to know how to use AIDS. For the right, it can be a chance to make America 'conservative' forever. We've gone against nature – the banal American nature of the fifties, built on the bomb and Hitler's mistakes. We've defied it and proved it. At times, I would take a kind of grim satisfaction in what was going on. For years, straight friends had been saying, 'Why fuss about rights? You're not badly off!' Now 'the right' (as if there was a left) were taking our deaths and using them, meaning them, willing them. They are giving them the meaning of political mass murder. We'd performed a kind of service in showing they were Fascists: their joy over AIDS had surprised it out of them before their *putsch* was ready. But it seemed a lot of people were waiting. The liberal America I'd loved, that I'd imagined in my nostrils, deep inside me, when I first came here to be charitable, it seemed to have stepped back, to be resting or recovering after the debacle of 1980. Waiting to see what would happen to us, thinking perhaps that a lot of gays may not be voting in the next election, that the whole embarrassment of gay rights will die away. It might make sense to hold off a little, wait and see where your principles might take you. What if the cause of

AIDS turns out to be just too scandalous, too obscene? Who knows where you are with these people, after all? And what can they expect? Now, while the liberals consult their principles, the police here arm themselves with masks and gloves, to tell the world what we really are.

Paul was more patient with it all than I was, partly because he was brought up with the extremes of American politics. Canadians may wish you dead – but they won't shout it in the street. I thought I'd got used to it, but I saw I hadn't when I was face to face with it. With this bestial shadow-America, I'd say, raging: America has the chosen people, with its own shimmering desert not far from here, its own covenant burned into the sky at Los Alamos and Hiroshima.

"But what good does that do, Jack?" Paul said once, when I was going on like this. Before his diagnosis: after that, of course I protected Paul from my anger.

"It makes me feel better, Paul. I'm mad at these people of yours."

"It would be just as bad elsewhere, Jack, or worse."

"Oh? Really. Maybe provincials like me are the last people who believe in America, Paulie," I said, furiously. "Huck Finn and Abe Lincoln – it wasn't for us up in the frozen north, but we believed that down here, there was something really happening."

Paul shrugged. "I haven't given up yet, Jack. And neither have you."

After a few weeks, Paul began to get restless. He wasn't feeling well, exactly, but he had no infections. He said he wanted to be doing something. He thought of getting some kind of easy work, to keep himself occupied. But then, almost on a whim, it seemed to me, he phoned to the Shanti project and went, that evening, to a group of people with AIDS. I didn't say it, but it must have been obvious I didn't want him to go. "It's just to see," he said. I thought he wanted hope, inspiration – and maybe knowledge, because who knows, perhaps there is some cure too simple for the doctors to believe?

He came back "in a different space," as he put it, datedly: he had a new intensity, a glow of hope. It wasn't because of any cure or treatment he'd learned about. He said he was glad he'd gone, though some things had been "Pretty terrible. Terrible." One member had bad, spreading KS for instance: Paul's face wrinkled in bewilderment. And people had talked about being fired, thrown out, not having money for treatments they thought would save them, being told by their families, "you made your choice."

The person he kept coming back to was the other new member. "A young guy named Ray, who just got his diagnosis. He looked healthier than I've ever been he's a body-builder, a hot man." Paul said this a little shyly, obviously taken with him. "And he was furious, seething. He was mad at us, as if we'd kidnapped him. But that was good to see: he's a fighter, he'll shake us up. Because a lot of people are depressed, really depressed."

I could feel an intention forming in Paul, but I didn't understand it yet. Going had been like coming out, he said. AIDS had been something you were alone with – "I'm sorry Jack, but it's true." – and then you saw there were others. People who shared it, who could understand.

"Do I have to get it to understand, Paul?"

Paul just gave me a long, rocking hug, while I tried to feel what was going on inside him.

He began visiting some of the group members – some of whom lived alone, in single rooms, hardly ever seeing anyone. San Francisco gay men weren't all rich professionals, and some of the rich professionals were made destitute too. He went to the next meeting, and came back looking very different. Ray hadn't come in: Paul had thought, disappointed, that he'd given up the group. Then a member who knew him came, looking shocked. He'd come from the intensive care, where Ray was on the respirator, with a tube down his throat. "I told him I was coming here, and I think he understood, I think he gave my hand a little squeeze."

Because anything can happen with AIDS, anything.

Someone said, "Maybe he's lucky. Maybe that's the best way." Ray's friend started screaming: there was a terrible shouting, wailing, tearing fight. With Paul not taking either side, soothing a man with tears running through the lesions – broken apart, understanding both sides.

I had to ask whether he really needed that. The stress of it must be wearing down his health, aside from the things he could catch. If Paul wanted to do something, why didn't we travel – go to Canada, to Vancouver, perhaps? I could easily get away from the store for a month or two.

But Paul's determination was only getting harder, grimmer. He—we – forgot the hedonism of before: it would be betraying Ray and everyone with AIDS. "I've got some real health, I can help."

"It's that damn church basement morality of yours, Paulie," I said. "You never got away from it. Why don't you think of yourself? There are other people who can help."

Paul just shrugged, somehow evoking Ray, who was suffocating while we talked.

"Things have changed a lot since then, haven't they? Who would ever have thought of this?"

For a while, Paul's work was a sort of vocation. You didn't see much of his group while you were here, because by then his strength had declined, he'd gone into another phase, psychologically. People from the group would come around the house. Or Paul and I would visit them in wretched little rooms or expensive apartments. Or in the hospital. Sometimes we would put people up in the apartment below ours. Paul was older than most of the people he took an interest in, and he became a sort of father figure to them. It was his school-teacher's instinct, to organize and educate and be patient. I admired this in Paul, very much, but I was terrified of where it was taking him. More and more we seemed to be in a world where AIDS was the only thing that mattered. At times, it seemed like a secret society, a blood brotherhood – even a new religion, small, underground, but growing, knowing its time was coming.

One day, just after Paul's second group meeting, I came home and met someone at the door, come to visit Paul. Terry: a tall man about our age, dressed in jeans and a Western shirt and stitched leather boots. He walked as if he had been riding all day, going up the stairs with macho stiffness. In the kitchen he began talking to Paul about his treatments. They seemed to be helping, at least he thought they were. And he pushed back the sleeve of his shirt. His arm was covered with KS: it seemed to be more stagnant, swollen blood than skin. I couldn't not stare. "You've never seen it before?" he said. I just shook my head, guiltily, though in fact I had. "It won't be the last time," he said, in a sort of brotherly or fatherly way: I was being initiated. Then he looked himself, as if seeing, perhaps, that the treatments really weren't helping. "There it is," he said, "and I still can't believe it." He looked back at me, with a funny kind of hope. As if I might be able to blink and wipe it all away: my disbelief, the old, safe world I still had, could say 'no, it's a bad dream.' But I could only feel a horrible, miserable pity: you wanted to apologize for being alive, for being determined to live, whatever happened to others. The life you clutched could do this to people. And then I felt a kind of anger from him. He seemed to hold the arm, to wield it, as if he wanted me to be shocked enough to gratify him somehow. The lesions were trophies, battle scars: they were his strength. I understood, but what I felt was a kind of weak resentment and turned away. Why was he doing this to me, to Paul?

I felt angry and guilty because I was angry with a dying man, guilty since I had no intention of dying myself, if I could help it. But I understood, too. What a strange fate, after all, to have to pioneer a new way of dying, to have disaster coming through you out of nowhere, while everyone watches. The unbearable strangeness of it. Paul never knew what he died of, what would happen, if the world would survive, or if it was really nothing in the end, a few thousand deaths, then relief: 'We're alive, thank God,' and forgetting. And the responsibilities – because gay men with AIDS are like our soldiers, like prisoners of war. At first it was their duty to escape, to get better and frustrate the people calling for their deaths. More and more, it's to die bravely. I heard one man with AIDS in his early twenties say that maybe it's a good thing, "Because at last we can show the world that we can do it, that we aren't weaklings." They aren't supposed to break down under torture, to give in and say yes, it's their fault, that they wish they hadn't been gay. Though every man with AIDS must think about that at times – Paul did, and talked about it. He could imagine having kept it secret all his life: getting married, having children. He would have been a wonderful, heart-breaking father: you could see that when he was with Cathy. There is, we all know, a place in the heart that it takes a hard prick to get to, but there are other things in life than that part of the heart, too, and Paul was good at them.

I was drawn into their world – hypnotized by it, seized by it. The rumours about treatments, the stories of strange, grotesque deaths, the medical terms, it all had its own light, like the horrible sticky colour of medical photographs. I was in over my head, with nothing under me. Because "with AIDS, everything is possible," as Nick, a friend of Paul's with AIDS, told me once.

He was about thirty-five, gaunt and rough-skinned with dark, bulging eyes. "Don't worry," he said, when I met him, "I always looked this way." When Nicholas was in the room, nothing else could be talked about. He would bring stories, rumours, deathbed statements, and deliver them in a blank, commanding way – a messenger from AIDS, a prophet. For instance, AIDS isn't rare at all, that is all bullshit: there are thousands of cases, tens of thousands, far more than CDC Atlanta will admit to. Really, AIDS is sweeping the world: ravaging Haiti, Cuba, all the Caribbean, it's all through Africa. It is devastating the Pacific Rim and Asia, destroying needle pushers, heterosexuals, women, babies. It might have been there in the jungle for centuries, and no one knew. For centuries, it could have been wiping out whole tribes at once, so no one on the outside would ever even know.

Paul knew better than to argue with him, but I couldn't help it. I wanted hope, not doom – not "whole tribes" – and also I wanted to hear more, I couldn't get enough. He didn't like to be argued with: he was a zealot, an Ayatollah. He seemed proud of his catastrophe, of the torture-God he served, death in its most majestic shape. "I'm going to die," he said once, looking right at me, and I was glad it was me and not Paul. "Maybe there'll be a cure someday, but I'm not fooling myself." And suddenly I was on the side of all the people who were fooling themselves, who were going to save their lives with brown rice or pumpkin seeds. Who were going to image KS or lymphoma away – image their old bodies back. Who wanted to live, foolishly, foolishly, whatever Nick said.

If you hear the resentment in this – well, he was horrifying. At other times I was a disciple. I sat at his feet. He'd look at me with those eyes and see something that had been in me always, an appetite for disaster, for death. But the resentment is real. I'm still angry at the world – it can't be at Paul, can it? – for his using his, our period of more or less good health the way he did. He didn't have to be a hero. Other people in that state try to forget AIDS, to live normally, ordinarily, as long as they can.

During this period, he looked more and more taut, even steely in a way – as if his bones were his hard will coming through. I began to feel he was somehow determined to get to the bottom of what was happening, not the biology or the politics, but simply the grief of it. He was trying to see how terrible it was, to take it all in. Death really does have its own domain, with its own space, its own unliving light, its own images—where corpses are inhabitants, citizens, where you see that corpses are the only real people. That isn't a myth. It's a fact. Some deep region of our brain we use for peering through to death, for trying to find the way out of life.

Anyway, it wasn't hard for Paul to see that something was wrong. So he was made to say, "If I do die, Jack, and I *haven't* given up, is that really so terrible in the end?"

Yes, Paul, it is. At times, to get away, or to spare Paul a bad mood, I'd go out into what felt more and more like a city under siege. Some men would still announce that there was no epidemic, "as far as I'm concerned," and another had killed himself because he mistook some minor blemish for KS. That last story is a rumour, but in a siege, rumours are living beings, more alive, more potent, than the miserable populace. They breathe up our fear, they thrive on it. So you hear about someone with AIDS fucking in the darkness of a backroom bar, saying, "If they get sick, it's their business. This is a free country." And you can't help believing it, because the story grabs the blackness of our situation, puts it right in front of you. People can't resist rumours like that. For example: the CIA did it. They went to the baths one night with needles and the virus, fresh from some government lab, found people asleep, drunk, drugged, too busy screwing to notice. "I saw it," someone says. "I saw those turkeys with needles: they had to be cops." I would try to argue, desperately trying to stay reasonable – not for the honour of the CIA, but to fight off the paralyzing fatalism. They've decided to wipe us out – we can't stop them – see you in the concentration camp!

Then I'd find myself on the other side, turned right around by some comfortable person saying, "That's foolish, nothing like that can happen here." Meaning camps, mass murder, genocide. And I would say, why not? If people with AIDS deserve it for being gay, then everyone who is gay deserves death: it's logic. Do you really think your good will, your kind heart, your moral courage run this country? Do you think you can face Hitler when he comes again? Do you know who you will be when you see him?"

But there were times when you couldn't argue. When Paul was in the hospital for the last time, I met someone with AIDS at some friends' house up the street. He told us he'd come to understand what was really happening. AIDS came out of all the psychic stress we'd taken on since Stonewall, the stress of coming out and being hated. It is a deep hunger for acceptance, a cry to the straights to love us. All over the country, certain gay men are somehow choosing themselves to get sick and send up this moral cry to our fellow humans to stop the hatred.

There are times when you think nothing is more horrible than the consolations. There was a long, awed silence. He had cryptosporidiosis: intestinal parasites that cause endless diarrhea. He was skin and bones, mostly bones. It looked as though his skeleton was terribly lonely and wanted to step out and join us. His eyes were pale and glittery, as if he'd been out in the desert sunshine all his life, hundreds of years. He was a fool, I thought. I saw he was holy too, in the way he'd transcended everything. He had taken everything, his suffering, his humiliation, his life turning into a river of shit, and given it all a shining, foolish transcendent sense. He was as foolish as a presidential smile and sacred in a way you could almost touch.

In that awed hush you couldn't argue and still I wanted to protest. "No, it's a virus, and a doctor in Paris has found it. You are dying of LAV, that is all. Your death means nothing, except bad luck." But of course I was silent too.

At the beginning of the summer, Paul was getting worse. He was thinner, and it was harder and harder to get him to eat. He would get bruises without bumping into things and they wouldn't heal. He began to develop yeast infections, little frothing glimpses into the mysteries inside him. But for a while he seemed to be getting more and more determined, as if he really could die in harness – drop on his way from the ICU or on the stairs up to some desperate small room.

I couldn't talk to him and I would get into states of dread and rage, going out to protect Paul and myself. Anger is like a kind of happiness, once you've forgotten the real thing. I would go through the city, guessing at the thoughts behind the faces, trying to see or smell through to the hidden crowd, the single faceless beast they could all become. What could we expect? People with AIDS were being thrown onto the streets. Gays in the streets are being attacked and beaten, and the cry now is AIDS. The police put on their gloves and masks, to redefine us – to tell everyone we are untouchables, vermin, and to make the next steps thinkable, feasible. And whatever the next steps are, closing baths or bars, individual quarantines, they will be to make steps afterwards thinkable, possible, not unreasonable. What could we expect? It was just the way I had always been hearkening to them, trying to see through the politeness or the expert authority or the logic – to what they *really* were. To what they really thought about the queer tilt we gave to their world. Sometimes I'd think that no one had ever understood them, the human crowd: either you are part of it or outside of it, either way you are insane. Whatever was going to happen, no reason and no paranoia could see through to it. All you could do was hold in your fear as long as possible – your fear which was their hope, their life, the breath in their nostrils. Now they've started showing pictures of children with AIDS, staring out with African eyes. We're killing children, and all the grown-up, unwanted, battered children, all the smiley Jesus-loves-me types – back to poor old unwanted Jesus himself – can try to get their revenge. *Children* – so even liberals can let go, and be free of us. What can we expect? *History*.

I'd go along thinking I wouldn't mind, that I would be happy to see it fall apart: I wouldn't mind being gassed to give this country its own holocaust, to let this fake, second-hand civilization get back to its real barbarism. Then I met a young man in a bar who said that he was going on with sex as before, and if he got AIDS he'd just buy a gun, an automatic pistol maybe, and go and blow away as many policemen as he could before they got him. "They shot Harvey, didn't they?"

He wasn't serious, but AIDS could have made him serious. I had to argue. Harvey wouldn't approve. Stay alive: we need you. And most of all, they would love it. They could give the dead policemen a state funeral and turn the Castro Valley into Beirut.

So, after all, I want the democratic illusions. I want this country to go on being America "whatever that is, Paul," as I said a long time ago in Winnipeg, in my superior northern way. Hoping he'd tell me, give me their secret at last. But he never did.

I stopped writing for a few days. I had to think about what I am really doing. The first time I read through what I'd written it seemed cold and shrunken in comparison with what is really happening. It is all about *ME*, Jack Durham, as healthy as ever, haven't been sick for years. Maybe, I thought, I should do something like what Paul did, in words, tell about all the people Paul and I knew, how they struggled, how they died or are dying, one by one. But I couldn't do that, nobody could.

The next time I read it, two days after, it was like a long scream. Is that what I want? Screaming isn't history: it isn't what happened. And that is what I want to get down and send out of here –twhat is really happening, the shock, the edge of it.

But then, I have to ask, how much of what I'm doing is just cherishing my own private fear? I'm still shaking from seeing how horribly the body desires to live, in spite of everything. There were times when I hated Paul's wretched body for the way it tortured him, when I wanted to kill it. When you see what your own body could do, how mindlessly it could hold on, you want to get up and walk away from it. And there's that other, greater, feelingless fear, of the moment when death reaches in and grabs, grabs you, grabs *this*.

Certainly fear is under everything. The fear that I would have to do what Paul had to do, try to make some kind of death out of all the dying, and then have that smashed too, become something they carry out in a black, zippered bag. All through this I was thinking, *I admire your courage, Paul, I'm in awe of it – but don't tell me where you got it, I don't want to know anything about it.*

And as well there is a kind of mortal chagrin – you'll understand this Bob, David. The whole crisis is like a wound to my pride, our pride: a deadly wound, you can feel the knife twisting. And only people who have never lived without pride, think it isn't essential to life. Here in San Francisco, here in America, after thousands of years, we were going to show that we could live as easily, as vitally, as everyone else. From the viewpoint of a lot of people, I had arrived here late, just before the end of the great days—I didn't even get a chance to say hello to Harvey Milk before they put him out of the way. But I didn't regret not coming sooner. I'm used to it: for me, arriving is arriving late. I didn't seriously envy the handsome boys: I was just deeply, profoundly proud of their living so well, so bravely. I was proud that we could *just live*. And then, with everyone watching, wondering if perhaps, after all, we could bring it off, death marks us out, death starts coming through our skins. The bitterness of having to cut back your pride, your hope. I can almost understand the gays who refuse to see that anything is happening. Like them, I thought I was going to see our freedom at last. Not hope for it, see it with my own bodily eyes. The last, most lost, most scattered tribe of all was going to find itself, know itself at last, here, in my lifetime, before my eyes. I was going to see young gays growing up like human children, noisily, brattily – or in perfect serenity if it suited them. But not in the mutilating silence we knew – the evil, pompous, nightmare silence patrolled by the experts and the law. And now all that is in doubt: now, at the least, it is going to cost infinitely more than we imagined. Now, all over the world, gay children are hearing, "Your heart will kill you: forget it."

That is there all the time, that wound in your pride like a knife being twisted. You rage like an old man – trying to rage away beyond arthritis and impotence – to shake your blood into life, to give your pride a last desperate flicker.

And there is another sin to confess to. At some point, I began to evaluate that Paul's sickness as a kind of opportunity. AIDS was history, was reality, that was clear soon enough. Paul and AIDS were as close as I would get in my life to seeing God, or something like him to seeing history. I was watching Paul covetously, making everything mine, taking it all in, as if anything, even the worst things – if Paul had gone crazy, had broken down, begged to live, begged to be killed – anything could be used somehow, because it would have the reality I wanted. I never quite felt any of this, I never quite hoped this, but a cold, inhuman, careerist ego was taking notes: the shades of KS, the sounds of pneumocystis, all the variegated foolishness of humans wanting to live. It was history, it was real, and I could make it mine. And can, perhaps – because if history is the *only* God left, how do you cut the rottenness out of your heart?

I should have found someone to talk to, obviously. At first, I'd had Paul, who was the sanest person I knew. But he was becoming more inward about certain things about what he finally thought about his death. And I didn't want to burden him, though I couldn't help letting my anger out at times, in bitter flashes. There are groups for people whose lovers have AIDS, but I was never good at groups. I didn't want to belong to people who read books on death and dying and called the desire to live denial. There are no books on death and dying, I would have said, not one. And anyone who breathes in is 'denying.' I would have been on Nicks' side, the side of the dying, on the side of the terror, the horror of their deaths, the grief they tear at us with, which is all they have against us, the living, that smug group.

So it's a good thing I met Jim Fields, the person I did talk to in the end, when it looked as if I might just give up talking. There are other people I might have turned to, I suppose, friends here, people at Shanti. But somehow Jim came from outside of it all.

Maybe Jim has told you how we met. Anyway, it was a few weeks after you left, in that little grocery store down the street. I heard my name, turned, saw Jim, and laughed. He was the same as ever, older, without the teenage glow, but still as handsome, as astonishing. It was like seeing Harvey Milk coming up Castro Street, laughing, clowning, with the cure of AIDS – Jim was that *beautiful*, almost, that impossible. I laughed and thought, you're late for your story. For your world. Because now love was trying to be human with failing resources: it had nothing to do with anyone's looks. Paul had developed herpes zoster – nothing rare and wonderful, just shingles, childhood chickenpox coming back, but it was painful, and frightening. There could be complications: encephalitis, meningitis. One of Paul's friends had died of herpes simplex, in other words a cold sore, eating through his skull, into his brain. You could feel grateful to people for having any face at all – and there was Jim.

At first, I simply didn't know what to do with him, about him, asked questions to put him off. He'd just moved into the neighbourhood, he was living alone, but he had a boyfriend over in Berkeley. They liked having two apartments. He was writing software, especially graphics programs. While I tried to muster courage, he tried to stimulate me by talking about fractal geometry, "something that would interest a philosopher, Jack." It was dizzying: he was talking about the jagged, the infinitely jagged edges of islands and how someone had found a geometry to measure them, while I wondered where to begin. Whether to begin.

We were out on the street before I got it out, staring at him savagely, because I'd seen 'AIDS' wipe years of friendship off a face in a second. He turned white and tried to catch his breath. It seemed incredible to me, but Paul was the first person with AIDS he had any sort of connection with. "Of course, I knew it was going to happen," he said.

After his shock, he was anxious to visit as soon as he could, to help in any way. And he became one of Paul's best friends – playing cards, bringing over the strange images he gets out of his computer. Science fiction landscapes, with the subtle texture of reality. Or "dragons," uncanny, apocalyptic shapes growing out of numbers. Paul would look at them and smile, like an old person delighted the world is still up to new things.

It was good for Paul to have someone who seemed to be from beyond AIDS. It was good for me too. But I could never have talked with him then about what I was feeling. I knew you would understand in your way, but that way was too intuitive for Jim, too angelic. I try to figure it out when I see you sitting at the terminal – intuitive without images, somehow, feeling your way in unseen, barely invented spaces – but really I can't. I suppose I wanted another paranoid gay man with a training in philosophy. Someone my own age, who was a good little boy just when Hitler's bridgework came crashing through into the cyanide capsule. If you were my age, David, perhaps but – we have that decade on each other.

In the last few weeks before Paul went into the hospital for the second time, I knew I needed help, that something was going to happen. But it was almost as if I thought going crazy would help Paul: destroying my mind would confuse the whole world and even death, get it so mixed up it would miss Paul. Once I forgot at the top of the stairs what you do with stairs and simply fell down them, thinking, on the way, 'Interesting: now I'm falling down the stairs. Will I break my neck?' And at the bottom, still alive, 'What a thing to do to Paul.' But I was only a little cut, a bit bruised, I hadn't wakened Paul from his nap, and I lay there among shoes and boots, resting, wondering what I really felt about life. I sat there entertaining myself with the possibility I had lost my balance because the virus was making its way up into my brain – into my thoughts. Who knows, after all, maybe some day you will read this and think 'That isn't really Jack anymore, that's the virus.' Maybe it's here now in this evil sentence – am I that cruel, that silly? I ought to cut it out, but I won't – it's cruel, it's cowardly, perhaps it's using up strength you will need later – but for some reason, I want you to know I had such thoughts. 'And the worst thing was, he could see it coming' – I overheard that in The Elephant Walk. And perhaps it's because at times I feel as if the only way to know what is going on is to give in to the mystery, let it into your blood, your nerves, up into your brain. That the only way to see AIDS is to follow after Paul and go blind from it. But these are dreams, imaginary fears – they let you avoid the unimaginable real thing. They let you feel excited and alive, while real fear is simply unfelt, pure, cold death.

I'd go out into the hilly streets, climbing the rocks that save us from the ocean, that were supposed to save us from the mainland, make us almost an island. I'd watch the city go by me and be amazed at how little it was affected by Paul's sickness, by what it meant, as if his wasting was a dream of mine, my nightmare devouring him in my sleep.

Once two boys went by talking in thrilled, excited voices, voices that had come from the hinterland, to be let go here, to flower in elaborate styles of insolence and sweetness. To speak as freely as if nobody ever died, because you could hear that in the pleasure down their throats: of course nobody dies, how could you bear to look at this sunlight if you knew anyone had to leave it? For a moment or two, from out of their voices – sweet, male voices going back and forth without the old ritual of threatening, the endless, straight-male haggling for power – I could see mortality lifting away. I was in the only city worth living in, or even giving a thought to.

But Paul had his claims, as if death was an idea he'd got into his head and couldn't get out now. I had to be loyal to that – to his stubbornness. He'd come to me, after all. *I was his first and only lover, his friend for dying with.*

But every so often there was the shock of seeing it wasn't my dream, that it was everywhere, that as the scandal spread it became normal, daylit. One afternoon, I was sitting in one of those plate-glass bars, and began to hear two men talking about 'another one.' Their voices were subdued, but not hushed: they didn't mind being overheard. They went through his symptoms, his tests, his diagnosis, what he'd said to his friends, his family, his lawyer, his lover and ex-lovers. Philosophical remarks, funny, brave remarks, courageous declarations, like Paul's but in a younger style. He'd written "courage!" on the mirror, and it was still there, you couldn't wipe it off. While I sat looking out through the glass, thinking, 'shtick, AIDS shtick, and they're using it all up. What are the ones after going to say?' Thinking about Paul and how he too had to die and keep up the conversation while doing it.

The story didn't stop. "Thrush," one of them said. "You know, the white spots down your throat." *Cheesy white spots* is actually how they put it. "After that, things just went from bad to worse." I saw Paul at the bathroom mirror looking to see if death was crawling up his throat that morning. The story went on, as if all the possible diseases were hurrying to get their chance at him before he died, "Ryan, his name was." The talker summed it up: "He died a horrible death." I got up and walked out.

Then – not suddenly, not surprisingly, without fuss – I heard a voice call my name, from up above. My adult name, and not an imagined voice in my head, but clear and high in the air off to my right, calling from a wide, tender sky of its own, a sky of infinite blue concern for me. For Ken, for Paul, for all torn human souls, but right now for me, for 'Jack'. I was hearing voices, I thought: and no wonder, I'd earned it. I longed to believe in the voice, to turn to it, to live under its sky, which was bigger, higher, more arching than the sky of the other people on the street, but so close, so intimate I could have reached and touched its face. I just went on like someone late for a meeting, grinding anger out inside myself. Not crazy, just dabbling in craziness. Not joining up with the drugged schizophrenics I'd begun to notice more and more everywhere photographing themselves, seeing themselves into my mind with sharp, sudden looks.

At night, kept awake by some new failing in Paul, or by numbers doubling up in my head like cells in a lab dish, seeing it all happening again in six months – in six months, everything, the same suffering, but a new cast – I'd get up and go out for striding, insomniac walks. One night I went past a tall, skinny young man who was sitting on a corner of a retaining wall in a street below mine: I'm sure you both remember it, you pass it on the way to the store. Jeans, leather bomber jacket, dark moustache poignantly historical now, that look, that moustache. Leaning back, against an iron fence, face up, eyes closed: drunk or stoned or getting himself desired or just taking a rest. It looked as if he had what not long ago I would have called tragic acne. Thinking of other things, I barely gave him a glance and then a few steps on, around the corner, I was grabbed by the thought it could be Kaposi's: AIDS, death, right there in the street. The day before I'd been listening to the radio, about people with AIDS, including some with nowhere to stay. People could phone in to say we should die. Or, if they were nice, that we should live. An old man called, a bitter, querulous old voice: he was a taxpayer, and saw no reason why taxpayers should do anything. "They screw in the streets, let them die in the streets." My ears pricked up, my scalp contracted, as if I'd been waiting for that voice, those words, all my life long. It was history phoning in from Beirut, from the war in all the cities. *"Let them die in the streets"* – it had me, it held me, going along and imagining there was a dying man or a corpse waiting at the foot of my street. I told myself it was impossible, insane, there were still only a few hundred cases in a city of millions. But I was half-asleep, and exhausted beyond anything sleep could do, and full of dreaming: the old voice, old and bitter as the race, opened on a whole world of dreaming. I was walking through the bombed-out cities of the past and the future, the waking nightmares we all have and don't let ourselves remember, cities of corpses which look at you with dried-up slits, which see through to the corpse in you. *"Let them die in the streets"*: I heard a kind of rejoicing in the voice, a call to celebration: there was feasting in that wise, loving, evil gaze, there was an infinite easing. I wanted to give in, to fall in love, to let death come spilling through me and flood the streets.

I made myself turn and go back. And began running towards him, towards the dead face in my mind. I came running around the corner, with my hands held out in case there was a sight I had to push away. Really, your friend, in your world, about two months ago. He'd gone, as if I'd dreamt him too.

I knew it was hysterical, that I had to contain it, that probably I could, unless Paul's AIDS had something too terrible in store for us – brain damage, a Paul who wasn't Paul, perhaps, looking and saying 'Who are you?' One afternoon I came home up the street, and stopped to see my house like a house I'd never seen before. As if I was so strong in dreaming I could fill it up to the skylights with other lives and go by Jack Durham in his forty-first year, starting afresh. Then I panicked. How was Paul? What if he died alone while I idled outside. I ran up the street, in and up the stairs, forgetting the end of the world – that luxury, that easy romance.

The herpes zoster was under control, which was a relief, and seemed to show that Paul still had some kind of immune system. But as he thinned out, losing weight, not eating, his skin seemed thinner, finer, transparent. His legs and arms were as frail as a young girl's. He walked with such care, as if he would fall over sideways at any moment. My God, you're sick, I thought one day, very surprised, somehow. It was my job to see the health in him. But he was simply waiting for his next infection.

What came was news. Phoning down to Los Angeles, he learned about a friend, an acquaintance, who had died. "Of cancer," his family said. Paul was sure it was AIDS, and almost sure that he had got his case from him. There was no way of knowing, but it was as if before he died he wanted to have some explanation. They'd gone one night to his place in West Hollywood for what turned out to be a one-night stand. "He collected old records, and he played some—Broadway musicals, mostly, he called them 'show tunes.' He fucked me, so that theory holds up. It was all right, I would have said it was great, but..." Paul shrugged: "Oh well."

I wanted to argue, but I couldn't. Paul wanted this story: he had to have something like this: the night he was killed. "Poor guy," he said. "Poor guy." With an odd fellow-feeling. "In the obituary – if there is one, I mean – put in *AIDS*, okay? If they let you."

We still went out for walks, though Paul tired easily. On the last one, I think he agreed only because he didn't want to say no. I couldn't see how sick he was, the way he couldn't see how little he'd eaten. It was still my duty to believe that things could be good for him, sun and air and new things to see, though the system for taking in 'good' was probably just gone. I had to be a sort of impresario: *sun, air, faces, all those touristy things – you'll love them, Paul, they're terrific. Life, Paul, life – everybody loves it.*

We got as far as a schoolyard at the bottom of the street, and Paul wanted to rest for a bit. There's a bench there, facing the playgrounds. Some teenage boys were playing basketball. Look, Paul, bare legs, bare chests: aren't we lucky? But I could see it would not work. Paul was past metabolizing young men in shorts. It looked as though sitting down had made things worse, set off some inner avalanche of fatigue and misery: he was sagging, pale and oozy with sweat. "My eyes are a little tired today," he said. And then, "I'm tired, Jack. I think you should get a cab."

I went to flag down a cab, afraid, desperate – what if he got worse, slid off the bench like a drunk, knew the humiliation of that? I was lucky, got a cab quickly and came back in it. There were the basketball players, grabbing every bit of good, driving it all through them into toes and fingertips, into leaping and shouting. They were on fire with sun and air. And there was Paul with an old silk rust-coloured windbreaker hanging around him, looking into the grass, not seeing it. From the battered cab, from soggy shock absorbers, it felt as though I could blink, my cruel hope for him could blink, and he would slide to the ground.

We got home all right, and Paul lay down: it was just a bad afternoon. I still didn't quite take in that the pace had changed, that we didn't have months anymore. Then Paul began coughing again, uselessly, from deep inside. If it was PCP, Paul had got over it once, but then, in comparison, he'd been thriving.

He went into the hospital and of course it was pneumocystis. And that is what he died of, five weeks later. So he never developed KS or lymphoma or herpes on the brain or cryptosporidiosis. There was no brain damage, not that I saw. Paul never hid under the sheets, screaming: he never looked at me and asked who I was. He had some luck. But in the last days his immune system had just gone: he was asked to do without one in a world alive with fungi and viruses. Herpes broke out on his face and wouldn't stop spreading. He began to lose his sight, and went blind with retinitis. I remember coming in one day and thinking, or imagining thinking, *that is it, no one could recognize you, Paul, I'm free*. You wanted to believe it was some creature Paul had left to do his dying for him, some animal. As his lungs turned into paper, into sand, he was put on the respirator, a tube rammed down his throat – *live* or *die, you faggot*, we just took it since he had no voice either, just his hand. Paul went through all this with courage – the courage you can't help, that you need just to get through, and some more. About three in the morning, he slipped into a coma, his hand letting go almost imperceptibly. His heart slowed, stumbled, thought, thought, decided not to go on.

It seems cruel to write this down – cruel to you, and I'm sorry, but you will know all this sooner or later – but I mean to Paul, as if he's still feeling it all, the suffocation, the body's struggling when the struggle is useless, the misery of being given over to death, left to its disposal, waiting.

Jim was with me through most of this, when Paul died and after. He took over, arranging things. The body was to be taken off for autopsy, and suddenly it seemed shameful they should open him up and try to find out how many kinds of death had been late for the feast. Whose side were they on? It seemed clear enough to me. I saw myself picking him up and running – he was light enough – maybe he could still breathe, see, talk, grow a face in the morning outside the hospital. I refused to take their tranquillizers – all they had to say about this death, this life.

Jim and Tom and other friends were reasonable for me. Jim phoned people. Phoned you. I'm sorry, but I had nothing I could say: I would have killed people rather than talk to them. It was as if I didn't like people who were alive.

The obituary did specify *AIDS*. Paul had wanted to be cremated: Jim arranged that too. There were some friends from LA, some of the men with AIDS Paul had come to know. Nick and Terry were dead: William was on the respirator. No family, Paul was the serious only child of old parents. I hardly noticed what was going on. Paul's dying had got worse and worse, as if it would go on forever, then broke off abruptly, nothing. Anyway, they got us to the cremation, and there he was going into fire that must have felt like winter sunshine, climbing away in smoke, with a chimney to himself. Jim invited me to his apartment to stay for a while. He works here, linking to his computer over the phone. I stayed inside for four days, then began going out. I would walk down to my house to see how it was, how it felt. I put the box of ashes on Paul's bed, to think, to be thought about. I'd go out around the city, watching it through the air Paul could not breathe, or fight to breathe. He'd escaped whatever was behind the faces, but what did they have in mind for the rest of us? While it was narrowing down on Paul, cornering him, AIDS had been widening around us, too, doubling, doubling. What could we expect? I looked at them, afraid they would smell my fear and like the smell, love it. In gay areas, I wanted to stop people, my brothers, the boys and men who'd fled Kansas and Bakersfield and Saskatchewan to live in a free country. I wanted to grab them and say, "Watch out, the sunshine is plate glass, you can drown in the air like fish." I went silently around our frail Zion, its walls one mucous cell thick, thinking *'Be careful. Keep from dying a horrible death. Keep from dying, because you are all as dear to me as a lover's sores.'*

When I saw people I knew I turned aside, in order not to talk about his death. It was as if his desperate breathing had pulled me in, as if he had lost so much, wasting, that it was disloyal to let go of anything now. But from inside all this it looked as though they were all ignoring Paul's death and what it meant with insane, cruel, swaggering insolence. All they cared about was sex. They looked as crazy as the kids in Iran, running over minefields, sure they'll be blown into paradise. At times, it seemed I should just give up, forget them all, not stay for the end. I should go and be a hermit in an abandoned cabin, live blindly in desert sunshine and forget about gays, including the one I'd been or tried to be. I wanted to turn my face away. At times I did, to save them from my thoughts. They were so arrogant and stupid I wanted to throw KS or herpes in their faces like acid. I hated them, they strutted so foolishly, cruelly, vulnerably. I'd think, *'Who can care about you? You are too stupid to live. You should all just give up. You should, we should do the only things we were ever really good at, flee and hide and cower. Turn and scuttle back up history's ass forever.'* And in the next second I was in love with all of them, they were all children, brothers, lovers, they were dying children of mine. They were life, pure life, so fragile and momentary that it was all dying too, second by second. I wanted to throw my arms at what was happening, to embrace it, to love it enough to hold it in, the Hiroshima I feel exploding through our blood. How crazy was I? There was no point in asking. No one was going to tell me. Paul was much too nice for the black, vicious, bone-breaking raging his death cried out for.

It's impossible to sum up, but I saw, I think I saw, how all my life they had been inside me, down my throat – the straights, the humans, power. They had been in everything I said, in all the meanings of all my words, in every tone of my voice. In my sarcasm, irony, cleverness. In my being wise and shrewd, a philosopher! In all my disillusioned lucidity: Jack Durham, conscious in unconscious times. How wise to shut up now, to push the plate of words away like Paul with no appetite, learn to live on silence.

They said AIDS was what we were: I wanted it to be what they were. I wanted it to be their last chance to be human, and I wanted to see them fail it, all of them, the humans, the Auschwitz species.

I'd thought I was fighting away from their world toward some kind of vision. There had to be some kind of compensation, there had to be: the colours of vision for my eyes, a shaman's flight for my bones, the bitter, cherished acids of prophecy in my craw. I had to be the prophet of the queer, scattered nation I found myself in, to talk to God and get our answer. Perhaps even to get an answer for the whole race, plainly desperate, dying for prophecy. And to think they would have to get it from us!

When it was beginning to get dark, Jim stepped in to see how I was. I still wasn't talking but I knew I was coming out of my silence. Standing and looking out, Jim talked about Paul. It was strange to hear him talked about in a calm, quiet voice. Jim mentioned things Paul had said when I wasn't there. He'd been worried about me, Jim said. He thought I'd be all right in the end, but he didn't know how it would come out. Poor Paul, I thought, to have to worry about that. I saw he'd been planting these things for Jim to use now. He'd arranged to be here now, and he was here, talking through Jim.

"Paul," I said to him, trying words again. Jim came over and sat beside me. There were tears on his cheeks, and I was furious. I said, "Do you think you've found the cure?"

He didn't answer.

"You saw him. You saw what they took out of there."

"Don't do that to him, Jack."

"There were people at the funeral, people who hardly knew him, crying their eyes out. And I thought, 'you're crying because you could get it too. You're crying to feel warm and alive.' That's rotten, it would be better to die."

Jim said, "But you don't mean that."

"I'll cry for the last one. I'll start when the last one has died."

If I send this letter, you'll understand: *we can't wait that long*.

If I send it – because should I decide now that I've used you, them, the thoughts of you, them, to get this monstrous thing out of myself, without really writing to you? Perhaps this is just to myself. Perhaps I should just put this away somewhere, to take it out twenty, thirty years from now, staring into that unimaginable century.

But I was writing to you two, holding on to you, real listeners, real friends – out across the human space – there. *Here*."

"Love Jack."

David looked up and out along the empty street, shining and leaping through tears, which were for Tim and himself as well as Paul. For his new-born, tender lover, out in the night, bearing Jack's rage alone: David could almost feel it killing them.

A tall, blond man came around the corner, but it wasn't Tim. 'Love, Jack,' and no sign of Tim.

It was only when Tim turned homeward – having walked as far west as the house where he had lived with Kelly – that he remembered Jack's letter had been left out on the kitchen table. He had been walking for hours, past all the places where he had lived. Now, remembering the letter, he started to run towards College Street and the red and black streetcar, the "TTC Comet". He must get home, across the city, before David woke. He thought of all the things he had done to David already: he saw him stretching above him, pounding his fists like a prophet angry at the sky, like a wizard demanding an entrance into a cliff.

Fast breathing brought up the grief in Jack's letter, as if it lurked far down in his lungs like pneumocystis. Suddenly he saw David was fine, was thriving. It was Paul who had done everything: in comparison, Jack's raging, David's worrying about him, Tim's wandering through the night, were nothing at all.

He stood under a tree on the dark street crying. He began walking again, and getting near College he pulled his T-shirt out and wiped his face with it. A streetcar was coming, he sprinted to catch it, wiping his face again as he stepped up into the light. The driver didn't notice. The car was empty.

He got off at Yonge, hoping to catch the all-night bus, not seeing it. He began walking north. The street was almost empty: it must be very late, close to dawn. But then, farther up, he saw a big man with iron-gray hair, going slowly up the other side—going gently, as if he carried something asleep inside himself. Getting closer, Tim knew what it was. Jack was back at last.

He had spent hours trying to walk away the fear of Jack's letter, of the familiar, angry voice that came from the pages. It had been as if he read everything else through his own dread. He had kept thinking of how Patrick in New York had got his diagnosis. He had been put to wait in a little room, alone. The doctor had walked in, said, "You have AIDS," and walked out, closing the door. Tim had been suspended in the fear the world could leave him alone and staring at the door, not knowing how he had got there, who he was. That was the core of the fear: there would be no one there, strong enough, inside him, to go through what Paul had gone through. After a life of pretending to be someone, AIDS would expose him as nothing, as no one.

He was drained now, his mind dulled, but talking with Jack could bring all that back. Who knew what Jack might say? Say or shout in the street? He should turn away, and wait to meet him at David's. They could throw regretful looks at each other across David's living room, and keep their safe, six years' distance. He might not even tell David he had read the letter.

Tim almost turned down a street that would take him over to Church. Then he found himself stepping onto Yonge. With the only cars far away, it felt uncannily empty, like a dry riverbed: he didn't need to hurry.

"Jack! What a time to meet!" he said, coming up onto the curb. In the quiet, he didn't raise his voice.

Jack turned, not recognizing the voice at first, looking surprised, and almost angry. It was because the lines of his face had gone much deeper, Tim saw. They were harsher, darker, and simpler too, more expressive. His iron forties had given him not a mask but deep, human lines.

"Tim Grey!" He smiled. "What on earth are we doing up?"

Tim had an impulse to embrace him, for being more formidably himself than ever – for being big and solid, for being ugly and beautiful with a generous, accomplished ugliness. Tim's hands reached and stopped, unable to reach through the frost of death still around him. He looked where his watch should have been.

Jack smiled a bit at this and started them walking again.

"So how are you these days?" he said.

"All right."

"Really?"

"Well I've been kind of in-between in my life lately."

"David said he didn't know whether you would be staying here."

"I've been thinking about that tonight. I couldn't sleep, like you I guess, so I went walking. And I ended up going to all the places where I've lived here, even the house where I was born. I wouldn't have thought you could do it, but I did."

He was getting out of breath, because he had to say something about Paul, now. He couldn't be left in silence any longer.

"I was thinking about Paul, too," he said, his voice almost breaking.

"Yes," Jack said.

"I'm so sorry, Jack. It was *so* – " Unfair, but David had already taken that away. Instead, he admitted, "I read your letter."

"Oh?" Jack looked guilty, or afraid.

"David suggested it."

"Yes. As soon as I sent that letter, I thought – " He hesitated, then explained. "Tonight, for instance, I've been thinking, 'All right, have your disaster, make it huge, make it terrible. But what did it have to do with Paul?' But maybe that's just a way of surviving – of taking a rest. What did it ever have to do with anybody?"

"But I understood all that," Tim said. "I've been through it too, in New York. There were times when you'd think, 'well, if I got it, why not? It's only what *they* want, it's what *they* always wanted.'"

"*Don't* think that way," Jack said, angrily. "Just don't."

"I know, but it's hard not to. I've been thinking, if I got it, what would I do? I don't even know who I'd be if I got AIDS."

Jack still looked angry, his mouth pressing tight. Then he said, "Paul went on being Paul. You'd go on being Tim."

Tim gave a joyless laugh.

"Maybe that's what I'm afraid of. It would have to be me—it couldn't be anyone else."

"But you *won't* get it," Jack declared, desperately. "I will *not* have any more of my friends dying."

"Well, all right, thanks, Jack," Tim said, fondly. It sounded almost as if Jack had got his anger so bright and clear it could burn the virus out of your blood. With his left hand, he reached and brushed Jack's shoulder – to know that Jack was solid, to brush strength from him, help, endurance. Jack smiled, feeling the touch, accepting it.

"No," he said, in a lower voice. "If it's up to me, you get to be old and crotchety and disenchanted. And *wise*, Tim – *wise!*" He said it angrily, angry at the word, angry at himself for loving it so much.

"Well, not too soon, please," Tim said. "Give me a few more years first."

Jack shrugged, agreeing perhaps.

"But what about you?" Tim said. "Are you moving back here?"

"I don't know. I was thinking about that when you came up. It's kind of a relief to be here. But at the same time you feel, *nothing* has happened. Not one deep breath has been taken since I left. I keep thinking, this can't be real."

He stopped for a moment, looking along the street. "This can't be it, you think. There is *another* Toronto than this." He shrugged. "But where are they hiding it? As for staying – it's too soon to decide. The house in San Francisco – can I leave it now, after Paul? And how will things work out with Bob? I mean, he is young, isn't he?" Jack laughed, fondly. "At times, he's almost young enough to be my father."

Tim smiled: Bob had been fathering him too. "Well, he'd be good at it, wouldn't he?"

"I suppose," Jack said.

They were getting close to the corner where Tim would turn to go home. Two very young men came down the street towards them, talking excitedly, unaware how late it was, how colourful they were in the empty night: billowy shirts and baggy shorts, rainbow socks and shoes. Coming closer, passing, the four gay men slipped one another little smiles. Jack looked after them, at the things dangling from their ears, at the lovelocks wagging over the napes of their necks.

"I'm over forty," he said. "And they're finding new ways of being pretty."

"Well, I don't mind!"

"Neither do I," Jack said. "Neither do I."

"But you know, Tim," he said, giving him a sad, shrewd look, "the truth is that no one knows what it is to be alive today. No one, nobody, not even handsome twenty-year-olds. Not that anyone ever did, of course, but they thought they did."

Tim's laughter went ahead along the street. "You're still at it, aren't you?" he said, glad to see Jack hadn't stopped playing philosophical games, games to get at truth. Jack was telling him that he had come through.

"To be alive, right now, right here. At the corner of Yonge and – " Jack looked for a sign – "yes, Gloucester. And to think *no one* knows what that is. It's exciting!"

He smiled, still gray and saddened, but pleased with himself. He'd burnished his irony, given it a new magnificence.

Tim chuckled, deep in his throat. "Well, Jack, be sure to tell us when you know."

"Of course. But I never will, though," he said, sadly. "If I say I do...well, be *careful*, listen carefully."

"This street goes over to David's place," Tim said. "And I'm worried he might have wakened up and be worrying. And I've been putting him through a lot lately."

They stopped. Jack looked north, then said, "I think I need to walk some more."

"Well, I'll see you at Bob's." Impulsively, Tim reached to hug him – to reassure his body that Jack still had a body too, then to welcome him, hold him back. He thought of Paul again, sobbing, and shaking Jack too.

"So," Jack said, standing back after a minute, looking down the sidestreet. "You two are lovers again?"

"Yes, we are. As of tonight, as a matter of fact."

"Tonight? Bob said he didn't know whether it had actually happened yet."

"Did he! Bob is always scheming, isn't he?"

Jack took a step or two, but without turning away.

"And this is your third time?" he asked, thoughtfully, as if he didn't know.

"Yes."

"And you couldn't really do it *four* times? Could you?"

Why not? Tim thought. Why not, if they wanted to, any number of times? But Jack was right: if they broke up after this, it would probably be for good.

Jack was smiling, shyly, but craftily too. It was as if Tim had never seen it until then.

"Jack! You want everything, don't you? You've got to have *everything*!"

"I thought you knew. *The journey is ALL*."

EPILOGUE
June, 1990

When the leaves came to the last of the trees in the valley, David collected his things together and took the ferry to the Island.

The price had gone up this year – again. He paid at the barrier and handed his ticket to the attendant just past it. *So silly.* He had to take a ticket and give it up five metres away. Why not just pay and walk through? Employment for the powerless, he supposed.

It wasn't that he minded the price. For that money he booked passage on the Thomas Rennie or the Sam McBride, pre-war beauties with two decks of polished wood, blue and white steel and smooth wooden railings to rest hands or elbows on. At this time of year they were almost always crowded with people. Mothers and their babies complained of the heat; old women with feet twisted from years of wearing high heels; teenagers in ragged cutoffs, over-sized T-shirts and caps on backwards, slick ghetto blasters blaring; earnest environmentalist trendy types with long hair and bicycles; cyclists in muscles, spandex, helmets and wrap-around sun glasses; children in packs of twenty or more, tended by harried day care workers; homosexuals who had taken the wrong ferry on the way to their 'secret' beach. David watched them all, and tried to avoid being pushed, shoved aside or trampled upon.

The passage began with the churning of water at the stern as the boat launched herself across the reflected sunshine of the harbour. Beneath the flashes of light, the water was turgid and green-brown. Bits of plastic or decaying paper were caught in the wash. Gulls hovered behind them, flashing suddenly down to snatch up hapless fish torn up from the depths by the strength of the screw. Propelled away from this scene of violence and death, the deep blue hull glided across the sunshine and the refuse to the islands at the edge of the lake.

David stood on the upper deck in the stern, legs and arms spread, hands braced against the wood of the rail, and faced back towards the heaving water, the carnage of the gulls and the towers of the city. It was his place to hold all of that at bay, to make the signs that mark the passage from one world to another—beyond the glistening waters of the harbour. Despite the absence of kin, clergy or colleague, he would fulfill his promise. With a quiet concentration, he bent his mind to that task with absolute dedication and certainty. During this sojourn, these serene islands would be free of the stains and stresses of the city.

When the ferry arrived at the dock, he waited until the howling babies, twisted feet, ghetto blasters, bicycles, spandex, children and stray homosexuals had all "debarked". Once they had landed safely on the island, when they were out of his way at last, David quit his post in the stern and made his way to the gangplank at the bow.

The men who worked on the ferry knew him. They had seen David and held off the crowds waiting to board for the return trip; they stood at a respectful distance.

When he reached the gangplank, he turned back to face the city. Ceremoniously, David raised his staff gleaned fresh from the valley floor that spring morning and sketched the circle of power in the air between those two worlds. He made the sign of the cross over the circle of power. Then, he spun one hundred and eighty degrees with the staff vertical before his face, dropping it straight down and tapping it three times on the dock of the island. Only then, did he disembark.

Centre Island has long been an amusement island. There was a village ('Centreville') with small buildings and animals for the children. As well, wooden paddle swans plied the pond, while gondolas swung on cables over the lagoon and then back. There were grandstands for rowing regattas for the lagoon, and restaurants for drinking beer. This island was the best spot after the city for holiday crowds, but despite all best efforts, it was corrupted with the dirt of the city. David wasted little time in making his way to the bridge that led to Ward's Island and the pier.

At the centre of the bridge, he tapped his staff three times again, then raised it overhead and uttered the words of power twice. He held this position while the veil of energy gathered, slowly coalescing around him like a brooding cloak spun of ebony and gold. At the precise moment that the veil achieved tension, he shrugged it from his shoulders and left it behind him to snap taut over the past history of Centreville, containing it and limiting any damage of immature souls that sought its titillation.

Before David lay the Avenue of the Islands – the broad, paved way between the beds of geraniums and the box maples – which led over the mat to the pier suspended high above the water of the lake. He made his way slowly, as he was wearied from the effort of invoking the veil, to the end of the pier. He drew strength from the purity of the air, the water and his goal – which seemed beyond the limits of man. *In remembrance...of you...and too many of our friends.*

He spent some minutes there, drinking in the vigor of the Primeval. Lake Ontario at this spot was innocent of pollution, refreshed by currents that swung along the shore from the east. Those currents had built the Islands, gouging materials from the sandstone bluffs of Scarborough to deposit there, a sacred offering to the people of Toronto, a sacred trust – which David felt obliged to honour and keep.

Boats, white sails billowing, drifted over the surface of the lake as white gulls and white clouds drifted across the porcelain sky overhead, mirror images of white on blue. Below him, the water slapped and sucked at the pylons which supported David there. The breeze blew across his face and chest, clutching at the cloth of his garments and tugging them gently outward behind him. That breeze gave him the stamina to continue on his journey to the particular grove – which was his final destination.

He made his way back from the pier to the beach, and then moved west along the sand. There were twelve stations between pier and grove, each of which required the demarcation of the circle of power and the chant of peace. At the first station (the point at which the pier met the beach) he did so and paused, motionless for one minute, before continuing. At the second, he repeated the process – but waited two minutes, then three minutes at the third station, and so on – until he had reached the grove. This was the twelfth station and the place where he stood, without motion of any kind, for a full twelve minutes.

The grove was a most sacred place. A screen of poplars, beeches and willows (among the most primitive of trees) shielded a strip of pure red sand, running down into the water on two sides. Ancient trunks, half in the water and half out, worn bare of bark and smoothed by the caress of countless waves, marked the limits of the *sanctum sanctorum*. The water that washed this strip of sand was the purest water on the islands. This was the point where the current ran closest to the land.

When the signs of obeisance had been made, David stripped off his clothing until he was clad only in the simplest of garments, burgundy–coloured underpants that clothed the central mystery of his being. Around his neck, hung a small leather pouch. His vestments, rancid with the stench of the city and the sweat of his body, were spread on the lower bows of poplar from east to west around the clearing. Once that half circle had been drawn, he walked to the edge of the water and fell to his knees in the red sand. He bowed his head once before the inviolate scene, and waded out until the water swirled around his hips, as his feet settled beneath displaced grains of sand.

When he reached this point, he removed the worn leather pouch which hung from around his neck, and gently, carefully, reverently opened it. He turned that receptacle upside down, bending low over the rippling, shimmering lake. Softly, Tim's cremated remains scattered over the surface, shattering his own reflection there. The gentle lapping of the waves carried the floating pieces away, while the heavier shards sunk silently to the sandy bottom. Smoothly, with great care, he reached down beneath the surface, pulling the molten image up towards his lips until it was taken up into him – held in his mouth between his tongue and his teeth – lifting his face to the clouds and the screaming gulls.

He held it there, until his gums became metallic and his tongue leather. But he would not drink it down. Instead, David slackened his jaw and let it flow out of the corners of his mouth. He let it be pulled down by the force of gravity – over his chin, to drip onto his chest – where it coursed along the curve of his breasts and gathered at the fullest point, just below his waist. The droplets hung there briefly – pausing in one last tender moment of contact – before returning to the lake.

There, again, one with the water of the lake, Tim's ashes swirled around his feet, legs, hips and groin, staining the burgundy undershorts the colour of the blood of Christ, and covering his mystery with the colour of divinity. This finalized the ritual which made him a unique servant of God, the appointed purveyor of Tim's cremated remains to Lake Ontario.

David's emaciated body heaved with grief and exertion as he clumsily flung the staff into the water. It reappeared, bobbed and floated on the swift current. Without warning, his dry cough returned, clutching at his chest, torturing, twisting and tearing at his insides. Light-headed, he tugged his clothing over his damp body, dressing with effort. Employing an uncertain, measured gait, David began his return trip – to the harsh reality that was Toronto.

He did not *dawdle*, along the way.

EXCERPTS FROM AN ESSAY WRITTEN BY BILL
A DEAR FRIEND OF GORDON'S

These excerpts were previously published in NOT A TOTAL WASTE: *The True Story of a Mother, her Son and AIDS*, (Lloyd, B.M., Mosaic Press, 1993, 1999).

In the end, Gordon was forced to watch, helpless, as the worst and most malignant of our nightmares waged war on his body; and yet he, as with thousands of other brave men before him, faced that nightmare with a courage, dignity and personal freedom that was, in the true sense of the word, awesome.

Yet he was not seeking comfort. He was seeking understanding. Gordon was fascinated by three things: puppets, architecture and the way children learned. He wanted to understand the structures of power and how they could be used, both for good and evil. For a child, a puppet can be a source of comfort, solace and learning. For an adult, it can describe the techniques by which we seek to destroy others. A building can be either a home or a prison; it all depends on who holds the key.

The road that Gordon took was not an easy one...He did manage to develop an enormous strength that came from knowing that he never flinched from life...Gordon did not succumb to trivial comforts at the expense of his own integrity. He would not deny who he was and what was happening to him. If he must die of a hideous plague, then he would do it on his own terms - and he did... His acute rationalism and his analytical tools allowed him to maintain his dignity in the face of an almost unbelievable assault. What was the source of that courage, that human wisdom?

Shortly before he died, Gordon bought that wonderful silk shirt. It was a funny, vibrant pastiche of colour. I think it summarized much of what he had lived for and something of what he had come to know. It was a celebration of spirit - an exaltation of larks - a joyful recognition that he was the master of his own spirit...Death may be merely an absence of constraints, a great gaping nothingness. But like Gordon's shirt - what a bright, glorious, *shimmering* nothingness!

THE TORONTO YOU ARE LEAVING
an Afterthought

The Toronto You Are Leaving is the tender, bitingly honest story of a young gay man's coming out and coming of age in the Toronto of the 70's and 80's. David is the university student, the bookworm who is just beginning the joyful, difficult transition of bringing his private self forward.

This novel is an entertaining, and valuable look into lives and relationships, as well as a moving and original perception of love. The reader gets to experience David's first crush on a straight friend, evolving with other friends' diverse romances and relationships. It introduces the reader to a host of very real, colourful individuals. Strong mentors and powerful self-evaluation shape David's views. The reader is offered a fresh perspective on lives lived fully and lost too soon.

Gordon's sensitive, often funny writing, replete with some ribald sexual moments, brings to life important issues such as homophobia, the effects that coming-out can have on a family, and the historical impact of the beginning of the HIV/AIDS plague upon the Toronto communities.

Warmth, eagerness, and vividly engaging characters are all here in the fascinating story of The Toronto You Are Leaving. It cannot fail to touch its readers.

B.M. Lloyd, Ed.D., Ph.D.
Author of *NOT A TOTAL WASTE: The True Story of a Mother, Her Son, and AIDS* (Mosaic Press, 1993, 1999)